Tilly Trotter Widowed

Tilly Trotter Widowed

a novel by
CATHERINE COOKSON

BOOK CLUB ASSOCIATES LONDON

This edition published 1982 by
Book Club Associates
by arrangement with William Heinemann Ltd

Printed and bound in Great Britain by
Richard Clay (The Chaucer Press) Ltd
Bungay, Suffolk

Contents

PART ONE

The Veneer

1

Mrs Matilda Sopwith stood against the ship's rail and watched the waters darken as the sun slipped behind the rim of the horizon. It had been an unusually calm day, in fact the weather had been clement for most of the journey, so different from that time almost three years ago when she had left Liverpool for America in this very same ship. Then, she and her small child and her friend, Katie Drew, had been tossed and tumbled about and made so sick that they had wished to die, and her small son had almost achieved this; yet the stormy sea and the plunging, rearing ship had not in any way affected her husband; he had seemed to revel in it, buoyed up by the fact that he was going back to the land he loved, the land, he had once said, in which he wished to die. And his wish had been granted him, but much, much sooner than he could have expected.

She swung her mind away from her husband and sent it spinning fast into the future that would begin on the morrow when the boat docked. She'd be met by her brother-in-law, John Sopwith, and his wife, Anna, both young, little more than boy and girl, at least to her mind; and there was no doubt that they would shower her with affection because she knew they were truly fond of her, for hadn't she been the means of bringing them together; two people who felt themselves scarred with defects over which they had no control, for what control had a young girl over hideous birthmarks? Perhaps in the man's case there was some measure for control for his cross was merely a bad stammer.

She could see them all taking the long journey back in the train; she could see the carriage meeting the train; she could see it bowling through the iron gates and up the drive to the manor house that lay on the far outskirts of South Shields; and she could already feel the welcome of Katie's mother, Biddy, and also witness the keen disappointment on her face when she realised that her daughter had not returned from America. But above all the pictures in her mind there stood out in sharp relief the faces of

3

the whole Drew family and of the other servants when she entered the house accompanied not only by her small son Willy but also by a smaller child whose features claimed the ancestry of a Mexican Indian.

"This is my adopted daughter," she would say to them. But why, their amazed gaze would ask, had she to adopt one such as she, for everyone knew creatures like her weren't really human beings, not like English human beings, and were merely born to be slaves.

Could she then say to them . . . could she even ever say to Biddy Drew, Biddy who, like her daughter Katie, knew all about her and had been her friend and confidante for years, could she say to her, "I did not adopt her, Biddy, she is my husband's bastard"? No, no; she could never put a slur on Matthew's name, although in the ordinary sense a bastard was no slur on the man, simply on the woman who bore her, that is if the child was white; but to be dark-skinned with strange unblinking eyes, a skin that seemed to flow over the bone skeleton beneath it, a mouth whose lips lay with gentle firmness one on the other seeming to forbid the tongue to speak, and then the hair, black, straight, its sheen making it shine like a military boot, and all encased in a tiny body. There could be no acceptance whatever for such.

Yet she wasn't worried so much about Josefina's acceptance into the house as she was worried about her effect on the villagers. It was unfortunate that the child, who was as far as she knew about four and a half years old, should have the stature of one hardly three, unfortunate because she knew what would be the outcome of the villagers' diagnosis once they looked on the strange piece of humanity: Tilly Trotter had been up to her tricks again. She could even hear their concerted voices: "My God! To think of it, having the effrontery to bring back another of her bastards. Wasn't it enough she had been the cause of the death of two men before disgracing herself by becoming the mistress of a man old enough to be her father? Then, when he was hardly cold in his grave, what did she do? She married his son and goes off to the Americas; and here she is come back as brazen as brass and showing off her latest effort."

As if she could hear the voices and see the faces, she turned sharply round from the ship's rail and leant against it for a moment before walking quickly away up the deck. As she made to go down the companion-way the captain stood aside at the

4

bottom of the steps and waited for her, and bowing his head slightly towards her, he said, "Only another few hours, ma'am. You'll be glad when the journey is over."

"Yes, I shall, captain; but I would like to thank you now, in case I don't see you later, for the effort you have made to make us comfortable during the journey."

"No effort at all, ma'am, it was a pleasure. And yet I wish I hadn't had the pleasure, that circumstances had turned out differently for you, for you've been so tried in your short time away from the old country. I remember your husband well. Pardon me for speaking of him, ma'am, I don't want to arouse any memories, but I'd just like to say we, my officers and the crew, thought he was a very fine gentleman."

"Thank you."

"Will I see you at dinner tonight?"

'Would you excuse me, captain? I don't like to leave the children for too long."

"I understand. Yes, yes, I understand; and I'll have something substantial sent to your cabin."

"It is very kind of you and I thank you." She inclined her head towards him, and he, in return, bowed his, and she went down the steps, along the corridor and into her cabin.

The cabin was the largest on the ship and one which the captain had allotted to her use much to the chagrin, she had discovered, of a Mr and Mrs Sillitt, a couple who were used apparently to making sea voyages and who had travelled on this particular ship a number of times.

It was as much to avoid Mrs Sillitt as her need to be with the children that had caused her to refuse to join the captain in the last meal on board. Mrs Sillitt was partly of French extraction and, therefore, her loyalties were divided. Scarcely a meal had passed during the voyage without she touched on the subject of the recent Crimean war, at times delving into it as if she had actually witnessed the battles of Alma, Balaclava and Inkerman. The lady hated the Russians with a fierce hatred, and some of her hatred seemed to have rubbed off on the English for which her husband bore the brunt. It appeared at times as if she was accusing the poor man of having ordered the weather to freeze the soldiery to death, for everything that had gone wrong was attributed to the British, and was not her husband English, in fact Dorset English; and being apparently ineffectual inasmuch as he

5

suffered in silence, he represented for her the inefficient British Command. The captain had at an early stage given up the fruitless argument, but not so the first officer who was a Scot. This man had confided in Tilly privately that he had little time for the English as a whole but God knew he had less time for the Frenchies whose main occupation seemed to be causing revolutions and making Napoleons. The latest one, who called himself Napoleon the Third, strutted around like a little bantam cock on a midden. No, the English, be what they may, were preferable to the Frenchies. And what's more, he could name a dozen women from the Liverpool dock front whom he'd be pleased to eat with in preference to sitting down opposite to Mrs Sillitt.

Mrs Sillitt's chatter had in a way floated over Tilly's head, that was until three evenings ago when she brought up the subject of "the blacks". She had brought Tilly sharply out of her reserve by saying in her naturally loud overbearing voice, "Do you think it's wise, Mrs Sopwith, to take a black child into the country? Although slavery has been abolished in England since the beginning of the century, there's still a suspicion in some quarters that black children are being used in the old way."

Her remark had stilled the conversation at the table and also caught the attention of the diners at the other six tables in the room.

Tilly had stared hard at the woman, then said stiffly, "I am returning home with my adopted daughter, madam," but before she could continue Mrs Sillitt, smiling tightly, said, "Yes, yes, I know, my dear, we know of your situation, but I'm only offering the suggestion that it may not be wise seeing that she will be brought up in close proximity to your son. Black and white don't go together. Never will. I merely put it as a suggestion. . . ."

"Then I would rather that you kept your suggestions to yourself."

This rebuff did not penetrate the hide of Mrs Sillitt, and she was about to make another retort when her husband, seeming to drag himself out of obscurity and making his entry as explosive as a gunshot, glared at his wife as he hissed, "Mind your own business, woman! Just for once, mind your own business and get on with your meal."

As the first officer said later, if everybody had burst into cheering he wouldn't have been at all surprised, but oh, he wished he could have put his ear to the keyhole when the couple were alone

6

in their cabin. Yet, he pointed out to Tilly, did she notice that the bold lady actually did as her husband bid her, although, mind you, she had looked as if she was going to burst asunder at any moment.

Since that meal a few nights ago the problem of Josefina had taken on a more definite shape in her mind, and the shape encompassed the years ahead and what might come out of the close proximity between the children. Mrs Sillitt had opened up another avenue of concern.

Yet as she sat on the side of the bunk and looked down on the sleeping face of Josefina she asked herself what else she could have done, and the answer came, she could have done what Matthew told her she must do, return home alone with Willy and leave his flyblow behind.

And it was strange to think now that that penultimate request of his had been unthinkable, whereas his dying request, the request that had made her swear that she would never marry again, had been easy to comply with.

She put her hand out and stroked the black shining plait lying over the small shoulder; then she rose to her feet and looked into the other bunk that was now on eye level with her. Her son was sleeping soundly, one fist doubled up under his chin. He was beautiful to look upon, so beautiful that the sight of him always brought an ache to her heart. Although when he was born he'd resembled his father there was now no trace of that resemblance in his features. He had her eyes. Oh, his eyes. The ache turned into a sharp stab that seemed to pierce her ribs. Perhaps in a very short while he'd be unable to see what she looked like; one eye was already sightless, the other gave him but dim vision, and yet no one looking into them would guess that they were not capable of normal sight. For a moment the incident that had injured his eyes rose before her. She saw herself in the market place, the child in her arms, and there was Mrs McGrath drunk and brawling, and when the sodden woman wielded the stick at her, she had ducked her head to avoid it, only for her son to take the blow. A baby of but six months he had been then.

Oh, those McGraths. They had been the curse of her life. All except Steve, the youngest of them and now the under-manager of the Sopwith mine. He had been her friend from childhood days. He had suffered for her, as his crooked arm proved, he had suffered for her because he loved her. Yes. Yes, Steve McGrath

7

had loved her. And three years ago she had almost taken advantage of that love and offered to marry him to escape the passion of Matthew, because even in her own eyes it seemed a sin to be marrying the son of the man to whom she had acted as mistress for so long and whose child she had only recently borne.

Would she be pleased to see Steve? She got no answer to this question, except to give herself another question: Would she be pleased to see anyone?

Although she had recovered from the breakdown that followed on Matthew's death, there was a great void in her which she felt would remain with her always for she could never see anyone filling it, except her son.

She now touched Willy's hair; it was getting fairer every day. She lingered a moment longer gazing at him, then she turned from the bunk and attended to the packing.

A few hours now and she'd be in England, home, home which meant Highfield Manor, the place where she had gone as nursemaid all those years ago, the place from which she had been twice turned out, the place to which she was now returning, not as mistress of Mr Mark Sopwith, or as wife of Mr Matthew Sopwith, but as a widow and owner of the house and estate and the mine besides. She was financially a very rich woman . . . rich in everything that didn't matter.

2

"S . . . s . . . soon be there, Tilly. S . . . s . . . soon be there . . . s . . . soon be home."

John Sopwith turned from the window of the swaying coach and looked across at Tilly and his wife sitting hand in hand; then with his arms out he encircled the two children kneeling up on the seat beside him, and when Willy, bobbing up and down, shouted excitedly, "Horses, Mama. Look, horses, galloping horses!" John said, "Yes, horses, my boy. Why are you so . . . so surprised? America is not the only pl . . . place that has horses."

"We had lots of horses, sir." Willy had turned and was looking up into John's face, and he, bending towards the child, said, "I am Uncle Jo . . . John. Say Uncle John." And the boy glanced at his mother, and when she gave a little smile and a small movement of her head he looked back at John and repeated, "Uncle John."

Josefina had now turned from the window and was looking at John, and she too repeated, "Uncle John."

Her words were clearly defined. She was speaking English yet the inflection of her voice stamped her as foreign as much as did her dark solemn appearance.

When she put up her hand and tapped John gently on the nose he burst out laughing. Then looking across at Tilly he said softly, "She's an unusual ch . . . child. I can understand why you wanted to br . . . br . . . bring her b . . . back with you."

Yet even as he spoke he knew he was merely being polite because for the life of him he couldn't think what had possessed Tilly to bring this coloured child, this strange looking coloured child, back home. This child did not look like any coloured person he had seen before. But he had seen pictures and drawings of American Indians, and there was something of the Indian in the hair and eyes. Yet she did not appear altogether Indian.

He now lay back against the quilted leather of the seat and with only half his mind he listened to his wife explaining the changes

9

she had made in the house and stating that she hoped they would meet with Tilly's approval. For the rest, a strange thought had entered his head and he was chiding himself for it, albeit at the same time expanding it. Four years old, Tilly said the child was, yet she had the stature of a child not yet two. To his mind she was too tiny to be four years of age, she was more like an infant. Tilly had left this country almost three years ago. . . . No, no! He now thrust the thought from him. There was the child's voice; she certainly spoke as a child of four might.

He centred his gaze on his wife now. She was so pleased to have Tilly back. There was little female company of her own age or station near the Manor. There were neighbours, yes, but Anna didn't make friends easily; she was still very conscious of her affliction, especially so with anyone outside the household. Yet looking at her now from his position there was just the merest sign of the purple stain rising above the lace collar of her blouse. It was only when she was undressed that the frightful birthmark covering one entire shoulder and part of her breast gave evidence of the burden she had carried since she was a child. Yet he loved every inch of her skin with a passion that seemed to grow in him daily. He had known when he married her that he loved Anna, but he had never imagined himself capable of the feelings that possessed him now. In a way he felt his feelings for his wife almost matched his dead brother's mania for Tilly. Why had Matthew to die? And how had he died? He was longing to talk to Tilly about his brother, to know every detail. All she had told them so far was that he had been wounded in an Indian raid and had died of his wounds.

"I never thought to see these gates again."

The carriage had turned into the drive and Tilly was now bending forward looking at the line of rowans, their greenery about to burst fresh and bright. Spring wasn't far off. For a moment she felt a stirring within her as if the coming season itself had touched her. Then it was gone, replaced now by a quivering anxiety, for in a few minutes she'd be meeting Biddy and, however pleased Biddy would be to see her, she wouldn't be able to understand that she'd come back without her daughter, for of all her children, Tilly knew, as strongly as she would deny it, Biddy had favoured the one she had chastised most. She had boxed Katie's ears as a child, shouted her down because of her chattering, ordered her about as if she were still a child when she was a full-grown woman, and had done all this to hide the fact from the rest of her family that she favoured this particular plain, podgy-looking daughter.

The carriage came to a stop at the foot of the steps and there they all were, all the members of the household, most of whom she recognised: all the Drews, Biddy looking the same as when she had left her, her work-worn back still straight, her big lined face, usually unsmiling but now with a look of bright expectancy on it that caused Tilly to gulp in her throat against the disappointment she was about to bring to her. There was Peg, the eldest of the girls – she must be near to forty and she was the best looking of the bunch. She had been married and widowed. And there was Fanny, the youngest. What was she, twenty-five? And Arthur, a sturdy man in his thirties; and he was the youngest but two of the seven Drew men. And that was Jimmy, who must be about twenty-eight now. Bill, she understood from one of Anna's letters, had left and had gone to sea. That had been a surprise. She had thought he might have joined his three older brothers in the Durham mines. Betty Leyburn was still here, and Lizzie Gamble. She had been engaged as under-housemaid just before they went to America. And there were two strange men. The younger of the two, a man of about forty, was now opening the door. He was the new footman then. And the portly man with the grey hair at the top of the steps must be the butler. At one time she would have smiled to herself at the evident way he was showing to all those present that he knew his place in the servants' hierarchy.

The children had scrambled to the open door of the coach and she watched the footman extend his arms and lift Willy down to the drive. She also noticed that he hesitated for more than a moment at the sight of the dark child, and that when he did place her beside Willy his eyes remained on her before he swung about and extended his hand to help her down from the coach.

Almost immediately now she was engulfed by the whole Drew family. This was not a meeting between mistress and staff, this was a meeting of friends. But as quickly as it had begun so it ended. With one arm around Tilly's shoulders, Biddy Drew looked towards the carriage and to where stood the young master and mistress she had served during Tilly's absence; and then she was looking at Tilly again and her voice was a whisper as she said, "Katie?"

"It's all right. It's all right, Biddy." Tilly was quick to assure her. "She's well and happy, very happy. I've got a lot to tell you. . . ."

"*She hasn't come back with you?*"

"No. No, but she'll be coming later on. She's married. Let us go in."

The Drew family gazed at one another, their eyes saying, Our Katie's married? Then at the children, particularly at the dark child, before they all followed Tilly and John and Anna up the steps.

At the front door Tilly was greeted by the butler. His manner as correct as one would wish, he bowed towards her, saying, "I am Francis Peabody, ma'am."

Again Tilly wished she could smile. How was she to address Francis Peabody? Call him mister or Francis, or merely Peabody? And this she did, but gently, saying, "Thank you, Peabody."

Then they were in the hall, and she stood for a moment looking around it. It was a beautiful sight, so beautiful. She hadn't realised before how beautiful this house was. Even in America when she had longed to return here she hadn't visualised it as she was now seeing it. Nothing had changed; Anna hadn't altered anything, not even to move one piece of furniture. She turned towards Anna and found her hand extended, and she gripped it, and she knew in this moment that here she could have a friend, a confidante; and yet she also knew that she could never talk to her as she had done to Katie, or as she would do to Biddy. She was the lady of the manor but beneath the veneer and the education that Mr Burgess, the one time tutor of her husband and his brothers and sister, had imposed on her was the child, the young girl, the granddaughter of William and Annie Trotter, two very ordinary people who had brought her up.

She looked down for a moment on the children. They were standing side by side gazing upwards to where the stairs led into the gallery. Their mouths were slightly agape, their eyes wide. The house was as new and surprising to Willy as it was to Josefina, for he could have no memory of it. And when he turned and, looking up at Tilly, said, "It is a big house, Mama," she said, "Yes, dear; it's a big house."

"Shall I take him . . . them upstairs, Tilly . . . ma'am? The nursery is ready."

She turned and smiled at Fanny Drew, who was as perplexed

as the rest of the household by the small dark addition to it, and in this moment too, so excited that she had forgotten that the old family friend, Tilly Trotter, was now their mistress. Of course, she had been their mistress for years before, but on a somewhat different footing.

"Yes, Fanny, take them up. Thank you. Their day things are in the small trunk, the other luggage will be following."

Fanny nodded and smiled and held out her hands to the two children; but her right hand being on Willy's left side he did not see it and she had to lift it up, and as the child was drawn forward he turned and looked towards Tilly, saying questioningly, "Mama?" and she, nodding towards him, said, "It's all right. Fanny will take care of you; I'll be up in a moment."

Following this, the servants, taking their lead from Biddy who had uttered no word since coming into the house, dispersed.

It was in the drawing-room when Anna was helping her off with her hat and coat that Tilly felt suddenly weak. Her legs gave way, her mind became a void, and the next thing she knew she was sitting on the couch with John and Anna bending over her, their faces showing their anxiety. "Wh . . . what is it, Tilly? D . . . d . . . do you f . . . f . . . feel ill?"

She shook her head. "No, no. Please don't worry; I'm not ill, it's . . . it's just reaction, relief I think that the journey is over."

"You almost fell, dear, and you've lost all your colour."

She caught hold of Anna's hand and pressed it gently.

"It's nothing. I . . . I was rather ill after Matthew died. My legs go weak now and again, I think I'll go and have a wash. And then I must talk to Biddy; I could see she was in a state. But" – she smiled weakly now – "before I do anything at all, do you think I could have a cup of tea?"

"*Of course. Of course. Of course.* What am I thinking about?" Anna rushed to the bell-pull near the fireplace and tugged at it; and presently, when the door opened and Mr Francis Peabody sailed into the room, she said, "Bring a tray of tea immediately, Peabody." The butler inclined his head and, gravely turning about, went from the room, and Tilly closed her eyes and it came to her that life could hold other problems besides those stemming from the big issues, such as the one of having two mistresses in the house. And then there was Mr Peabody. No, not Mr Peabody, merely Peabody. How would he react to her sitting at the kitchen table chatting to the cook, laughing with Peg and

Fanny. But then, after all, the latter needn't trouble her for she didn't think she'd ever laugh again. . . .

After drinking a cup of tea she did not go upstairs immediately; instead she went into the kitchen where it looked as if Biddy was awaiting her entry, for she was standing to the side of the table looking down the long room towards the green-baized door. Her hands, joined at her waist, were gripped so tightly that the knuckles showed white. Peg and Fanny Drew were also in the kitchen and they too stood waiting for Tilly to approach.

Going immediately to Biddy, Tilly pressed her hands apart and gently pulled them from her waist and, holding them tightly, she said, "It's all right. It's all right, Biddy, Katie's all right, I've a lot to tell you. But first" – she now glanced at the girls – "I want to say how glad I am to see you all again. I . . . I never thought I would. . . . Sit down." She drew Biddy to the settle, and when they were seated both Peg and Fanny came and stood in front of them, and Fanny in her soft voice said, "You weren't just sayin' she was married, were you, Tilly? She's not dead, is she?"

"Dead! Don't be silly, Fanny. Of course not! She's married." Tilly now turned and looked at Biddy and she shook her old friend's hands up and down as she said, "She's married, Biddy. It . . . it all happened at the last minute. She wasn't going to stay. You see. . . . Oh it's a long story. After Matthew died I had a kind of relapse and I wasn't aware of very much for months, and then when I got on my feet my one thought was to come home, and the very day before we left – Katie was all packed, not a word about staying – Doug came to me, Doug Scott. He's a cowboy. Not like an English farm boy, oh no. Anyway, he told me that he loved Katie and Katie loved him, but that she wouldn't stay because she felt her duty was to come home with me. Well now, Biddy" – Tilly dropped her head slightly to the side – "what could I do? Could I have said yes, she must come home, when I knew where her heart lay? And what's more, Biddy, she'd never get a chance again like Doug." She turned and smiled at the girls now, saying, "He's a handsome fellow and seems twice her size . . . well, I tell you, he's six foot three. And Luisa, she's Mr Portes's daughter who now owns the ranch, is promoting him and giving him the house that we lived in. We had it specially built for ourselves. She's very fortunate, Biddy. But the main thing is she's happy, and she says they'll come home next year, or perhaps the following one, because Doug's not short of money."

Biddy sighed now, then said, "I was looking forward to seeing her, Tilly."

"I know you were, Biddy, but she would never have got such a chance here."

"Nobody'd get such a chance as that here." Peg's head was bobbing as she spoke. "I wish you had taken me with you, Tilly."

"Be quiet you!" Biddy, sounding her own self, now turned on her daughter, saying, "And not so much of the Tilly, I told you all yesterda'. You'll forget yourselves one of these days, and in front of company."

"Oh." Tilly now flapped her hand towards Biddy, saying, "It's lovely to hear my name again."

"People should know their place; they've been told often enough." Biddy now rose abruptly from the settle and went towards the open fire, and Tilly pulled a small face towards the girls and they both grinned at her.

It was as Biddy bent and lifted the teapot from the brass kettle-stand that she said, "I was sorry to hear of your loss, lass," and her daughters nodded their heads confirming the statement. When their mother passed them and added as she placed the teapot on the table, "You seem fated, lass, for sorrow," the pain that seemed to lie just beneath Tilly's ribs stabbed through and she lowered her head and bit on her lip, and when Peg's hand came on her shoulder it took an effort to stem the tears gushing up from the back of her throat and into her eyes, and she said thickly, "I'll go and have a wash. I'll be down again later."

"Aye. Aye." Biddy had not turned towards her, and the girls stood silently by as she walked between them, her head still bent, and went up the kitchen, through the long passage and into the hall.

Seeing the hall empty, she stood for a moment, her hand about her throat, trying to compose herself.

"You're fated, lass, for sorrow." It would seem that Biddy was right; in fact she had merely voiced the thought that had been in her own mind since Matthew died. Oh, Matthew! Matthew! Would the longing for him never leave her? . . . And yet it was little more than four years ago that she had stood in this very hall and said, "Oh, Mark! Mark!" after Matthew's father had been carried out.

And then there was that day in the far past when she had run to Simon Bentwood, the farmer, after hearing that his wife had

15

died, feeling that his arms would be widespread to greet her. And what had greeted her? The sight of him naked in the barn consorting with a woman far above his station, and her as bare as on the day she was born. That first love had died as cleanly as if it had been cut off with a knife. Yet it had been love, a love that she had fostered from when she was a child.

There had followed the twelve years with Mark as his mistress and mistress of this house. And she had loved him too. Oh yes, she had loved him too. But was that love anything compared with what she gave to his son? There was no way to measure love against love. When it was present and filled the time, it was all. But how many times could one love? She didn't know. What she did know was, she had loved for the last time.

3

The days that followed were, in a way, tranquil. She fell into a routine. Three weeks had passed and she had never been outside the gates; nor had the children, but they were content, in fact in their element. The garden had become a world to them. They were spoilt by Arthur and Jimmy Drew and also by the new coachman, Peter Myers. He had taken the place of Fred Leyburn who, with his wife Phyllis and brood of children, had moved to Durham where a windfall of a cottage had been left to Phyllis by an aunt.

Then there was the stable-boy, Ned Spoke. Peter Myers had already threatened him with a beating for running with the bairns and acting the goat as if he were a bairn himself instead of a thirteen-year-old lad.

It was at this time that Tilly, fearing that the children were beginning to run wild, spoke to Anna about the matter of their education. This she had decided to take upon herself, as there seemed nothing for her to do, for as much as Anna made an effort to let go the reins of the household, the habit of the last few years was strong and when the young matron found herself giving the orders she nearly always ended with, "Oh, Tilly, I'm sorry, I'm sorry," until the apologies had become rather embarrassing, making Tilly feel inclined to take the easy way out and say, "You carry on as always." But then, where would she be? What would her position become in this household? She owned the house, she owned the estate, she owned the mine. . . . That was another thing, the mine. She had only a few days ago expressed the wish to go to the mine and this had seemed to shock both John and Anna. The mine was no place for her now, not in her position. In any case, it was being run very efficiently by the manager and his under-manager.

They seemed to forget, that is if they ever remembered, that she had once worked in the mine.

And about the under-manager. She thought that in some way

Steve might have made a point of coming to the house to welcome her back. Was he not a tenant in her cottage? Yet why should he wish to bring her back into his life? From the beginning she had played havoc with his feelings, not intentionally, oh no, never, for she had made it plain to him that she would never feel for him other than as a friend. And who knew now but that he was married or at least might have someone in his eye.

She was feeling very unsettled in herself; as Biddy would have exclaimed if she had confessed her feelings to her: "You don't know which end of you's up, lass." And there was Biddy herself. She was the same yet not the same. She still did not seem to have got over the disappointment of Katie not returning, although she'd had a letter from her and one enclosed from Doug. Her only comment on this had been, "He seems a decent enough fellow." Then she had added in her caustic manner, "But I can't see our Katie on a horse, she'd look like a pea on a drum."

But now she was talking to Anna about the children. "I'm going to engage a nursemaid," she said; "someone sensible, young enough to play with them but old enough to keep them in their place when needed. In the mornings I'll take them for lessons, Willy already knows his ABC, but Josefina doesn't take too kindly to learning I'm afraid."

"They're so very young yet, Tilly, and they're enjoying the garden and playing. Must you start them on lessons?"

"I don't think you can start them too soon, Anna. You know, when I first came here John was four years old and Mr Burgess had him reading nursery rhymes. The first one I heard John read was 'The Little Jumping Joan':

> Here I am, little jumping Joan,
> When nobody's with me I'm always alone.

And when he finished it he always put his head back and laughed."

"Did he stammer then?" Anna's voice asked the question quietly, and Tilly lied boldly, saying, "Yes, much more than he does now. Oh" – she shook her head – "much more because now he can reel off sentences without a hitch, and that's all your doing." She inclined her head towards Anna, and Anna replied simply, "I hope so because I love him, I love him dearly, and I never forget that I have you to thank for him, Tilly."

"Nonsense! Nonsense! You would have met up without me."

"No, we shouldn't and you know it. When you asked me to come back that day I had intruded on you, hoping like some simpleton that you could give me a cure for my birthmark, I know now your mind formed a plan of bringing us together. John needed someone and I needed someone." She leant over and gripped Tilly's hand. Then after a moment she said, "There's only one thing bothering me, I . . . I show no signs of having a child."

"Oh, there's plenty of time, that will come. Remember I was with John's father for twelve years, well . . . eleven years before it happened to me, so don't worry your head, just go on being happy."

"Oh, I am happy, Tilly. I never imagined there could be such happiness in life. I. . . ."

They both turned as a knock came on the door and it opened, and Peabody was standing there.

"A messenger on horseback has brought this letter for you, madam. He says it's urgent," he said, holding the letter out as he walked slowly towards Anna.

Getting up, she took it from him and opened it. She read a few lines; then her face showing her concern, she looked at Tilly, saying, "It's from Aunt Susan. It's Grandma. She has taken a bad turn; I must go at once."

"Of course. Of course." Tilly now looking at the butler said, "Tell the messenger to return and say Mrs Sopwith will be there as soon as the carriage can take her."

"Yes, madam." Peabody inclined his head towards Tilly. Then as he went to turn away she stayed him, saying, "Order the coach to be got ready immediately, and then send word to the mine and ask Master John to return home as soon as possible."

She noted herself that she did not say "The master" because there could be no master of the Manor until Willy took his place, and that would be years ahead. . . .

In the confusion of the next few hours Tilly seemed to step back over the years. It seemed as if she had never been away from the house. The reins were in her hands once more and from the moment she saw Anna and John into the carriage she knew with that strange knowledge that could be termed intuition, or foresight, or even witchery, that they had gone to stay, and that for the first time she could now act as mistress, legal mistress of the house.

4

A fortnight later Anna's and John's belongings were taken to their now permanent residence in Felton Hall, beyond Fellburn. The old lady had had a stroke and Anna felt that she should be near her. Tilly was under the impression that John wasn't too happy at leaving the manor; but wherever Anna was there he wanted to be, and as he said to Tilly, what made her happy satisfied him. John seemed to have matured greatly since he married.

The day following their final departure, Tilly interviewed a girl from the village. Her name was Connie Bradshaw. She was the daughter of the innkeeper who, so she informed Tilly without much regret in her voice, had died last year, and her mother was no longer at the inn but living in a cottage on the outskirts of the village. She was a sprightly girl, free spoken, as Tilly found out when she questioned her.

"How did you know I was enquiring for a nursemaid?"

" 'Twas round the village, ma'am."

It was odd, Tilly thought, how a whisper in the house could travel to the village, and that over two miles away and none of the staff seeming to visit it.

"Have you just left a position?" she asked the girl.

"Well, not rightly a position, ma'am. I was workin' in the bar for me mam after me da died, but she gave me no pay an' then she got slung out."

"Slung out? . . . Why?"

"Drinking more than she sold, ma'am."

"Oh!" The candidness of the girl caused Tilly's eyelids to blink and she looked to the side for a moment. She only faintly remembered Mrs Bradshaw and had a picture of a blowsy woman, loud-voiced and running to fat, and so she could understand this girl wanting to get away from her parent and to better herself.

"Your name is Connie?"

"Aye, ma'am."

"Well, Connie, I shall take you on trial for a month. Your temporary wage will be two shillings a week. Should you suit at the end of that time then your wages would be ten pounds a year, together with uniform and your choice of tea or beer as refreshment. You will have leave to go to church on a Sunday if you wish, and one half day holiday a fortnight and one whole day a month."

The girl's face was bright as she replied, "Eeh! that sounds good to me, ma'am. I hope I'll suit. I'll try anyroad."

"I'm sure you will. Good-day, Connie."

"Good-day, ma'am."

She had interviewed the girl in the morning-room and after allowing enough time, as she thought, for her to get along the passage and to leave by the kitchen, which way she had entered, she herself left the room and made for the kitchen, meaning to give Biddy the orders for the day's meals, but she stopped just before she opened the kitchen door to hear the girl exclaim loudly, "I've got it! On trial for a month I am. Ain't there no housekeeper here? She asked all the questions hersel'. Well, I suppose she knew all the answers seein' as she was in my place once."

"Get yourself along, miss, and it'll surprise me if you reign a month."

That was Biddy's voice, and Tilly remained for a while standing where she was before turning about and going back into the morning-room.

She had made a mistake in engaging that girl, yet she had felt sorry for her having to work in a bar for nothing, and then putting up with a drunken mother. But she was from the village, and she should know by now that no villager wished her well, except perhaps Mr Pearson. Yet what had his son done? Appeared out of the blue in the wilds of Texas and exposed her past to all who would listen. But she couldn't blame Mr Pearson for that; you should never blame the parents for what their offspring did. Look at Mark's daughter, Jessie Ann. She had been the sweetest child but she had turned out a little Tartar of a woman. What would be her thoughts now, she wondered, knowing that her father's mistress, whom almost literally she had thrown out of this house, was back in it as its rightful mistress this time. It must be gall to her.

About that girl. Well, she had only taken her on for a month; she would wait and see. But now she must arrange her days, at least her mornings, in the schoolroom and the first thing she must do was to get suitable books. There wasn't a book in the library that she could use to instruct Willy and Josefina. At one time there had been dozens in the nursery, but when the second Mrs Mark Sopwith decided to leave her husband and take the children with her they had taken their books along with them.

But she knew where she could lay her hands on books of instruction for the young, in the attic at the cottage. After Mr Burgess died she had spent days clearing the rooms downstairs and packing the books under the roof; all she had to do was to go along there and select what she needed. . . . And risk running into Steve? Well, she'd have to meet him sometime. And why need she be afraid of meeting him? No need whatever.

She would go along one afternoon between one and three because if he was on the back shift he would likely still be down below, and if he was on the fore shift he would most likely be on his way there. Still, why try to evade a meeting, they were bound to come across each other some time; so the sooner the better and get it over with.

She left the room and went to the kitchen and the first words Biddy said were, "I think you've taken on something there, lass."

"I've told her it is only temporary, for a month."

"That's just as well. Doubt if you'll put up with her for a week, she's all tongue. And you know who she is?"

"Yes, she's Bradshaws' daughter from the inn."

"A pair if there ever was one. He died of drink an' she's goin' the same way."

"So I understand, but the girl didn't seem to want to follow in her mother's footsteps."

"She's got her mother's tongue. . . . Anyway, it's your business but I'm tellin' you this, lass, if she starts any of her antrimartins back in the hall" – she inclined her head towards the wall and the servants' hall next door – "I'll slap her down quicker than you can spit."

Tilly smiled as she said, "You do that, Biddy, it'll save me a job." It was odd, she thought, yet comforting how she dropped into the old colloquial way of speaking when talking to Biddy. "Now about me dinner, I don't feel very hungry today so. . . ."

"If you ask me, you never feel very hungry. Now look" – Biddy pointed – "there's a lemon sole that'll melt in your mouth. There's some veal cutlets an' all. Now I'm gona do those for you and you're gona eat them. Do you hear me?"

"I hear you."

"Here." Biddy jerked her head, a sign for Tilly to go and stand close to her, and now Biddy's voice was a mere whisper as she said, "Has his nibs been at you?"

"Peabody?"

"Aye. Who else?"

"No. Why should he be at me?"

"To get his daughter in here as nursemaid. The footman, Biddle, let on about it."

"He has a daughter . . . Peabody?"

"Four."

"No!"

"Aye. And you know what he was aiming to do just afore you came home?"

"No."

"Get the lot of them here. His eldest one's tickin' forty and she's a housekeeper in Newcastle somewhere. He'd been on to Master John about a housekeeper sayin' that it wasn't right for an establishment like this to be run by a cook." She now thrust her thumb into her chest. "Then his second eldest daughter is a widow with one bairn, and the other two are in service. The youngest, just on seventeen, would, he imagined, be just right for the nursery. Oh, when he knows about our Miss Connie Bradshaw the poker 'll drop down his spine and right out of his backside, and he'll crumple up 'cos, let's face it, that lass's as common as clarts. He thinks my brood's bad enough. Oh aye, he does." Biddy nodded vigorously at Tilly who now bit on her lip and lowered her head; for the first time in many, many months she had the desire to laugh.

Oh, it was good to be home, good to be with Biddy, good to be with real people. Not that John and Anna weren't real. Not that Matthew and Mark hadn't been real. But there was something about Biddy and her brood that presented life without veneer. There was no pretence. You hadn't to act in her presence, you just were. But she knew that if she were acting correctly as the mistress of this house she should not be standing hobnobbing with her cook; nor should she have the desire at this moment to fall against her and put her arms around her and say. "Oh, Biddy! Biddy! hold me close, comfort me." In fact she shouldn't be in the kitchen at all, she should, as that girl had said and as Peabody expected, have a housekeeper and leave the ordering to her, for was she not Mrs Matthew Sopwith.

No, no; she wasn't, not really, not underneath. Under the façade she knew who she was, and always would remain so, she was simply Tilly Trotter.

The sun was shining when, a week later, she rode out of the court-yard, and not side-saddle but astride the horse. It was the first time she had been on a mount since she had returned, and she was aware that the men were watching her covertly from the stables, as was Biddy and most of the staff from the kitchen windows.

She sat relaxed, as Mack McNeill and Matthew had taught her. The stirrups were long, her legs almost straight. Her riding breeches were grey, her high boots and coat brown; except for the bun of white hair showing behind her soft felt hat, the one that she had worn when riding out from the ranch, she could have been taken for a young man, a slim, straight young man.

As Biddy, her face close to the window, muttered to her daughters: "In the name of God did you ever see anything like it, the change a pair of trousers can make in a woman! And it'll do her no good at all to be seen ridin' like that, astride a beast for all the world like any man."

It was Jimmy Drew who opened the gates for her. He had been working at the end of the drive trimming the hedges, and, what was unusual, he never spoke as he watched her ride through, although she said, "Thanks, Jimmy. Thanks. . . . Lovely day, isn't it?"

She wasn't unaware of the stir she had made in riding out in such a fashion, and she knew her slouched hat, which was at variance with the smartness of her coat and breeches, would itself cause comment should she meet any rider. But what matter, she was used to comment. And this is how she had been taught to ride; and this is what she had worn when riding side by side with Matthew.

Oh Matthew! Matthew! If only he were here. Last night she had dreamed and the dream had been so real that she had turned in the bed and snuggled into him and just as always happened when she had turned to him he had loved her, and she had woken rested and put her hand out to feel him, and when realisation hit her she had pressed her face into the pillow and sobbed.

24

But crying was for the night; you faced the day calmly. You had two children to educate and a house to run . . . a difficult house to run, a house that was staffed partly by her friends and partly by professional servants. It hadn't been difficult for Anna and John to keep the harmony between the two factions but it was going to be so for her, for she knew she wouldn't be able to favour her friends without annoying her professional staff, few as they were.

She put her horse into a canter and rode so until she came to the lane leading from the main coach road. Here she quickly drew the animal to a walk as she saw in the distance a woman and three children scrambling up the bank. They had been gathering wood, which was made evident as they pulled the bundles into the narrow ditch at the side of the road, and when she came abreast of them they stared up at her as one, their eyes unblinking.

"Good afternoon." She smiled at them, and it was after a moment that the woman replied, "Afternoon, ma'am," at the same time bobbing her knee.

As she rode on there came over her a strong feeling of nostalgia for the days when she herself had gathered wood, not only gathered it but limbed it from the trees and sawed the branches up before dragging them home, and then had the satisfaction of seeing a roaring blaze at night as she sat before the fire between her granda and grandma. But that was another life, another world.

When she eventually turned a bend in the narrow lane and came within sight of the cottage it was to see a horse tied to the gate post, and her acquired knowledge of horseflesh told her it was a good animal and beautifully saddled. She also noticed that the hedge bordering the side of the cottage had been allowed to grow to almost twice the height she remembered it, although the top had been kept trimmed, but as she turned from the lane and rode up by the side of it she could just see over it and towards the front door of the cottage.

She was pondering in her mind whether to ride on and return later when the door of the cottage opened almost abruptly and a woman stepped on to the pathway, and following her came Steve. She did not immediately recognise the woman but she recognised Steve, although his head looked to be bandaged and his face was smeared with coal dust. The woman had turned and was looking up at him where he was now standing on the step above her, and it was with a start of amazement, not untouched with horror, that Tilly now recognised her.

It must be all of seventeen years since she had last set eyes on this woman, and then she had been lying naked in the barn with Simon Bentwood. Strangely, it was this woman who had decided the course of her own life; in a way, it was her she had to thank for the position that she now held as mistress of the Manor, for if on that day she hadn't seen her lying with Simon Bentwood, he and she herself would have come together and she would have been a farmer's wife and happy to be so. . . . Life was strange, terrifyingly strange. But what was that woman doing here? Indeed, what else but trailing a man! She was noted for it. She remembered her nickname, Loose Lady Aggie.

Tilly slid from the horse and took its head to keep it quiet. She did not want to be found here by either of them and it was no use riding on because the path which simply circled the garden would eventually bring her back into the lane and in full sight of them.

She listened as Lady Myton spoke. Her voice was as she remembered it, high, haughty, the words clipped. "You're foolish, you know that," she said.

"I don't see it that way, m'lady." Steve's voice sounded cool.

"It's a good position, you'd be in charge of the stables. There are nine hunters in there altogether."

"As I understand it you have very good stockmen already."

"Yes, I had, but Preston has left and his place is open."

"Then why not move the next man up?"

"He's not capable enough."

"Well, I can assure you, m'lady, he'd be much more capable looking after hunters than I would. My knowledge of horses is practically nil."

"I saw you riding the other day, you handled the animal well."

"Oh, him!" There was a slight note of laughter in Steve's voice now. "Only because his back's as broad as a fireplace settle, and he's too old even to trot. His days were over in the pit and he was on his way to the slaughterhouse; I felt he would save my legs the three-mile walk twice a day, so I took him on."

"You're making light of your achievements."

"Not a bit of it, m'lady."

There followed a pause now and Tilly heard their footsteps going down towards the gate; then Lady Myton's voice again: "You are turning down a great opportunity. Do you know that? And anyway I understand you were thinking of leaving the mine?"

"I think you've been misinformed, m'lady."

There was another pause before her voice came again, saying, "It's a tinpot mine, doesn't even pay its way."

"Again I think you've been misinformed. It's doing very nicely for all concerned."

"Until it's flooded again. And look at your head. I understand there was a fall this morning?"

"Just a slight one. These things happen every day in mines."

"And two men taken to hospital?"

"Just broken bones, nothing to worry about really."

Again there was a pause, and when the woman spoke Tilly could only just make out her words. "When we last met I indicated that I could be of great help to you; and you know, you are the kind of person that could be of great help to me. It would be a reciprocal situation."

There was a longer pause before Steve's voice came to Tilly, saying, "On that occasion, m'lady, I'm sorry to remind you, I pointed out that you had picked on the wrong man."

There was now the grating of the horse's hooves on the rough road and the sound brought a feeling of panic to Tilly. If the visitor rode back in the direction of the mine all well and good, but if she decided to take the coach road then she would pass by the path and almost assuredly she would glimpse her.

As there came to her the words "You're a fool, Mr McGrath. Do you know that?" followed by Steve's answer, "Yes, I'm well aware of that. Have been for years," she pulled the horse forward and was making quickly up by the side of the hedge when she heard a loud, "Well! Well!" and, looking over her shoulder, she saw Lady Myton sitting on her horse staring towards her. As they looked at each other over the distance Tilly realised that the woman had recognised her, and this was made evident when her ladyship's voice rang out, saying, "Mrs Sopwith, about to enter by the back door. If I remember rightly you have a habit of turning up at inopportune moments. The way is clear now." She thrust out one arm in a dramatic gesture. "He's yours, for the time being at any rate. I've always balked you, haven't I? Ha! Ha!"

As Lady Myton spurred her horse up the path, Tilly was aware that Steve had parted the top of the hedge a little way back and was peering at her in amazement; then almost instantly he seemed to be by her side.

"Oh, I'm sorry, Tilly, I never expected you. I mean . . . well"

27

– he haunched his shoulders and spread out his hands – "what can I say? Here; let me turn him about."

He turned the animal about and into the lane and tied it to the gatepost where Lady Myton's mount had been fastened a moment ago.

Now they were walking up the path to the cottage and she hadn't as yet spoken.

"Here, sit down." He pulled a chair from underneath the table, and she sat down thankfully and looked at him as he bent slightly above her. He was smiling, his eyes shining, his black hair above the bandage was ruffled, his shoulder muscles were pressing against his shirt; the belt that supported his trousers didn't cover a stomach bulge; he was a very presentable man and she could understand how he attracted Lady Myton.

As if he had picked up her thoughts he put his hand to his head where the bandage was stained as he said, "That woman! She's a menace, and she's as brazen as a town whore. I'm sorry." He flapped his hand now. "But I'm so surprised to see you. Of course I knew you were back and we'd come across each other some-time, but to be on the doorstep so to speak."

"And at the wrong moment." It was the first time she had opened her lips and she smiled at him and he smiled back at her as he said quietly now, "Aw, Tilly, it's good to see you and to hear your voice. How are you?"

"Oh, getting along, adjusting."

"I hear you had a rough time of it out there." His eyes rested on her hair where it showed under the turned-back brim of the hat, but he made no remark on it.

"Yes, you could say that, Steve."

"I was very sorry to hear about Mr Matthew, very sorry indeed. You can believe that, Tilly, I was."

"Thank you, Steve." She looked to the side for a moment; then her glance went round the room and she said, "You haven't altered anything."

"No; why should I, it was just right to begin with."

"You still like living here?"

"Nowhere better. In one way I've never been so contented in me life. Look, I'll just have a sluice and then I'll make you a cup of tea. The fire's bright." He thumbed towards it, and impulsively she said, "You go and have a sluice and I'll make the cup of tea."

"You will? Aw, Tilly!" He jerked his head at her. "It's as if

28

the years have dropped away. I'll do that. Do you remember the day the bucket fell down the well?"

"Yes, yes." She laughed at him as he went down the room and out of the bottom door. She didn't, however, go immediately to the fireplace but stood looking around her, and for a moment again nostalgia hit her and she had a longing to be back in this cottage with Mr Burgess sitting on the couch there nodding over his books, and Willy lying in the wash-basket by the side of the fireplace. She hadn't realised how peaceful she had felt during that interlude between Mark and Matthew.

Automatically her hand went to the mantelpiece for the tea caddy; and yes, when she opened it there it was half full of tea. As he said, he hadn't altered a thing. Dear Steve. But she must be careful, very careful, she must raise no hopes in that quarter again.

A few minutes later when he came into the room his face was clean and shining; his hair was combed back and the bandage was off his head showing a two-inch cut across his brow sealed now with dried blood, which caused her to exclaim, "Was the fall bad?" Then turning her head to the side, she muttered, "I couldn't help overhearing some of your conversation."

"I'm glad you did, Tilly, else you might have thought otherwise . . . got the wrong idea like. . . . But about the fall. No, it was nothing. Two fellows were trapped, one got his shoulder put out, the other . . . well, I think his leg's broken but it'll mend; we got them out quickly?"

"Is the mine paying?"

"Aye, yes. Oh yes, especially this last year. Master John has done a good job. He belies his looks that young fellow if I may say so, and the men think highly of him. There's hardly a day goes by but he shows his face, and that's something in a mine owner. Well, what I mean is" – he gave a quick jerk of his head – "I know he's actin' for you, but the men look upon him as the boss and although he's got a longer trek now comin' from his wife's place he still turns up."

"I'm glad the men have taken to him. He's a good young man in all ways, but I'm sure things couldn't have worked out so well without the help of you and Mr Meadows. By the way, were you thinking of leaving?"

"Er . . . well no. No, no, not at all . . . and leave this cottage and everything? I'd be daft now, wouldn't I?"

She stared at him, this Steve McGrath whom she had known

29

from a boy who had pestered her with his attention until she had shocked him off by becoming the mistress of Mark Sopwith. That Steve had been a kindly nondescript character, persistent in his attentions, but nondescript; but this Steve, well, he could be a man of the world. Put him in different clothes and she could see him talking with the best of them. He sounded confident, knowledgeable, which thought brought her to the reason for her errand here. And so as he turned from her, saying, "You've mashed the tea then. I'll pour out. And you still take milk?" she said, "Yes. Yes, please. And . . . and I must tell you the reason why I came today. You see I'm in need of books, school books; I'm going to start teaching the children."

"Well, you've come to the right place, Tilly; they're all just as you left them. Well, that isn't quite true." He now paused with the big brown teapot in his hand. "You see I've been going through them, at least some of them. I'd have to live a couple of lifetimes afore I'd manage to read that lot up there" – he lifted his head towards the ceiling – "but the more I've read lately the more I've realised what a learned man Mr Burgess must have been, because most of the pages have pencil marks or queries on them. He must have read most all the light hours of his life."

"Yes, I think he did, Steve. As for me, I've always felt indebted to him and that indebtedness increases with the years because besides teaching me so many things, he taught me what to read. You can waste so much of your time reading stupid matter."

"You're right there; but I don't think he possessed a book that you could put the name stupid to. You know, I think he would have made a good member of parliament, and on the side of the working man too. Did you ever read the notes that he made on Malthus? By! some of them were scathing, especially those touching on what Malthus said about catastrophes, wars and famines and such being the natural means of preventing overall starvation. . . . My! if he'd had his way there wouldn't have been any bairns born because every bairn meant another mouth to feed. He was a stirrer was that Malthus. I used to sit here at nights" – he pointed to the rocking chair now – "and get all worked up about him, real hot an' bothered." As he put his head back and laughed Tilly gazed at him, her face straight. She hadn't read anything about Malthus but she remembered the name now and hearing Mr Burgess explaining to Mark the Malthus theory, his idea being to bring about an ideal life for the few.

"Is your tea all right?"

"It's lovely, thanks. Have you read any of Shakespeare?"

"Oh aye. Oh yes. By! there was a writer, wasn't he?" He now sat down at the opposite side of the table to her and, folding his arms on it, he leaned towards her, saying, "I can put this to you, Tilly. You see I can't talk to anybody else about it because I'm like a being set atween the devil and the deep sea. The lads back there" – he jerked his head – "wouldn't understand what I was getting at, even those who are now learning their letters on the quiet, and if I was daring to open my mouth to me betters" – he made a face here – "you can imagine their reaction, can't you?" He now straightened his back and took up the pose of a man sitting at a table with an enlarged stomach and his voice matched his stance as he said, "What the devil is the fella on about? Give them an inch and they take a mile. Only way to manage 'em is keep 'em down. Keep 'em down."

Tilly put her hand over her mouth and laughed quietly and as she did so she felt the tense muscles in her body relaxing. Oh, it was nice to talk to one of your own sort, an intelligent one. And now he was speaking again.

His arms once more folded, he said quietly, "As I was about to put to you, did it ever occur to you when you were reading a lot, Tilly, of just how ignorant you were of all the things that went on in the world afore your time, and just how ignorant everyone else around you was? Did it? Did it?"

"Oh yes, Steve, yes." She shook her head slowly from side to side. "I know I'm still ignorant. I think you only start to learn when you realise you're ignorant, it's your ignorance that drives you on."

"Yes. Aye, yes" – he nodded at her – "that could be true. Yet I was thinkin' the other day when I was listening to the lads down below, if they all had the chance to read and write would it get home to them that they were ignorant? Would they take advantage of it? Do you know I doubt it, I doubt it, Tilly. I think some men are made in such a way that they cling to their ignorance. 'I know nowt but I'm as good as thee, lad'. You know, that sort of thing, sort of 'I'm not gonna learn, on principle.' Mind your eye, I don't think women would take that attitude; I think if women got the chance they would learn."

"Oh, I don't know if I agree with you there, Steve. All a woman really wants, in the first place that is, is a husband and a

31

home and bairns. All the ordinary woman wants is warmth and enough to eat for herself and her family. A woman will work all her life to get security, as it were, for those belonging to her."

He sat back in his chair now and his lips went into a twisted smile as he said quietly. "What about the Lady Mytons?"

"Oh, they're a type on their own, bred of their own class."

"Well now, it's me that doesn't agree with you there, Tilly, for I don't think they're a type on their own. Her type is found in every class of society from the gutter upwards."

"Well, you certainly sound as if you know." She was smiling at him but when she saw the colour rise to his brow she actually laughed aloud, and he self-consciously with her, and he said, "Well now, Tilly, don't get me wrong: I didn't mean I'd had experience with people like her in every class. But I do keep me eyes and ears open, and all I can say is she's not alone. And when you do get somebody like her she's worse than any man. . . . Eeh!" He rose to his feet now, saying apologetically, "I shouldn't be talkin' to you like this."

"Why not?" She looked up at him. "We're old friends, Steve, we've known each other for a long, long time, and we're not children any more."

"Yes, you're right there, Tilly." He stood gazing down on her. "And eeh! by! it's lovely to see you again an' to talk to you. And it goes without saying you'll be very welcome in your own house" – he spread his arms wide – "any time you've a mind to come, because I'll not be able to take the road the other way unless I come as a messenger, will I?"

She wanted to say again, "Why not? You may call any time you like," but what had she warned herself of just a short while ago? They were old friends but the friendship must remain old and not be renewed in any way. She rose to her feet now, saying, "May I go up and sort out the books?"

"It's your house, Tilly." His voice was level and slightly flat now. He pointed to the ladder, then added, "When you've got what you want give me a shout and I'll bring them down for you."

"Thanks, Steve."

She had her foot on the first step of the ladder when he said quietly, "That outfit suits you. You don't see the like of it round here."

"No, I suppose it is surprising, but it's common in America and it's a very comfortable way to ride."

He nodded at her and she went up the ladder and into the attic where his bed was. It had been roughly made and there were no clothes lying around. He was naturally tidy, like a sailor might be, one who was used to a small space. Well, thinking back to his early days he had been used to a small space, a cubby-hole in the roof, if all tales were true. Yet that being so it was a wonder he hadn't gone the other way and strewn his things far and wide. He was a surprise was Steve in all ways; there was not the slightest connection between the man and the boy.

She went to the far corner of the attic and she could see at once that the books had been sorted over but she quickly found what she wanted. A moment later she knelt down on the floor and called, "Steve! Would you take these please?"

Having reached up and taken the books from her, he placed them on the floor, then, his arms extended, he steadied her as she came down the ladder.

It was the first time in years that she had felt his touch, in fact she couldn't remember him ever putting his hand on her; she could only visualise him standing suppliant and pleading for her love. Now, surprisingly, he must be so self-sufficient he didn't need love of any kind or else he would surely have been married before now.

"How you going to carry these, you can't tuck them under your arm? Look, I'll make two slings and they'll hang at either side of the saddle."

"Yes, yes, that's a good idea. Thanks, Steve. And I'll have to be getting back." She took a fob watch from the pocket of her short riding jacket. "Twenty to three. Dear, dear, how the time flies. The children will be racing round looking for me."

"How is the boy?"

"Oh, Willy? He's fine."

"Are his eyes improving?" He asked the question quietly and she looked into his face which was straight now and then her head drooped as she said, "The sight has completely gone in one eye and the other is somewhat affected, but I'm afraid time isn't on his side with regards to his sight going completely."

"I'm sorry. Oh I am, Tilly. I'm sorry to the heart. And I can tell you that feeling isn't unmixed with guilt when I think me mother is responsible. By! the things our family have to answer for. I want to stop believing in a hereafter except for the fact that if there's no justice beyond they'll get off scot-free. I used to think

33

our George was decent, or would have been if he'd got the chance, but his youngster, Billy, is another Hal by the things I hear he gets up to." He looked down towards the floor now as he said, "Me mother turned up at the door here one day. I didn't ask her in, and I said things to her that day that she would have brained me for a few years earlier. You know" – he smiled wanly now – "when I was a lad I used to imagine she had stolen me as a bairn because somehow I didn't seem to link up with any of them in that house. And when our Hal gave me this" – he now lifted his left arm which he was unable to straighten from the elbow, he added with bitterness, "I swore that one day I'd get me own back on him, and I did, didn't I?"

"Oh, Steve!" She swallowed deeply in her throat. "I was to blame for that."

"No! No!" The words were emphatic. "I would have done it some time or other; I meant to kill him and I haven't the slightest regret. Perhaps I'll have to pay for that too if there's a beyond, but I'll willingly do it. He would have died in any case that night left out alone as he was on the fells, with his back broken, but I saw to it that I despatched him afore the weather got him. Now don't worry, Tilly" – he put out his hand towards her but didn't touch her – "I've never lost a moment's sleep over it. I became a man that night, and it's odd but I seem to have grown from then on both upwards and outwards. I feel free of the lot of them now."

As she stared at him she wondered if he really had forgotten what he had said when he came to propose to her. "I killed our Hal for you, Tilly," he had said. "What I did to him I did for you." Had the years blotted out that memory? She imagined it must be so, and it was just as well. Oh yes, it was just as well.

During the time it took him to rope up the books neither of them spoke, and it wasn't until they were going down the path that she said, "I'm so glad that you're settled in the cottage, Steve. I would have had to sell it, or let it to someone who wouldn't have looked after it as you have."

He half paused as he turned to her, saying, "You'd sell it?"

"I don't know. I don't think. . . ."

"Well, we can talk about it later, can't we?"

"Yes, yes."

"Talking of buying cottages or houses, I had a stroke of luck a few years ago."

"Yes, what was that?"

They were standing by the side of the horse now. "Well, you know the people I lodged with when I worked in Durham, a Mr and Mrs Ransome? Well, the old lady died, and he was lost without her, and one Bank Holiday he took me with him to a cottage right out in the wilds of Northumberland, nothing but hills around it, and on the hills nothing but sheep. He had been brought up there. It wasn't much more than a little but and ben, nothing like this one" – he jerked his head backwards – "two small rooms, a loft and a couple of shippams and most of the place dropping to bits. Well, from that day we got into the habit of going up whenever we could and doing a bit of repairing. I could have got a job as a stone-mason by the time I'd finished; and oh, it was and still is lovely up there, in the good weather that is. By heck! come the winter it would freeze the nose off a brass monkey. Anyway, to cut my long story short, when Mr Ransome died what did I learn but he'd left it to me, the cottage and ten acres. Sounds marvellous doesn't it, but you've got to see the land. It's all stone and you can't do anything with it except run sheep on it, and then only a few. But there you are, Tilly, I'm a landowner. Doesn't that surprise you?"

"It does, it does indeed, Steve; and I'm very happy for you."

"Funny thing life, isn't it? Neither of us had a brass farthing or as much as a penny to start with, and now we're both well set, you most of all. And there's nobody more pleased for you than I am, Tilly."

"Thank you, Steve. Thank you."

They stared at each other for a moment, both smiling. Then without further ado he bent down, took the sole of her high boot in the palm of his broad hand and the next moment she was astride the horse, and he was looking up at her, saying, "You make a fine pair. I'll swap him any day for the old dodger back in the field."

She laughed, saying as she did so, "Bye-bye, Steve," and he answered, "Bye-bye, Tilly."

The horse had taken but a few steps when she turned and looked at him. He was no longer smiling and for a moment she seemed to recognise the expression that was usually on the face of the boy he had once been, and it disturbed her. But only for a short while, until she reached the Manor.

*

35

She had handed the horse over to Peter Myers and when Biddle met her at the top of the steps she had allowed him to relieve her of the books, but she had no sooner entered the hall when Josefina, jumping down from the second stair and evading Connie Bradshaw's hand, rushed towards her, crying, "Mama! Mama! she slapp-ed Willy. Mamma, she slapp-ed Willy.'

Taking hold of the child's hand, she said, "Quiet! Quiet! Josefina." Then looking towards where Connie Bradshaw was holding Willy by the hand she asked quietly, "What is this about slapping?"

"I just tapped his hand, ma'am.'

She stared at the girl for a moment; then reaching out, she took her son's hand and drew him to her side, saying to him now, "Have you been slapped, Willy?"

The boy hesitated a moment as he peered up at her, his lids blinking over his brown eyes, and he replied, "I was naughty, Mama."

She had noticed this about her son that he never answered a question by yes or no but generally gave a reason. It was a queer trait in a child and it nearly always pointed to his attempting to avoid trouble both for himself and others.

"Why were you naughty? What did you do?"

"I pulled at nurse's chain. . . ."

"He touch it, Mama, she nasty, grab it and slapp-ed him. She slapp-ed him hard, Mama."

"I didn't, I didn't. I tapped his hand, that's all."

Tilly looked at the girl. She wasn't wearing a chain of any kind. Naturally she wouldn't while on duty. She didn't, however, go into the question of what kind of a chain Willy had been pulling, but instead said, "Please don't raise your hand to the children again. If they're naughty come to me immediately and I shall deal with them. You understand?"

"Yes, ma'am."

"Well now, take them up to the nursery. I'll be there shortly."

"She naughty, Mama. She naughty."

"Quiet! Josefina. No more. Now be a good girl, go along with Willy."

Both the children went dutifully away with their new nurse, but not silently, for Josefina's mutterings could be heard even when she reached the gallery.

Tilly turned now to where Biddle was still standing holding

36

the books and she said to him, "Take them to the nursery, please."

"Very good, madam."

As she watched the footman ascending the stairs she wished Anna hadn't gone to the expense of rigging out both him and Peabody in such flamboyant uniforms. Breeches and gaiters didn't somehow go with the atmosphere of this house.

She sighed and pondered for a moment whether to go into the kitchen as she was or go upstairs and change. Having decided on the latter, she slowly mounted the stairs and as she made her way across the balcony and along the broad corridor, Josefina's high piping voice came to her, and she smiled to herself ruefully. Things didn't change all that much; it seemed no time since Matthew and his two brothers and his sister had run wild up on that floor and chased each other screaming down the stairs and along this very corridor.

Again she thought, Oh, Matthew! Matthew! for Matthew had loved her from the first moment he had seen her; he had been ten and she sixteen, and later he had died loving her; but he had laid the rest of her life heavily on her.

Immediately on entering the room she stopped and looked towards the bed on which she had lain with his father, but never with him, and she asked herself why she should have thought that, Matthew had laid the rest of her life so heavily on her, for hadn't she made up her mind she could never love again and so the promise she had made to the dying held no burden for her. . . . Or did it?

She had got out of her riding clothes and put on a dressing-gown, and, sitting before the mirror, she pondered the fact that she was only thirty-five but her hair was as white as driven snow. It was the hair of an old woman, yet she hadn't a line on her face. As she rose from the stool, pulling tight the cord of the dressing-gown around her thin body, an impatient voice within her muttered, What did it matter what she looked like? One needed to have pride in one's looks only for a husband or a lover, and she'd had both and now she had neither. So be it.

5

"Look, Ma, I saw her shaking little Willy as if he were a rat. If the other one had been there there would have been hell to pay, but Miss Josefina had run down to the lake. I saw it all out of the gallery window."

"Well, if she had really hurt him he would likely have yelled out."

"He doesn't, Ma. I've noticed that about him, he doesn't. Miss Josefina makes up for it, I'll give you that, but he holds his tongue about things. He's funny that way, an' it's sort of old for a bairn of his age."

"Well——" Biddy went on straining the stock through a sieve as she said, "Give her enough rope and she'll hang herself; you can't do anythin' without proof and don't you go carryin' tales, our Peg."

"I don't go carryin' tales, but I hate to see little Willy. . . ."

"Master Willy."

"All right, Ma, Master Willy. And anyway, I don't forget meself beyond the kitchen door, and I'm not talkin' to anybody but you. Now. . . ."

"An' mind who you are talkin' to." Biddy stopped her straining for a moment. "Don't use that tone to me."

"Oh, our Ma, you never change."

"No; that's one thing about me; as I was yesterda' I'll be the morrow. An' when I'm on, what were you and Myers gassing about in the yard a minute ago when you should have been about your work?"

"Oh, he was tellin' me that he had met up with the Mytons' coachman when he stopped for a pint in the Black Horse t'other night. And what do you think of the latest, Ma?"

"Well, I won't know till you tell me, will I, lass?"

"You know who her ladyship is after now? You'd never guess."

"No, I'm no use at guessin', so spit it out."

"Steve McGrath."

38

Biddy let the strainer drop into the clear liquid, then jerked it out, saying, "Never!"

" 'Tis true. She does, she is. She waylays him on his road back from the pit."

"She's a maniac, that woman . . . Steve McGrath. Eeh! who in the name of God will she have next? She had the master at one time, then she had Farmer Bentwood; and now Steve McGrath of all people. . . ."

"Oh, them's not all. Their coachman told Myers that one of the stable lads . . . well, he wasn't all that young, he was nineteen, but he did a bunk one night 'cos she kept coming up in the loft after him, supposedly wanting to have her horse saddled, sometimes around two o'clock in the morning." Peg started to giggle and Biddy said, "God above! She should be locked up."

"An' speaking of bein' locked up." Peg now nodded at her mother. "That's what she's tried to do to his lordship. The coachman said she'd had a doctor there to have him put away, in fact two of them, but the old boy talked so sensible like an' acted the same way that the doctors were flummoxed an' said they could do nothing until he became dangerous, an' dangerous he's become if the rumour is right."

"What rumour?"

"Well, the coachman said the old fellow's taken to ordering the coach practically every day and he takes his shotgun with him. He's known all along about her carry-on, but till now it's just seemed to slide off him. But since the doctors came he's changed. The coachman said it was funny 'cos although he seemed to talk more sensible like he acted more mad, if you know what I mean."

"No, I don't." Biddy now took the strainer and threw it over into the sink as she called into the scullery, "You, Betty! These dishes will be walking out to meet you if you don't clear the sink . . . and now!"

As the voice from the scullery shouted, "Comin' Mrs Drew, comin'," Biddy walked to the far end of the kitchen towards a round baking oven set in an alcove, and opening the door gently she peered in before closing it as gently again. Then turning to find Peg at her elbow and sensing that she was intent on imparting something of a private nature, she asked under her breath, "What is it?"

Peg now glanced down the long kitchen towards Betty and she waited until the girl had scooped up an armful of dirty dishes and

39

disappeared into the scullery again before she said, "I hear they're startin' on about Tilly again . . . in the village."

"Startin' on about Tilly! What now?"

"About the little one."

"Well, what about the little one?"

"Aw, Ma!" Peg's voice was a mere whisper now and she shook her head from side to side before she added, "Well, you know Tilly says she's well on past four, but I ask you, does she look it? She's so tiny and she hardly looks on three. Of course, she talks older but that's with being a foreigner and learnin' her English from Tilly."

"What you gettin' at?"

"Well, Ma. Aw, don't you see what they're sayin'? They're sayin' it's hers."

Biddy drew her head back away from her daughter's and into her shoulders and said, still in a whisper, "Don't be so bloody soft."

"I'm not, Ma, I'm not soft. And don't put on so much surprise either, 'cos hasn't it occurred to you it's funny that she should bring such a bairn back with her? Even our Arthur said the other night, white people don't do that kind of thing, pick up Indian bairns, I mean adopt them when they've got one of their own, and he says by what he hears from fellows who've been over there that the Indians are looked on worse than the niggers."

"But the bairn's not Indian, just Spanish or Mexican or some such."

"Aye, you've said it, Ma, some such. Mind, not that I'm blamin' Tilly. She could have been raped. Aye she could by all I hear, 'cos, as our Arthur said, women are classed no better than cattle over there. And he's worried about our Katie."

"He's not the only one." Biddy turned and went back down the kitchen with Peg close on her heels. But at the table she stopped and, her face grim, she looked at her eldest daughter as she said, "This business about the little dark 'un being Tilly's, well, I'd stake me life on it there's not a happorth of truth in it. Why, seein' how Master Matthew doted on her he would have murdered anybody who touched her."

"Perhaps he did, Ma. How are we to know anything? She doesn't talk about what happened out there. The only thing we can gather is it must have been pretty awful to turn her hair white. Anyway, it doesn't matter what we think, it's them villagers, you know what they're like, nothin' seems to change them, father to son, mother to daughter. The witch business still clings to her."

"What's that?" Biddy cocked her ear to the side and Peg said, "It's the little 'un screaming; you can hear her a mile off."

"Well, I've never heard her from down here afore. Look, get yourself upstairs and see what's afoot."

As Peg hurried out of the kitchen and into the hall Tilly came out of the library and they looked across at each other before both running to the stairs and up them. As they reached the gallery the screams came louder, mingled now with Willy's childish crying and the voice of Connie Bradshaw.

Tilly was first up the nursery stairs and as she rushed through the open door into the day-room she stopped for just a second to take in the scene before her. Willy was lying on the floor nursing his hand and crying loudly, but in the far corner of the room Connie Bradshaw was shaking Josefina in the same way a terrier would shake a rat, and the child was screaming and kicking out with her feet.

"*Put her down this minute!*" Tilly's voice thundered through the room, and Connie Bradshaw actually dropped the child to the floor, and Tilly, rushing forward, picked her up and cradled her in her arms while she glared at the nursemaid, crying, "*How dare you! How dare you!*"

"She tore at me, she tore at me face. Look!"

Tilly looked at the girl's face. There was a long scratch down one cheek, and it was actually bleeding.

"You must have done something very bad to her that she should react in that way," Tilly said emphatically.

"Ma-ma. Ma-ma." Josefina had her hand on Tilly's jawbone stroking it rapidly – it was a gesture she always used when she wanted her whole attention – and now through her crying she spluttered, "Beat Willy. Beat Willy, Mama."

"I didn't, I didn't, you little liar you!"

"Be quiet! And don't you come out with such terms here."

"Mama! Mama!"

Peg had picked Willy up from the floor, but pressing himself away from her hands, he groped towards Tilly, crying, "Your box. Your box, I was looking at your box."

"What box, dear?" Tilly now put Josefina down and picked up her son and again said, "What box, dear?"

"From the toilet, on the table, Mama, the pretty box."

"In her pocket, Mama, box in her pocket!" Josefina was screaming the words now as she pointed at the nursemaid, and Tilly, looking at the girl, demanded, "Show me what you've got in your pocket."

The white starched apron that reached from the girl's waist to her ankles and which had a bib with the straps crossing over her back and buttoning on top of her hips, had two large pockets. Connie Bradshaw now stuck her hands into them, saying as she did so, "I've got nothin' in me pockets but what's me own."

"Then you needn't be afraid of letting me see what belongs to you."

The girl's jaw tightened and she thrust out her chin as she said, "I've got a right to what's mine. Me ma says everybody's got a right to what's theirs. I know me rights, you can't search me, I've got nothin' belongin' to you. You'll get wrong if you accuse me I have."

Tilly now looked towards Peg and said, "Ring the bell for both Peabody and Biddle, please."

Peg now went to the corner near the fireplace and pulled the rope twice before pausing and pulling it again three times.

It was Biddle who entered the room first and he stopped within the door and stared at his mistress, then at the scene before him; but he said nothing, and neither did Tilly. Presently, the butler arrived puffing slightly, and he, too, stood without speaking for a moment. When he did speak, all he said was, "Madam . . . you rang?"

"Yes, Peabody. I want you to witness Peg searching this girl."

As Peg moved towards the nursemaid, Connie Bradshaw backed from her, saying, "You lay a hand on me and I'll scratch your eyes out."

"We'll see about that." As she spoke Peg's hand came out and caught the girl a ringing slap around the ear, and before she could retaliate Peg had her up against the wall and was thrusting her hand into one of the pockets. Then she pulled out a small enamel trinket box. It wasn't more than an inch across and about the same in depth, and as she handed it on her open palm to Tilly she said, " 'Tis off your table, ma'am."

Taking the box, Tilly stared at it; then shaking her head, she said, "No, this one is from the china cabinet surely in the drawing-room?" Turning now, she said, "Biddle, will you please go across

42

to this girl's room, take Peg here with you, and search her belongings."

"I'll have the polis on you, yes, I will. I didn't take that box, I didn't. It was that little black sod picked it up from off the table, and I took it from her and was gona take it back, I was."

"Do as I ask." Tilly nodded from Peg to Biddle, and they left the room.

She herself remained standing awaiting their return, the children pressed tightly against her skirts, and Peabody, standing apart, kept his gaze on the still defiant girl as if he were viewing something that smelt.

The five minutes seemed endless before Peg and Biddle returned, when the footman, holding out his hands to Tilly, said, "She had made a hole in the underside of the mattress, ma'am. These were in it."

Slowly Tilly picked up from his palm the locket and chain that Mark had given her years ago, it was one of the few pieces that his wife hadn't managed to take with her. The locket was silver with a gold filigree surround, the chain supporting the locket was of fine gold. She hadn't missed it because it was kept in a box among other trinkets in the bottom drawer of her dressing-table. From his other palm she took up, first a miniature portrait of a baby. It showed Mark's father at the age of one year. It had lain from the time it was painted until now in one of the cabinets downstairs. Next and lastly, she took from his hand two gold rings and a brooch. The rings had been presents from Matthew. They, too, had lain in a box, or rather in a velvet case, at the back of the top drawer of the dressing-table.

She turned slowly and looked at the girl. She must be stupid. How did she expect to get away with this? But then of course, anyone with access to the bedroom could have been blamed, Peg or Fanny, Lizzie Gamble or Betty. On Sunday, which was her half-day, she would have taken the things home and her mother would have disposed of them, and she would have returned as brazen as brass. No, she wasn't stupid, she was cunning.

"Do you wish to call in the law, madam?" Peabody did not say "the police" or even "the polis", but "the law", and she looked at him for a moment before saying, "No, Peabody; we won't call in the law but I would ask you and Biddle to go into her room again to make sure there is nothing more there."

"Very good, madam."

Both men inclined their heads towards her and left the room; and now Tilly, looking at Peg, said, "You will stay with her, Peg, until she is outside these gates."

"I want me money afore I go; I've been here over three weeks."

"You have forfeited any right to your probationary wages; you are lucky you won't find yourself in the house of correction this night."

"Aw! you. I'll have me ma on you for me six shillings, she'll sort you out. Anyway, I wouldn't have stuck it here. Me ma always says you shouldn't work for them worse than yersel."

The girl moved from where she had been standing against the wall down towards the nursery table and as she went to pass Tilly she glared at her as she said, "It's right what they say in the village about you; not satisfied with havin' a blind bastard you had to go whorin' with a bloody nigger."

For a moment Tilly seemed to stop breathing. Then there rushed through her body a torrent of anger. It was like fire in her veins. She was facing Alvero Portes again, diving at him, tearing at his face; she was firing point blank at the Indians. The girl before her seemed to sprout buffalo horns, her face was painted, and she sprang at her, delivering a blow first to one side of her face, then the other. What she would have done next she didn't know had not Peg torn her back from the girl and thrust her down into a chair before almost flying to where Connie Bradshaw was leaning against the wall holding both sides of her head with her hands and with tears now raining from her eyes, and she shouted at the girl, "Out! Out" and swinging her round, she pushed her out of the door and on to the landing; and there meeting the butler and the footman, she cried at them, "She went for the bairns!" and then added, "and . . . and the mistress."

"She did?" Peabody drew himself up to his full height and, looking down on the spluttering girl, he said one word, "Scum!"

The word seemed to return the girl to her defiant self and she yelled at him, "I never did! I never did! She hit me. Like a mad 'un, she was, crazy. But I'll have her. Me ma 'll have her for it, you'll see. . . . Aye. Aye, just you wait 'n see." Her voice trailed away as Peg pushed her down the stairs.

Peabody and Biddle entered the nursery, and the sight of his mistress sitting at the table, her head held in her hands while the children, crying loudly, clung to her waist, caused the butler to

44

become ordinary and human and to say softly, "Come, madam, come. Don't distress yourself. You, Biddle" – he turned to the footman – "take the children downstairs; Mrs Drew will see to them. Put them in the servants' hall." Then turning to Tilly again, he said, "Take my arm, madam. This has been a most unfortunate occurrence."

"I'm all right, thank you. I can manage." Tilly rose from the chair and stood supporting herself against the table for a moment; then she looked at the elderly man and said, "Thank you. Thank you, Peabody. I . . . I think I will go to my room. And yes, if you would see me there I should be grateful. And then would you ask Mrs Drew to come up to me, please?"

"Certainly, madam. Certainly."

As she walked, with the aid of Peabody's arm, she felt that her legs were about to give way beneath her. Those waves of rage always had a weakening effect on her. Dear God! what she might have done to that girl if it hadn't been for Peg. But the knowledge that the village had started on her again had made her lose control. Would anybody believe her now if she were to say that the child was Matthew's, his byblow? No. The only one who could speak the truth was Katie; and it wasn't likely that she would ever come back to this country again. Although she had promised Biddy that Katie would come on a holiday some time, she knew in her heart there was little chance of it. Katie could not endure the sea and Doug Scott could not endure to be away from the life to which he had been bred.

Scandal had touched her once again and this time it would be worse than before. To brave the scandal of a white bastard had been bad enough, but to have a dark foreign one added to her score was something she didn't know how she was going to contend with. Matthew had been right. Oh Matthew! Matthew!

6

"Bloody trollop! Put the devil on horseback an' he'll ride to hell.
Never was a truer word spoken. Bash me daughter, would you,
you dirty trollop! Come out o' there an' I'll sort you out!"

Peabody was at the hall window looking over the terrace down
on to the drive where stood the drunken woman, and as Biddle
came hurrying up to him, he turned his head towards him and
said, "It's that girl's mother and she's as drunk as a noodle. What
do we do with her?"

"Get her away before the mistress hears her, I hope."

Biddle made towards the front door. Biddy came hurrying out
of the kitchen and across the hall, saying, "Hold your hand a
minute. Leave her to me; I can deal with the likes of her. You go
out there an' she'll have your fancy toggery off your back quicker
than it took you to put it on, I can tell you that."

"But she sounds a vicious woman, Mrs Drew."

"Well, what am I just telling you, Mr Peabody? But if she
starts any of her games with me my two lads will be behind me,
and they'll give her the Highland fling down the drive and out of
the gates, I can assure you of that. But I'll be obliged, Mr Peabody, if you'd see that the mistress stays up in the nursery until the
coast's clear."

"As you say, Mrs Drew. As you say."

There was no doubt who was in charge of this situation and
when Biddy pointed towards the door, Biddle almost jumped to
open it. And then she was standing on the terrace looking down on
the bloated face of the prancing, shouting and gesticulating
woman.

"Aw! she sent ya out, has she? Frightened to face me, is she?
The dirty, whorin' upstart!"

"I'll give you two minutes to turn an' get yersel' down that
drive and out through them gates, Bessie Bradshaw. And if you
don't make a move I'll have you carried out."

"My God! look who's talkin'." The woman put her head back

46

and laughed loudly. "Daft old runt! You know what they say in the village about you? You close your eyes to the goin's on to keep your family set-in. But I'll not close me eyes, no, I'm goin' to the polis. She battered my lass. You should see her face." She slapped at her own cheek now as she ended, "Out here."

"Your girl attacked her."

"Bloody liar!"

"There are witnesses. And let me tell you something, Bessie Bradshaw, if it wasn't for the mistress your lass would be in the house of correction this minute for the stuff she stole."

"*What!*" The woman now stood swaying, her head poked forward. "What you say? My lass stole? You're a damned liar!"

"I'm no liar. Two of the staff – and they weren't my lot either – searched her room and found a number of valuables stuffed in the mattress."

"My lass stole?"

It was evident to Biddy that this news had come in the form of a shock to Bessie Bradshaw, for the woman screwed up her face as if in protest, then said, "You tellin' the truth, Biddy Drew?"

"Aye, I'm tellin' the truth. And there's those inside there" – she jerked her head back towards the house – "who would go to court an' swear to it an' all. And it would be nothing less than three years she'd get, and lucky at that."

The woman now half turned away and looked about her. She saw the two men standing at the entrance to the stable yard, she saw the faces at the hall windows; then, her eyes lifting slowly upwards she saw the lone figure outlined against one of the narrow windows that bordered the top of the house and, recognising it, her anger returned and she rounded on Biddy again, crying now, "Aye, well, about this 'ere last business, I'll deal with Connie. But there's one thing she hasn't done yet, she hasn't stood without her shift on cryin', Come on, Tom, Dick or Harry, this way, this way. Tis a whorehouse she should be in, your missis. Worn hersel' down to skin an' bone with it, she has. All in together, girls, never mind the weather, girls. Shameless bitch, bringin' her black bastard here."

Biddy was down the steps facing her now and crying, "Shut your mouth and take your trip!" the while pointing down the drive. "Now get goin' or I'll do what I promised first off."

"Aw, to hell with you! An' the lot of you. You'll sizzle in hell's flames. Drink's one thing, but loose livin' 's another. I'm no

47

loose liver, never have been. Nor me lass. Stealin'! Don't believe a bloody word of it." She shook her head before she turned about and shambled away, her voice receding with her steps.

Biddy waited until the woman was lost to her sight round the bend in the drive; then, beckoning her sons to her with a jerk of her head, she said, "Take a dander down there and see she gets out. And I'll have a word to say with you, our Jimmy, as to how she got in. Those gates should be locked."

"They are locked, Ma. She must have got over the wall down by the wood; it's no more than four foot there."

Biddy shook her head. "Well, go on after her," she said; "and see she goes out the same way she came in."

Her sons hurried away to do her bidding, but she did not return to the house by the way she had come out; instead, she walked slowly through the courtyard and so into the kitchen, and there, looking at her daughter, Fanny, she said, "I wonder what next. At her very door! Aye, I've said it afore and I'll say it again, that lass draws trouble towards her as a flower draws the bee. She never goes out to meet it, it just comes to her. Like the season that brings God's little apples it comes to her."

"You're right there, Ma. You're right there." Fanny nodded. "I'll make a fresh pot of tea, and I've set her tray. Will I take it up?"

"No; I will."

"Well, I'll carry the tray up the stairs for you."

"Aye, you can do that, for of a sudden I feel tired, sapped."

Fanny picked up the tray and preceded her mother out of the kitchen, along the passage, across the hall and up the main staircase, but when they reached the gallery, Fanny turned and whispered, "Will I put it in her bedroom or take it straight up to the nursery?"

Biddy thumbed upwards, and by the time she reached the nursery floor she was panting and so she stood and inhaled a number of deep breaths before following Fanny into the day-room.

Tilly was alone, the children were having their afternoon rest, and when Fanny put the tray on the table and went to pour the tea out, Biddy shooed her away with a wave of her hand.

Neither of them spoke until Biddy, taking the cup of tea to Tilly, where she was still standing in front of the window, said, "Here, lass, drink this."

But Tilly did not turn to her and take the cup from her, she raised her arm and, leaning it against the edge of the deep frame of the window, dropped her head on to it and began to sob.

Quickly putting the cup down on the ledge, Biddy turned her about and, holding her tightly in her arms, murmured, "There, lass. There, lass. Take no notice, she's scum. They're all scum in that village, every blasted one of them. The devil's run riot through their beds for years, for every one – man, woman and child – in that damn place has got him in them. Come on, lass, come on. There, dry your eyes. Look." She pressed Tilly away from her and with her bare fingers rubbed the tears from her cheeks, saying loudly now, "You're the lady of the manor, lass, you're above the lot of them. You can buy and sell them; with the money you've got you could buy the whole damn village and turn them out on their backsides. Just think of that now. Here, come on, sit down and drink this tea."

Tilly sat down and she drank the tea, and after a moment or so she looked at Biddy and said "How am I going to live down this latest, Biddy?"

"Be yourself, lass. Go out and hold your head high. Take them both with you wherever you go. If you've got nowt to be ashamed of, it won't show in your face."

Tilly became still as she looked straight into Biddy's eyes and said slowly, "Josefina isn't mine, Biddy; she is the offspring of a Mexican Indian girl, a very young girl, and a white man."

"A white man?"

"Yes, I said a white man."

"Somebody you knew?"

Tilly's gaze did not flicker, she made no movement for almost thirty seconds, and then she said, "Yes, someone I knew, Biddy."

Slowly Biddy's gaze fell away from hers and, picking up the silver teapot, she poured out another cup of tea, and when she handed it to Tilly she said, "You've got nothing to be ashamed of, lass. If you ask me, much to be proud of. You'll win through. You'll win through."

49

7

On the following morning Tilly had another visitor and his presence caused a greater stir than had that of Bessie Bradshaw.

She'd had a disturbed night and had slept late – on Biddy's orders no one had attempted to waken her – and it was almost ten o'clock when she came down to breakfast, but not before she had visited the children in the nursery.

The morning was soft. She looked towards the long window at the end of the breakfast-room. It gave on to the side terrace and the sloping lawn that led down to the lake. She could just glimpse the sheen of the water and she thought how peaceful it all looked, but empty, solitary; yet she realised that this was but a reflection of her inner feelings.

Last night she had lain for hours pondering on her life, a life that could be said to be uneventful looked at from the outside, but which underneath the surface had been filled with tragedy since she was a child: her father dying in strange circumstances; her mother fading away afterwards; then herself being brought up by her grandparents on stolen money that had lain hidden for years; her persecution by the villagers, through which, inadvertently, she had been the cause of the death of two men; her succumbing to the love of the owner of this manor, and her constant attendance on him for twelve years until the day he died; then her bearing him a child, and finally marrying his son.

She had fallen asleep before her thoughts had begun to revive memories of this last episode in her life; and for this she would have been thankful, for what she tried not to think about at night were those short years spent in America because then, just as her husband had had nightmares about frogs, so she would have nightmares about Indians and mutilated dead people and a child's brains splattered about a post.

There was a tap on the door and Biddle came into the room, almost scurrying towards the table in his haste, and in a voice little above a whisper he said, "Madam, there . . . there is a visitor."

"A visitor? Who, Biddle?" Her voice was flat.

Biddle swallowed. "It is Lord Myton, ma'am," he said.

She rose to her feet, repeating, "Lord Myton!"

"Yes, ma'am, and . . . and I think you should be prepared for the fact that, that he is . . . he is not quite himself, ma'am."

She was moving towards the door as she said, "How did he arrive?"

"By coach, ma'am." Biddle seemed to spring forward now and open the door for her. And then she was in the hall looking at what she termed an apparition, for there stood an old man dressed in a heavy riding coat which covered a long blue nightshirt. On his feet were bedroom slippers and on his head a high riding hat. His face was unshaven and his wrinkled chin and cheeks showed a stubby bristle of some days' growth. His eyes set in deep dark hollows appeared bright but their light was lost as he screwed them up when inclining his head towards her and doffing his hat, which showed his pate to be quite bald. But what caught Tilly's attention more than his appearance was the gun he carried under his left arm.

"Ma'am . . . sorry . . . to trouble you . . . ma'am." His words were spaced. "My card." He fumbled in the breast pocket of his coat; then looking to the side, he said, "Howard. My card for . . . for the lady."

Stepping forward and playing up to the situation as if he had practised it daily, Peabody said, "Madam has your card, my lord. She would like you to come this way." He looked at Tilly, his eyes wide, and she, making a small motion of her head towards him, said, "Yes, of course." And now holding out her hand to Lord Myton, she directed his shuffling walk into the drawing-room.

"Kind of you, kind of you."

"Not at all. Do please be seated." Tilly indicated an armchair, then watched the old man slowly lower himself down into it. He still held his hat in one hand and the gun under his other arm, and when Tilly said, "May I take your hat, sir?" he handed it to her, muttering, "Yes, yes." But when, without speaking further, her hand reached out to the gun he pressed it tightly to him, saying now in a high squeaky voice, "Oh no! Oh no! Not that. Not that. Sit down. Sit down."

She sat down opposite to him, and she remained quite still as he peered at her. Then seeming to have come to a decision in his mind, he said, "You're all right; don't look like a whore. She's one. Oh aye, all her life. . . . Is she here?"

"I don't know to whom you are referring?" Tilly lied now.

"Her, of course, me wife, the bitch. Always a bitch, but gone too far this time. My God! Aye. Aye." He now leant towards her and, his voice dropping to a hissing whisper, he said, "Trying to put me away. D'you know? Trying to put me away, insane." He bobbed his head once more, then repeated, "Insane. And you know" – again he bobbed his head – "I must have been all these years – insane. But I laughed. Didn't matter, didn't matter . . . long as she was at t'other end of table, amusing, made me laugh. Oh yes —" He drooped his head, and it was some seconds before he repeated, "Made me laugh." Raising his head again, he grinned at Tilly now as he added, "A sense of humour. Bawdy, aye, like a man, bawdy. That's why I took her, good company, bawdy." Again his head fell forward and now he muttered, "I was no use to her. Didn't matter, didn't matter . . . No. No; but not with a pit fella. Aw now, not with a pit fella!"

The last words had ended on a shout and he repeated, "Pit fella, lowest form of life. Sunk to that, pit fella. . . . Kept tag of her amours. Aye, yes. An earl'n a guardsman in town. Gentlemen. Gentlemen. Always gentlemen in town. But here. God Almighty! Like a stag in the rut. Sopwith first one. . . . Your man, wasn't he, your man? Mistress to him. Kitchen slut they said you were . . . come up. Don't look it. Don't look it. He did a damn good job on you if you ask me. Then the farmer. Oh aye, the farmer. Then Turner and Drayton and on and on." He turned his head to the side and looked around the room and, his mind diverted for a moment, he said, "Nice . . . nice. Taste here. Good taste." Then bringing his watery gaze on to her he said abruptly, "You do this?"

It was some seconds before she could answer. "Just the upholstery and drapes."

Again he was looking around him. "Very nice. Very nice. But her. Yes, her, aye." He nodded at himself as if recollecting his thoughts; then pointing his finger at her, he said, "John Tolman. Yes, John Tolman. His wife, you know . . . you know Joan?" Tilly shook her head.

"She nearly tore her hair out . . . Agnes's. Scrapped like fishwives. Yes, aye, they did." He began to chuckle now. "Then Cragg, Albert Cragg, you know. You know what?" His body began to shake with his chuckling and he bent almost double but still keeping his eyes on her as he said, "She must never have looked at faces. God! no, 'cos you know Cragg?"

Did she know Cragg? And did she know Tolman? Yes, she knew them, but more of their wives, the women who had looked upon her as if she was mire beneath their feet.

"Three good stable lads. Aye, three good stable lads I lost. But what matter? Menials are there to be used. What's good for the goose is good for the gander." His body was again shaking. "Should be what's good for the gander 'tis good for the goose, eh? . . . Eh?"

Suddenly becoming still and his voice issuing in a growl from his throat, he said, "Where is she? She's here!"

"No, I'm afraid she's not, milord. Your wife is not here."

"Don't lie to me. She knew I was after her 'cos she had sent for those damned fellows again to have me barred up. Burton said she had ridden off to the pit fella's cottage, but when I got there they were gone. Lad said he had seen them riding towards here. Now, don't you hide 'em. It's the finish, I've stood enough. Disgrace, a pit fella!" He drew saliva into his mouth and looked for somewhere to spit, but after a moment he fumbled in his pocket and drew out a green silk handkerchief. Having spat into it, he made an attempt to pull himself to his feet. But Tilly was already standing in front of him and, her voice soothing, she said, "Lord Myton, please listen to me. I can assure you on my word of honour you wife is not here, and I can assure you too that you are mistaken about . . . about her association with the . . . the pitman."

"No? No?" His lower lip curled so far over that she could see the stumps of his diseased teeth in the side of his gums.

"I swear to you, Lord Myton."

He looked up at her now for some seconds before asking in a childlike voice, "Well, where can she be?"

"I have no idea."

"I'm dry."

"Oh, I'm sorry, I should have offered you some refreshment. What would you like?"

"Brandy."

"Brandy it shall be." She hurried to the fireplace and pulled at the bell rope, and as if Peabody had been standing outside the door it opened and she said to him in a voice that appeared calm, "Would you please bring the decanter of brandy?"

53

"Yes, madam."

It all sounded so normal, and the normality was continued when a few minutes later the butler placed a tray by the side of his lordship and poured out a good measure of brandy which he handed to the old man. Lord Myton gulped at the brandy, and after he had emptied the glass he shivered, smiled a weak smile and said, "My drink, brandy." He handed the glass back to Peabody who looked at Tilly, and she made a small motion with her head towards the decanter and he again poured out a good measure, but this time he left the glass on the tray. Looking at it, the old man did not pick it up immediately but he said, "Good. Good."

The butler was turning away when he hesitated as there came the sound of voices from the hall. They had caught Tilly's attention too and she, looking hard at Peabody, said, "Will you please stay and attend to his lordship for a moment?"

"Yes, ma'am."

"Excuse me." She bowed towards the old man, and he, picking up the glass of brandy, said, "Yes, yes." At the moment he seemed oblivious of where he was except that perhaps he thought he was at home for, looking at Peabody, he muttered, "Should be a fire in the grate."

"It's warm outside, milord."

"It ain't warm inside, not inside me t'ain't."

By the time Tilly had closed the drawing-room door behind her he had already thrown off the rest of the brandy.

In the hall stood Biddle, Peg, and the visitor, who should be none other than Steve.

Walking towards her and, straight to the point, Steve said, "Is the old man here?"

"Yes." And she added in a whisper, "And where is she?"

"When I last saw her she was haring back home to Dean House where she expected to find the doctors. Apparently she sent for them first thing this mornin'. The old fellow had been on the rampage all night looking for her. He had a gun."

"He still has and he's in a very odd state. Come in here a moment." She turned abruptly and led the way into the dining-room, and when she had closed the door on him she said immediately without any lead up, "He suspects you and her."

"Me!" He screwed up his face at her.

"Apparently you are her latest choice, and she has made it pretty evident, hasn't she?"

54

"Now look here, Tilly; you believe me, there's nothing. . . ."

"You needn't protest, Steve; I believe you, but the old man'll take some convincing. Have you met him?"

"Never. Never set eyes on him."

"Well, that's one good thing because . . . well, I really think he means business if somebody doesn't get that gun away from him."

"What brought him here anyway?"

"From what I could gather he understood that she and you were making for here."

"*What!*"

"That's what he said. One of his men told him that she had gone to your place. He must have got it out of the man at gunpoint I should imagine. Anyway, when he didn't find you or her he questioned a boy on the road, who said he had seen you both riding towards here."

"I rode with her as far as the coach road and I told her plainly I wasn't accompanying her any further but I'd have a look round for the old fellow on my own. The last time I saw her, as I said, she was haring back towards Dean House, and it was as I was making me way roundabout like to the mine, 'cos I'm on turn in an hour, that I met Richard McGee and I asked him if he'd seen anything of the Myton coach. He said he had passed it not fifteen minutes gone heading for here; at least it was on this road and so I put two and two together. . . . Look, Tilly, as he doesn't know me, do you think I can persuade him back into the coach because I can't see you handling this on your own?"

She paused a moment, staring at him, then said, "Yes, perhaps you could help. If once you could get the gun away from him he'd be easy to handle, but whatever you do don't let on that you work at the pit. Miners in his estimation are the lowest form of life and it's because he thinks his wife has" – she lowered her chin whilst keeping her eyes on him – "an association with one such that has created the last straw."

"Oh!" He raised his eyebrows while making a small nodding motion with his head as he said in mock politeness, "Thank you very much for telling me, Tilly."

She smiled wryly at him now. "He's just finished his second large brandy and he's in the state that he might have thrown it over me had he been told that I, too, once worked with the lowest form of animal life."

"Yes. Aye" – Steve's face became serious – "that takes some

remembering. I can't imagine you ever being down below, Tilly."

"Oh I can. I can remember every moment of it vividly still. But come on —" again she smiled at him and made her first attempt at a joke for many a long day as she said, "I do hope he hasn't shot Peabody, we were just beginning to understand each other."

"Aw, Tilly." He pushed her lightly on the shoulder and they stopped for a moment and, looking at each other, laughed quietly; then, her voice serious now, she said, "I don't see how I can find any amusement in this situation."

"It'll be a bad day when we don't see the funny side of things, Tilly."

She nodded now and led the way out of the dining-room, across the hall and into the drawing-room, and it was immediately apparent that Lord Myton was giving Peabody a lesson on his long sporting gun. It was evident too that their presence was very welcome to Peabody for, moving quickly out of range of the pointing gun, he glanced from one to the other as he almost stammered, "W . . . will I serve some re . . . refreshment for the gentleman, madam?"

"No, thank you, Peabody; I'll call you if I need you."

Bowing slightly, the butler made his escape, and both Tilly and Steve looked towards Lord Myton who was sitting leaning forward, his left hand cupping the long barrel of the gun, while the forefinger of his right hand stroked the trigger. He was looking towards the fireplace as if aiming at the banked flowers stacked there.

"Would you care for another drink, milord?"

"Oh. Oh" – he looked at her – "it's you. No, no; I don't think so. No —" he smiled a toothless smile now as he added in a normal tone, "if I start on it too early I don't enjoy me dinner and I do like me dinner. Never lost me appetite. Strange that, isn't it?"

"No, not at all; I'm very glad to know you still have a good appetite. Would you care to stay and have a bite with us?"

He seemed to consider for a moment, then said, "Well, yes, ma'am, yes, and thank you kindly. What are you having today?"

What were they having?

Oh yes, yes; she recalled quickly, then said, "It's rather a plain meal but very appetising; there is spring soup, saddle of mutton, asparagus and the usual vegetables" – she nodded at him – "and we'll finish with baked gooseberry pudding and cheeses."

56

"Sounds nice, very nice, not wind-making."

Tilly swallowed and glanced at Steve before she said, "I don't think it'll be wind-making."

"Strong digestion. Always have. . . . Who's this?" The question was addressed pointedly at Steve, but before he could answer Tilly said, "He's a friend of mine, milord, a . . . a lifelong friend."

"Workman?" He turned his eyes on her. "Lifelong friend?"

"Yes, milord, a lifelong friend. I was once a working woman, you remember?"

"Oh aye, yes," he chuckled; "from the kitchen, from the kitchen. Yes, yes. Don't sound it though." Of a sudden his joviality vanished and he demanded, "Where the hell is she? She's not going to make a fool of me this time. Where's she, eh? Her fancies have caused her to stoop low in the past but not as low as this, no, no."

As his left hand jerked the barrel upwards Tilly said softly, "Would you like to rest, milord, before you eat? There's a comfortable couch in the little sitting-room off the. . . ."

"All right here. You want me out of the way?" His white brows were beetling.

"No, no, no, of course not, milord."

"Pleasant woman." He turned now and addressed Steve. "Pleasant woman. I like pleasant company; but one can't always be laughing. What do you say?"

"You're right, milord; one can't always be laughing."

"You sound like a workman."

"I am a workman, milord."

"What are you?"

"I am an engineer."

"Oh. Oh, engineer?" The old man's eyes widened, the wrinkled skin stretched as his head bobbed. "Engineer. Bridges?"

"Er . . . yes, milord, bridges."

"Oh indeed! Bridges. Railroads; they need bridges over and under. Oh yes, yes."

"Could I help you into the next room, milord."

"Help me? Why do you want to help me, you're not of my household, are you?" He now narrowed his eyes at Steve, then shook his head, saying, "No, can't recollect seeing you before. No, of course not, you're the workman, engineer, building bridges, yes. Aye." He now swung the gun round and laid it across his knees, where his great coat had fallen open exposing more of his

57

nightshirt. Then raising his head, he looked at Tilly and in the politest of tones he now said, "Would you please leave the room, madam, I wish to go to the closet?"

Tilly showed no surprise, she neither blushed nor swooned, the reactions one would have expected from a lady of the manor, but what she said was, "The closet is at the end of the corridor, milord. If you would allow my friend to assist you, I will show you the way."

The old man stared at her again, then made a chuckling sound in his throat before saying, "Ain't no lady, that's evident; no lady'd show me to the closet! Funny, but that whore of mine could sport naked, oh aye, aye" – his head was wagging now from side to side as if throwing off denial – "I say, an' I know, sport naked she could, but throw up her hands in disgust if she opened the door and saw me on the closet. But you wouldn't, would you, ma'am?"

"No, milord."

"No, she wouldn't." He now nodded to Steve, but just as Steve was about to make some remark his attention and that of Tilly's also was brought to the door from beyond which there came the sound of an altercation. But it didn't penetrate to the old man until the door was thrust open and there, seeming to fill the whole frame, stood his wife. She was arrayed in a plum-coloured riding habit, a high velour hat perched on the top of her dyed hair. Her face looked suffused with anger. Behind her were standing two men, their heads and shoulders alone visible to those in the room until she moved forward; and then their sober dress proclaimed them to Tilly immediately as doctors.

The old man did not move from his seat except to turn his head in his wife's direction; that was until she marched forward crying, "Stop this capering and come on home this very minute!" and then he spoke, his voice sounding so ordinary and sane that Tilly's eyes were drawn from his wife and on to him as he said, "Stay where you are, Agnes! Stay where you are!" and as he spoke he slowly moved the gun into a position in which it was pointing straight at her.

When the two gentlemen accompanying her now made a move towards him, he said sharply, "You, too!" and he shifted the barrel of the gun just slightly but enough to encompass the three of them. Then he spoke to the nearer one, saying, "Brought the papers with you, all signed and sealed, eh, to put me in the mad-house? Is that it?"

58

"Now, sir." The voice sounded oily. "We just want to see you well settled in your bed, nothing more."

"You're bloody liars, sir. And don't move! I'm warnin' you. You see, what you've all forgotten is that I've nothing to lose, I'm near me end and I know it. But I thought to go out of life as I've lived it, laughing at it on the side. And I would have done, but she went too far. Pit fella she took a pit fella. Me grooms I'd tolerate, but a dirty pit fella! And you threw him in me face, didn't you? Bragged you could get 'em from the top to the bottom."

As the old man's lip curled, Steve drew in a long breath and cast his glance down towards the floor; but his head jerked upwards almost immediately as Agnes Myton's voice, screaming now, cried, "You're mad! You don't know what you're saying. Doctor —" she turned to the man at her right hand, crying, "This is what I've told you about, delusions, delusions, accusations, all lies, lies. He's got to be restrained; I can't stand any more of it."

"Did you hear what she said?" The old man now turned his head slightly towards Tilly, while keeping his eyes on the three in front of him. "She said she can't stand any more. Ain't that funny? By the way, I wanted to go to the closet, didn't I?" He paused, then gave a sound that was like a high laugh before he added, "Doesn't matter, not now, doesn't matter. Wind'n water, that's all we are, wind'n water."

"Give me that gun." His wife was stepping slowly towards him now and he said, "Yes, I'll give you the gun, Agnes. Aye, yes, I'll give you the gun 'cos I'd hate to enter hell alone."

Tilly heard herself scream out as she saw the quivering finger pressing the trigger, then at the moment the explosion rocked the room she watched Agnes Myton clutch with both hands at the bosom of her habit. She watched her mouth open wide as if in amazement. She watched the woman's head move from one side to the other as if to look at the doctors as they held her, then slowly slump in their embrace. But they had hardly laid her on the floor before there came another report, and as Tilly looked towards the old man she again screamed for she was back in the Indian raid. In a way she was seeing what she had imagined Alvero Portes to look like after the Indians had finished with him, for Lord Myton had placed the gun under his wrinkled chin before firing the second barrel.

8

Well, it was to be expected, wasn't it? Wherever she is somebody dies. Two of them this time. A lord and lady, a murder and a suicide. Well, as they all said in the village, it proved it, didn't it? There was something odd about her. It went right back on her great-granny's side; they'd all been touched with witchery.

They counted up the deaths and tragedies that lay at her door, they recalled her immoral doings, they reminded each other that she had ruined Farmer Bentwood's first marriage, then when his wife died and he didn't ask her to marry him she had put a curse on him that turned him to drink and whoring. Now he was married again with a little daughter of his own and had gone steady these past three years. Well, he had done right up to the time Tilly Trotter, or Sopwith as she was now named, returned from the Americas. And what had happened? He had gone on the spree again. Oh yes, there was something about her, something bad, and folks were wise to give her a wide berth.

And those sentiments were also expressed by old Joe Rawlings's daughter to the second Mrs Bentwood herself. Peggy Rawlings had called at the farm for some milk and in a roundabout way had brought up the tale of the coroner's inquest last week on the two dead gentry. "Miscarriage of justice, that's what me dad says, Mrs Bentwood. He said they should have brought that madam up for indirect murder like she should have been brought up years gone by, for people die like flies when they're near her. It's witchery me dad says."

The second Mrs Bentwood had surprised Peggy Rawlings by saying, "I don't believe in witchery, witchery is just ignorance."

As Peggy said to her dad later on, "She was a bit snotty, so I got a bit snotty with her and I said to her, Farmer Bentwood believes in witchery, her witchery. He suffered from it, and you watch out you don't an' all." Then she had added, "She looks the quiet sort, his second wife, but I think she's deep under it. Well, I've warned her, so it's up to her. . . ."

Later that night Lucy Bentwood, looking at her husband across the supper table, said, "What happened at the inquest last week?"

"What happened? How should I know?"

"You went; I know you went."

"All right, if I did, what about it?"

"Nothing, nothing." She smiled at him. "I just want to know what happened."

"What always happens at inquests, they prove the people dead."

His wife continued to stare at him for a moment before resuming her eating and she wasn't surprised when he pushed his plate away from him before he had finished his meal and without an excuse got up and left the table. She watched him through the open door making for his office at the other side of the small hall, and she herself stopped eating and sat with her hands folded on her lap.

She loved this man and she had imagined that he loved her, not that she thought for a moment that she was the be all and end all in his life. She knew that he'd had other loves, many of them, if all the hinting tales were true, but this Mrs Sopwith, Tilly Trotter as she once was, seemed to have been the first love in his life and she'd always had a strange influence on him, being responsible, so she understood, for turning him from a kindly generous-hearted man into a drunken, roistering boor. Yet since they had met on that momentous night outside the theatre in Newcastle when she had slipped on the icy pavement and he had caught her and held her he had become for her the man he once was, kindly, thoughtful and loving. He was ten years her senior and she had known that she was past the acceptable marriageable age; but he had treated her like a young girl, and she had felt like a young girl and given him a daughter. And this had seemed to bring an added joy into his life, that was until two months or so ago when Mrs Sopwith returned to the manor, a widow now.

Three times in the last month he had got drunk. Could there be any truth in the tales of her power? Had she put a curse on him?

She almost overbalanced her chair as she sprang up from the table. She was no ignorant villager, she was well read, thanks to her parents' care; also she was sufficiently cultured to pass herself quite well on the piano and at the embroidery frame. She wasn't going to let such stupid thoughts get a hold in her mind. If Simon was returning to drink, then there was a reason for it, and it would have nothing to do with witchery. . . .

Simon, sitting in the office and drawing hard on his pipe, might not have agreed with his wife at this stage in his life. Years ago as a young man he had defended Tilly Trotter against the accusation, but having experienced the effect she had on men, particularly himself, he was beginning to think along the lines of the villagers. There was some strange quality in her that upset a man's life. All those years she had been Mark Sopwith's mistress he himself had gone through the tortures of the damned; and when Sopwith died and she was turned out of the manor, her belly still full of him, he had offered to father her bastard. And what thanks had he got in return? Scorn. Yet at one time she had loved him; oh yes, he was sure of that, she had loved him. When he looked back he realised that she had loved him even before he had come to the knowledge of his love of her. He had imagined that his feelings were merely those of a big brother protecting the young sister, but on the very night of his first marriage, to Mary, his eyes had been opened, and he hadn't been able to close them since.

He had just about managed to face up to that situation when she was shameless enough to marry the son of her late keeper, and her six years or more older than him! By! that had shaken him to his very core. What he would have done if she hadn't gone off to America right away he dare not think. Gone and set the whole bloody manor on fire likely because he had seemed to go mad at the time. Then he met Lucy and he had to admit that Lucy had resurrected some remnants of decent manhood in him. Under her love he saw reflected the man he had once been, the young, outspoken, upright farmer who would do a good turn for anybody; and then when she had given him a daughter life had taken on a new pattern, a new meaning. He had sworn on the day his child was born that he would cut out drinking altogether, and he meant it. But what happened? Tilly had to come back a widow now, and free to marry again; that was if anybody would take her with a second bastard at her skirts. The tale that the black piece was older than her son wouldn't carry water. It was rumoured that young Sopwith had died through the wounds he got in an Indian raid. That, too, was just hearsay; likely he died fighting over her as other men had.

God in heaven! He rose from the chair and began to pace the small room. Why couldn't she have stayed where she was over there What was it in her that got into a man, turned his brain?

When he had heard the rumour that her hair was white, as

white as the driven snow, he had thought with some comfort, Well, she'll look like an old woman now, but last week, standing at the back of the crowd as he had done many years ago when she had appeared in another court when the judge had asked if she was a witch, he had seen her come out on the arm of the young Sopwith, and her hair was indeed white, but she was no old woman. If anything the whiteness had added to her fascination. He had never thought her really beautiful, she was too tall to be beautiful, taller than most men, yet there was something in that face that outstripped beauty; there was a magnetism about her eyes that looked at you yet didn't seem to see you for they were looking through you, into you, and beyond. And who should be walking behind her but young McGrath. He still thought of him as young McGrath, yet he was a man, taller and broader than himself now, except round the middle. He had always been her shadow, had Steve McGrath, since he was a youngster spewing his calf-love all over her. Was he in the running now? No; Master John Sopwith wouldn't, surely, tolerate that association. And yet what, after all could Sopwith do, she was mistress of the whole place, and she must have come into quite a packet too from her husband. It was incredible that she, Tilly Trotter, whom as a child and young lass he had at one time kept from starving, should now be in this position. It maddened him, really maddened him.

He stopped now in his pacing and stood near the corner of his small desk with his finger nails digging in the underside of the wood. He knew he had come to a turning point in his life, that either he could revert to his drinking bouts which would likely cause her nose to curl, or he could go on upwards, which would mean that he could do what he had wanted to do all those years ago and buy the farm. With what Lucy had brought with her he now had more than enough, and for extra land at that. But buying the farm would mean getting in touch with her. Aye, well, that's what he would like to do, come face to face with her and show her that whatever power she had wasn't strong enough to ruin him.

The decision made, he sat down again and, placing his elbows on the desk, he dropped his face on to his hands, and his teeth ground against each other and his lips pressed tight to stop her name escaping, but this mind groaned at him, Tilly Trotter! Tilly Trotter! God blast you!

9

Tilly made the acquaintance of Lucy Bentwood one day towards the end of June. They came upon each other in the middle of Northumberland Street, Newcastle, and, strangely, they took to each other, although they exchanged only a polite greeting.

Tilly had been persuaded to leave the house to accompany John and Anna to the city. Anna was to see her lawyer with regard to her grandmother's estate. Her grandmother had died a month ago, and from that day her daughter, Anna's Aunt Susan, who was in her late forties, had taken to her couch and decided she was in decline, and so it was left to Anna and John to settle all the legal affairs.

Tilly had left them at the solicitor's office in Pilgrim Street, the arrangement being that they would meet in an hour's time and have lunch together. In the meantime, she herself was bent on doing some shopping for the children.

She had not wanted to leave the house at all for since the day of the inquest she seemed now to have dropped back into the lethargy of the time following Matthew's death. She was aware that if it wasn't for the children she, like Anna's Aunt Susan, would have needed little persuasion to take to her couch for then she would less likely become involved in another's life.

Over the past few weeks she had almost come to believe that there must be something in what the villagers said about her, inasmuch as she seemed to attract death. She had heard Biddy going for Peg who had been repeating some gossip from the stables that it was odd how Lord Myton had chosen her drawing-room in which to commit murder and suicide; why hadn't he done it in his own house? And what was Steve McGrath doing there? Hadn't she been poison to the McGraths all her life?

It was as she turned from looking at the display behind the great new plate glass window of a shop that she came face to face with Simon Bentwood and his wife.

At first she did not look at the young woman but at the man

who had been her first love. He was now in his middle forties but he looked fifty or more; his face was florid, his girth on a level with his chest. His clothes were good – he had always dressed well – but there was no semblance of the young man who had touched her heart all those years ago. As she glanced at the woman at his side, who looked young enough to be his daughter, she hesitated, not knowing whether to go on or to stop. The decision was taken from her when Simon said, "Hello, Tilly."

She swallowed before she could answer, and then, her voice low, she said, "Hello, Simon."

"This is me wife." He put his hand to the side and Lucy Bentwood, staring at her, inclined her head, then gave the slightest bob of her knee. This gesture seemed to incense Simon, for having first spoken in an ordinary tone, he now almost growled at his wife, "No need for knee bobbing here, woman. Tilly and me know each other too well for that. Isn't that so?" His face had taken on a deeper hue, and because she felt sorry for the woman she answered him in a quiet level tone, saying, "Yes, we were well acquainted when I was quite young."

"Acquainted!" He laughed now, his head jerking up and down. "Funny word to use that, acquainted."

When into his laughter his wife's quiet tone came, saying, "I am pleased to meet you, Mrs Sopwith," Tilly looked at her and, seeming to ignore Simon completely, answered, "And I you, Mrs Bentwood."

Lucy Bentwood smiled now at the tall lady, because that's how Tilly appeared to her, a lady, and aiming to make amends for her husband's manner she proffered: "We're up for the day. I'm going to shop for some material to make dresses for my little girl."

"That is a coincidence." Tilly smiled towards her. "I, too, am shopping for my children. How old is your daughter?"

She did not include Simon in the question and his wife answered, "Just on two, ma'am."

Again Tilly was aware of Simon's displeasure at this latest address, but this time when he broke in on their conversation his tone was less aggressive: "I've had it in mind to come and see you these weeks past, Tilly," he said.

"Yes?" She turned an enquiring glance on him.

"It's about business."

"Oh!"

65

" 'Tis about the farm."

"You want repairs done?"

"No; more than that. I'm thinkin' of buying it if that meets with you."

"Oh!" She raised her eyebrows, at the same time turning her gaze for a moment on his wife; then she said, "Well, it's something that needs to be looked into, but if you would just let me know when you are coming we could discuss the matter."

"Fair enough."

Tilly now stepped to the side and, looking at Lucy Bentwood, she said, "Good-bye, Mrs Bentwood."

"Good-bye, ma'am."

Tilly made no formal farewell to Simon, nor he to her, she merely inclined her head, then walked on, but she was hardly out of earshot before Simon Bentwood said to his wife, "You drop the ma'am when speaking to her, she's no better than she should be."

"I don't think I could."

"Why?" He paused again and stared at her; and she, with the strength of character which he had already come to suspect lay under her quiet, even serene demeanour, said, "Because no matter what is said about her, she appears a lady. Before opening her mouth she appears a lady, more so afterwards."

"My God!" He looked as if he were aiming to toss his head off his shoulders; then leaning towards her, he said, "You know what they say about her, don't you?"

"Aye, yes, I've heard it all, but as I see it, so to speak, Simon, it's nothing but second sight. My grandmother had second sight: she saw my grandfather dead six hours before they brought her the news, and he had died not half an hour's run from her door. The horse shied, the carriage wheels went back on him and that was the end, and she had seen it and told me mother, as I said six hours afore."

"Oh, be quiet!"

"Just as you say, Simon. Just as you say."

"And don't use that laughing tone at me."

"Did you think I was laughing, Simon? Well, I can tell you I wasn't. I'm only trying to keep a calm head in a very odd situation because that lady just gone back there caught more than your imagination years gone, not only from what I heard and the little you told me yourself, but from the look on your face whenever her name's been mentioned and in your eyes as you looked at

66

her not a minute gone. No, Simon, I'm not laughing. And what I'll say here and now should be, I think, kept for a private place, not in the middle of Newcastle, but it's in me mind and here at least you can't bawl your denials, so I'll say it, and once it's said I'll mention it no more. 'Tis this. The part of you she once had I fear she's still got, but she had it afore I met you, and I've given you a child. And again I say this, 'tis no place to tell you in the middle of a street but I'm bearing you another."

She was pulled to a stop and he stared down at her, into her kindly eyes, and he knew shame as he had never known it before; and he cursed Tilly Trotter and her returning into his life, for here before him was his wife, a young woman whom he had been lucky to wed, and she was wise and good. Yes, very wise and very good, for at this moment he recalled how Mary, his first wife, had taken his affection for Tilly Trotter: it had poured vitriol into her veins and made her mad at times with jealousy.

He did not say, "I'm sorry, Lucy," what he did do was to take her hand and draw it through his arm as he muttered, "Let's go home; we can shop another day."

Meeting Simon had in a way been equally disturbing for Tilly. She no longer found that the sight of him disgusted her; she had looked into his face without seeing the picture that had been in her mind for years, that of his nakedness sporting with the plump white body of Lady Myton. She must already have accepted that his conduct had been no worse than that of her going to Mark, or, what must have appeared worse still, of her marrying Mark's son. And was he any worse than Matthew lying with that small enigmatic looking Mexican girl, whose child she had taken on to herself, the child who had already brought her trouble by the fact that she herself was being named as its mother?

No, what was past, was past with Simon; he was a man as other men. That he had grown coarser was a pity, but now that he had taken to himself a wife, and such a one, augured good for his later years. . . . And he wanted to buy his farm.

She remembered vaguely her granny saying that it was the desire of Simon's life to own his own place. Well, if he came in a proper way and offered a reasonable sum, and she would not quibble over the amount, he would own his own farm. But in granting his desire she knew she would be doing it not so much for him but for his wife, that young woman with the pleasing manner, the open honest face, the young woman who had addressed her as ma'am. She liked her; under other circumstances she would have wished for a closer acquaintance. But that was impossible.

She did her shopping; met Anna and John, and after a substantial lunch, which she didn't enjoy, she expressed the desire to return home. In a way she knew she was disappointing Anna for the arrangement had been that they should visit the galleries; but all she wanted was to get away from this city that reminded her only of police courts, and men who looked at her from top to toe the while their eyes seemed to strip her of her clothing.

It was a fortnight later when Peabody announced, "Mr Simon Bentwood, ma'am."

Tilly rose from the seat in the drawing-room. She did not say, "Hello, Simon," for he would surely have replied, "Hello, Tilly," she just inclined her head towards Peabody, which motion told him his presence was no longer needed.

When the door had closed on him, Tilly, looking towards Simon who was standing just within the room, said, "Please take a seat, Simon. I've had the fire put on" – she motioned her hand towards the fireplace – "this last week of rain has called for fires."

"Yes, yes, indeed." His tone was polite, even deferential, and if he had owned to the truth he was at this moment feeling a little awed; it was the first time he had been inside the manor house. His yearly rent had always been collected by one servant or another; not since his father's time, when the manor boasted a steward, had anyone from the farm gone to the house to pay its dues.

The carpets and furnishings were making an impression upon him, and at the back of his mind he was telling himself that these had been her surroundings for years, and in a way she had taken on the patina of the furniture about her, a veneer that had caused

68

Lucy to call her ma'am. Yes, yes, he could understand that one would become different living in these surroundings.

When he was seated he looked to where she was standing to the side of the hearth with one arm outstretched, her hand resting on the marble mantelshelf, and standing like this she looked at him and said, "What can I offer you to drink? Would you like something hot or a whisky, or rum perhaps?"

She watched the muscles of his cheeks working as his tongue pressed his saliva into his throat. "A cup of tea would be welcome, thank you."

She half turned and, lifting her hand from the mantelshelf, she extended it backwards and pulled on the piece of broad thick tasselled red velvet that hung down by the side of the wall.

A moment later the door opened and she looked towards Peabody and said, "A tray of tea, Peabody, please."

"Yes, ma'am."

She does this every day, Simon thought. It comes natural to her. It was unbelievable when he looked back to the lass she had been, sawing, humping branches twice as big as herself, digging that plot of land. How would she have turned out if he'd had her? Not like this for sure, she'd have been a woman, a mother of a family, respected, whereas now, for all this grandeur, her name was like clarts, and she was feared and hated, aye, you could smell the hate of her in the village, when her name was mentioned. If she had known what was to become of her, would she have picked him or this?

Peabody brought the tea in, she poured it and handed him a cup and he drank it, and then another, and still he hadn't brought up the reason for his visit. It was she who had to say, "You have come about the farm, Simon?"

"Aye, that's it, I've come about the farm."

"Well, I've been thinking it over and I've talked it over with John because he helps me run the estate" – she smiled deprecatingly now – "and I have decided that you may have the buildings together with fifty acres."

"Fifty acres!" His shoulders went back. "But there's all of seventy-five acres to it."

"Yes, I know, and the rest can still remain for your use but as rented land. You see in this way it will in fact square the land off as the farm and those fields just out on the east side of the estate."

"I'd rather take the lot."

"Yes, I suppose you would, Simon, but that's all I have to offer. It's up to you to decide if you want it or not."

"Oh yes, I want it, that's why I'm here. If you think back to the early days, Tilly, you'll realise I've always wanted it."

She made no reference to the early days but said, "With regard to the price, of course the stock's your own but the outbuildings are in good repair and Mr Sopwith . . . Senior" – she swallowed here – "had, I remember, two new byres put up for you, and also a small barn."

She immediately wiped from her mind the picture that the mention of a barn conjured up, and went on, "Then there's the house. John tells me that it was repointed for you some two years ago. A new well, too, was dug. And so his suggestion of four hundred pounds would not be exorbitant."

John had suggested seven, it was she who had brought it down to four, and Simon before he had left the farm this morning had said to Lucy, "They'll want eight for it, if a penny." But then, of course, he had expected the whole amount of land.

Tilly watched him rubbing his chin with the side of his hand as if considering her offer. It was a man's way. He must know that the terms were favourable, but this she supposed was business, and no one ever thanked you for giving them a bargain.

"Well, aye, yes, I suppose I'd be willing to settle for that."

"I'm pleased. It's good to feel you own your own home."

"Aye, it is. Well, you should know, Tilly."

He slowly turned his head and looked about the room, and she said stiffly, "In a way this is only entailed to me, it will be passed to my son when he's twenty-one."

As he stared at her she felt the colour rising to her face. She knew what he was thinking: her son had no claim to a stick here, he was an illegitimate child. Her voice sounded cool and her words clipped as, looking back at him, she said, "It has been arranged in law, he will inherit."

"Oh. Oh, well, that's good enough." He now rose slowly to his feet and, again looking round the room, said, "'Tis a splendid room. The ceiling in itself is something to look at." He was staring upwards at the medallions linked with garlands within ornate squares when there came the sound of high delighted screeches, seemingly from above his head, followed by the soft thumping of steps running down the stairs.

Looking at him with a slight smile now, Tilly said, "The

children, they're on the rampage. This is what happens if I leave them for too long."

"Do you look after them yourself now?" The "now" indicated that he knew all about Connie Bradshaw and she answered, "Yes, in the meantime, but I have a new nursemaid coming next week."

He looked towards the door when the squeals came from the hall and he said, "They seem to be enjoying themselves."

He'd hardly finished speaking when the door burst open and Willy ran into the room, one arm extended, his head to the side, an action he used nearly always when he was running. "Mama!" he cried. "Mama! Josefina is going to whip me." He was laughing as he flung himself against Tilly's legs; he then ran behind her as Josefina came racing up the room like a small dark sprite, and for a moment there was a game of tig about Tilly's skirts, until she cried, "Enough! Enough, children! Do you hear me? We have a visitor. Willy, stop it!" She slapped at her son's hand and he became still; then she caught hold of Josefina's arm and, shaking her gently, said, "Enough! Enough! Now, no more!"

Their laughing and giggling died away and they stood now, one on each side of her, looking at the guest.

"Say how-do-you-do to Mr Bentwood, Willy."

The boy paused a moment, put his head back on his shoulder and to the side, screwed up his one good eye; then, his hand outstretched, he said politely and slowly, "How-do-you-do, sir?"

There was just a second's pause before Simon reached out and took the boy's hand and, his voice sounding gruff, replied, "I do very well, youngster."

"Are you a rela . . . relation?"

"No."

"Are you from the mine?"

As Simon was about to reply again, Tilly, reaching out, drew Willy back to her side, saying, "Don't be inquisitive, Willy."

"I was only asking, Mama."

"I know you were, but it isn't polite." She now half smiled at Simon; then looking down at Josefina, she said, "This is my adopted daughter. Say how-do-you-do? Josefina."

It was Josefina who stepped forward now and, as politely as Willy had done, she too said, "How-do-you-do, sir?"

Simon made no reply, he just stared down at the tiny elfin figure below him, searching the brown face, the black eyes, the straight hair for some resemblance that would connect her with

Tilly. And he imagined he saw it in that indefinable something that Tilly possessed; added to which the child looked much younger than her son and was hardly half his size. The fact that she spoke clearly mattered nothing: children often spoke well at two years old, and the strong foreign burr gave the impression that she was older. But she wasn't older than the boy. Anyone with half an eye could see that.

He almost started as the child said, "Don't you want to take my hand, sir?"

He looked at Tilly. She was looking at him, her face stiff and just as he was on the point of putting out his hand the child suddenly and impetuously threw herself against him and, gripping his leg below the thigh, looked up at him as she cried, "You are very big man and you smell like Poncho. . . ."

The next second the child would have landed on her back on the floor had not Tilly sprung forward and caught her. In one motion she swung the slight form up into her arms, and glaring at Simon, she said bitterly, "You should not have done that!"

"Why not? I could understand that one" – he nodded towards Willy who was now squinting up at him, the lid of his good eye working rapidly – "but I think you went too far with this one. I've heard it said that the Indians rape women; well, if they did you, then you should have come into the open and people would have understood. You must think folks are simple, or as ignorant as pigs, but the dimmest knows that no white adopts a black bairn. Buy 'em for slaves, aye . . . or house boys as they are called, but adopt, no! And for you to look down your nose on me for my one mistake. My God! you've got a nerve. I'll say you have that. . . ."

"Get out!"

"Aye, I'm going. I knew this would happen."

Tilly again reached out towards the bell rope, and as she did so he turned towards her, his lip curled in disdain. "You needn't ring for your lackeys, I can walk out without them aiding me. An' let me tell you one thing afore I go. I'm sorry I ever put the word love to you. Beddin' with your own kind I could understand, or being taken down by a wild man I could understand that an' all, but not to try to pass it off as you're doing. Do you know something, Tilly?" Glaring at her, he thumbed towards Josefina. "That makes me want to spit."

He had pulled the drawing-room door open, but he did not close it behind him, and she watched him marching past both

72

Peabody and Biddle. She watched him turn his head and bark some words at Peabody, then he was gone.

She didn't move until Peabody entered the room and, closing the door behind him, said softly, "Are you all right, madam?"

Slowly she lowered Josefina to the floor, saying, "Yes, thank you, Peabody."

He came and stood quite close to her. "Are you sure, madam? Look. Sit down, madam, and I'll pour you a cup of tea" – he put his fingers on the silver teapot – "it's still hot."

She sat down and when he handed her the cup he said, "Do not trouble your mind about such a man, he's no gentlemen. It is the first time in my career that I have been referred to as a lackey."

"I'm sorry, Peabody."

"It's not your fault, madam, that some men cannot help but behave as louts. I will take the children now, madam, and see that Biddle takes them walking in the garden. The rain has stopped. We'll wrap them up warmly."

"Thank you, Peabody. Go along, children." She made a small movement with her hand and they both quietly did her bidding.

Alone she sat with her eyes closed. She saw herself sitting in the wagon supporting Matthew's blood-stained body, and she could hear his words, "Go home. Take Willy, and leave her behind." Matthew had known what he was talking about. Yes, yes, indeed, he had known what he was talking about.

10

Christine Peabody turned out to be a very good nursemaid and a girl with a pleasant personality, so much so that she overcame Biddy's initial dislike of her; she happened to be the butler's youngest daughter and Biddy had prophesied she was the thin end of the wedge for his other three daughters, but that remained to be seen. The girl was very good with children. She could be playful, but she could also be firm. She was so good with them that Tilly had a great deal more free time on her hands, and this enabled her to read more and . . . ride more. She was finding an increasing enjoyment from her association with horses. Accompanied by Peter Myers and Arthur Drew, she even went to a horse sale. Myers, having dealt with horses all his life, had a knowledge of horse flesh and on that occasion helped her to choose a three-year-old mare well broken to the saddle. The mare was lively and needed exercise, which necessitated her taking it out daily.

On a number of occasions during the months that followed she met other riders. The first time it was a group of six gentlemen, all well mounted but both horses and riders bespattered, indicating they were returning from the hunt. They all moved to the side of the road to allow her to pass and each one of them doffed his hat to her while keeping his eyes riveted on her face, albeit vitally aware that she was wearing breeches and sitting astride a horse like any man.

The occasion she met up with a party of four, two ladies and two gentlemen, the gentlemen again moved to the side, but the ladies had kept to the middle of the narrow bridle path, and in order to pass them she had to take her horse into the ditch; true, it was a shallow ditch, but the fact that they would not make way for her told her more plainly than any words how she was considered by the gentry of the neighbourhood.

There was a joy in riding: the feel of the horse's muscles beneath her legs, the power of its stride, the idea that it was soaring her heavenwards when it jumped a hedge and the exhilaration it created in her as it galloped over a free field, the wind whistling past her ears, down her throat and up her nostrils seeming to have a cleansing effect on her. However, after a time her rides became merely physical exercises, so leaving her mind free to grope; and she knew she wanted a companion.

Anna preferred to ride behind the horse in the comfort of a carriage; when she sat on the back of one it was merely to trot. But John sometimes accompanied Tilly; and these occasions she found most pleasurable, the end of the rides finding them panting and laughing, very rarely talking.

There was, she knew, another companion she could have had on her rides.

Sometimes, when returning from a ride she had come across Steve, and he had accompanied her back to the coach road, but no further, for almost always he would be black.

The last time they had met in this way he had said laughingly, "I'm getting a feeling for horseflesh; I think I'll go to the market one of these days and get me one with four legs, not that I'll do away with old Barney here because we've come to an understanding. We have long conversations, you know, old Barney and me."

It was strange about Steve, he could make her laugh. This mature Steve could make her laugh whereas the young Steve had mostly irritated her; but this she knew had been because of his pesterings of love.

Of late, she'd had to curb a desire to take a ride or even a walk to the cottage and just to sit quietly there. She knew where he put the key. It was the same place where she herself used to leave it, a good hidey-hole. There were no doubts in her mind why she wanted to go to the cottage and to talk to Steve; it was simply for the company, someone of her own ken as she put it, someone who understood her language, the language she used when she hadn't to stop and think. But that was as far as it went, and this being so she knew it was unfair to put herself into his presence unless there was a good excuse for doing so, for after all, at bottom, he was still Steve and underneath the man was the lad who had loved her. And he might still be there; it wasn't fair to bring him to the surface.

*

Biddy said, "Why don't you have a party at Christmas, lass, and come out of yourself? Look; you've been in black long enough. As long as you still wear black you're still in the grave with him. Let the dead bury the dead, as the saying goes. Get Master John over and Miss Anna. And don't tell me she can't leave her aunt, her with two nurses to see to her. They could, you know, wrap her up and bring her over. The bairns would soon bring her out of herself and get her off her couch if I know anything. How old is she anyway?"

"Oh, late forties."

"God Almighty! and puttin' herself on a couch. But then it always happens. I've seen it again and again: women who've never had a man, they've got to have attention from somebody, so they take on a sickness, and other people, mostly their relations, have got to run their legs off up to their knees an' are often in their own boxes afore their charges. Oh aye, I've seen it happen, in mud huts and in mansions."

"Oh, Biddy!" Tilly looked across the settle where she was sitting in the kitchen to where the big-boned elderly woman was rocking herself briskly backwards and forwards in the rocking chair. This was the time of day she looked forward to: the children were in the nursery asleep, the rest of the staff had gone to their rooms, except perhaps Peabody or Biddle or whoever's turn it was to lock up, and at this time of the evening she would sit opposite Biddy and they would talk; or rather she would listen, for Biddy seemed to store up all the odds and ends of the day and pour them out on her and, as was her wont, she would jump from one subject to the other. But no word she said was idle chatter; there was always the wisdom of common sense in most of what she said or, as now, a subtle hint, a subtle plea for one of her daughters.

"It never did anybody any good to live unto themselves. Gives them too much time to think about what's not happenin' or what's going to happen. There's only one thing sure in this life and that's death, but most people meet it half-way, even get ready for it in their middle life by making a nightgown for their laying-out or a shirt for their man. Then they sit and think about it comin'. Half the trouble in the world comes through people who have time to think. As me mother used to say, our mind's like a hen's nest, every egg you put into it is hatched. If the egg's been tread properly then the chick will be all right, but if it's not, sitting on it, brooding on it, what do you get? Just a big stink. What I'm

76

sayin' is that it's not right to live alone, nor live in the past. . . . Now there's Steve over there in that cottage living by himself. 'Tisn't right. If our Peg had her way he wouldn't be long alone." She nodded at Tilly, saying, "Aye, that's how it is with her. And she been married and widowed. But the want is strong in a widow. And it's funny, isn't it, it was the same with our Katie. Our Katie would have walked on hot cinders for Steve but he never looked the side she was on. Of course, there was you in those days, Tilly." Again she nodded. "But now things are different, positions are different. Our Peg would make him a good wife if he had the sense to see it. I think he only wants a nudge, somebody to tip him the wink. Aye well" – she looked at the clock on the high mantelshelf – "it's about time I was making for me bed. Aye." She pulled herself upwards and ran her finger round the shining globe of a copper pan, one of a set of eight all in a row on the mantelpiece, and she nodded her head at it, saying, "I'll get that Betty working on those pans the morrow. Look at that dust on them!" She held out her finger towards Tilly, but Tilly could see no difference between the colour of the gnarled finger and any dust. Rising to her feet she said, "You're too finicky, Biddy."

"Aye, well, you'd have something to say, ma'am, if you found a dirty kitchen." Biddy had said the ma'am with a grin and Tilly flapped her hand at her, replying in kind, "All right, my woman, see that they're clean tomorrow."

They smiled broadly at each other before Tilly, turning away, said, "Good-night, Biddy."

"Good-night, Tilly lass. By the way. . . ."

Tilly paused and Biddy, loosening the strings of her white apron, said, "Don't you think it's about time I had a letter from our Katie?"

"Oh, I shouldn't worry; you'll be gettin' plenty of mail for Christmas and more than mail I suspect."

"What do you mean by that, more than mail?"

"Never you mind. Wait and see."

"She's not comin', is she?"

"No, no; not that, Biddy. I told you perhaps next year."

"Aye. Aye. Good-night, lass." She turned away on a sigh, and again Tilly said, "Good-night, Biddy."

In her room, Tilly sat before the dressing-table taking down her hair, and she paused with a hairpin in her hand and stared into the mirror. What was she to do, give Steve a hint that Peg was there

77

for the asking? Perhaps he was aware of it already. Anyway, from what she knew of the man Steve, he wouldn't appreciate any hints like that; if he wanted something he would go after it. If he had wanted Peg he would have had her before now.

Yet it was right what Biddy said, nobody should live alone. But she'd have to live alone. Yes, for the rest of her life she'd have to live alone. But then not quite, she had the children, she had her son, her own son, and she had in a way a daughter, a little dark much-loved and loving daughter. Yes, and one who would one day grow into a dark young woman, with all the needs of a young woman, perhaps intensified by the nature of that very colour.

The eyes looking back at her through the mirror became large and as if they had spoken she said to them, "Sufficient unto the day is the evil thereof."

11

November was mild. It was all agreed they were having better weather these past two weeks than they'd had at times in the middle of the summer. On two consecutive Sundays the sun had shone and she had ridden through the park with the children as far as the spot where the cottage had once stood.

She had already told the children that she had once lived at this spot, and each time they came to it they forced her to stop and plied her with questions about it; as today, when Willy, sitting straight on his pony, his head to the side, looked to where the old outhouses still stood almost obliterated now by the undergrowth and asked, "Would my grandmama and grandpapa have loved me?"

Tilly, surprised at such a question, looked at her small son and said, "Yes, yes, of course; they would have loved you dearly, Willy."

"Would they have made a fool of me?"

"A fool of you?" She narrowed her eyes at him. "What do you mean, make a fool of you?"

"Well, I heard Jimmy say that grandparents always made a fool of grandchildren."

"Oh, Oh" – she smiled broadly at him now – "what Jimmy was meaning to say was that all grandparents spoil their grandchildren."

"Oh."

"Mama."

"Yes?" She turned to Josefina.

"Would they have loved me, Willy's grandpapa and grandmama?"

"Oh, yes." Tilly, her voice very gentle now and her head nodding, gazed at the diminitive figure on the small pony and said, "Very much. Oh yes, they would have loved you very much."

"Even because my face is different from Willy's?" The child took her hands from the reins now and tapped her cheek.

79

The smile slid from Tilly's face as she said, "They would have loved you for yourself."

"Not because you are my mama?"

It was a strange question, and Tilly paused a moment before answering this wise and perceptive piece of humanity. "No, not simply because I am your mama but because you are yourself."

The child now turned her gaze away from Tilly who was peering at her and, looking straight ahead, she repeated, "'Cos I am myself." Then looking back at Tilly, she asked, "Do people always throw stones at people who are not the same colour?"

"No, no, of course not. But who has been throwing stones?" She looked now at Willy, but he remained silent; then again she was looking at Josefina and repeating, "Who has been throwing stones?"

"Christine said not to trouble you, she said they were silly boys."

"When did they throw the stones?"

Josefina pursed her lips an shrugged her small shoulders but remained silent, and Tilly turned to her son and, her voice stern, demanded, "Willy, tell me, who has been throwing stones."

"Some children, Mama, from beyond the gate."

"When?"

He considered for a moment, then said, "Sunday."

"Last Sunday?"

"Yes, Mama."

"And before that?"

"Yes, Mama."

"Can you remember when?"

"On . . . on fair day, when they were on holiday, they had on their Sunday suits." He nodded at her.

She now reached out and moved aside the hair covering an inch long scar on his brow, just above the jagged line left by the rough stitching of the wound that had caused his near blindness, and she recalled a day some weeks ago when she had come into the hall and found Christine Peabody talking rapidly to her father. The children were standing between them and when she enquired if there was anything wrong it was Peabody who had answered, saying, "Master Willy ran into a branch, madam, when he was playing. He has cut his brow a little."

"Did a stone do this, Willy?"

The boy's eyelids were blinking as he muttered, "Yes, Mama.

But it wasn't Christine's fault, she ran out of the gates and chased the boys."

Tilly felt her body slumping down into the saddle for a moment, but only for a moment; then she was sitting bolt upright. All her life she had suffered from the village and the villagers and because of Josefina they had another flail with which to beat her back. But Josefina was one thing, and her son another. The village, in the form of Mrs McGrath, had blinded her boy in one eye, and that stone could have taken the little sight that remained in the other, for the cut in his brow had gone deep and it was just above his right temple. Another half an inch or so and it could have been the eye itself.

As she felt the old surge of temper rising in her she swung the horse around, saying to the children, "Come! we're going for a ride."

Obediently they turned their ponies and trotted by her side, and when they cut on to the main drive and went towards the main gates neither of them cried as they might have done excitedly on another occasion, "Are we going to ride far, Mama?" They remained silent.

At the lodge she drew rein and called, "Jimmy! Jimmy!"

She knew it was Jimmy's day off, and when he appeared at the door dressed only in his trousers and shirt he quickly buttoned up the neck of his shirt as he came down the path, saying, "Yes, Ti . . . ma'am?"

"Would you mind going back to the stables and telling Arthur or Myers, whoever is available, to saddle a horse and follow me as quickly as he can."

"Yes. Yes, ma'am, yes, of course. Which way will I tell them to go?"

"I'm making for the village."

The young man's eyebrows shot up as he said, "The village!" and he repeated in amazement, "The village!"

"Yes, Jimmy, the village. Tell him I'll wait at the turnpike. Go at once will you as I'm in rather a hurry." As she spoke she took out her watch and looked at it, and after gaping at her for a moment, Jimmy turned and, just as he was, he rushed up the drive.

Her watch said half past eleven. Most of the villagers would be at the service, and all the children too, and if Parson Portman was anything like the usual preachers it would be three quarters of an hour before the church emptied.

Jimmy, in obeying her orders so promptly, had forgotten to open the gates, and she had to dismount and open them herself. It did not matter for, not wearing a habit, her remounting proved no obstacle.

Out on the road, she walked her horse, and the children's ponies followed suit. They had gone some distance when Willy asked tentatively, "Are you vexed with me, Mama?"

She turned her face towards him and swallowed the lump in her throat before answering softly, "No, my son, I'm not vexed with you."

"Who are you vex-ed with then?" This question came from Josefina, and Tilly, now looking at her, said, "Not you, my dear, either."

"Are you vex-ed with the village?"

"Yes. Yes, I suppose you could say I am vexed with the village."

"Are you going to chas . . . chas . . . ?"

"Yes, I suppose in a way you could say I am going to chastise them, dear." And she added bitterly to herself as she looked ahead, "And not before time. For once I'm going to live up to my name. God forgive me!"

They hadn't been waiting long at the turnpike when Tilly heard the sound of galloping hooves behind them and Arthur Drew came riding up to them.

Drawing his horse to a halt, Arthur breathed deeply for a moment before he asked, "You all right, Tilly?"

"Yes, yes, I'm all right, Arthur."

"There's something you want me to do?"

"Yes, Arthur." She paused. "I want you to ride say two or three lengths behind us as I go into the village, and when we stop you stop. I simply want you as a show of strength, if you get my meaning, sort of prestige, the lady of the manor taking her children for a ride accompanied by the groom. Do you follow me, Arthur?"

He didn't quite, but he knew she was up to something. The Tilly he knew never put on airs, but she was playing the lady now all right, and he'd support her with everything in every way he knew how.

"I should have got rigged up in me best," he said.

"You're all right as you are." She looked at his breeches tucked in his top boots. The boots could have had a better polish on them, but what matter, he was the servant following his mistress. That's how it should be today.

"Have you got a large white handkerchief on you?" she asked.

"Aw" – he made an apologetic movement with his head – "I've got a hanky on me but I'm afraid it isn't very white."

"Oh, it doesn't matter, Arthur; I have the very thing." She unloosened the top button of her riding jacket. It was without revers and was made very much in the style of a Texas Ranger's coat, buttoning right up to the neck. Pulling a narrow cream silk scarf from around her neck and leaning towards Willy, she said, "Take off your cap, dear."

She now proceeded to wind the scarf twice around his head, slanting it downwards to cover the cut at his temple, and when he protested, saying, "But, Mama, it isn't bleeding," she said "I know that, Willy, but I want you to keep this on. Here, give me your cap." She now placed his cap to the back of his head leaving the scarf much in evidence.

Again she looked at her watch, saying now, "There's plenty of time, we'll take it slowly." She glanced back at Arthur explaining, "I want to be in the middle of the village when the church comes out."

Arthur made a slight motion with his head. His mouth opened and closed, and then he said, "Why? Why, Tilly?"

For answer she said, "How long will it take us to get there, fifteen minutes?"

"Aye, that should do it."

"Very well, off we go. And children" – she looked from one to the other – "don't ask any questions until we are back home. You understand?"

Willy was the first to say, "Yes, Mama."

But Josefina said, "No questions, Mama?"

"No questions, Josefina, not until we reach home."

"Yes, Mama."

"Well now, come on."

Her head up, her back as straight as a ramrod, she now urged her horse forward. It could have been that she was leading an army into battle, and in a way she was. She knew that when she faced her enemies what she would put into them would not be the fear of God, but that of the devil. It was the only weapon she had, and she meant to use it for the sake of her children.

The village street was curved. Some of the houses were very old, their foundation stones having been laid over two hundred years past. The houses at the end spread out to form a square in the middle of which was a large round of rough grass where at one time had stood the market stone, but all that remained of it now was a flat slab, itself almost obliterated by the grass. At one side of the square were small cottages fronted by gardens, the opposite side was taken up by a number of shops, in the middle of which stood the inn.

Not all the villagers attended church, some went to chapel. The church and cemetery lay back from the road at the east end of the village; the chapel, a new erection, was, as it were, cut off from the village by being situated down a side lane; but whether by accident or design both services began at the same time on a Sunday and also ended approximately at the same time. It was laughingly said that the minister of the chapel had a runner waiting outside the church to inform him when the parson was drawing the service to a close. However that may be, both sets of worshippers, at least those on foot, generally managed to straggle into the village square at the same time as they made their way home.

So, as usual today, in twos and threes they emerged in their dark Sunday best either from the side lane or through the lychgate, but all of them stopped in their tracks, only to be nudged forward by those behind them, for there in the middle of the green was a woman sitting on a horse; she was flanked on each side by a child on a pony, and behind her at a respectable distance sat a man in the clothes of a groom.

It took but a few minutes for the older inhabitants among the thickening throng to recognise the rider. The younger ones had to grope in their minds, but even they soon realised this was the woman that all the stir was about.

After their first pausing some of the villagers began to move towards their respective houses, defiance in their step which was lacking in their faces, and it was as the first couple entered their gate that Tilly, in a voice that was not loud, but each word clear and distinct and which carried to everyone present, turned to her son and, pointing across the square, said, "That is the inn, Willy, where Mrs Bradshaw used to serve. You know, her daughter came to look after you and struck you and stole my jewellery, so I had to dismiss her. And next to it is the baker's shop. The Mitchams lived there."

She was aware that her son was straining to stare at her, his mouth slightly open, his face red. She was also aware that most of

84

the people had stopped and that they, too, were staring at her, and most of them too had their mouths agape, and their eyes stretched wide. But as if she were unaware of them and now moving her arm to the side, she said, "Willy, where you see the board swinging that is the wheelwright's shop. The wheelwright's name was Mr Burk Laudimer. His son has now taken his place." She could have added at this stage that these people blamed her for killing his father, but she went on, her finger now pointing here and there, "That is the carpenter's shop. Mr Fairweather owns that and he lives in a cottage" – she turned her head and her body moved slightly in the saddle as she pointed behind her, adding, "over there." In her turning she saw Arthur Drew's face. His eyes, too, were wide, almost popping out of his head.

She was again pointing in front of her, but now leaning towards Josefina as she did so and saying, "You see that cottage there, Josefina? There lives the gravedigger. You know what a gravedigger is? He is a man who buries the dead."

She could see that Josefina was on the point of asking a question, and so she turned from her and went on naming names, pointing out houses; and lastly she pointed along the street to where at the end of the row of shops was the blacksmith's, and it did not escape her that outside the door stood George McGrath and his son, taller now but whom she recognised as the boy who had broken the cottage window and accused her of killing his Uncle Hal and calling her witch.

She had lost count of the people she had named, she only knew they were all standing transfixed gazing at her, as they might have done at something at a fair, but without the enjoyment that sight would have elicited. And it was at the precise moment when she was about to give them an ultimatum that there pushed through the crowd, his black robes flapping, Parson Portman.

She had, of course, heard of Parson Portman but she had never met him; apparently the manor was out of bounds to him, but now there he was standing not three yards from her looking up at her and she down at him.

When she spoke to him her voice was polite and had the inflexion of the gentry, which surprised him. He had heard so many tales of this woman and none good, yet she had the face of a . . . he dare not say angel, so substituted in his own mind, a beautiful creature with the strangest eyes he had ever seen in a woman.

Parson Portman was an educated man. He was a bachelor from

85

choice, for he had seen too many of his kind struggling to support a wife and yearly increasing family. He loved the creature comforts which included good food, wine and a large fire, and a man in his position didn't usually come by these things unless he had been able to buy himself into the church. Being one of eight brothers, his people had educated him but that was all they had been able to do for him. And so, knowing on which side his bread was buttered, he aimed to keep in favour with his more wealthy parishioners and no one of these but had held the Manor and its occupants in disdain for years.

He had been assigned to this parish following his predecessor's departure in disgrace through his wife's escapades, joint escapades, so he understood, with this very woman here. She had corrupted the parson's wife, so the tale went, but now working it out for himself, this woman in front of him could have been little more than a child or a very young girl when the incident happened. Yet from the look of her he could imagine that she could have a strange power over both men and women: possessed of the devil they said she was, and that death attended her wherever she went.

What was he to do? How was he to deal with the situation? Why was she here, attended by her children and her groom? What did his parishioners expect him to do, put a curse on her?

What she had said to him was, "Good-morning, sir." And now some moments later in answer to her greeting, he replied, "Good-morning, madam. Can I be of any assistance to you?"

She seemed to consider for a moment, then said in no small voice now, "Yes, oh yes, Parson, you could be of great assistance. You will I am sure have heard of me, and, of course, you will know that I am a witch and have been persecuted because of my particular talent." She now looked over his head and around the gaping faces; then looking down on him again, she went on, "Not only have I been persecuted, but my son also. Perhaps you are aware that my son" – she put out her hand now towards Willy – "is almost blind. This was done by one of your parishioners. He has just a little sight left in one eye. Well, not satisfied with this, the children of the village have been sent . . . directed apparently to finish what their parents started." Now she swiftly put out her hand and whipped off Willy's cap showing his bandaged head and, her voice rising and again looking at the scattered crowd, she cried in a voice that the young Tilly might have used "A well aimed stone tried to finish the job. Well now, sir," – once more she lowered her head and looked at the parson – "I have come to the village to give them an ultimatum: the persecution stops or else I shall use the powers that they ascribe to me, and the first one in future who lifts his hand against us, or even his tone, I shall deal with in my own way."

The whole square was silent; the fact that a mongrel dog stood immovable on the edge of the green staring up towards her only added to the eeriness.

When she turned her fierce gaze down on to the parson's face it looked blanched. She saw him wet his lips, move his head in bewilderment, then put his hands out as if he were about to appeal to her; she did not allow him time for she dug her heels into the flanks of her horse and the beast turned obediently and moved off the green on to the roadway. The children following suit came slightly behind her. Lastly, after he had stared, in his turn, in amazement at the fear-filled faces of those nearest to him Arthur Drew followed his mistress out of the village.

Tilly, as after any emotional experience, expected to feel slightly sick. She expected her body to tremble, her legs to be so weak that they would not support her, and in this particular case that they would have possessed no strength with which to guide the horse. But she felt none of these things, what she did feel was a great sense of elation which lasted all the way back to the Manor. And when as soon as they were inside the house the children wanted to clamber about her and ask questions, she quietly passed them over to Christine and, saying to Peabody, "Have a glass of wine and some biscuits sent up to my room, please," she walked steadily across the hall and up the stairs.

But Arthur Drew in the kitchen sat at the table and wiped the sweat from his brow and looked at the faces of his mother and his sisters as he said, "Ma, it was the weirdest thing I've ever experienced. I tell you, she sat there on that horse and the things she did! She named everybody in that village, at least all of them that had had a go at her. And then it was like the heavens had opened and there was the parson, and she talked to him, called it an ultimatum. But I tell you, every soul in that village knew she was offering them a curse. Eeh! Ma."

"Here, drink that." Biddy pushed a mug of ale towards him, and she watched him drain the mug dry before she sat down and said, "I can't take it in, the very fact of her going into the village. What brought it on do you think?"

"I don't know, Ma. The only thing is, as I said, she bandaged young Willy's head up just as if it had happened this mornin'. But 'twas the way she spoke. I tell you, Ma, I wasn't on the wrong side of her but she still put the fear of God into me. You know, I can't help but say it, there's somethin' in her . . . Tilly."

"Don't be so bloody soft, our Arthur!"

"I'm not being bloody soft, Ma." He had risen to his feet. "You weren't there."

"Well, she's no witch. God! you've known her long enough."

"Aye, I have, an' there's nobody I like better, but I tell you, Ma, she's got somethin' that the ordinary woman hasn't. And I can't put me finger on it no more than anyone else can, but it's there."

"Aye, it's there, and it's nowt but attraction as they call it. Some women have it and some haven't; she's got a bit more than her share, that's all."

"Well, have it your way, Ma; the only thing I can say again is you weren't there. But I'd like to bet me bottom dollar that there won't be any more trouble for some time in the village."

"Well, that's something to thank God for this Sunday anyway. By! I'll say it is 'cos she's had more than her share." It was Fanny nodding at him now. "From as far back as I can remember people have been at her. I only wish I'd been there."

"I only wish you had, our Fanny, instead of me. Yes. Yes" – he nodded slowly at her – "I only wish you had. But I'll tell you this, I wouldn't want to sit through that again."

"What did the parson say to her?"

Arthur had made for the door and he turned. "Nowt. Nowt. He just looked as if he had been struck dumb or put under a spell or somethin'. Aye, that's it. Like the rest of 'em, put under a spell."

"Good for Tilly, 'cos he's never crossed the door. It would queer his pitch with the pious nobs he toadies to. Good for her."

"Ma, I'll say again, you weren't there, and to my mind it wasn't good for anybody."

12

There was a change in Tilly. The Drews had remarked on it, Peabody had remarked on it, and Tilly herself remarked on it. Since the Sunday she rode into the village square and prophesied doom and tribulation for anyone who would dare to persecute her or hers in the future, she had, as it were, brought to the surface her fear of the villagers, and with such a melodramatic effort too, for she was fully aware that she had played on the melodramatic and used it to aid the effect of her warning. Yet as she had ridden out of the village there hadn't been a vestige of the old fear left in her; in fact, she had the idea that she had distributed it among all those present that morning.

The change in her was made evident when she no longer by-passed the village on the way to Shields but ordered Ned Spoke or Peter Myers, whoever was driving the coach, to go directly through the village. Also, at times she rode horseback through it, but never alone, always she would be accompanied by one of the men acting as groom. But quite frequently she rode alone to visit Anna and John.

It was Anna who said to her a few days after the eventful Sunday, "Is it true what I'm hearing, Tilly, that you went to the village on Sunday and waited for the church coming out and addressed them?"

Tilly could not help but laugh at the term used for her haranguing Parson Portman's and Mr Wycomb's congregations and she answered, "Yes, quite true, Anna. But I wouldn't say I addressed them, rather put the fear of God in them . . . or the devil. Yes, the latter is more like it, the devil. They've associated me with him for so many years that I felt it was about time I gave them proof of his power."

"But why? Why?" Anna had questioned, her head shaking from side to side. "There has been no trouble lately."

"No? Willy was struck in the head with a stone; in fact it was almost on his eye, his good eye. I was unaware that the stone

89

throwing had been going on for some time; it was kept from me so I wouldn't worry. Well, that's how these things start. The next move could be setting fire to the barns . . . or even the house. Oh, don't shake your head like that. Remember . . . or perhaps you don't but I've already been burned out once. They have persecuted me for years and if I intend to go on living at the manor, and I do Anna, I'm not going to have the children brought up in fear. If anyone's going to hand out fear in the future it'll be me."

Anna's eyes had widened, her face had stretched as she said, "It sounds so unlike you, Tilly. You've always seemed to crave peace and you've never been the one to retaliate."

"That was because I was so fearful of them, petrified of them and what they might do. Yet on looking back, I remember after they burned the cottage down and my granny had died because of it, I lay on the straw in the woodshed and I can recall vividly imagining myself standing in the middle of the village screaming at each one in turn, denouncing them and instilling fear into them. It has taken a good many years for that desire to bear fruit. You know, they say if you wish and think on a thing hard enough you'll get it in the end, but that saying doesn't take account of the work, and in my case the anxiety and fear in between."

John, too, was a little shocked at the stance Tilly had taken. His concern, however, was mainly with regard to her safety. "They c . . . could have set about you, Ti . . . Tilly. There're still some w . . . wild ones in that village," to which, touching his shoulder, she had answered with tenderness, "John, you know that some brave men are afraid to walk through a graveyard at night. Well, I've turned into the graveyard for that entire village," and to this all John could say was, "Oh, Tilly! what a simile, you . . . you a graveyard. Oh Tilly!. . ."

However, one person, but only one, saw the funny side of the incident, and that was Steve.

During the past month Tilly had made two visits to the mine, once accompanied by John, and once on her own. John, in a tentative way, had suggested that she did not visit the mine unaccompanied. "It wasn't seemly," he had said.

To anyone else she would have answered, "Why not? I'm the owner, it belongs to me, why shouldn't I visit it and speak to the men who work there?" But she merely smiled at him and said, laughingly, "Remember, John, I'm no lady." And to this, he had screwed up his eyes, tossed his head to the side and, his stammer more evident again, he had spluttered, "D . . . don't say su . . . such things. Tilly, you are as g . . . g . . . good a lady as ever I've . . . . I've met. It m . . . maddens me when you dep . . . dep . . . deprecate yourself. I am con . . . concerned for you simply, be . . . be . . . because you are a l . . . lady."

Dear John. Dear John. Sometimes she thought, of all the Sopwiths he was the best and the kindest. Perhaps, she told herself, she thought that way because he was uncomplicated, he had inherited none of the passions of his father or his brother. In a way he and Luke were alike in temperament, as Matthew and Jessie Ann had been.

They would see Luke soon. He had written to say he was coming, that he was getting leave from his regiment at Christmas and would spend a few days with them. He had never seen Willy since she had returned home and, of course, he hadn't set eyes on Josefina, and she naturally wondered not a little just what his reaction to the child would be. Yet it didn't trouble her.

On this particular visit to the mine, she had talked with the present manager, Mr Meadows, and she sensed that he, like John, didn't welcome her presence. On this occasion the men were coming out after doing a shift and a half, and she had wanted to know why they had been called upon to do the extra work. There was a little water coming in on the B level, Mr Meadows had said. And she had surprised him by answering, "There was always a little water coming in on the B level. In my opinion it's time that area was closed off."

The sharp retort the man was about to make was checked by his remembering that this woman had once worked down this very mine and had for days lain with the owner behind a fall, the same fall that caused the man to lose both feet. And so he said, "There's been a lot of work, repair work, done on B section, madam."

"Then why are you still having trouble?"

God! he thought, the questions women asked. "Because, madam," he said slowly, "this whole mine runs by the side of and in some parts under the river."

"I'm afraid of that, Mr Meadows," she had answered; "and that's why, I repeat, that section should be shut off."

"Then you'd better talk the matter over with Mr John, madam."

She looked at the men who were passing her. They were not only black from head to foot but they were also wet, the wet coal dust was covering them like a black glaze.

She stopped two men. "What's your name?" she asked, looking at first one then the other.

"Me name's Bladwish, ma'am, Bladwish."

'Bill Thircall, ma'am," said the other one.

She smiled at them now before saying, "How bad is it down there?"

"Oh, not all that bad, ma'am. Bit of water. We've got it in time; it'll take somethin' to get through that now. The river'd have to burst its banks first." He laughed.

She looked from one to the other. They must have been down there sixteen to eighteen hours; they looked worn out yet they could still smile, still have a cheery word. And what were they going home to? A two-roomed cottage, a hovel really, like the Drews used to live in, which at one time she had gladly shared with them. Well, that's something she could do, and would do: she'd build a new row, two rooms up and two rooms down, and a dry closet in the yard. Yes, that's what she'd do.

As the two men touched their foreheads and moved away she turned and was about to speak to the manager, whose expression was anything but pleasant, when she saw Steve coming up the drift towards her. He was accompanied by three workmen. They were talking and nodding at each other, but when Steve glimpsed her he seemed to pause for a moment before leaving the men. Coming towards her, he touched his cap and said, "Good-afternoon, Mrs Sopwith."

It was the first time he had addressed her formally, and she answered in the same vein, "Good-afternoon, Mr McGrath. I hear you're having some trouble."

"Oh, nothing to worry about." He glanced towards his superior. then said, "There's one thing sure, wherever it comes in it won't be in that spot again."

"Don't you think that section should be closed?" she now asked.

"No, no." He shook his head in a wide movement; then looking at Mr Meadows, he said, "You don't think so, do you, sir?"

"I've already had my say to madam." The manager now turned to Tilly, adding, "If you'll excuse me, madam, I must be about my business;" then glancing at Steve again, he said, "I want you in for the fore shift."

It was a moment before Steve answered, "Right;" then looking at Tilly, he said, "Can I give you a step up on your mount, Mrs Sopwith?" and she answered, "If you please, Mr McGrath."

When she mounted she looked down at him and said, "Thank you," before turning the horse around and taking it up the muddy bank past the stables, the lamp house, and the office.

She had noted Steve's hesitation when Mr Meadows had told him he expected him to be at work for the fore shift. Like the men, he had likely been below sixteen or eighteen hours. It was now late in the afternoon, in fact it was dusk, and the fore shift went in, she knew only too well, at two o'clock in the morning. From where he lived it would mean getting up at one if he intended to make a meal before going out; and what he would have to do, the men would have to do. Nothing seemed to improve in mines, time, pay or conditions. She had heard of men in other pits striking and she could understand why. Oh yes, only too well she could understand why.

In a thoughtful mood she walked her horse, thinking, I've enough money to raise their wages, I could cut down their hours. Yet she knew, as kindly as John was, he'd be very much against this, for any alteration in pay or lessening the men's time would bring other coal owners, such as Rosier, about their ears. Bonded men were little better than slaves; in fact, looking back, she considered the four male slaves on the ranch in Texas had in many ways lived better than some of her own miners.

But she could alter things, give them decent places to live in, and rent free, she must talk to John about it or perhaps Steve.

As if her thinking had conjured him up, she heard the clip-clopping of the hooves of the old horse on the road behind her and, turning, she drew her horse to a standstill to allow him to come abreast. He was riding the animal bareback and as he jogged to a halt, he said, "That's the first time he's ever trotted. Do you know, I think he could gallop if he was put to it. There's life in the old boy yet."

She smiled at him, then said, "You must be very tired."

"Oh, not too bad; not too tired to brew a cup of tea if you'll come in?"

"No, thank you, Steve. It's getting dusk, and if I'm not back before dark they'll have the bellmen out for me."

93

They rode on in silence for a few minutes, and then he said, "Nice to see you taking an interest in the mine, Tilly."

"Yes." She half turned her head towards him. "It's one thing taking an interest but another thing entirely, I imagine, to get anything done, I mean make changes."

"Oh" – his chin jerked up – "you mean Mr Meadows. He's a stickler for the rules. I suppose I shouldn't say it but he's frightened of the death he'll never die. To my mind he shouldn't be in this business at all; either you're made for it or you're not. Not unlike being in the army, where you've got a better chance of surviving if you come up from the ranks, so to speak. It's all right being conversant with the technical stuff but if you don't get the feel of a seam before you touch it, then there's something missin'. Still, the way things are suits me: I see to below and he sees to up top, most of the time anyway. You're sure you won't come in for a cup of tea? It won't take a couple of minutes."

They were nearing the cottage gate now and she shook her head, saying, "Another time I'd be very pleased to. In fact I must come again and gather up a few more books, if that's all right with you?"

"Oh" – he jerked his head – "now don't be silly, Tilly . . . if it's all right with me, it's your cottage. By the way" – he put his head slightly to the side – "you're looking better, brighter. Your riding likely does you a lot of good. And as I haven't seen you for some time, I must congratulate you on one ride you took."

As she returned his gaze she pretended she didn't know to what he was alluding and her voice had a query in it as she said, "Yes, and what ride was that?"

"The day you put the fear of God into them in the village."

"Oh that! Do you think that's the right term?"

His laugh now rung out as he answered, "No, somehow I don't. An' there's one thing I can tell you, you acted like a dose of senna on half the churchgoers that morning. And through the bits of tittle-tattle I've heard here and there I don't imagine you'll have much trouble from that quarter in the future. Your fame's spread even as far as Pelaw. On the way back from Newcastle last week I dropped in at The Stag to have a drink. I've never been in that pub afore, so they didn't know me, and talked freely among themselves. And I can tell you this, Tilly, they were mostly for the stand you made, for you know, like the way Shields feels about Newcastle, Pelaw and up the line feel about Shields, and the villages."

"Well, that's good to hear anyway, it means I won't have a hunting party coming from Pelaw."

"No; nor nowhere else, if you ask me. As one of the fellows said, he had seen you once and he wouldn't mind having a witch like you sitting at the other end of the table any day. Aw! Tilly" – his voice suddenly full of concern, he put in quickly, "I just said that to reassure you. I mean. . . ."

"I know what you meant, Steve. And don't worry, the name doesn't trouble me any more, in fact I think I'll cultivate it. Yes" – she nodded her head – "that's what I'll do. Anyway they've dubbed me a witch for so long I feel there must be something in it."

"Never! You've got as much of the witch in you, Tilly, as I have blue blood."

"You think so?"

"Sure of it."

"Then tell me, Steve" – her voice was serious now – "why has the name stuck to me, why have I been persecuted because of it?"

"Oh" – he leant forward and stroked the horse's grizzled mane, then moved his lips one over the other before slanting his eyes towards her and saying, "It's because you've got something, a sort of an appeal. No, no" – he now shook his head – "that's not the word. Attractiveness, I suppose, would be better. Better still" – his voice sank on to a low note as he ended – "fascination. Aye" – he nodded his head – "I think that's the word that fits you, fascination. You've always had it. Don't ask me what it consists of, I don't know, it's just you."

Her voice as quiet as his, she said, "It's an attribute I could have well done without, Steve."

"Aye, from your point of view you would say that, but not from others, Tilly. No, not from others."

She lowered her head and remained silent, which prompted him almost to shout, "Look! we're out here nattering when we could have been indoors in the warmth, you're sure. . . .?"

She was sitting bolt upright, the reins tight now in her hands as she said, "Bye-bye, Steve. I'll pop along one day for the books."

He didn't speak until the horse had taken a few steps, and then he answered "Do that, Tilly. Do that." His voice was so low that his words came only faintly to her.

She put the animal into a trot and then into a gallop, and all the while her mind kept pounding with the rhythm of its hooves: fascination, fascination; and she knew that the fascination for her still held with him, and she told herself once more that she must keep clear of him for his own sake, and that if she visited the cottage it would have to be when he was out. But, on the thought, the feeling of loneliness welled in her; of all those about her, with the exception of Biddy, with whom she would like to be on friendly terms it was him; because whatever the tie was, it was there and had been since they were children.

13

Christmas was a gay affair, made so not only by the children but by their new Uncle Luke. This tall man who crept on all fours and chased them and elicited from the children screams of delight as he pretended to be a monkey and sprang on to couches and over chairs. Not only did the children enjoy him, but so did John and Anna and Tilly, and indeed the whole of the staff were for him: was he not a soldier who had fought the Russians, those strange and terrible people who lived on another planet? Besides that he was a gentleman, a gentleman who had a civil word for them.

As they said in the kitchen, they doubted if this house had ever heard such laughter and known such gaiety. And they themselves added to it. From Betty up to Biddle and Peabody they each in his own way contributed towards the happiness that prevailed in the house during the holiday.

It was only at night when lying alone in her bed and the echoes of the laughter had died away that Tilly would whisper, "Oh, Matthew! Matthew! If only you were here." Yet at the back of her mind she knew that if Matthew had been present, the atmosphere might not have been so gay, so free. Matthew had to dominate the scene, he would have had to set the pace, play the practical jokes, as he had done from a boy; yet like most practical jokers he was unable to accept being made a fool of, of being laughed at in return.

John, for instance, had always been laughed at because of his stammer. He was used to it. And Luke, she had found during the last four days, possessed qualities that had hitherto lain hidden. His way with children was delightful. He let them rumple him, climb all over him. This was new to them, for the man that Willy faintly remembered as his papa had never played with him, and the man that Josefina remembered as her papa had hardly ever looked at her. This uncle was certainly a revelation to them and, like all children, they took advantage of it, so much so that on

97

Boxing Day there were tears when Christine was ordered to take them to the nursery and prepare them for bed.

For the first time that Tilly could remember Willy had dis-obeyed her, saying openly, "I don't want to go to bed, Mama, I want to play with Uncle," whereupon Luke put in, "If you don't do what your mama tells you then I'm going to pack my bags and call for the carriage and ride away, right to the sea, and there I'll board a boat and you'll never seen me again."

The response had been quite unexpected for both Willy and Josefina had thrown themselves upon him, the tears flowing freely and crying, "No! Uncle Luke. No! Uncle Luke."

When peace was restored and the four adults were left in the drawing-room, John, nodding at his brother who was now lying flat out on the chaise, said, "I think it's just as w . . . well you've only g . . . g . . . got another f . . . few days, otherwise Tilly would have to give . . . give you notice and. . . . Just l . . . l . . . look at you! For a sol . . . sol . . . soldier of the Queen, you are a mess . . . mess."

"Oh." Luke stretched out his legs and put his hands behind his head as he said, "It's wonderful to be a mess, this kind of a mess;" and rolling his eyes backwards, he looked up at John who was standing at the head of the chaise and, his voice quiet, even serious now, he said, "Don't put a damper on me, little brother; you have no idea what this spell has meant for me." He brought his head down now and looked towards where Tilly and Anna were sitting on the couch that ran at right angles to the fireplace, the open hearth showing a great bank of blazing logs, and he asked, "You don't mind, Tilly, do you?"

"No, Luke, I don't mind. Of course I don't mind."

"I suppose I have gone a bit far . . . daft."

It was Anna who spoke now, saying, "I wish more people could show their daftness in a similar way."

Luke rose on his elbow now and grinned towards her as he said, "Thank you, sister-in-law. And if you'd care to engage me when your family comes along I should be delighted to offer my services free."

When Anna hung her head slightly, John's eyelids blinked rapidly and, his stammer evident now, he said, "You're a f . . . f . . . fool, Lu . . . Luke. Always were and . . . and . . . and always will be. Come on, Anna, let's go and s . . . see the children to bed, then g . . . get on our way."

He held out his hand to his wife, turning his head and glaring at his brother as he did so.

As soon as the door closed on them, Luke swung his legs from the chaise, pressed his shirt into shape under the lapels of his coat, ran both hands over his skin-fitting trousers, then smoothed his hair back before saying, "Did I say something wrong?"

"No, not really." Tilly gave a slight shrug of her shoulders. "Anna is just a little conscious of the fact that there is no sign of a family yet. But as I've told her" – her smile widened now – "it took me almost twelve years."

"Yes, yes, it did." He nodded at her, and their laughter joined.

It was strange but she found she could talk very easily to Luke. Of the three brothers she would have said she liked him the least. He had always appeared a very self-contained person; he knew what he wanted to do and he did it with the minimum of fuss.

She watched him now rise and come towards her, and when he sat down in the corner of the settee he looked at her for a few moments before he said, "This is the first time we've been alone together since I came home. Funny that." He raised his eyebrows. "I said home. Although I spent all those years away in Scarborough, then in the army, I still look upon this house as home."

"I am glad of that."

"Tilly."

"Yes, Luke?"

"I've never mentioned Matthew, being half afraid it might be too painful a subject to bring up. . . . Is it still?"

"No, Luke, no. Talk about him if you want."

"John tells me he had a terrible time. What I mean is you both had, I think you most of all."

When she remained quiet he wetted his lips before lowering his head and muttering, "You're more beautiful with your white hair."

And again she made no answer.

He raised his eyes to her as he said, "You'll marry again of course?"

"No, Luke, never."

"Oh." He jerked his chin to the side. "That's nonsense. Anyway, I can't see you being allowed to remain single."

"Nevertheless, I shall."

"Why?"

"I can't tell you why, only that I shan't, I won't . . . I. . . ."

"Don't be silly, Tilly." He leant forward, one hand pressing deep into the pile of the cushions as he brought his face almost within an inch of hers. "Love doesn't last a lifetime. It can't, not unless there's someone on the other end to keep the fire stoked. You loved Matthew, all right, I admit that, and he loved you. No . . . no" – he now made a single swift movement with his head that spoke of denial – "he didn't love you, his feelings for you could only come under the term of mania. He was so eaten up by you, even as a boy, it wasn't normal."

"Don't say that, Luke."

"I must say it because it's true, and you know it's true. He would have put you in a cage if he could just to keep you to himself. And in a way, yes" – he nodded at her – "in a way I can understand his feelings. But it wasn't ordinary love, and you shouldn't let the memory of it rule your life. Tilly" – he caught at her hand and she let him hold it – "I'm going to ask you something, a question, but I think I already know the answer. . . . It's simply this, why did you adopt Josefina?"

All the muscles in her face seemed to be twitching at once, she couldn't take her eyes from his. Her mouth was dry and she ran her tongue round her lips before saying, "Because her mother didn't want her and . . . and she was such a tiny thing so, so in need of care."

"No other reason?"

Again she moved her tongue around her lips before saying, "No."

"You're lying, because I know that nobody in their right senses adopts a dark child, not one such as her, except a missionary might. She's not an African, she's not Chinese, she's not Spanish, nor is she pure Indian or Mexican. There'd have to be some very grave reason for you to take such a child into your life." He released her hand now and, turning from her, he lay back against the couch and spread one arm along the head of it as he said, "When Matthew came back from America we met only once. We had a long day together and as usual when two men meet the conversation reverts to the pleasures they have had or missed. I asked him what the American women were like. I remember his answer wasn't very flattering. One of the ranchers had three hefty daughters and, excuse the coarseness, but I remember he referred to them as three mares waiting to be sired, but not without the ring. He said the only beautiful women were half-castes. I asked him if he had known any of them, and by using the term 'known' I was indicating something deeper, and I remember he made a face before using a certain expression which told me that he had been in contact with at least one of these women. Then the fact that he refused to enlarge upon her, and that his manner became abrupt, seemed to suggest his association with one person had had consequences that he wished to forget. Well now, Tilly," – he turned and looked at her – "I must admit when I first set eyes on Josefina she gave me a bit of a shock and I asked myself the question that everyone must ask when they see you and her together, why did this woman adopt such a child, a child that looks like a little foreign elf, a beautiful elf, but a strange creature? Why? And after thinking back I knew I had the answer. She's Matthew's, isn't she, Tilly?"

Her eyes were wide and unblinking and when her lips trembled he caught at her hand again, saying, "Poor Tilly. Dear Tilly, to shoulder his flyblow. . . ."

"She's not a flyblow!" The sharpness of her reply almost startled him, and he said rapidly, "I'm sorry. I'm sorry. Believe me, Tilly, I'm sorry."

"If she's a flyblow so is Willy."

"Tilly! Tilly!" He had pulled himself towards her and was gripping both her hands now. "Tilly, you are the most wonderful woman on earth. Do you know that? And I'm going to say this to you. I won't ask you to forget about Matthew because you never can, but don't hang on to the past. Marry again. Promise me" — He shook her hands up and down now as he repeated, "Promise me you'll marry again for I can't bear the thought of you being wasted."

She slumped back against the couch now and her voice was weary as she said, "I can't. I can't, Luke."

"Tell me why. Is there a reason, not just your feeling for Matthew?"

It was on a long drawn out breath that she said, "Yes, there's a reason."

"Can you tell me it?"

She turned her head and looked at him. If she didn't give him a reason he would probe.

He broke into her thoughts, saying urgently now, "It isn't that you're ill in any way?"

"Oh no, no." Again she let out a long breath, and now she said,

"I promised Matthew on his death-bed that I would never marry again."

He drew his chin tight into his neck and screwed up his eyes as if getting her into focus before he exclaimed, "You what!"

"I don't need to repeat it, Luke, you heard what I said."

"I hope I didn't. You said that you promised Matthew on his death-bed not to marry again? Don't tell me he asked you to give that promise."

Her lids were lowered, her chin was on her chest when he said, "Good God Almighty! But yes, yes –" He let go her hands now and sprang up from the couch and paced the length of the long rug that lay before the open hearth as he cried, "I can hear him doing it. Yes, I can hear him doing it. Promise me no other man will ever touch you, Tilly. Let me take my mania to the grave with me."

"Luke! Please, Luke."

He was standing now, his legs apart, his arms spread wide, silent, just standing gazing at her; then his arms flapping to his sides and his heels almost clicking together, he said, "Damn him! He was my brother and I say to you, Tilly, damn him wherever he is for the selfish, self-centred maniac he was. As for you to give him that promise, what were you thinking of?"

"I was thinking of him dying. And under the same circumstances I would do the same again." Her voice was quiet.

He bent towards her as he said, "You've got a long life before you, Tilly. You are lonely; one can see it in your eyes. You laugh with everything but your eyes. And think of the years ahead. Knowing this, can you say you would give the same promise again? By God! if I wasn't your brother-in-law, Tilly, I would see that you broke that promise. Do you hear me? A man can't marry his brother's wife, and even if he could you might think that to run the whole gamut of our family was a bit too much, but if it was within the law, Tilly, I tell you that I'd wear you down, because I, too, have loved you, not like Matthew, that maniac, or like my father in need of solace, but as an ordinary man loves a woman. . . . Oh, don't press yourself away from me like that. Nothing can happen between us, I'm well aware of that. And I haven't lived a saint's life because I couldn't have you. Oh no; I've enjoyed a number of women; and it's because I've done this I know what you're missing. And let me tell you" – he poked his face towards her – "that's what you need at this very moment.

And because I'm sure of this I beg of you, forget your death-bed promise and take yourself a husband, a man who'll be a father to those children because that's what they want. Their need in a way is as great as yours."

When he straightened his back the sweat was running down from the rim of his hair over his temples and, his voice quiet now, he said, "This is the moment I should apologise I suppose and say I'm sorry, but I'm not a bit sorry, Tilly." He took a step back from her and they surveyed each other in silence until he said, "I'll leave you to think over what I've said. Tell yourself, Tilly, that the dead are dead, and there's nothing as dead as a dead man. I am haunted at night by the dead I have seen and by the fact that there can be nowhere for them to go: the heavens couldn't hold all the dead that have died in battle and by plague and massacre. There's no place for the dead in which to survive even in spirit, Tilly, so they have no power over you. Matthew is dead. He will never know whether you have kept the promise he extracted from you or not. Your struggle to keep faith with him is as senseless as if I were to say to you now, I am going to shoot myself because I remember that my friends dropped dead around me."

Her head was bent again and she felt rather than saw him walk up to the head of the couch, and when she heard the drawing-room door close she opened her mouth wide as if she were about to scream; then she pressed her hand tightly over it, but she did not now say, "Oh, Matthew! Matthew!" rather, her mind cried, "Oh dear God! help me. Help me."

14

The children cried when Luke departed. Dressed in his uniform once more he did not look the same man who had clambered over the furniture like a monkey, chased them up and down the stairs, rode the rocking horse in the nursery, and generally enchanted them; yet the uniform did nothing to hide the man from them, the father figure, and they clung to his legs until they were forcibly removed by both Tilly and Christine.

When the nursery door closed behind them, Tilly led the way down the stairs, saying, "You have spoilt them," and he answered, "If playing the father to them has spoilt them, then I am found guilty."

She did not answer this, but hurried on across the gallery and down into the hall. It was the first time he had made reference to the conversation they had held in the drawing-room four days previously, four days which she had found to be very uncomfortable. She had no doubt within herself that if it hadn't been for the law Luke would have pressed his suit, and then what would she have done? Father and two sons. No! No! It wasn't to be thought of. Anyway, she had no feeling for Luke other than as the brother of her husband and the elder brother of John. She had more, much more tender feeling for John than for Luke. She was glad he was going, but he stirred her mind in the most uncomfortable way, and not only with regard to the children. But it was right what he said, they missed the presence of a man, a father; but as she would never be able to supply that, she must in some way endeavour to bring into their lives the male element.

The thought of Steve was rejected at once, yet it was the first name that came into her mind, for she imagined Steve would be good with children. No, she knew what she was going to do once she was rid of Luke. And now here they were standing face to face at the front door. The carriage was waiting on the drive. Myers had lowered the steps, Biddle was standing on the terrace; Peabody flicked a speck from the back of Luke's collar, then moved back and stood at a respectful distance. Luke took her hand and, his voice soft, he said, "Good-bye, Tilly. This has been a most memorable visit for me." And out of politeness, she said, "You must repeat it as soon as possible."

He made no answer, but leaning forward, he put his lips to her cheek, and as he did so a shudder passed through her body because for a moment she imagined him to be Matthew: he had the same body smell, his mouth was the same shape.

Her fingers felt crushed within his grasp. She could have winced with the pain but she made no sign, and then he was gone, running down the steps. He did not turn and look at her again, but she saw him looking up at the nursery floor; then the carriage was bowling down the drive.

Biddle came hurrying up the steps and into the hall and, closing the door quickly after him to shut out the bitter wind, he was about to chafe his hands when he noticed his mistress standing in the middle of the hall. He stopped and looked at her enquiringly; then he could not keep his eyebrows from rising slightly as she said, "I would like to speak with Ned Spoke. Bring him to the morning-room, please."

. . . . "Yes, ma'am."

As Tilly made her way across the hall to the corridor leading to the morning-room she was well aware that Biddle and Peabody were exchanging glances and wondering why she wanted to see the stable boy.

She had already given everybody their Christmas boxes, generous with them, too, she had been. What was she wanting with Spoke?

Young Ned Spoke, too, wondered this as he was thrust into the changing room by Biddle, told to take off his boots and to choose a pair or slippers that were likely to fit him from a row set against the wall, then ordered to lick down his hair, straighten his jerkin, and to mind his manners when speaking to the mistress.

Ned Spoke had not answered Mr Biddle. Mr Biddle was a foot-man and you didn't backchat footmen, but he followed him obediently through the kitchen, past Mrs Drew who wanted to know what was up but got no reply from Biddle, and into the corridor, then into the hall, across it and there he was standing in what he termed a grandly room, the carpet so thick he felt that the large slippers on his feet were lost in it.

"Thank you, Biddle."

Biddle went out and closed the door and Ned Spoke stood looking at the mistress.

"Sit down, Ned."

"What! I mean, should I, ma'am?"

"I've told you to."

Ned slowly lowered himself down on to the very edge of a chair and stared wide-eyed at his mistress, and he would have said that his eyes couldn't stretch any further but they did as he listened to her talking.

"You used to like playing with the children, didn't you, Ned?"

"Aye, ma'am."

"Why didn't you continue to play with them?"

"Mr Myers stopped me: I was wasting time, ma'am."

"Well now, in future, Ned, I want you to play with Master William every morning for at least an hour. If it's bad weather you can go into the big barn, but if the weather is at all mild I prefer you to play outside."

"Play ma'am?"

"Yes, play, Ned, wrestle and. . . ."

"Wrestle!" The end of the word seemed to jerk the boy's head up and he gulped, then gulped again before he whispered now, "Wrestle, ma'am?"

"Yes, that's what I said, wrestle."

"But I can't wrestle properly, ma'am. Well, what I mean is, not like me Uncle Phil. He's got prizes for it."

"Your Uncle Phil had prizes for wrestling?"

"Aye, ma'am; he's a champion."

"Indeed! And where does he live?"

"Hebburn, ma'am."

"Hebburn, so near?"

"Aye, ma'am."

"When is your next leave, Ned?"

"I had it last week, ma'am."

"Well now" – she smiled at the boy – "you may take another leave tomorrow morning and I want you to go and ask your uncle to come and see me with the idea of giving you real lessons in wrestling so that when you wrestle with Master William you won't hurt him in any way, but he'll learn from you. Will you do that?"

The boy's mouth was agape, his eyebrows, which were inclined to points, seemed to be straining to disappear into his hair line, and again he gulped before he said, "He works in Palmers, ma'am; he . . . he could only come on a Sunday 'cept in the summer when the nights are lighter."

"Well, tell him he can pick his own time. And when we meet we can arrange his fee."

"Wh . . . what, ma'am?"

"I mean we can discuss what he will charge for his lessons. Tell him that."

"Aye, ma'am."

"And another thing: while you are playing with Master Willy, Miss Josefina will be skipping and playing hop-scotch."

When the boy's face took on a look of utter perplexity, Tilly said on a gentle laugh, "I won't expect you to play hop-scotch or skip with Miss Josefina, Christine will be there to see to that; but I'd like you to be altogether when you are . . . well, having a game."

"Yes, ma'am." His next words, however, seemed to come out of the mouth of a very small boy, not of this gangling thirteen-year-old youth, when he said tentatively, "But Mr Myers, ma'am?"

"I shall see to Myers, Ned. Don't worry about that. I shall also tell him that I want you to learn to ride so that you can accompany Master William when, later, he is able to ride out on his own."

When Tilly got to her feet, the boy came up from the chair as if he had been stung, and he walked two steps backwards before bowing his head to her and saying, "Thank you, ma'am," and, his face breaking into a broad beam, "Thank you, ma'am."

She knew she was being thanked not for the wrestling part of his order but for the fact that he was going to be given the chance to ride a horse, and for a moment she recalled the negro slave, Number Three, whose life was saved because he had sneaked out at night just to touch a horse, for if he had been in his hut he would have been massacred with the rest in the Indian raid.

Ned Spoke almost ran across the hall, the passage, then the kitchen, oblivious of the staff waiting to know what the mistress had had to say to him, for he was telling himself that only last week he had been about to give in his notice because his father had said he could make more in the pit. He hadn't wanted to go down the pit, but there was little excitement in his present job, and Mr Myers was always at him, but now, by golly! every day to play with the young master and then to learn to ride. Eeh! he couldn't believe it. . . .

Nor could the rest of the staff when they heard. Even Biddy was strong in her protest to Tilly, saying, "Is it true what I hear, you're goin' to get the bairn learn to wrestle?"

"Yes, it's true, Biddy."

"But he's little more than a baby yet?"

Tilly stared at Biddy for a moment before she said quietly, "In a few years more, Biddy, and under other circumstances he'd have been able to go down the pit."

"Oh" – Biddy had swung herself round – "those days are past now. And anyway, seeing who he is he should be brought up like a gentleman. That's my opinion, if you want it."

"I'd rather see him brought up like a man, Biddy. He's already handicapped but he's going to grow big and strong. Well, I want him to be able to use that strength should the occasion arise. And what is more —" She had turned away and looked out of the window on to the stable yard as she ended, "I have learned over the holidays that he needs more than a nursemaid and a tutor, he needs a man's company, a boy's company."

"Well" – Biddy now flounced back again – "a lad like Ned Spoke isn't to my mind edifying company for the likes of him."

"For what I need Willy to learn Ned and his uncle are the right people to teach him."

"And the little youngster is going to skip and play hop-scotch an'll?" There was a sneer in Biddy's voice. "Might as well have her brought up in a back lane; or perhaps you could find some flags and chalk up a hop-scotch on them for her."

"Yes, perhaps I could, Biddy" – Tilly was smiling tolerantly at the old woman now – "but I'm afraid I'd have a job. Still, the next best thing is the stone flags in the corner of the barn. I'll have them cleared and they can play on them there."

"My God! I've heard it all. It would never have happened if Master Matthew had come back with. . . ."

"No, it wouldn't, Billy." Tilly had turned on her now, her voice conveying deep hurt and anger. "Everything would have been different if Matthew had come back as you say; but he didn't come back, I'm on my own, I have the lives of two children in my care and I'm doing what I think best for them. I said Willy was handicapped, but not half as much as is Josefina. For the first time in our acquaintance, Biddy, you're not being very much help."

As Tilly stormed her way up the kitchen, Biddy leant over the table, her head bowed deep on her chest, and although she said aloud, "I'm sorry, lass," it didn't carry. The flouncing figure went out of the far door and now Biddy groaned aloud as she muttered, "You've gone too far this time. You should practice what you preach, woman. You're always on to the others about knowin' their place." Putting out her hand, she now groped towards a chair and, flopping down on it, she muttered, "I'm tired. Oh God! but I'm tired."

It was the first time in her life that she had ever expressed those words aloud.

The following morning, like any housekeeper or ordinary servant, Biddy knocked on the morning-room door, and when she was bidden to enter she went in slowly and, standing some distance from Tilly, who although she had finished her breakfast was still seated at the table, she stared at her for a moment before swallowing deeply and saying, "I've come to apologise —" she was on the point of adding "lass" but substituted "ma'am", and on this Tilly closed her eyes tightly, gave such a hard jerk to her head that a bone cracked audibly in her neck, before getting to her feet and, taking Biddy by the shoulders, she actually shook her, saying, "Don't! For goodness sake, woman, don't! Never, never do that Biddy. Never apologise to me, not you! There'll never be any need for that between us. Oh! you old fool." Now she pulled the older woman into her arms, and Biddy returning the embrace, they held tightly for a moment; then almost embarrassed, they pushed away from each other, Tilly, her voice almost rough now, saying, "Sit yourself down."

"No, lass; I've got a lot to do, I'm up to me eyes in the. . . ."

"Sit down. That's an order."

When Biddy was seated Tilly took a chair opposite her; then leaning forward, she gripped Biddy's hands as she said, without any lead-up, "It was Luke. You see, when he was here he had such an effect on the pair of them" – she jerked her chin upwards indicating the nursery – "and we had . . . well we almost had words about them. He —" She looked away now as she went on,

"He said that they both, not only Willy but Josefina too, needed the presence of a man in the house, they were surrounded by women, they were being brought up by women. Anyway, he set me thinking, and the best I could think of was that Willy should have a playmate who could also instruct him in games. You see, Biddy, I'll never be able to send him away to school. As things are, all I'll be able to teach him in the physical line will be how to sit a horse, and he can do that already, so I want him to be able to box, run, wrestle with the best of them. Do you understand?"

"Aye, lass, aye; yes, I understand now."

"And it won't hurt Josefina to be able to stand physically on her two legs either."

It was Biddy who smiled now and said "Well, I doubt she'll ever be more than a bantam-weight, Tilly." When they laughed together, Tilly said, "No, perhaps not; but she's wiry and she's smart up here." She tapped her forehead. "She's miles ahead of Willy in that way."

"Huh!" Biddy was on the defensive. "You're not sayin' Willy's dim?"

"No, no; far from it, but she's got a brightness of mind that is ... well, the only way I can explain it is by saying it's very un-English, she's as knowledgeable and keen witted as a child twice her age and she has a sort of sensitivity, a kind of knowing that is very unchildlike. Anyway" – she squeezed Biddy's hand – "I have no intention of sending them both to the fair or the hoppings."

"Well, that's something to be thankful for." Biddy now rose to her feet and, changing the subject completely, she said, "About New Year, is Master John and Miss Anna coming?"

"Not to stay, Biddy. They wanted me to go across there, but I couldn't really think about leaving the children for a couple of days, so they are popping over on New Year's Day for dinner, that is, weather permitting. There is a smell of snow in the air. Don't you think so?"

"Yes, I do. I was just saying the very same thing to meself this morning when me bones began to rattle when I got out of bed."

"Well, that's your own fault." Tilly now pushed her towards the door. "There's no need for you to rise before eight in the morning, Peg can take over nicely."

"It's a habit, lass."

"Well, it's a habit you'll soon have to break."

"When that time comes order me a wheel-chair, will you?"

"Go on with you!" Tilly pressed her out through the door and into the hall and as she watched her walking away it dawned on her that Biddy was an old woman. She must be seventy if a day, but she wouldn't admit to any age. The saddening thought came to her that if Biddy retired or died there would be a gap in her life that no one else could fill, because, whether she had realised it or not, from the first time she had met her she had looked upon this woman in the light of a mother, and as they had been drawn more and more together Biddy had taken the place of a mother, the only real mother she had ever known.

As she made her way up to the nursery she told herself she would get Peg and Fanny to one side and tell them that they must lighten their mother's load in the kitchen and see that she kept off her legs more.

Her granny used to say work never killed anybody, not perhaps outright but it led them by both hands to the edge of the grave.

15

They were preparing for a New Year's party in the servants' hall. Lizzie Gamble and Betty Leyburn had been infected with the giggles from early morning and by afternoon had passed them on to Peg and Fanny; even Christine Peabody, when out of her father's sight and hearing, hugged herself at the thought of the fun they were going to have at the party.

Peter Myers's brother who played the fiddle had been invited and he was bringing along his friend who played the concertina, and both these males were unmarried; also Biddy's eldest son, Henry, and his wife and their two children were coming, and Alec and his wife, and Sam and his wife.

So it must have appeared to Mr Peabody that the Drews were having the monopoly in the coming entertainment, for he had approached the mistress to ask if it would be possible to invite his brother and his wife, who lived in a village outside of Hexham in Northumberland, to be his special guests. But having come so far would it be in order that they could be accommodated for the night? And to this the mistress had replied, most certainly. Some of the Drew family too would be staying overnight and so he could give orders that rooms were to be aired and beds warmed in the west wing.

This left only Biddle; and he surprised everyone by asking if he could bring his mother and father. As Fanny laughingly said, fancy Biddle having a mother and father. Well, she supposed he had been born at one time. She had then gone on, still giggling, to relate to her mother that Biddle had said he would like to invite his parents because he had no female appendage. She had made great play on the word and mimicked him. Then her laughter becoming filled with a self-conscious embarrassment, she had added, "He asked me if I would dance with him, an' all."

Biddy had looked at her daughter for a long moment before she said, "Well, he's a man underneath his uniform and I suppose you could do worse," which had elicited a great, "Oh, our ma!

Me and Biddle?" And Biddy had repeated, "You and Biddle. Beggars can't be choosers, not when they're gettin' on a bit, they can't." And again Fanny had said, "Oh, our ma!" then stormed out of the kitchen, the skirt of her stiff print dress bobbing with each movement. But in the passage she had paused for a moment and looked towards the stillroom where Mr Peabody and Mr Biddle usually had their morning tea. Then she looked back towards the kitchen door as if viewing her mother through it; after which she wagged her head and hurried along the corridor, a tight smile on her comely face. It could be a leg up, he could become butler if old Peabody snuffed it. It was worth considering. She gave a little hitch to her step, pulled the waist of her apron straight, patted the back of her starched cap, then went into the servants' hall where two long tables were covered by starched white cloths, and on them Betty and Lizzie were laying out the extra crockery, cutlery and glasses, all loaned from the diningroom. . . .

Tilly, of course, had promised to attend the party and to see the New Year in with them, but not wishing her presence to put any restraint on them, she told herself that after drinking in the New Year she would take leave, for once she was gone then, she knew, the fun would start.

While Mark was alive, she had often listened to the laughter and song seeping up through the thick walls into their bedroom. A servants' party was allowable on New Year's Eve, and if it continued on into the early morning of New Year's Day it would have been a very mean master who would have checked it.

Mark had been no mean master but she knew that he had been irritated by the sound of gaiety and the distant thump, thump as they danced their way through the night. Of course, she had understood that the prancing about must have been a special kind of agony to a man who had been deprived of his feet, and never once during the eleven New Years that she lay by his side did she by word or sign show how she longed to be down in that hall among the Drews dancing in the New Year.

It was strange, she told herself, that she had never been to a New Year's party, not where there was meat and drink and dancing. She had seen the New Year in standing between her granda and her grandma; she had seen it in from the window of this very bedroom year after year. Then she had seen it in in America; but never, like other folk, had she known any jollity, and so in a way she was looking forward to tonight and the party. She would, under the circumstances as mistress of the house, not be able to let herself go as she once would have done, but nevertheless she told herself she would enjoy the happiness of those around her, especially the Drews, for besides being her friends, they were, she considered, her family.

She was coming down the lower part of the main staircase when she saw the dining-room door open and Fanny start to run across the hall, only to pull up at the foot of the stairs and, with head slightly bent, say, "I'm sorry Til . . . ma'am."

Tilly looked down on her for a moment; then, her head shaking as her lips compressed, she walked to the foot of the stairs before she said, "And so you should be. Thank your lucky stars I'm not Peabody."

The words were uttered in an undertone and issued with mock censure which caused Fanny's head to lower still further and her teeth to clamp down hard on her lower lip before, sedately now, she continued walking across the hall towards the kitchen.

Tilly was smiling to herself as she went towards the drawing-room, then her head turning to the side, she glimpsed between the heavy tapestry curtains draping one of the long windows, a rider dismounting on the gravel below the terrace. Going sharply to the window now, she recognised John and was also aware at this moment that Peabody had appeared as if from nowhere and was making his way towards the front door. It was as if he had smelt a visitor, or perhaps his hearing was so acute it was attuned to any unusual noise outside.

He had the door open as John came hurrying up the steps, and as Peabody reached out for his hat and cloak John thrust him aside with a wave of his hand, while addressing Tilly, saying, in a more than usual flustered fashion. "Glad I f . . . f . . . found you in. Thought you might have g . . . g . . . gone to New . . . Newcastle."

"What is it, John?"

She looked at his bespattered clothes, even his face showed streaks of dirt. He was leading the way now towards the morning-room – he seemed to have forgotten for the moment that he was no longer playing master – and Tilly, after a quick glance at Peabody, followed him, and not until they were both in the room and the door closed did he turn to her and say, "It's the mine. I . . . I thought you should know. There's b . . . b . . . been an . . . an accident."

"Oh no!" She put her hand across her mouth, then asked, "Is it bad?"

"B . . . b . . . bad enough. One man dead, three . . .b . . . badly injured. B . . . B . . . But there are still f . . . f . . . four others down below."

"When did it happen?"

"This . . . this morning. L . . . L . . . Last shift. They ge . . . ge . . . get careless at holiday times. It's always the way." He stumped round from her and walked to the end of the room, his hand now gripping his brow; then coming back to her again, he stood before her and his body seemed to sag as he said, "I d . . . d . . . didn't want to trouble you but off . . . officially you are the owner, Tilly, so you had to know."

"Of course. Of course. Where . . . where has it happened, which road?"

"Number four."

"Number four?" she repeated. "That's right opposite to where it happened to . . . to. . . ."

He nodded now at her, saying, "Yes, Tilly. It's a f . . . f . . . faulty seam. And McGrath w . . . w . . . warned us. Well, at least he told Meadows. I c . . . c . . . came upon them discussing it, but Meadows w . . . w . . . wouldn't have there was anything wrong. I've never had m . . . m . . . much faith in Meadows; he never w . . . w . . . went down enough, left it all to Mc . . . McGrath. McGrath is a good enough fellow but he hasn't the responsibility and n . . . now they're b . . . b . . . both down there. . . ."

"What do you mean, both down there?"

He swallowed deeply, then swallowed again, before he said, "They've been cau . . . caught, and two other m . . . m . . . miners, they were fur . . . further along the road."

One hand cupping her cheek now as she stared at John, but without seeing him for she was in the dark again holding Mark's twisted body, groping for stones in the blackness to support his back, tapping endlessly on the wall of rock, dropping off to sleep only to be woken by Mark's groans and at times his screams; and now Steve was down there hemmed in. Was he, too, trapped by the arms and legs . . . or his complete body?

"I'll have . . . have to get back, Tilly, but I thought. . . . "

She gave a jerk with her head as if coming out of sleep; then putting her hand on his shoulder, she said, "Sit down a moment;

you must have a drink. And . . . and listen, I'm coming back with you."

"No! No!"

"Yes." The word was definite. "I'm the owner, and being so I should be there. But look" – she turned her head now towards the door – "I've got to give them all" – she now waved her hand backwards – "some other excuse for leaving because they're having a party tonight and they are all excited and if they knew about the fall it would spoil everything because the men would go immediately along there. As you know, they were all miners once. But they can't do anything, can they?"

"N . . . no, no. All that c . . . c . . . can be done is being done."

"Well now, listen." She wagged her finger at him. "I'm going to ring for Peabody. He will get you a drink. In the meantime, I'll tell Biddy and the rest that . . . that Anna is not well and she wants to see me, eh?"

"Yes, yes, you c . . . c . . . could do that. B . . . B . . . But they'll find out t . . . tomorrow, if not before."

"Yes, I know they will, but let them have a bit of jollification tonight. You see they've invited families and friends and they've talked of nothing else for days. I . . . we mustn't spoil it now."

She reached out and pulled on the bell, and almost immediately there came a tap on the door and Peabody stepped into the room. But he didn't speak, he just looked at Tilly and waited, and she began, "It is most unfortunate, Peabody, but Mrs Sopwith isn't well and she would like to see me. I'm sorry that I'll miss the party but I'll leave it all in your hands. You must see that everybody enjoys themselves."

"Yes, madam. Of course, madam." His eyes flicked from her to John, taking in his bespattered apparel, and she knew by the look on his face that he had not entirely believed what she had told him and so, on an impulse, she put in quickly, "We must take you into our confidence, Peabody. What I have said is merely an excuse, there has been an accident at the mine. But if I let this be known to the staff, you understand that they will feel it their duty to postpone the party."

Peabody stared at her for a moment, then said, "I understand, madam, and I shall do as you wish. May I say that I hope the accident isn't serious."

"I am afraid it is, Peabody."

"I'm deeply sorry, madam. And may I add that I think it is

very commendable of you to consider your staff in this way and that your gesture will be appreciated."

She nodded at him as she said hastily now, "Please get Master John a glass of brandy, and on your way give orders for my horse to be saddled. I shall step into the kitchen and tell them before I go to change."

"Very good, madam."

A few minutes later Peabody returned to the morning-room with a tray and a decanter of brandy and, after pouring out a good measure, handed it to John, saying, "May I ask, sir, if there are any casualties?"

"One d . . . d . . . dead and three injured so f . . . far."

"Dear, dear! And on New Year's Eve too. Strange, strange —" He shook his head before adding, "You would have thought that death would have left madam alone on this particular night of the year at any rate. Now wouldn't you, sir?"

"What? Oh yes, yes."

John sipped at the brandy, then watched Peabody walk slowly from the room. Odd fellow, but then any man must be odd to want to become a butler. What had he said? You would have thought that death would have left Tilly alone on this particular night of the year. What a strange thing to say.

16

The light had already faded when they reached the mine, a slight drizzle was falling and it lent a lustre to the numerous lamps swinging backwards and forwards among the men milling around at the entrance to the drift.

After dismounting, Tilly and John pressed through the crowd of women forming a rough half circle between the stable block to one side of the drift entrance and the offices and storerooms at the other. The half circle was broken by the rolley way that led down into the drift from the level land above, and John had to make way for Tilly as she walked it until the way was blocked by waggons and the women crowded to the side of them. There must have been thirty or more women and children on one side of the waggons alone, yet there was no sound coming from them. Not even the children were crying or whingeing, and Tilly recognised the anxiety that creates silence, and she didn't break it as faces turned towards her but looked back into the wide staring eyes with understanding.

Then they were at the mouth of the drift and John was asking, "Anything fur . . . further?"

One of the men said, "We're making progress, sir. We've just come out for a breather, the other lads have taken over. Can't work more than four abreast down there and . . . and the air's heavy."

When Tilly, without speaking, moved past them to make her way into the drift, one of the men put his hand on her arm and said, "Oh no, ma'am, no, 'taint safe in there yet. They're propping up as they go but it ain't safe."

"How many men are there down there, I mean in the rescue team?"

"Oh" – he turned and looked at his mates – "about twelve of ours and half a dozen Hebburn men."

"Hebburn men?" she repeated. "No one from Mr Rosier's mine?"

"No, ma'am. An' there would be more from Hebburn I think but they're scattered like. You see it's a night for jollification an' there's only the safety men left, and ten to one they'll be bottled. But Rosier's fellows would have come if they'd known, no matter what he says, but as I said, ma'am, they go visitin' the night and nobody'll likely go back till middle shift the morrow."

She now looked past the man and up the slope to where the band of women were divided by the waggons and, nodding towards them, she said, "What about the women?"

"What do you mean, ma'am?" It was another man speaking now.

"Couldn't they take a turn going in and helping?"

"Huh! you've never been in there, ma'am; you're up to your waist in water in parts an' your sweat's helpin' to raise the level. You've never seen owt like it, ma'am."

"Yes, I have seen something like it, and so have those women standing there." She turned abruptly from them and, looking at John now, she said, "Come along."

It was he who had hold of her arm now, saying sternly, "Oh no! Til . . . Tilly. No!"

"Yes, John, yes." Her voide was as loud and as stiff as his and, wrenching her arm from his, she surprised one of the bystanders by grabbing his lamp from him and hurrying into the darkness.

John was stumbling by her side now protesting all the way, and she stopped abruptly and, her voice quiet, she said to him, "I know more about this mine than you do for the simple reason that I've worked in it. I've walked along this very road, day in day out for months. And I've experienced a fall. You seem to forget that. Now let us go and see what the trouble is."

Fifteen minutes later she saw what the trouble was. At first the men took her for another man, seeing that she was in riding breeches, but when she spoke they gaped at her open-mouthed and one of them, straightening his back after lifting an enormous piece of rock and handing it to his mate behind him, said simply, "Ma'am."

"How's it going?"

"Slow, ma'am."

Her voice had caused a pause in the rhythmic passing of the stones, and in the light of the lamps she looked at the wall of rock some yards ahead, then asked, "Have you heard anything?"

"Oh aye, ma'am, aye." Several of them nodded. "They're there all right, but it's far back. There's a lot down, it'll take some time yet."

She looked down at her feet, she was standing calf-deep in water but, unlike the rest of those present, she didn't feel it for the soft leather of her riding boots came up to just below her knees. But the men around her hadn't only wet feet, they were wringing to the skin right up to their waists, and their upper bodies were naked. She turned to John who was speaking to one of the men. He was saying, "How long do you think . . . think it will be before you g . . . g . . . get through?" and the man answered, "Couldn't tell sir, not at the rate we're goin'. The road's narrow and the stones have got to be moved well back, else as you see they would soon block this way."

While John and the man went on talking she stared at the wall of rock before her and beyond which were Steve and the manager and two other men, and it wasn't likely with a fall such as this that they would have been able to save a light. And then there was the lack of air. Half an hour could make all the difference; five minutes could make all the difference between life and death when you were short of air. If anything should happen to Steve she would have lost her only lifelong friend. The thought came to her like a revelation. There was no one alive now that she had known as long as Steve, there was no one in her life had been so faithful to her as Steve, there was no one she could talk to now as she did to Steve. If anything should happen to him a new aloneness would enter into her being; only Biddy and Steve were her kind of people and Biddy was old and could die tomorrow. But Steve was young . . . well, in his full manhood, and he could die tonight.

When she turned about and ran stumbling back through the water of the drift John, coming behind her, cried, "Ti . . . Tilly! Ti . . . Tilly! wait. What is it?"

So swift was she running that he still hadn't overtaken her before she came out of the drift and into the open air. Straightaway, pushing her way through the men, she made for the women and, lifting her lamp high, she yelled into their amazed faces, "How many of you have worked down below?"

To her surprise no one answered her for the moment; but then a hand went up here and there and a voice said, "Me, ma'am. Me, missis." Of the crowd on this side of the waggons not more than eight responded; and when, having squeezed herself between two bogies, she put the same question to the women on the other side, she wasn't aware that she was speaking in a voice no longer representing Mrs Sopwith but that of Tilly Trotter, the girl before she had come under the guidance of Mr Burgess, the tutor, and what she cried was, "Will you come below an hour at a time an' help move the stones back?"

"Ay, aye. Oh aye, ma'am. Anything's better than standin' here waitin'."

But when the women moved up abreast of the men near the mouth of the drift they were halted with gruff cries of, "No bloody fear! you're not goin' in there," and "Those days are gone." And "It's men's work. Now get back, the lot of you!"

"If I can go in there they can." Tilly was facing them. "For the first turn I'll take eight women with me. We'll do an hour at a time."

Of a sudden silence fell on them again, at least on the men. They stood stiffly staring at this woman who had made a name for herself, and a queer one at that, but she owned the mine and was willing to go in and hump with the rest, which was something when all was said and done, and her living soft for years.

When the women pushed their way through the menfolk there were no more protests and Tilly said quietly now, "Just eight of you." And on this she went ahead, John again by her side and muttering now, "My G . . . G . . . God! Tilly. If anything should hap . . . happen to you." And now looking at him tenderly and because of the concern on his face, she whispered under her breath, "Nothing can happen to a witch, John, that she doesn't want to happen."

And as he said, "Oh, Tilly, things li . . . li . . . like that c . . . c . . . can court dis . . . disaster," she thought painfully, Yes, maybe you're right. All her life she had courted disaster and this might be just one more time, and a voice cried from deep within her and from out of the pit blackness she remembered so well, "Hang on, Steve. Hang on." And it sounded as if she were talking to Mark, encouraging him to live, to keep breathing.

*

The first shift of women worked like Trojans. They passed the stones back right to the junction of the roads where they were piled up against the walls.

Against John's protest, she also accompanied the second batch of women in; but within a short time she had to come out and rest. It wasn't because her arms or her back were aching, it was the constriction in her chest. Her lungs has been free of dust for years and she was taking badly to it now. She sat in the office quite alone for a time to recover herself. John had gone in again with another shift of men and what was most gratifying was that pitmen from other mines were making their appearance in ones and twos having heard in a roundabout way of the disaster. There were men from as far away as Felling who had walked the six miles in the rain to help.

When she looked at the round-faced clock on the office wall she thought there must be some mistake for it couldn't be twenty minutes to eight. Sure she hadn't been here all of four and a half hours.

The thought brought her to her feet and she picked up the lamp and went out into the night again. The rain was coming down steadily now but she found it cooling on her face. As she neared the entrance to the drift she felt the excitement: there was no silence now but a combined chatter.

"Ma'am! Ma'am! I think they're nearly through. They can hear the knockin' clearer."

She said nothing, but hurried through them and, almost running down the rolley way, she came to the junction where the women turned to her with their sweat-smeared faces eager with the news. "They can hear 'em plain, ma'am. Heard a voice they did."

She passed through them and into the water which now flooded into the top of her boots, but which did not make her shiver for it felt warm, and she looked to where a man was shouting into the stone: "That you, sir? You all right, sir?"

She did not hear the mumbled reply and she only just stopped herself from shouting, "Ask if Mr McGrath is all right."

A man turned to her now and said, "Another hour, ma'am, at the outside should see us through."

"Good. Good." She nodded at him and smiled, and he jerked his head at her and with renewed energy began to lift the great blocks of stone as if they were house bricks.

*

122

It took more than the hour to get through to the trapped men. It was quarter to eleven when they pulled the first man through. He was unconscious but still alive. The second man had a smashed arm and a broken ankle. The manager was in a very bad way, having been pinned down by a beam. The only one who had apparently escaped injury was Steve, but after he had helped to ease the manager through the hole and had himself crawled through he swayed as the men helped him to his feet. But saying, "Thanks, lads, thanks. I'm all right, I'm all right," he stumbled unaided towards the junction. And it was there that Tilly saw him, and he saw her. He might have passed her but for the fact that, hatless, her white hair, now looking a dirty grey, caught his eye. He paused before walking towards her and saying casually, "What do you think you're up to?"

And she, swallowing deeply and blinking at him, said just as casually, "I'm after a job." The men and women around laughed, but their laughter was high, and had an unnatural sound.

When John, addressing Steve, said, "Are you . . . are you all right, Mr McGrath?" there seemed to be a pause before Steve answered, "Yes, yes, I'm all right, sir."

Tilly's eyes now travelled over Steve. There was no sign of injury on his arms or face but she could see that he must have been up to his neck in water for a time for he was still wearing his shirt and there was a deep rim of black scum around the collar, and she knew enough about the pit to remember where the water last touched it always left its mark. As she stood there the years fell away from her and she was back in this junction watching tiny children crawling out of the side roads, some of the roads no higher than three feet, which didn't allow for a child to stand up, not if he or she was over six years old. She saw them dragging the iron harness from between their legs or pulling the leather band that was attached to the skip from their foreheads and then dropping where they stood, some of their faces wet with sweat, others with tears, and surprisingly one or two here and there had laughter on their lips.

The law had been passed in 1842 prohibiting children from working in the mines but little or no notice was taken of it in many quarters, for who was to know what went on down below, and inspections, like miracles, happened rarely. Often, too, the men of the family were with the masters in this, for how, they reasoned, could a man be expected to bring up a large family on a pitman's wage. No; a shilling a week was a shilling a week, however it was earned.

When she herself had come to work down here late in 1838 the sights, the stench, the weariness, the labour, the long hours in dimness, the vileness of the language, the exposure of the human body in all its undignified postures, and the almost animal viciousness of some of the workers, coupled at the same time with a comradeship which would herd them together in times of stress, brought into her awakening knowledge a side of humanity dragged out of human beings by the environment they were forced to live in. Only in after years, when looking back, had she realised the lessons she had learned in those long months below ground.

"C . . . C . . . Come, you're all in."

She blinked and turned to John who had taken her by the arm, and when he said, "I'll ge . . . get you home and then. . . ." she cut him short, saying, "No, no; there's no need. I'm all right; Anna will be waiting for you and worrying. I'll . . . I'll ride back part of the way with Steve."

She turned her head to where Steve was walking a little behind her and she asked, "Will you be fit to ride?"

"Aye." His answer was brief.

And now John turned to him and said, "W . . . W . . . Would you be able to see Mrs Sop . . . Sopwith home, McGrath?"

Again Steve paused before answering, when he merely said, "Aye," not even adding "sir" now.

Tilly cast her glance back at him and because of the dirt covering his face she could not see the expression on it nor that in his eyes for his head was bent slightly foward and his gaze directed towards the rough track as if, she thought, he was making sure of where he planted his feet. Once more she wanted to ask, "Are you all right?" but John was speaking again: "I really think I sh . . . sh . . . should go b . . . b . . . back with you at this time of night; McGrath w . . . w . . . will want to get cleaned up and rested. It must have been a pretty stiff time in there." He turned and glanced at Steve, but Steve was still looking towards his feet.

"John, please" – she tugged at his arm – "I'll be perfectly all right. It's you who needs to get home and rested. Now say no more, Steve will see me to the gate and with a bit of luck I may be able to join the New Year party after all."

"The staff p . . . p . . . party? Yes" – John nodded at her – "and we have guests c . . . c . . . coming too as you know. But this has certainly put the damper on it for me. If only that one hadn't died, and Mr Meadow in s . . . s . . . such a bad way." He hung his head. "The others, well, they can be p . . . p . . . patched up, but I hate to lose a man in the m . . . mine."

She nodded at him in silence now; she had forgotten about the first man they had brought out. What was his name? Fox. Andrew Fox. Well, she would see to his widow and children. She could do that, and she could erase the fear of the family being turned out on the road. She would give the wife a pension.

As she walked up the rise into the open air where the sky was high with stars now for the rain had stopped, she looked upwards for a moment as she thought, It's as if I had just come back.

"Now you're sh . . . sh . . . sure, Tilly?"

"Oh, John" – she shook her head impatiently at him – "get on your horse and get home. Tell Anna a happy New Year from me. I'll pop over as soon as possible. Come along, let us get the horses." She made to move away, but then stopped and waited. The women and men who had followed them out of the drift, seeing her standing there, stopped one after the other; and when the last one had put in an appearance she spoke to them, saying simply, "Thank you very much. Thank you all very much. And I'm sure you men will realise what a great help your women have been to you tonight. And those you have rescued will I am sure want to thank you, too, when the time comes. Please tell Mrs Fox not to worry, she and her family will be seen to. What is more I can tell you now, I intend to build two new rows of cottages in order to house you in better conditions."

No one spoke until she said, "Good-night to you all," when, as she turned away there was a chorus of, "Good-night. Good-night, ma'am. Happy New Year ma'am. Thank you, ma'am."

When they reached the office, John, as if just remembering something, turned to Steve and said, "What about the p . . . p . . . pumps? that water is deep down there."

"I'll see to that afore I leave, sir. Sanderson, Briggs, and Morley will deputise for the night; they'll see to things and I'll be back first thing in the morning."

"Oh, well. Thank you, McGrath. Thank you. You've had a l . . . l . . . long ordeal and must be very tired."

"Not when you reckon some of the falls, sir. This one was just a matter of a few hours. I'm sorry about Fox though; he was a good man, in many ways."

"Yes, yes he was. And you yourself were lucky to c . . . c . . . come out unscathed."

Steve did not reply for John had turned to Tilly asking, "Now are you sure . . . ?" only to be cut off by her voice, weary-sounding now, saying, "Yes, yes, John, I am sure. Now please get yourself home."

"W . . . W . . . Well, if you insist. Good . . . Good-night, my dear."

"Good-night, John." She put her hand on his arm and guided him to the door where he turned and called, "Good-night, McGrath."

"Good-night, sir."

Alone with Tilly now, Steve, pointing to a chair, said, "Sit yourself down, Tilly; you look just how I feel. Would you mind waiting another ten minutes or so?"

"Not at all. Go and do what you have to do."

Without further words he left the room. With his going her body seemed to slump, and she bent forward and looked at her hands. Like her clothes, they, too, were black with coal dust. When she touched her face she could feel the grit on it and she guessed that her hair would no longer be looking white. Of a sudden she felt weak, almost faint. Twisting her body round, she put her forearm on the rough wooden desk that fronted the window, the window at which she had stood and given her name before making her first trip into the mine. "Tilly Trotter . . . spinster," the keeker had said. That memory seemed to belong to another life. But tonight's memory was fresh in her mind and it was with a deep sorrow that she thought: Why do people have to work and slave like that, to run the risk of being trapped or of dying in the dark? And the answer that came to her was simply, money. Yes, that was it, money. Wasn't she herself making money out of the labour of these people? Yet were she to close the mine tomorrow, would it help them? No, their condition would be worse than that which they suffered when working down below, for if they were allowed to spend their days above ground the majority of them would starve for there wasn't enough work to be had for them.

Sighing now, she leant her forearm on the desk and laid her head upon it. . . .

It was some twenty minutes later when she was startled by a touch on her shoulder and Steve's voice saying, "You all right, Tilly?"

"Oh yes, yes. I . . . I must have dropped off."

"And no wonder. Well, the horses are ready. Come on." He took her elbow and raised her up; then lifting the lantern from the table, he led the way out.

The horses were standing in the yard and after fastening the lantern to the side of his saddle, he came round to where Tilly had one foot in the stirrup and, putting his hand under her other heel, he helped her to mount. . . .

When they reached the cottage she drew her horse to a halt, saying, "Come no further, Steve, you're worn out. Just give me the lantern and I can make my way."

When he didn't answer her, she peered at him, saying, "What is it, Steve?" and when her hand went out and touched his shoulder and he visibly winced and drew his head down, she said again, "What is it?"

"Nothing, nothing. Come on." He went to urge the horse forward, but she swiftly leaned across and pulled on the reins, saying, "You're hurt. Your shoulder? Get down. Get down." Without further ado she dismounted and went to his side and tugged at the bottom of his coat, saying, "Come on, get down."

Silently now he obeyed her; then leading his horse, he took it through the gate and up the path, and she followed.

When the animals were housed in the rude stable and he muttered, "They've got to be seen to," she said, "Go on in, I'll see to them." Again she was surprised when he obeyed her. Quickly she brought water and hay for the beasts, then hurried into the house. Steve was sitting in the old rocking chair to the side of the banked fire. He was leaning forward, his elbows on his knees, his hands slack and joined between them. Without any preamble she stood in front of him and said, "Where are you hurt?"

Simply he answered, "My back."

"Here, let me get your coat off."

When he pulled himself to his feet she eased off his coat. His striped blue shirt was black, and she noticed right away that the front of it hung loose but the back seemed stuck to his skin, and when she touched it she saw his teeth clench and his face muscles knot.

"Why didn't you say?" she said harshly. "You should have gone to hospital with the rest and seen the doctor. Was it the stone?"

He moved his head once, then said abruptly, "Aye, it pinned me for a time."

Swiftly she went to the fire, took the bellows and blew into the bottom bars. Then she lifted the lid of the big black kettle that was standing on the hob, dipped her finger into it and, finding it hot, took it up and, hurrying into the scullery, she groped in the dark for the tin dish that in her day she had kept under the sink – as Steve had once told her he had never altered anything – and so she found it immediately.

A few minutes later she set the dish of warm water on the mat before the hearth, then said to him, "Get on your knees."

Slowly he obeyed her.

Again and again she wrung out the towel and placed it across the torn shirt on his back, taking off the coal dust while at the same time soaking the garment loose from his skin.

When at last she was able to pull the shirt over his head, her own features screwed up at the sight of his shoulders. There were three deep cuts on them and, added to this, the skin had been sheared off for some six or eight inches across the shoulder blades.

"Oh, you are a fool you know, Steve. What do you think you're up to? Playing the brave man with a back like this! It looks flayed."

He gave no answer but made to rise from his knees, only to be checked by her, saying, "Look, stay where you are; these cuts have got to be cleaned or else you're in for trouble. I must get some fresh water."

When she returned from the scullery, he was no longer on his knees but sitting on a low cracket in front of the now bright fire, and when she began to bathe the raw coal-dust-infested flesh he made no movement whatever. She had been about to say, "Am I hurting you?" but she knew that to be a silly question. He must be going through agony for she was having to rub at the raw flesh to get the dust free. What he needed was to lie in water. Now if it had been summer he could have gone into the river. But it wasn't summer, it was New Year's Eve. Strange, but she had forgotten it was New Year's Eve.

After she had cleaned the wounds as best she could, she said, "What I need is fat. Have you got anything at all like that?"

"There's a jar of goose dripping in the cupboard." He jerked his head, and to this she said, "Oh, good, good. There's nothing better."

Gently now, she pressed the goose fat into the raw patches of flesh; and then she asked, "Where do you keep your clean shirts?"

When he pointed to the bedroom and said, "In the chest," she looked towards the far door, saying, "I'll have to take the lantern for a minute."

She was surprised when she lifted the lid of the chest to see what she imagined to be about a dozen shirts lying in a neat pile. He looked after himself, did Steve. And that was good. She liked that.

In the room once more, she went to put the shirt over his head but he took it firmly from her hands and, getting to his feet, he put it on. Then for the first time he spoke lightly, saying, "I'm not going to tuck it into these," pointing to his dirty trousers, and he walked from her towards the bedroom. But there, in the doorway, he turned, saying, "You could do with having your own face washed, Tilly."

"Yes, yes." She smiled warily at him. "I think I'll do just that. And then a cup of tea wouldn't come in wrong, would it?"

"No, you're right there, it wouldn't. Take the lantern into the scullery with you, the fire is enough light for me."

"Yes, yes, I will, Steve. . . ."

It was about fifteen minutes later when they sat, one each side of the hearth, sipping gratefully at mugs of steaming tea that had been laced with whisky, and after Steve had drained his mug he leant forward and, looking towards the fire, said, "I've known some New Year's Eves but this is the strangest."

"I think I could say the same, Steve. What time is it?"

They both lifted their gaze to the high mantelpiece and almost simultaneously they said, "Ten to twelve."

"We should be hearing the hooters soon."

She nodded at him, "Yes, yes. I've forgotten the sound of the ships' hooters. . . . How you feeling now?"

"Much better; a lot of fuss about nothing."

"Nothing!" She turned her head to the side. "Good job you can't see your back. And you won't be fit to go in in the morning."

"Oh, don't you worry. Never fear, I'll be there in the morning."

"I think you should see a doctor."

"After you've been at me?" He smiled at her. "I don't need any doctor now. Anyway, I've got good healing flesh, it'll be as right as rain in a few days."

"That's as may be." She reached out now and put her mug on the wooden table, then said, "There's one thing I do know, you're not moving out of this house tonight again. I'll make my own way home."

As she rose to her feet he too rose, saying quietly, "And there's one thing I know an' all, and that is you're not making your own way home. What will happen if you meet up with some of the lads out on the spree bringing in the New Year from here to Gateshead?"

"I can be home within half an hour, and I don't suppose they'll start their rounds much before one.

She had been smiling gently but now the smile slid from her face as she saw the expression on his, and when he said quietly, "Stay and see the New Year in with me, Tilly," something in his voice caused her to lower her gaze. Stay and see the New Year in with me. It sounded an ordinary request; but what happened when the church bells rang and the ships' hooters blared, when the factory buzzers shrilled into the night? You shook hands, you looked into faces as you said a happy New Year, a happy New Year, and those you loved you kissed. Yet she couldn't be so churlish as to refuse his request. And anyway, they would see the New Year in together were she to allow him to accompany her home. Yet she knew in her heart it would be a different thing to stand in a room, the door closed, waiting for the first sound to herald in the New Year, the year that was to bring happiness, work and money galore, the seeming fervent desire of every ordinary Northerner, for hope sprang eternal in their breasts.

Her decision was, however, taken from her when from a distance, like that of a hunting horn, came the sound of a ship's siren, and Steve, turning and looking at the clock, said, "It must be slow. Come. Come on Tilly," and took her hand and drew her to the door and there, pulling it open, they stood looking out into the starlit night, with the sounds of sirens, hooters and bells filling the air.

Her hand still in his, they had stood for some seconds silent when, turning to her, he looked into her face and, his voice soft, he said, "A happy New Year, Tilly."

"And the same to you. A happy New Year, Steve."

He had caught her other hand and was holding them tightly against his breast now and when he murmured, "Oh, Tilly, Tilly!" she went to withdraw from his hold, but he gripped her hands still more firmly, and with the sound of a break in his voice he muttered, "Every New Year that I can remember, Tilly, I've wished only for one thing, and you know what that is. No, no; let me speak, just this once."

Still retaining his hold on her, he drew her back into the room, pushing the door closed with his foot as he did so, and now to her bent head he said, "Part of me, the sensible part of me keeps ramming it home that the situation for me is hopeless, worse than ever it was, you the lady of the manor, me little more than a hewer down the pit . . . well, only a couple of steps up and likely to remain there. Forget her, I've said. Marry, I've said. and I've tried; God knows I've tried. Twice I've been on the verge of it, only to withdraw because it wasn't in me to make another woman's life a hell. One can put up with one's own hell but inflicting it on somebody else, that's another thing. But now for the other side of me, the side that lives in a dream. This side sees a man who doesn't work down the pit, who speaks well, dresses well, can carry himself in any company. This man can go to the lady of the manor and say, "I love you, Tilly. I've always loved you. Marry me." But this fellow only comes alive at night, and he's never there in the morning. But it's night now, Tilly. . . . No! No! Keep still; just let me hold your hands, just this once, please!" His voice had risen from a murmur and the last word was not asked in the form of a plea but more of a demand, it was as if he were saying, "You owe me something for my constancy over the years," and it brought her head up and her eyes, misty now, looking into his. And as she stared at this man whose love had been an irritation to her in her youth, there came over her the most strange feeling, and somewhere in the far recesses of her mind a voice was repeating: How many times can we love? It was a question she had asked herself on the very day Matthew expressed his passion for her, and she knew that she loved him although she had loved his father, and once long, long ago she had loved Simon Bentwood too. And now this feeling was rising in her again, this warmth, this desire to enfold, to be enfolded, this longing to be at one and the same time a wife, a mother, mistress, and friend. . . . But she knew that all she could ever be to this man, to this man whom she was seeing with new clear eyes, all she could ever be was a friend.

Yet more than friendship must have seeped upwards into her eyes for the next moment she found herself for the very first time crushed within the circle of his arms. The thumping of his heart reached through her clothes and penetrated her skin, and when his lips fell on hers and covered her mouth she neither succumbed nor resisted. She was only aware that at one point she had the desire to put her arms about him but told herself that his back was sore – she hadn't said to herself, "You mustn't do this."

After he released her lips he still held her tightly, his breath seeming to come from deep within his lungs, and it was some time before he said, "I'm . . . I'm not going to apologise, Tilly, I've done it. It'll likely be all I'll ever have of you, but it's something to remember."

When his arms finally released her, she staggered and he had to clutch at her again. Then he was sitting her in the chair near the fire once more. He did not sit opposite her but remained standing, looking down at her; and now he said, "Say something, Tilly."

When she didn't speak he said, "I'm going to tell you something. Deny it if you like, but I know it's true. You in your own way are as lonely as I am. And another thing I'll tell you. You've changed your opinion of me of late. Once you saw me as a sop of a lad, at least soppy over you. I pestered you. If I'd had more sense I might have made better weather of it. And yet, no; you have to work out your own destiny. But now you're back, not where you started, true, yet on the same ground. But at the top of it. Master John, though, and all his kin, no matter how good they are, they're not your type, Tilly, not your people. You look like a lady now, you talk like a lady, you act like one, but underneath I still see you as Tilly, Tilly Trotter. Will you tell me something truthfully? Look at me, Tilly."

Slowly she raised her head to him, to this Steve McGrath who looked every inch a virile man, and the beat of her heart quickened, and what he was saying now was, "Imagine you had come back, but not in a high position, and I was as I am today and you were seeing me differently, would there have been a chance for me?"

She closed her eyes tightly now and her head was bowed again as she said, "Oh Steve! Steve! don't ask me such a question, because I cannot answer it. I . . . I can only tell you I'd be happy to have you as a friend."

"Aye well" – he gave a short laugh and sighed deeply – "that's something. But that'll only be until you marry again."

Her head jerked up quickly now and, her face straight, her voice sharp, she said, "I'll never marry again, Steve."

"Don't be silly."

It was odd but that is what Luke had said, don't be silly; and now Steve went on almost to repeat Luke's statement: "You won't be able to help yourself. Anyway, men won't let you," he too said, adding, "I'd like to take a bet on it that within two years' time there'll be a man in the manor sitting at the head of your table."

"You'd lose your bet, Steve, definitely you'd lose your bet."

He bowed his head towards her and his eyes narrowed now as he said, "You seem very sure of that, Tilly."

"I am, Steve."

"Why? There must be a reason."

"There is."

"Can you tell me?"

Could she tell him? Twice in a week could she divulge the promise she had made to Matthew? Yes, she could. She would have to, if only to stop him hoping. Looking up at him, she said, "I promised Matthew on his death-bed that I'd never marry again."

"*You what!*"

It was odd, men's reactions seemed to be alike. Even his features had taken on the expression which had been on Luke's face.

"You mean to say your husband asked you not to marry again?"

"Yes."

"Well" – he shook his head slowly from side to side – "all that I can say now is that you must be slightly crazy if you stick to it."

"A promise to the dying is a promise, Steve."

"Aw, to hell with that!" He swung round from her, then back again, pointing at her now and saying, "Look, Tilly. It nearly broke me up when you married him. I hated his guts then; that was nothing though to what I feel about him at this minute. But I'm going to say this, rather than live your life alone I would come to your wedding the morrow. What kind of a man was he anyway to make you promise such a thing? A selfish bugger at best. That's swearing to it, but that doesn't describe his mentality. To my mind it's just as well he died because he would have had you caged."

It was really uncanny how alike his reactions were to Luke's. She rose to her feet now, saying wearily, "I'm tired, Steve, very tired," and the sound of her voice and the look on her face made him immediately contrite and he said, "I'm sorry, too, Tilly. I've forgotten what you've been through an' all the night. You're the one who should have been taken home and washed and seen to. I'm sorry, I really am."

133

"Don't be, Steve. I'm glad it's in the open, and you're right when you say I'm lonely. I'd be happy and proud to have you as a friend, Steve, always, but at the same time I don't want you to waste any more years on me. There are so many women who would jump at the chance of you."

"Aye well, you'd better get them lined up and I'll sort them over." He smiled a twisted smile; then holding out his hand, he said, "I say again, Tilly, a happy New Year."

As she put hers into it she replied, "And to you, Steve, and to you, and many of them."

PART TWO

Below the Skin

1

Lucy Bentwood straightened up and looked down at the broad expanse of her husband's naked back and she said, "For goodness sake, Simon, stop whingeing like a bairn without a bottle!"

"Don't you dare use that tone to me —!" The next word, "woman!", was stifled by a sharp cry as he tried to turn from his face to confront his wife. Resting on his elbow, his body now half turned towards her, he gasped, "You think you've got me where you want me, don't you, half paralysed? You wouldn't have taken that tone a few. . . ."

The flat of her hand on his shoulders thrust him downwards, and with laughter in her voice now, she said, "I've always taken that tone with you, and you know it. If I hadn't, I wouldn't have been able to suffer you."

When he made no comment on this statement, the smile slid from her face and, reaching out for a bottle of liniment, she poured some on to the palm of her hand, then applied it to his spine, and as she rubbed her hand rhythmically up and down his back she thought with a sadness that she never showed to him of how true her words had been, for if she hadn't laughed at him she would, many a time, have cried because her patient and happy nature had been sorely tried by him in so many ways; not alone by the scrapings of his love that he gave her but which she felt was compensated for by the son and daughter she had reared, but with the knowledge that his mind was filled with the want of the woman who had beguiled him from her very childhood and whose memory until a few years ago had driven him again and again to bouts of drinking.

The night he fell off his horse in a drunken stupor and lay in the cold ditch for hours she took to be a blessing, for from that time his back had been affected, so much so that he was in constant pain, there were times when he couldn't move for days on end. Even when he was mobile he found it agony to walk the farm. No longer could he ride a horse, and the jolting of the pony trap was agony to him, so his visits to the village and the inn were few and far between. But what she was more thankful for was that he could not now keep an eye on his daughter.

He had always been possessive of Noreen, but from the day her young brother inadvertently told his father that they had met up and talked with Mrs Sopwith's pair, life had hardly been worth living. Noreen was only fourteen at the time and her brother not yet twelve, they were mere children, but his reaction was such that, had he heard they had been behaving indecently with the young couple from the Manor, his wrath couldn't have been worse. What her daughter's life would have been like if her father hadn't happened the accident, Lucy didn't dare to think because Noreen had inherited some of his own independent spirit and from the beginning had baulked at the bit he had put in her mouth.

But now she was riding free – Lucy turned her head and looked towards the bedroom window as her thoughts followed her daughter – she hoped not too free. She knew where she was at this minute and she dreaded with a great dread that the knowledge of what her daughter was about would ever reach the ears of her father. Yet if she knew Noreen, the time would come when she and her father would stand face to face and the truth would be out. And then God help them all.

Noreen Bentwood was of medium height; her hair was a deep rich brown and thick with a natural wave to it; her eyes were hazel and set in sloping sockets in her oval-shaped face; her skin did not look delicate but slightly weathered; her cheeks were red, as was her large well-shaped mouth. She carried herself straight and placed her feet firmly, her walk always suggesting she was off to some place. And on this particular Sunday afternoon she was certainly off to some place for she was going to the burn, to what she termed the little island. It should happen that the little island was the same spot hidden by the half-circle of scrub where Steve McGrath had fished as a boy, and where one day he had sat watching a salmon, protecting it as it were.

Every Sunday for the last two years, except when the snow lay so thick that it was impossible to get to the bank, she had made this journey, and on each occasion she had met and talked with Willy Sopwith, sometimes for minutes only, other times as long as an hour.

Nearly always, on her journey, she would recall the first time she had come upon him. She was then almost fourteen, and it was on a Sunday too. She and Eddie had been walking by the river bank. They had rounded the curve by the bushes and there saw this young man sitting fishing. She remembered how he lifted his head upwards at their approach; then rising from the bank, he had stood peering at them with his head to one side. And she knew this was the son of their landlady, the woman who had made a name for herself, the woman whom her father hated because he had once loved her and she had turned him down. This information she had managed to get out of her mother only recently, when she asked the question, "Why does Dad hate Mrs Sopwith?" and her mother, who was always honest with her, told her why. The information lowered her opinion of her father yet another peg because she considered her mother to be a wonderful woman and her father a fool for still entertaining thoughts of a notorious lady while possessing a wife such as he had.

Noreen had always felt that she was older than her years and when on that Sunday the tall fair-haired young man said, "Hello, little girl," she forgot, or chose to ignore, the attitude a tenant-farmer's daughter should pay to the gentry who owned their land and answered, "Little girl yourself! I'm coming fourteen, and there's nothing I can't do on the farm, and I intend to learn blacksmithing."

She had expected him to laugh at her but what he said was, "I'm sorry. I didn't realise you were such an age, or so talented, but I wouldn't go in for blacksmithing if I were you . . . well, not if I had your voice."

At this she had ignored her brother's tugging at her arm and replied, "What's wrong with my voice?"

"Nothing, nothing at all; it sounds a lovely voice, I'm sure you must be able to sing."

She had paused while staring at him, then had said in a modified tone, "Well, yes, yes I can sing. I sing in the choir and I've sung solos."

"I wasn't wrong then?"

She had found nothing to say to this and she had been about to walk towards him to see what he had caught when around from the far end of the bushed riverbank there came "the other one from the house". She had seen her before from a distance, in fact she had seen them both from a distance but never close enough, as now, to speak to. She transferred her stare to the slight figure approaching them, and noted with amazement that the girl, who was about her own size, which was then five feet, appeared much smaller because she was so thin. Everything about her was thin, her body, her face, her hands, her feet, she looked like a large chocolate-coloured doll, a beautiful chocolate-coloured doll. When she spoke it was not to her but to her adopted brother, so called, her father said, and her words, clear and high sounding, were, "What have we here? Did you catch them, Willy?" Then she laughed, and her laughter, like her voice, was something that Noreen had never heard before, they were both strange, musical, she couldn't put an exact name to the sounds except that they re-called some of the notes Mr Byers struck on his harp. But what she did know instinctively was that she didn't like the dark indi-vidual. She guessed she'd be snooty, high-handed, and this urged her to shout, "No, he didn't fish us up, miss, but he could have you, by the looks of you." And on this, she grabbed her brother's hand and, turning about, walked quickly back round the bend and along the bank, her step causing Eddie to run and to protest, "Aw, give over, our Norah, you're pullin' me arm out."

It was this incident that Eddie had related innocently in his father's hearing which evoked such wrath as they hadn't before witnessed in him. . . .

It was a full year later when Noreen next met Willy Sopwith. She was with the dogs at the far end of the land. A sheep had become caught up in the wire fencing and she was trying to ex-tricate him. The wild barking of the dogs had drawn the attention of a rider on the top road. Glancing up, she saw him and she knew by the way he turned his head that it was young Sopwith.

He dismounted and came down the bank towards her, but she went on with what she was doing, and Willy said, "Can I give you a hand?" and to this she answered briefly, "You'll have to get over the fence and push him from yon side."

And this he did; and after the sheep was free and racing down the field bleating with relief, they stood looking at each other. She had grown considerably during the past year and he remarked on this, smiling as he said, "I had better not make the same mistake I did at our last meeting," and she, finding herself smiling back at him, said, "No, you'd better not." Then peering towards the wire, he said, "Couldn't one of your men have come and done this?"

"They're at the market, and Father has hurt his back."

"Oh, I'm sorry."

It was on the point of her tongue to say, "I'm not," and she knew she would have been speaking the truth because over the past year her father had hardly let her out of his sight. He had always wanted her alongside him, much more so than he ever wanted Eddie, which seemed strange to her. But of late she hadn't even been allowed to go to church on her own. Although he himself never entered the place he took her there and waited for her coming out again. As she had remarked to her mother, he had become like a jailer. But this last week she had known freedom and had revelled in it, as she was doing at this moment.

Looking up into Willy Sopwith's face she saw that he was beautiful and a great pity arose in her for his condition. She knew the cause of it had been them McGraths from the village, yet some of the older folk said it would never have happened if his mother hadn't been a witch. She had seen his mother out riding but to her the odd things about her were her hair which was very white and that she sat a horse like a man and wore breeches. Otherwise, like her son, she had a beautiful face.

He had asked, "What is your name?" and she had answered, "Noreen. But I don't care much for it, I prefer Norah."

When he said, "I'm Willy Sopwith," she answered, "Yes, I know." And then he had laughed. He had put his head back and laughed, and while one part of her felt annoyed, another was amazed that with his handicap he could be so cheerful. He seemed a happy individual. She didn't know many men who were happy, in fact she didn't know any men who were happy.

When she had demanded, "What's funny?" he had stopped, then after a moment said, "You know, really I couldn't say, it was just . . . well, how you took the wind out of my polite introduction."

There had followed a pause, and then he had said, "Do you go to the games?"

"Yes, sometimes."

"I might see you there then?"

"Are you showing something?" she had asked.

"No, no." He shook his head; then added, "I like to watch the wrestling."

"Wrestling?" A memory was stirring in her. She had heard that the almost blind fellow from the house boxed, or fought, or did something like that with one of the hands.

"You sound surprised."

"Yes, well, I am a bit. I . . . I thought it was only the rough 'uns who went to see wrestling and things like that."

"Well, perhaps I'm a rough 'un."

"You don't look it, you don't look . . . well. . . ."

"Well what?"

"Well, the type that would be interested in wrestling."

"Oh! Now let me tell you, miss" – he had assumed a pompous air – "it is said that I am quite good at the game, myself, depending upon my sparring partner."

"Indeed! Indeed!" She too, had now assumed an attitude and when she added, "My! My! the things you hear when your ears are clear," he laughed again and she with him.

And that's how it began.

During the following year they might not meet up for weeks, and then it would be only in passing, but she learned a lot about him during that time. She learned, to her further amazement, that he did a stint at the mine, some three days a week, and that he also went into Newcastle to study engineering. But how he managed this with his one good eye, which didn't seem to be all that good the way he had to peer through it, amazed her. But what surprised her most was his cheerfulness. With a handicap such as his she wouldn't have been surprised if he had been morose and had shunned people; but he seemed to like company, and he was never at a loss for an answer, or to ask a question.

Then came her sixteenth birthday. Her mother had bought her a new coat and bonnet. The coat was grey cord with blue facings and a cape to the shoulders, and the bonnet was blue velvet trimmed with grey. She had never had anything so smart in her life and she felt that all eyes were on her when she stood up in church to sing on the Sunday morning. When the service was over she had hurried away because there was no father waiting to escort her home; not even Eddie was there to accompany her, for he was in bed with a cold. So she was alone when she met up with Willy.

He wasn't astride a horse today, nor was he sitting on the bank fishing, he was walking slowly along the road accompanied by a dog; and it wasn't a presentable animal, not like their own sheepdogs. He was the first to speak, saying, "Why, hello. It's you, isn't it?"

"Yes, it is me," she had answered pertly. "Who else?"

"Well, you must excuse me if I didn't recognise you at first, you look dressed for town and very pretty."

"Which means I suppose that when I'm not dressed for town I don't look pretty?" She was smiling as she spoke and she expected him to laugh, but on this occasion he didn't. With his face to the side he stared at her before saying, "I meant no such thing. I've always considered you pretty, more so, rather beautiful at times."

She could give no answer to this; no one had ever told her she was bonny, let alone beautiful. The little mirror in her bedroom had assured her that she was . . . all right, perhaps not as pretty as Maggie Thompson from the village, but much better looking than the Rainton twins.

Into her silence he now asked quietly, "Will you be out walking this afternoon?"

"I may be," she said; "I cannot promise. My mother will be making me a tea, it's my birthday."

"Oh, may you have many, many more. How old are you? Seventeen?"

There was a moment before she said with apparent reluctance, "No, sixteen."

"Yes, of course." It was as if he were recalling the day she had stated emphatically that she was nearly fourteen.

The dog surprised her now by coming up and sniffing at her and when he licked her gloved hand she patted his head, saying, "He's a friendly fellow. What breed is he?"

"An Irish hound."

"What's his name?"

"Pat. You couldn't call an Irish hound anything else, could you?"

"No." She laughed gently, then said, "I must be on my way. Good-bye."

"Good-bye."

She knew that he hadn't walked on but was standing still and this caused her step to go slightly awry and she had to check the desire to run. But she told herself, she was sixteen and her running days were over, she was a young woman and from now on must act the part, no matter how she might feel inside. . . .

She didn't manage to see Willy that afternoon. Her father was out of bed and he never let her out of his sight, not on that day or for some weeks that followed. But when at last they did meet again by the burn it was as if only hours had passed since they had spoken for, standing close to her, he held out his hand and she placed hers in it; then they sat side by side on the bank and talked.

And so it would happen whenever they could meet he would take her hand, that is if the dark one wasn't with him. But as time went on she seemed to be there more often than not and when this happened Noreen would merely pass the time of day with them, then walk on. Strangely the dark girl now never spoke in her presence, even though she stared at her all the while.

This form of occasional Sunday courtship continued. She would be eighteen on Tuesday and today she was going to the river and she prayed that she would find him alone, for the time had come, she knew, for something to be said openly between them. Of late she had felt that if he didn't speak and so enable her to declare her love for him her body would burst asunder. She knew that he liked her, more than liked her. She could feel it in the touch of his hand, she knew it by the way his narrowed gaze lingered on her, yet he had never spoken one word of love, not even of tenderness. Perhaps, like her, he was afraid of the consequences of a declaration. She knew that her father's wrath, should he ever hear of her association with this particular Sopwith, would be something that her imagination could not even visualise. And on Willy's side there was his mother.

His mother she knew wasn't a good woman, well not morally good, everyone said so. For years she had been carrying on with the manager of the mine and, as people pointed out, she could build all the cottages she liked and give her pit folk pensions and their bairns boots and baskets of food at Christmas, but that wouldn't wipe out her sin in the eyes of God. Apparently she had always been a bad woman. Hadn't Willy himself been born out of wedlock after she had been mistress to his father for years. And when he died she went and married his son. And when the son died she returned home with a brown baby that she said she had adopted. Taking all that into account, she was really an awful woman, and yet she must admit that the glimpses she had had of her seemed to belie all these facts. She wished she could meet her and form her own opinion of this woman. She wasn't afraid of meeting her, not like some of the villagers who'd walk a mile rather than run into her.

Well, if Willy spoke she'd have to meet her, wouldn't she? And oh, she hoped it would be soon because every time she was near him the feeling in her was like that of a smouldering fire, which only needed the touch of his lips to burst into a flame. But when that happened the flame, she knew, would engulf not only her but a number of others; and there would be screams of anguish from all sides, particularly from her father. But she felt strong enough to face the consequences, any consequences, if only Willy would speak.

2

It was on this same Sunday morning that the matter of Willy's association with Noreen Bentwood was being brought into the open at the Manor, and not by Willy or Tilly, although she wasn't entirely unaware of what was going on, but by Josefina who, in an unusual burst of rage, had screamed her denunciation.

It should happen that Josefina had made arrangements to go and visit John and Anna who were entertaining for the week-end Paul and Alice Barton, a brother and sister whose home was in Durham. The Bartons were what was known as a county family and whereas the county didn't visit Mrs Tilly Sopwith, there was no such barrier at the home of Mr John and Anna Sopwith.

Josefina found Paul Barton good company; he was a foil for her wit. Besides playing a good game of whist and croquet, he was good to watch at cricket.

Of late there had been a great restlessness in Josefina. She couldn't herself put a name to it, she only knew that she was tired of the Manor and the way of life in it. No one with the exception of John and Anna ever visited. If she or Willy wanted to meet people they had to go out, not that that really worried her because she didn't care much for people. With the exception of Willy and her mama there was no one she really cared about. And then the feelings that she had for these two people appeared, as it were, to be set on different platforms in her mind.

For her mama she had an affection, but the feeling she had for Willy she knew to be that which a woman has for a man. She also knew that Willy did not view her in this light but looked upon her more as a sister. And this, coupled with her knowledge that her mama was not really her mama, had caused to grow in her the feeling that she did not belong to anyone in this country. And so there had formulated in her mind a decision concerning her future. Her life presented her with two roads: if she could not walk the one she desired, then she would take the other stoically,

146

and in doing so she might in the end be compensated and the strange void in her be filled.

But in her cool reasoning she had forgotten to take into consideration that in her small exquisite body were traits of mixed heritage, whose reactions civilisation had merely dampened down.

The arrangement of the house had been altered over the years. Tilly continued to use the bedroom which had always been hers, and the dressing-room adjoining and the closet. She'd also had a guest room turned into a private sitting-room and it was here she spent most of her time, here she kept the books that concerned the running of the household and also those concerning the business of the mine. Gradually she had taken on the management of the mine, though not the practical side. This she still left to John and Steve and his under-manager, Alec Manning; but over the years she had come to know more about the business side of it than any of them, and this knowledge she had gradually imparted to her son. She had also encouraged him to take an active part in the running of the mine, for from a boy he had shown interest in it, and knowing that a choice of careers for him would be limited she saw his interest as a godsend to them both, imagining that whatever happened she would always have him by her side. Even if he married he would want her to remain on here. Well, where else could she go? or would she go, even though there were times when she wished she were miles away.

All her life she seemed to have been alone; yet not quite alone, for it was true what Steve said, all her life he had been there, and was still there. And for many, many years, too, there had been Biddy.

Biddy had been dead these last ten years, but as good as Fanny and Peg were, they could not make up for their mother. They had not the wisdom or the warmth. Loyalty, yes. Oh, she couldn't ask for more loyalty than she still got from the Drew family; and since Fanny had married Biddle, he, too, had joined the clan, as it were, and defended her name against slander.

It was odd that her name had still to be defended. And yet what had she done over the past sixteen years that would call for defence of her except that she had made an open friend of Steve.

When in the quiet of the night her body ached for the closeness of another human being and she imagined a face looking at her from the pillow, she told herself she was a fool, all kinds of a fool, and cruel into the bargain, for what had she given this man in return for a lifetime's devotion? Nothing but her hand, and at rare odd times her tight lips.

Yet she knew that if she were to stand up before the altar and swear unto God that nothing else had transpired between them, God would not believe her. And after all, who would blame Him?

She wondered at times how Steve managed to continue in this situation. She wondered if he had a woman on the side, someone whom he took up to that cottage in the hills. Twice he had taken her there but on each occasion the tenants had been present. They were a Mr and Mrs Gray. Peter Gray had been a lead miner who had had to leave the mine when the lead began to poison his system, but he was a man who was very handy and he had extended the cottage on both sides and made a fine job of it. Over the eleven years he had lived there the cottage had grown to twice its size with the addition of a washhouse, a cow byre and a stable, and all built lovingly with the stones he and his wife had gathered from the hillside. But two years ago Peter had died, and Nan, his wife, now an old woman, had gone down into the valley to live with her son. And not once since the cottage had become empty had Steve suggested that he take her up there. Yet she knew that every other week he took leave from the late shift on the Friday night until the Monday morning. She also knew that he paid not infrequent visits to an inn on the Gateshead road, and the reputation of this particular place was anything but savoury.

And what did all this amount to? That he had a woman. And who could blame him? Not her; although the thought of it stabbed at her and created a pain of jealousy which she would have attributed to a young girl and not to a woman of fifty. But she didn't look fifty, she didn't look anything like her age. Nor did Steve. Steve was a year younger than herself but he could pass for a man in his late thirties. There was not a grey hair in his head and his body was straight, which was unusual in a man who had spent so many years going down the drift. But he looked after himself did Steve. As he had once said laughingly to her when she had seen him running across the hills, "I've got to keep up with you."

He often ran with Willy. Willy had to have a guide when he was out running, for the sight of his good eye was slowly deteriorating, and it gave her a keen pleasure to see them both together. Willy liked Steve. But then Willy liked most people. His nature was so kind and embracing that she feared for him at times. Only the good die young, it was said, and she was afraid that the gods might claim their own.

And then there was Josefina. Josefina liked Willy, and Tilly sensed at times that she might even more than like. Yet you never really knew what Josefina was thinking. As a child she had been open in her love, demanding affection, but as she grew to girlhood and then touched on womanhood a strange reserve seemed to have settled on her. She looked a lot but said little. She had formed disconcerting habits: one such was sitting perfectly immobile for an hour or more at a time. It was as if the real being in her had gone away and left the outer casing without life. On one such occasion she had touched her shoulder, and Josefina turned and looked at her and said enigmatically, "Why did you do that, Mama?"

"Do what?" she had asked her.

"Bring me back."

"Bring you back?" Tilly had repeated. "From where?"

"I don't know." Josefina got up and walked away leaving Tilly very troubled. Yet within a short while she had returned to her sharp-tongued witty self. And the incident was forgotten, until it happened again. . . .

Of late there seemed to have been a barrier growing up between them. She was worried about Josefina. And now on this particular Sunday the years were rolled away by a succession of shouts that were touching on screams, and they were coming down from the nursery floor. Tilly's head jerked backwards. It was as if there were two children up there again and Josefina was having a tantrum because Willy was laughing at her. But there were no children up there now. The whole nursery floor had been given over to Willy. The old school and playroom was now a music room because he loved playing the pianoforte. Also he was quite proficient on the violin. His bedroom was next door.

The room across the landing, where Tilly herself had once slept, he had turned into a small museum in which every article was made of brass, from coal scuttles down through candlesticks and horse-brasses to miniatures of all kinds of animals. Everything was brass. It was a strange hobby, one which was started by Ned Spoke's uncle, the man who had taught him to wrestle. On

Willy's fourteenth birthday, Ned brought him a brass horseshoe for luck; and with that the collection had begun.

When something heavy hit the floor above and Josefina's voice rose to a shrill scream, Tilly ran from the room, along the corridor, and up the stairs to the nursery floor, and for a moment she put her hands over her ears as the voices of both Josefina and Willy came at her. Then she was in the music room and amazed at the sights before her, for there was Josefina flinging music books and sheets here and there, tearing some in the process.

"Stop this! Stop it this instant!" Tilly was herself yelling now. "Josefina, do you hear me! I say stop it!" At this the girl paused for a moment; then suddenly lifting up the violin that was lying on the top of the piano, she swung it in an arc and sent it flying against the oak cupboard that stood against the far wall.

"*Oh no! No!* You're mad. You're a bitch. Do you hear? You're a bitch."

Tilly became still as she stared at her son now who was on his knees on the floor, his hands searching for the pieces of the broken violin that John had bought him on his sixteenth birthday and which was an excellent instrument and had cost a great deal of money. But it wasn't that that was freezing her emotions, it was that this gentle son of hers should be so aroused that he would call the girl he thought of as his dear sister, a bitch. She had never heard him use a swear-word or an uncouth sentence in his life.

Her head swung towards Josefina, who had rushed across the room and was standing over him. She had taken no notice of Tilly's presence, it was as if she considered they were still both alone, for now she shouted, "I'm a bitch, am I, not to be classed with your pig and cow girl? All right, I'm a bitch, but you, Willy Sopwith, are a bastard, a stupid one-eyed bastard."

There were times in Tilly's life when she knew that she herself had been so consumed with rage that she became unaccountable for her actions, like the day she sprang on Alvero Portes and tore at his face. And how she had sprung again and had gripped Josefina by the shoulders and actually swung her from her feet into the middle of the room, and was shaking her as if she were a rat as she cried at her, "Don't you dare! Don't you dare use those words to my son! Do you hear me?"

Josefina's head became still for a moment. Fury still spitting from her eyes and her lips, she yelled. "Well, he is, he is a bastard. Besides his sight you have kept him in the dark . . . about that, and other things an' all."

Tilly gaped open-mouthed at the slight, dark bundle of rage wriggling in her grasp; then she thrust her away with such force that the girl almost overbalanced, only saving herself by gripping the edge of the piano, at the other side of which Willy was now standing, the broken violin in his hands but not looking at it, for his face was turned to the side, his head moving slightly as he took in the two misted figures before him.

The sudden and unusual burst of temper was ebbing from him and flowing into him now was a deep sickness lined with sorrow, not so much for himself and what he was hearing, but for the two people that he loved and who were stabbing each other with words, for now his mother was crying at Josefina, "He's no bastard, but you are. Do you hear, girl? You are! You are my late husband's bastard. Why did I adopt you? Not because your mother didn't want you, for she knew she would be able to make use of you. No; I took you because I thought it was my duty. But I'm going to tell you something now, girl, and you've brought it on yourself: I don't think my husband fathered you. He swore he didn't but your mother and her father and brother wanted money, so they named him. And your mother was a loose woman. Now think on that, who's the bastard?"

My God! My God! Tilly put her hand to her head and, turning about, staggered to the wall and leant her face against it. What had she said? What had happened? In a few minutes of anger she had destroyed the girl's life. Their association had been wonderful until this very day. . . . No, it hadn't. A denial came at her. For some time now Josefina had been changing and the girl's attitude towards her had at times been marked.

Slowly, she turned about and now leant against the wall again and looked from one to the other. Their faces were no longer convulsed with anger. Both seemed to be holding the same expression as they stared at her, and the only word she could put to it was, amazement.

Piteously now, she said, "I'm sorry. I'm sorry," then letting her gaze rest on Josefina, she said softly, "Forgive me. Please forgive me."

Josefina blinked her eyes, then turned and glanced at Willy before looking at Tilly again, and when she spoke it was as if she hadn't been screaming her head off minutes before for her voice sounded cool and calm and what she said appeared as if she had given the matter great thought, not that it had been thrust upon her only minutes before. "There is nothing to forgive. I, too, should say I'm sorry. And what you have told me is not such a surprise as you may imagine, only I wish I had acted as I felt inclined to some time ago and brought the matter into the open. The only difference your revelation has made is for me to re-appraise how I feel inside, and how I appear outside, for I have realised that I am not wholly Indian or Mexican or even Spanish, but I have never imagined there was English blood in me. I'm inclined to believe what you said that your husband did not father me. If he did it would make our relationship" – she now glanced at Willy – "rather complicated, and I don't know how you would term it. Seeing that Willy was born of one man and I of his son, we cannot therefore be half-brother and sister. I don't know what we can be" – she shrugged her shoulders – "that is if I was born of your husband, which, if I am to go by my inner feelings, I would repudiate."

Tilly stared into the small, exquisite face. The way she spoke, the words she used, were alien to how she looked, but if ever she'd had doubts before she doubted it now that Matthew had ever sired this girl. And so what was their relationship? If there was nothing of Matthew in her then she would be free to have Willy . . . to marry Willy. There, it was out, the secret fear that she had kept hidden for years, because she had known that Josefina loved Willy. This had been demonstrated since he had met up with Simon's daughter, not only met up with, but become very interested in. This, too, had been a source of worry, even more so than Jose-fina's affection for Willy, for she could imagine how the bitter, frustrated Simon Bentwood would look upon his daughter favouring her son, and he with his handicap.

She wondered if ever life would run smoothly for her, that she'd ever have a day to call her own, go where she liked, act how she liked. Yes, act how she liked. And if she could only act how she liked at this moment she would take up her skirts and flee from this house to the cottage and throw herself into the arms of Steve. Yes, yes, throw herself into his arms, into his bed. Strange how years could alter one's feelings. Of all the loves in her life there had never been one like the present, one that exchanged so little yet was so fiercely strong on both sides, like a subterranean torrent ever flowing in search of an outlet.

"May I speak to you alone . . . Mama?" The last word came

hesitant from Josefina. This didn't go unnoticed by Tilly, and she stared at this girl who had in a way ceased to be her daughter even by adoption and, looking towards Willy, she said, "Would you excuse us, Willy?"

Willy scrutinised them both for a moment through the narrowed lid of his eye, then turned abruptly and left the room. And now Tilly and Josefina were alone, and almost immediately the girl began to speak. "Don't look so worried, Mama," she said; "it all had to come into the open sooner or later. It's really later because I've been thinking a lot about my beginnings for a long time now and waiting for the opportunity to talk to you about the matter. But I'd rather it hadn't been in this way."

"Well," Tilly sighed, "why did you bring it about then? Why were you screaming at Willy?"

"Oh that!" Josefina now turned her back completely on Tilly and, walking to the window, she stood looking out for a moment before she said, "I wanted him to ride over to Uncle John's with me. The Bartons are going to be there, Paul and Alice." She turned her head slightly now in Tilly's direction. "You know Paul is the only man who has shown any real interest in me; not that I imagine he could ever bring himself to ask me to marry him, but his manner is natural when talking to me. He does not treat me like a black servant when I don't speak, or show embarrassed surprise at my intelligence and choice of subjects when I do. If you remember, Mama, for a time a few years ago the county doors were opened slightly for us to squeeze through, but apparently their curiosity being satisfied, they were closed again, that is with the exception of the Bartons. But it really didn't matter because —" She turned her head to the window again and paused before continuing, "I was quite happy to be at home here as long as I was with Willy. He was all the company that I wanted. But I suppose you know, Mama, I love Willy and if, as you say —" Again her head moved so that she could see Tilly, and then she ended, "If, as you say, you don't think your husband was my father, then I am no relation to Willy and there would be nothing to stop us marrying, except one thing: he has always seen me as a sister and he has been led to think of me that way. But —" She now walked towards where Tilly was standing and her body seemed to become even smaller with the admission that she dragged from her lips as, with bowed head, she said, "There's another thing, he loves that Bentwood girl."

If in an unemotional moment Tilly had been asked which girl she would choose for her son she would, if she were to answer truthfully, have said, "Neither." But at this moment, if forced to make a choice, she would have plumped for this dark exquisite creature before her, who was now wringing her heart with the unusual expression of sadness on her face, for with this girl Willy's choice would bring no repercussions, except perhaps raised eyebrows from the county folk and expressions of "Well! what do you expect of that set-up?" from the villagers. But for the Bentwood girl, she guessed that Simon Bentwood would rather see his daughter dead than married to her son. The jungle telegraph worked both ways and over the years she herself had inadvertently, and sometimes deliberately, listened in as the messages dropped into the kitchen quarters. Simon's tirades against his daughter in his drunken bouts was general knowledge, but it never ceased to amaze her that such love as he professed for herself could turn into a red raw, deep uncontrollable hate. That his wife held no such feelings she had personal evidence of, for on the four occasions they had met during the last fifteen years they had stopped and spoken amicably, both enquiring after the other's children and both knowing that under different circumstances they could have been friends.

Of the daughter in question Tilly knew nothing, except that she was a bonny girl with an open countenance. She had passed her when out riding but they had never exchanged a word. She wondered now how she would react to this girl if she ever became her daughter-in-law and, presumably, mistress of this house.

Her whole body jerked, whether at the thought that had come like a violent stab into her mind or at the shock of Josefina's words, for she had just said, "If I can't have Willy, I am going back to America to find my people."

Tilly's mouth opened and shut twice before she brought out, "You . . . you won't find them in America. Well . . . I mean not the America from where I brought you."

"Why not?"

"Because they are . . . they are mostly white people there now."

"And I wouldn't be accepted, is that what you're saying?"

"Yes, that's what I'm saying, you'd never be accepted, not as an equal."

"Well, I could find my own people and be accepted there I suppose."

"You . . . you could not endure the life of your own people."

"What about the Spanish? I can remember speaking Spanish fluently when I was little."

"That . . . that was the language a lot of Mexicans adopted because they were integrated."

"So, no one would have me, is that what you're saying?"

"I'm being truthful, Josefina, for your own good. You are here, you belong here. You. . . ."

"No, I don't! That I do know." The anger was back in her tone. "I have known for a long, long time that I've no place here, and that only Willy could have made my life tolerable. Well, say what you like, I mean to go back and find out for myself how I'll be received. I won't have to ask you for any money, you have been more than generous to me with my allowance over the years, and I have spent very little of it, seemingly because, well, I suppose that some day I knew the time would come when I would leave. And the time has come."

"Josefina!" Tilly held out both her hands towards the small figure, saying pleadingly now, "Wait! Wait! If you must go back then you must, but . . . but let me make arrangements. I've kept in touch with Luisa McNeill over the years. And there is also Katie. She will welcome you and help you."

Josefina remained silent. Her dark eyes looked bright but not with the moisture of tears. Tilly had never seen her cry; not even after tumbles as a child she had never cried; yelled and fought, yes, but never given way to tears. But now she saw her throat swelling and she watched her gulp before she spoke. "Will you write to them straightaway?" she asked quietly.

"Yes, this very night."

"Thank you."

As Josefina turned away, Tilly had the desire to pull her back and into her arms as she had done when she was a child. As a child she had demanded to be held, to be petted, to be loved; but there was nothing of the child in Josefina now, only a cool aloofness that held one at bay and which was the result of deep conflicts of colour and race, a race that had its beginning in the past so far back that all that surged to the surface now was a strange uneasiness.

After the door closed on Josefina Tilly sat down on the music stool in front of the piano. About her feet were slithers of broken wood, some a polished brown, some showing a plain surface. As she stared down on them, the thought came to her that they represented her life, for every now and again back down the years something had broken her happiness, dashing it to smithereens. Superstition, jealousy, death had all played their part, and now love, young love had suddenly flared into passion with the result that not only was she going to lose her adopted daughter but there was every possibility that she would soon lose her son. And he was the only human being she loved in life. . . . Except, of course, Steve. The "of course" passed through her mind as if her feelings for him were an established and open fact instead of a secret pain known only to herself.

When she heard the handle of the door turn, she looked over her shoulder and watched Willy enter the room. He did it slowly, turning and closing the door and seeming to pause a minute before making his way towards her. Then one hand resting on the side of the piano, he stood peering down at her. She did not return his gaze but kept her eyes lowered towards the floor once more; nor did she raise her head when he said, "Is it true that I was born out of wedlock, Mama?"

The question sounded so precise, as if a character in a book had suddenly become alive and was speaking his lines. She almost gave voice to a shaky laugh. "Is it true that I was born out of wedlock, Mama?" Not as one of her own people would have said, "What's this I'm hearing! Look! I want the truth, am I a bastard or am I not?" but, "Is it true that I was born out of wedlock, Mama?"

In an ordinary way she should have been amazed at this moment that her son was still in ignorance of the true nature of his birth. He was nearly twenty years old, he was a man, a big, handsome looking man; not even near-blindness nor the scar across his brow left by the blow that had inflicted him with the blindness detracted from his good looks, and all his life, at least since she had put him in the care of Ned Spoke, he had shown a desire to mix with people, and mix he had. He had attended the fairs and the hill races and the markets. This being so, you would have thought that somebody would, perhaps when in drink, have referred to him as a bastard; but apparently no one had. Perhaps the condition of his eyes had evoked pity; added to which the very fact that he went down the mine and showed that he wasn't afraid to use pick or shovel when learning the ins and outs of the business had caught the admiration of other men.

Yet it wasn't only with the common man he had mixed, he had, through John and Anna, met members of the county and these, as she knew only too well from personal experience, could convey an insult while smiling into your face, or the inflexion they laid on a few simple words could set a mind wondering. Yet he had escaped all this and here he was asking a question, the answer to which, had she been wise, she would have given him years ago.

She raised her head and, looking up into his deep brown eyes over which the lids were blinking rapidly now, she said tensely, "Yes, it's true. I lived with your father for twelve years and I nursed him every day of that time. He had, as you already know, been in an accident at the pit which deprived him of his feet. His wife would not divorce him. When she died he wanted to marry me but I said no. I was of a different class. I felt unfit to take on the position of his wife . . . that is legally. You were conceived very late in our association. I would have married him then to give you a legal name but he died."

"And then you married his son?"

These words were ordinary sounding now, but with a note of condemnation in them, and she replied more stiffly still, "Yes, I married his son. I married him because I loved him and he was a young man. I had never known the love of a young man." At this moment she did not think of Steve, but apparently her son did for his next question brought her up from the seat so swiftly that she almost overbalanced and her voice was loud as she cried at him, "No! I am not having that kind of association with Steve."

"You're not?"

"No, I'm not!"

"Well, I'm surprised that you aren't because he cares for you."

She was silent for a moment before she said, "And what gives you that idea?"

"Well —" He sighed and turned from the piano now and walked away from her towards the table as he said, "I may be almost blind but I can still see a little; and then again I don't discount my hearing. He talks of you. I have learned more about you from him than from anyone else. At one time I imagined he was my father."

"Willy!"

"Oh" – he swung round now – "don't say it like that, Mother, as if you were shocked. I've always imagined that nothing could shock you; you know so much of the world, and have gone

157

through so much. It would have been the most natural thing that you two should come together now and again. I understand it must have been difficult for you both, you in your position, he in his, but I thought . . . well" – he shrugged his shoulders and stretched out his arms while she stared at him.

The young man confronting her now seemed a different being from the one who had entered the room a few minutes ago and said, "Is it true that I was born out of wedlock, Mama?" And now she watched him sigh deeply as he went on, "What does it matter how we were born, where we were born, and even who begot us, it's how we act that matters. You, I think, have acted for other people's good all your life and without much thanks. Most people seemed to have wrought havoc on you, and I'm, apparently, going to be no exception when I tell you that I'm in love with Noreen Bentwood and mean to marry her, that is if she'll have me."

He took a step nearer to her, his face to the side now, with one eye peering at her, his voice soft as he said, "I'm sorry if I'm hurting you. I never want to hurt you. I know how you view Bentwood and I've never got to the bottom of why he hates you so much except that you turned him down more than once, but I suppose that would be enough to make any man hate. She's . . . she's a nice girl, Mama, a lovely girl . . . say something please."

She had to force herself to bring out the words, "If . . . if she makes you happy that's everything. Have you spoken to her?"

"No. Oh no."

"No?"

"No, not a word. And . . . and I don't think I've given her a sign because . . . well" – he gave a short laugh – "I'm not exactly the catch of the season."

"She'd be the luckiest girl alive to get you, and I would think she knows it."

"I wish I could think like that. She's been kind to me and —" He turned away now and walked towards the window saying, "There's no one I've known that I've felt more at ease with." He did not add, "except yourself" and she closed her eyes tightly and bit on her lip. "We've sat on the river bank and I've held her hand, just held her hand, and it's filled me with a feeling of. . . . Well, I can't explain it. I suppose one could say peace, and yet no, not peace because there's a turmoil inside me when she's near. And what's more, she takes away that awful feeling of being disabled. I feel whole when I'm near her."

He stopped speaking and she saw his face tilted back as if he were looking towards the sky. He seemed gone from her entirely, and the pain in her chest was as if a mill was grinding against her ribs. She had never imagined he felt himself handicapped, he had always been so cheerful, so outgoing as if he took his lack of sight as a natural thing. Her pain increased as realisation seeped into her that her son had not gone from her this day but rather some long time ago; perhaps the very first time he had met up with Noreen Bentwood.

"Say something."

She had not realised that he had turned from the window but she could not do as he asked, and now taking her hands, he pleaded, "Please, don't be upset, nothing has changed between us. What has happened today doesn't matter. I'm only sorry it has had to happen this way. If Josefina wasn't such a spitfire none of this would have come about. I'm sorry I called her a bitch but I was so mad at her when she broke my violin, and all because I wouldn't go to Uncle John's with her."

Tilly bowed her head. It was strange how some men could be so inwardly blind. He had no idea of Josefina's true feelings for him; and it was better that he should remain in ignorance.

When he put his arms about her and kissed her she held him tightly for a moment before saying, "Go and make your peace with her, she's very unhappy." She did not add, "She won't be here much longer;" enough was enough.

When the door had closed on him she stood perfectly still in the middle of the room, then lifting her hand, she pressed it tightly over her mouth as if to prevent the words escaping from her lips, for her mind was crying, Oh Steve! Steve! He was the only rock in her life, the only being who had never changed. She wanted to fly to him, fling herself into his arms and cry, "I'll marry you, Steve. I'll marry you." At this moment the promise she had made to a dying man appeared foolish and futile, and her reason for not having broken it earlier was, she knew, because she'd had two children to bring up, then two young people to see to and guide; but now both of them were gone from her life, cut off as surely as if they had packed their bags and taken separate coaches to separate railways, they had gone.

She must see Steve, she must. Perhaps he hadn't gone to his cottage. Well, if he had she would stay and wait for him. Oh yes, she would wait. Whatever time he came back tonight she would be there waiting. Had he not waited for her for years?

From the top of the stairs she called down to Biddle and gave him orders to have her horse saddled. Then going to her room, she swiftly changed her clothes. Fifteen minutes later she was galloping down the drive, through the main gates and on to the coach road. But she did not continue along it to the turnpike as she had done at odd times before, she jumped her horse over a ditch, then over a low field gate, rode him around the border by a dry stone wall until they came to a part where the wall had broken down. Taking him gently over this, she set him into a gallop down a shallow valley and up the bordering hill. On the top she drew him to a stop for a moment, not only to give him a breather but to view the surrounding land. Away in the far, far distance to the right of her she could see a narrow silver streak, that was the River Tyne. Away to the front was soft undulating farmland. Then her eye was drawn slightly to the left and below her where the land dropped again, and her gaze became rivetted on two riders. One was unmistakable, as was his mount. Steve's horse was a fourteen-year-old mare which ten years ago she had helped to choose. She was broad in the back and made for weight, but the horse walking alongside her was a sleek animal, evidently a hunter, and its rider was sleek too. But she wasn't a young girl. She had her face turned towards Steve and she was laughing, they were both laughing, he into her face and she into his. The sound of it came to her as if carried on a patch of wind, and now the mill grinding against her ribs worked faster as she saw Steve lean from his saddle, his hand outstretched. She could not see what he did with it, but its direction left little to the imagination – he was placing it on that of his companion.

On God! God! She turned her horse slowly about and the seemingly unaffected part of her mind said, "Why do you always say, Oh God! God! when you're upset? You never pray, so why do you appeal to Him now?" But appeal to Him she did and, looking upwards, she asked, "What have I done this time?" and the answer seemed to come to her from every corner of the wide expanse of sky, saying, "You left it too late. You left it too late."

3

Noreen was sitting by the burn gazing into the water. She had been sitting like this for almost an hour now and she told herself she would wait another five minutes and then she would go.

She waited ten, fifteen, and she had risen to her feet when she heard the rustle of footsteps in the dry grass, and the snuffling of the dog, and quickly she put her hands to her bonnet, straightened it and dusted the grass from her coat, and then he came round the corner and towards her.

"Hello."

"Hello."

"I'm . . . I'm late."

"Yes, you are."

He laughed gently now. Any of the other young misses he had met he was sure would never have given such a forthright reply. They would have said, "Oh, are you? Well, I've just come," or some such nonsense. He held out his hand to her and he knew it was trembling, and when her fingers lay within his palm he knew that she was trembling too. His head to the side, he bent down towards her and as he did so it seemed for a second someone had lit a lamp in front of her face.

"You've got a new bonnet on," he said.

"You can make that out?"

"Yes, yes. I see it plainly in my mind. And you too. You're . . . you're very beautiful."

"No." Her voice sounded flat now. "I'm pretty but not beautiful."

"I think you're beautiful."

"Well, I'll not argue with you."

"No, you'd better not."

They both laughed; then he said, "Am I allowed to say that blue suits you? It is a new coat and bonnet, isn't it?"

"Yes, my mother bought them for my birthday . . . it's my

birthday on Tuesday, but it being Sunday she gave them to me today to wear."

"Yes, I know when your birthday is."

"I never mentioned it to you so how do you . . .?"

"You told me the day you were sixteen, and you had a new bonnet and coat on then."

"Did I?"

"You did and you know you did. You pronounced it as if you had gained a century." Again they were laughing; and now he drew her cautiously towards the river bank and, as they had done so often before, they sat down side by side on it.

She reached out now and drew a paper-covered parcel towards her, saying as she did so, "I've brought your books back. I like the Dickens stories, but they're sad, aren't they?"

"Yes, they are; but they're true to life."

"How do you know because you've hardly been away from the big house?"

"I've been to London."

"You have!" There was awe in her tone now.

"I have." His tone was deliberately pompous. "And what's more, I have heard Mr Charles Dickens reading his own stories from the stage."

"You haven't really."

"Yes, I have. My Uncle John and Aunt Anna, Mother, and Josefina, we all went to the St James's Hall one night and listened to the great man. It was most enthralling. I felt so sorry when he died; 'twas as if I had known him personally."

"He is dead then?"

"Yes, he died about three years ago."

"Aw, I'm sorry too. I hate to hear of people dying. I never want to die, I want to go on living and loving. . . ." She stopped suddenly and her fingers jerked away from his.

After a moment he leaned towards her and said softly, "You love someone, Noreen?"

Her head was bent, her hands tightly clasped.

"Yes." Her head was nodding now.

"Do I know him?"

There was a pause before her answer came. "Yes."

"What's his name?"

When she didn't answer, he asked gently, "Can't you tell me his name?"

"No" – she was shaking her head now – "he's got to speak first."

"Perhaps he's afraid to, this person you love. You see I know all about being afraid to speak my mind because I, too, love someone very, very dearly. But I'm . . . I'm handicapped. I couldn't imagine her ever really loving me, being sorry for me yes, being a companion to me, a friend, but I couldn't ask her anything more until . . . well, I wouldn't want to frighten her and lose her friendship."

"Willy." She was kneeling by his side now gazing at him, and he swung himself round so that he, too, was kneeling, and as he whispered her name she said again, "Willy. Aw Willy." And then their arms were about each other and his lips were on hers, hard, tight, and she was clinging to him as if she would never let him go.

It was minutes later when, still clinging together, they sat once more on the edge of the bank; and Willy now brought from his pocket a small box and, handing it to her, he said, "A happy birthday, my dear, dearest Noreen."

Slowly she pressed the spring and when the lid opened there lay a brooch in the shape of a half-moon and lying in the crescent was a star. The moon was set with small diamonds, the star too, but at its central point there lay a ruby.

"Oh! . . . Oh! . . . Oh! Willy. I've never seen anything so beautiful. Oh! thank you. Thank you." Her arms were about him again. Once more their lips held; and then he said in a tone full of emotion, "You'll marry me, Noreen?"

"Oh aye, yes, Willy." Each word seemed to be balanced on wonder, and again she said, "Oh yes, yes."

"When?"

Slowly now she sank away from him while still retaining hold of his hand, and she looked across the water as she said one word. "Father.". . . .

From the thicket behind them a prone figure slowly edged itself backwards and if the couple on the bank heard the rustle of the grass they put it down to a rabbit, but the dog heard it and when he made towards it, Willy commanded him to stay.

Randy Simmons was more of the weasel type than a rabbit, and he grinned and nodded his old head as he muttered to himself, "Aye, aye, *Father*." News of this would mend his back for him. Aye, by heck, it would. He could see his master skiting up to that

163

Manor and tearing it apart. Just let her say it to him once again, "You're as lazy as you're long, Randy Simmons," and he'd put the shackles on her all right. He'd split on her, her father'd hear about it in any case, sooner or later.

Father. She had a good right to say it like that, the little trollop.

By! it'd make a story in the pub, the witch's blind bastard and Bentwood's lass. 'Twas about time there was a bit of excitement round here, things had been too quiet of late. Aye, much too quiet.

"Girl! look at your coat. It's all grass stains, you'd think you had been kneeling in it."

"Mam! Mam!" Noreen pushed her mother's hands away. "Stop fussing and listen, I've got something to tell you . . . listen . . . listen . . . Willy has asked me to marry him."

"Willy?" Lucy screwed up her eyes as if she had never heard the name Willy before, and one thing was sure, she had never heard it from her daughter's lips.

"Willy Sopwith."

"Willy Sopwith?"

"Mam, don't act on as if you didn't know."

"Well, I didn't know it had gone this far." Lucy's voice was now a harsh whisper and she glanced about her as if afraid of being overheard. Then grabbing her daughter by the shoulder just in case this fear should be realised, she thrust her forward, saying, "Get upstairs."

When they were standing in the back bedroom Lucy peered at her daughter as if she were finding difficulty in seeing her. The light in the room was dim, it being the original upstairs room of the once two-roomed cottage that had first stood on this site, and on the brightest day the light merely filtered into the room through the two narrow windows that were set like armoury slits in a castle wall; and the walls, all of two foot thick, did resemble those built as a fortification. Noreen could have had any of the other three vacant bedrooms in the house but she preferred to stay in the one which had acted as her nursery when a child.

"You're mad, girl. You know that, you're mad."

"All right, I'm mad, but we're going to be married."

"When, in the name of God?"

"I . . . I don't know exactly, but we are. He . . . he wanted to take me to see his mother today, and when I wouldn't go he wanted to come here. . . ."

"Come here! Oh!" Lucy held her head between her two hands and she rocked herself from side to side as she said, "He'd go for him. You know that, he'd go for him."

"Well, he might find his match if he did, Willy's no weakling."

"He's almost blind, girl, at least from what I hear . . . Is he?"

"Yes." The answer had come firm and clear, and as Lucy looked at her daughter she recognised that she wasn't arguing with or trying to persuade a young girl, because Noreen neither looked nor sounded a young girl, she was a woman. She had always been older than her years and much wiser than one would expect from someone of her age, but the revelation did not deter her in her pleading, in fact it seemed to make it imperative that her daughter should see sense before it was too late. "Look," she said now; "give yourself time. Tell him you must think it over, have time. . . ."

"I have thought it over, and for a long time now, and I've given him my word. Anyway, I want to marry him. If I don't. . . ."

"*Oh no! No! Oh girl, no!* Lucy had put her hand up as if to ward off something fearful, and now she cried almost in anguish, "Not that, girl. Don't tell me that you *must* marry him. How could you!"

"Mama!" The word was almost a bellow. "You're barking up the wrong tree."

Lucy closed her eyes and her body seemed to slump; then looking at her daughter again, she said, "I'm sorry, lass, I'm sorry, but I could stand anything except that. The disgrace of that, at least for you. Aw no! No! Aye —" she managed to smile now as if in relief — "things will work out, at least I hope to God they will. But do this for me, lass, don't mention anything yet. And don't go running off because that might be all right for you and him but your dad will go up to that house and there would be murder done. I tell you you don't know how he feels about . . . about that woman." Her head was down now and her lips were trembling and it was Noreen's turn to feel concern. Putting her arm around her mother's shoulder, she said, "I . . . I do know and . . . and I think he's mad, mad in so many ways, mainly for not appreciating what he's got in you, for what I've seen of her . . . she's got no figure, nothing, she's as flat as Willy himself."

They stood in silence for a moment, Lucy her head still bent, Noreen looking towards her bed. When she spoke she asked a question: "Do you think, Mam," she said, "that Dad's not right in the head, because nobody sane could act like he does about something that happened years and years ago, and be normal?"

Lucy now moved from her daughter's hold and towards the door and she had the knob in her hand as she said, "He's sane enough in one way but mad in another, because some women have the power to turn men's brains."

"I don't like her."

Looking sadly at her daughter, Lucy said, "Well, if you're hoping for her to be your mother-in-law it's a sad look out for the future, because there's an old adage that says, a wife is but the second woman in a man's life." And on this she went out.

4

For the past two months Tilly had avoided meeting Steve except when she visited the mine, and even there she managed to arrange for a third party to be present.

She knew she was afraid to be alone with him, in case she might upbraid him for enjoying another woman's company and in doing so reveal her own feelings towards him. And this she knew would be most unfair for the situation between them was of her own making. She could have married him any time within the last sixteen years but now it was too late.

A meeting had just taken place in the office with regard to the building of new repair sheds, also the renovation of the stables. There had been present John, the under-manager Alec Manning, Steve and herself. Some of the under-manager's remarks had been disturbing. He was a modern young man, not afraid to open his mouth, and he said openly that it was very little use spending money on new buildings when the roads inside were almost worked out. Better, he thought, to open new seams.

She had been surprised that Steve had not downed him. His silence on the point seemed to suggest he was of a similar way of thinking. Then why, she thought, hadn't he spoken up. Her own thoughts became agitated as she realised that his mind was not wholly on the business in hand.

John had been emphatic against spending more money on exploring new drifts until he was absolutely sure there was nothing more to be had out of the present ones.

The meeting had ended with nothing settled because no two of them seemed to be in agreement on any point.

She came out of the office and stood talking to John, aware at the same time that Steve and his under-man had gone into the lamp house. Steve hadn't spoken to her privately except to wish her a good morning.

John brought her attention to him swiftly by saying, "Mc . . . McGrath is not . . . not himself these days. I fear there m . . . m

". . . might be some . . . something in the rumour after all."

"What rumour?" Her voice was sharp.

"Oh, just that I heard he was th . . . thinking of leaving the pit and taking up f . . . f . . . farming. I understand he's got some kind of a f . . . f . . . farm."

"It's merely a cottage."

"Oh yes, yes" – he looked closely at her – "I f . . . f . . . forgot you've b . . . been there. And it isn't a f . . . farm of any k . . . k . . . kind?"

"No. The land's useless for farming. A few sheep perhaps but that's all. When did you hear this?"

"Oh, s . . . s . . . some time ago, in fact I c . . . c . . . can't remember wh . . . wh . . . where it was or who m . . . mentioned it. But there, I think he w . . . w . . . would have told you about it, w . . . w . . . wouldn't he, Tilly, if there w . . . w . . . were any t . . . t . . . truth in it?"

There was un underlying meaning to his words which she wasn't slow to recognise, but she ignored it, saying, "Well, I happen to be his employer, but then it is often the employer who is the last one to be brought into the picture. . . . How is Anna?"

"Oh, as usual." He looked to the side before returning his gaze back to her and saying, "I've s . . . s . . . suggested to her that we adopt a b . . . b . . . baby."

"How did she take it?" Her voice was soft now, sympathetic.

"N . . . N . . . Not at all well, T . . . T . . . Tilly. In fact, it brought on one of her ner . . . ner . . . nervous bouts again."

"I'm sorry. But you know, John, children besides bringing blessings also bring pain."

She watched him shake his head sadly now as he said, "She, and I too, would gladly su . . . su . . . suffer the pains."

"Has she talked the matter over with her doctor?"

"N . . . N . . . No, Tilly, and I w . . . wouldn't suggest it to her, n . . . n . . . not again. I d . . . d . . . did once allude to it but it's such a de . . . delicate matter. You understand?"

"Yes, yes, John, I understand. Well, give her my love. And I'll expect to see you both on Friday. Insist that she comes, won't you, John, because it will be the last time she will see Josefina."

"Th . . . Th . . . That girl, she must be m . . m . . . mad and ungr . . . gr . . . grateful in . . . into the bargain."

"No, no, John. It's natural I suppose, she wants to see her people and the country from where she sprang. It's a natural desire. And she can always come back. I've told her this is her home, she can always come back . . . Well, there's Robbie with your horse." She pointed, "Good-bye, John."

"Good-bye, Ti . . . Ti . . . Tilly. See you Fr . . . Fr . . . Friday."

They parted: he mounted his horse and rode away; she now went to the stables.

As she approached the wide double doors she was met by Steve leading both her own and his mount out. Without a word he assisted her up into the saddle and the next minute he was riding by her side, and not until they were clear of the pit head and on the road did she speak, and then she said, "You've changed the shift?"

"Yes, some days ago."

Again there was silence. At one point the road narrowed until their mounts had to walk close together, and when his knee touched hers, he said, but without looking at her, "Why have you been avoiding me, Tilly?"

"Avoiding you?" She had turned her head towards him, and so she was aware of the angry hue that had come over his face before he exclaimed, albeit in a lowered tone, "Oh, for God's sake, Tilly, don't put on your drawing-room manner and your polite asides. I say you've been avoiding me, you know you've been avoiding me, and I want to know the reason."

So he wanted to know the reason. Being Steve, he wouldn't settle for anything else. Well, what would she say to him? Tell him the truth: I've been avoiding you because I'm jealous, because I can't bear the thought of you being nice to another woman? And what would his answer to that be? "You're too late, Tilly, you should have thought about this years ago, even a few months would have made all the difference. I'm a man, I need someone." And she had no doubt that he slaked a particular need during his not infrequent visits to his cottage on his long weekends and to the inn on the high road. And she couldn't blame him for that, oh no.

"Come in a minute."

She turned to him in surprise. She hadn't realised they had ridden so far in silence. She allowed him to help her down, watched him as he tied her horse to the gate post, and then she preceded him up the path and stood aside while he placed the key in the lock, turned it and opened the door.

When she entered the room the proceedings went as usual. He put the bellows to the fire, he took up the black kettle from the hob, went into the scullery, and in a short while returned with it and pushed it into the heart of the coals, then went again into the scullery, and she sat listening to him getting the thick of the coal-dust from his hands and face. But today his ablutions seemed to take longer and when he came into the room she saw that he had also washed his hair; it was lying flat and gleaming on his head.

He came and stood in front of her, but he did not speak for some seconds; and then his words were directly to the point. "Out with it, Tilly," he said; "you owe me this at least."

Well, here was something she could make use of without giving herself away, so she repeated his last words, "I owe you that at least, you say. Well, perhaps you owe me something too, Steve. If you are thinking about changing your job, shouldn't I have been the first to know?"

"Changing my job? Where did you hear this?"

"Does it matter? . . . Is it true?"

"It is and it isn't, so to speak. It could be true but on the other hand it could be just a rumour."

"As is the fact that you may be thinking of getting married?"

There, she had jumped in with both feet but without giving herself away. He was looking down at her, straight into her face; but his expression told her nothing. His next words did however: "Yes" – he inclined his head towards her – "I've been thinking about it for some time now, some long time in fact."

"You could have told me."

"Yes, I suppose I could, but what would you have said?"

"I —" She kept her eyes fixed on him as she took her spittle over the lump in her throat, then continued, "I could have wished you happiness, you deserve happiness."

"We very rarely get what we deserve, Tilly."

"May I know her name?"

"Oh" – he pursed his lips – "her name doesn't matter very much." He was turning away as she said, "Well, I've seen her face so I would like to put a name to it."

He stopped in the act of making a step; then his right foot seemed to descend slowly to the floor and he remained immovable for a moment not speaking. When he turned, it wasn't towards her but towards the fireplace where the kettle was spluttering its boiling water on to the new glowing coals, and he lifted it up and placed it on the hob, then straightened his back and reached for the tea caddy from the mantelpiece before he asked, "When did you see her?"

"Oh, you were out riding together some time ago."

The tea caddy in one hand now, he stretched out the other hand for the brown teapot which was standing on a corner of the delf rack to the side of the fireplace, and he said slowly, "Ah yes, yes; that would be one Sunday about seven weeks ago. It was the first time we had ridden together."

He turned his head now and looked at her over his shoulder and his face was bright. He was smiling, the lines at the corners of his eyes were deep, his mouth was wide and the expression on his face pained her to such an extent that she wanted to cry out against it. She couldn't remember ever seeing such a look on his face, not even on that night long ago when they watched the New Year coming in together, and he had taken her in his arms and kissed her.

"Well now, where's that milk? As if I didn't know." He went to the cupboard beneath the delf rack and took out a can. Lifting the lid, he sniffed at the contents and said, "It should be all right, I only got it last night, 'tisn't turned yet."

She watched him pour the milk into the cups, then take up the brown teapot and pour out the tea. After handing her a cup, he picked up his own and, taking it from the saucer, he raised it as one would a glass of wine in a toast, and he waited as if he expected her to do the same. After a moment she did so and forced herself to say, "I wish you every happiness, Steve. You know that."

"Not more than I wish myself, Tilly. Not more than I wish myself." The smile slid from his face and he was placing the cup on the table when the sound of a galloping horse drew his eyes towards the window, and, bending his length downwards, he said, "It . . . it looks like one of your lads. It is, it is. It's Ned Spoke. What now?"

She had risen swiftly to her feet and they were both at the door when Ned came running up the path. He stood gasping for a moment before he could say, " 'Tis trouble, ma'am. I . . . I was on my way to the mine, then I saw Bluebell." He thumbed back towards the horse.

"What is it?" She had gone down the step and had hold of his arm now, and again he gasped before he said, "Mr Bentwood, he . . . he came crashing in. Mad he was, clean mad like a raving bull. He knocked Mr Peabody over, clean over. Then Biddle tried to tackle him. 'Twas then that Master Willy came on the scene. He . . . he, Mr Bentwood, sprang on him and got hold of him by the throat, so Peg said, but Master Willy, being good at throwing people off, got free. But he didn't raise his hand to him. He tried to speak, Peg said, to calm him down. But then Mr Bentwood came at him again and knocked him flying."

Tilly now ran down the path calling as she did so, "Is . . . is he hurt?" and Ned, coming after her, cried, "His face is busted a bit and he hit the bottom of the stairs and went out like a light, but he came round again."

"Wait! Wait! Tilly; I'll be with you." Steve was now running to the stable, buttoning his shirt neck as he went, and he mounted his horse almost at the same time as Tilly did hers, and within seconds was galloping after them. . . .

The house seemed in chaos, it was as if the whole staff had gathered in the hall. It was Biddle who came forward now to her, saying, "He's all right, madam. Don't worry, he's all right. He's recovered. We put him in your room."

She did not stop to ask questions but flew upstairs and into the bedroom to see Josefina holding a cold compress to Willy's face. He was sitting on the edge of the bed and since the compress was covering his good eye he turned in the direction of the opening door and, sensing her before she spoke, he said, "Don't worry, don't worry, it's all right."

"Oh my God!" Tilly had lifted the compress away and looked at the darkening surface of the skin from the top of the eyelid to well below his cheekbones, taking in the split at the corner of his upper lip which was still bleeding. "We must get the doctor."

"I've already sent for him."

She turned and looked at Josefina who added harshly, "But who *you* should send for is the police. That man should be locked up, he's mad."

"We want no police . . . or a doctor." They both looked at Willy as he finished, "Just leave me alone and I'll be all right."

"You can't be left alone." Tilly's voice was almost a bark. "Have you any idea what has been done to your face?"

"Well, whatever it is it can't be worse than what has already been done to it, can it?"

172

They were the first real words of bitterness she had heard from his lips. Before, whenever he had referred to his blindness it was with acceptance. His nature was innately placid or had been; but over the last weeks she had noticed a change in him, a hardening. It seemed to date from the day of the upset with Josefina.

There was silence in the room for a moment, the only sound being that of water dripping into the dish as Josefina wrung out another compress. When she placed it against his cheek, she said, "Well, this should bring home to you the fact that if you want to survive you'd better give up whatever thoughts you're harbouring concerning that gentleman's daughter."

The reaction of his hand coming up and tearing the compress from his face was so rough that he almost caused Josefina to overbalance, and his voice now matching his action, he cried, "He, or no one else, is going to stop me seeing Noreen and —" he paused and his eye searched for his mother and held her gaze as he finished, "marrying her."

Again there was a short silence, ended by Josefina turning hastily away, saying with bitterness equal to his own, "I hope you live long enough to accomplish it, that's all."

As the door banged Tilly wrung out another compress and when she placed it on his face and he said, "What's wrong with her these days?" she could have answered, "If you don't know you are indeed blind. Can't you understand that the girl you have treated as a sister all these years is in love with you, deeply in love with you?" She could not have made a comparison, saying, "And to a greater extent than Simon Bentwood's daughter," because as yet she had no way of gauging the feelings of the girl, she only knew that she had so ensnared her son it could in the end be the death of him; and her mind gave her no other word but ensnared.

When a tap came to the door she turned her head, saying, "Come in," and when it opened Biddle stood aside to allow Steve to enter, and what struck her immediately was the incongruity of the two men, Steve in his coal-dust-stained shirt, a leather belt holding up his trousers, and Biddle in his grey and blue well-fitting gaitered uniform.

"How are you?" Steve was standing at the other side of Willy, and he, lifting his head, said, "What does it look like, Steve?"

"Pretty rough to me."

173

"Well, that's how it feels."

"Something's got to be done about that man." Steve was looking across at Tilly now, and Tilly asked simply "What?"

"I'm not having the police brought into this, Steve." Willy made to rise from the bed while Steve, staying him with a hand on his shoulder, said, "No; well, there's no need for that, not as yet. But if he thinks he can put the fear of God into you and everybody else he'll go on doing it. You've got friends haven't you? Phil Spoke, and Ned an' all, are not to be sneezed at when it comes to a knockabout."

"I don't want that."

"No! Well, you just might have to agree with it in the end. What I can't understand is how he got at you; using one of your holds you could have had him on his back because he's gone to wind. He's big but he's soft bodywise; you could have tossed him."

"I didn't want to toss him."

Steve let out a long breath and as it ended he said, "I can understand that. But now, I think, looking at your face a steak wouldn't come in wrong until the doctor gets here."

"A steak! I never thought of that, I'll get one immediately." Tilly almost ran from the room; and with her going Steve lowered himself down on to the edge of the bed to the side of Willy and, his voice changing, he said, "You'll have to be careful, lad; he'll not let you have his girl, not as long as he's alive."

"Why? Why, Steve? All because of some silly thing that happened years ago."

"Silly? Well, I wouldn't call it silly. What would you say if I came along now and took your lass away from you, from under your nose, and you had to watch her being happy with somebody else?"

"But it was so long ago; and he was so much older than Mama. I can't understand it."

Steve gave a short laugh, then he said, "You can't understand it? Knowing your mother, being with her all these years, and you can't understand what it is about her that gets hold of a man?"

Willy bowed his head now; then his voice a mere murmur, he said, "I can't bear the thought of her having had so many men."

"Oh, you mustn't look at it that way, lad. Fact is, it isn't her who's had the men, t'other way round, they've had her, pursued her, persecuted her. One or two courted her, but they were few compared to the ones who would have liked to. Your mother is a unique woman, Willy, haven't you realised that? What do you think's kept me running after her, at her beck and call so to speak, since I was a lad?"

Willy slowly turned his disfigured face towards Steve and he peered at him for a moment before saying, "You're a good man, Steve. She's lucky to have you . . . for a friend. I've . . . I've often wondered why you haven't married her. I've thought perhaps it might be . . . well, the difference in position, but knowing that much about her I know she doesn't lay much stock on position . . . You've never married, Steve?"

"No, never."

"It's a pity, I think you should be."

"Yes, you're right, I should be, and I intend to be."

"Married?" There was a quick and interested movement of his face which caused Willy to wince and put his hand up to his cheek and, as the door opened, Steve was saying, "Yes, I hope to be married and not in the very far future. There's only one hindrance but I hope to overcome that."

The room was quiet again and Tilly placed the steak over the whole surface of Willy's right cheek, and it seemed a long time before anyone spoke, and then Willy, his tone quiet, said, "Steve has just been telling me he intends to be married."

"Yes, I know."

"You didn't say."

"Oh, it wasn't all that important."

The reply could have been taken as a slight insult or as merely an expression of ingratitude for a life of devotion, but to both the younger and the older man they conveyed neither of these things. Strangely, the same thought entered both their minds.

5

The instigator of Simon Bentwood's memorable visit to the manor was Randy Simmons. He had for some long time been looking for an opening through which to inform his master of what was going on between his daughter and "that one up there's son" without exposing himself as a peeping Tom, or of bringing himself further into the black books of his mistress, for Mrs Bentwood had made it plain right from the beginning that she didn't savour him or his ways. However, because he had been so long employed at the farm he knew he stood well with his master.

So when it should happen that a letter was placed in his hands he, later when explaining it to the mistress, put it in his own words that inadvertently the master had twigged it.

As Tilly's grandmother had often said to her, no big event ever came about of its own accord, it had to grow, and such events matured from little acts or coincidences or, as in this case, just the changing of a sailing time of a boat going to America.

Josefina was due to leave Liverpool on Thursday, the nine-teenth of June, but because of boiler repairs not being completed on the particular ship the passengers had been transferred to a sister ship sailing on the high tide last thing on Sunday night, June the fifteenth.

Willy, who, of course, would be accompanying Tilly to Liver-pool to see Josefina off, felt he must get word about the changed arrangements to Noreen. But how? He put it to Ned Spoke who had over the years become his friend and confidant, and it was Ned who said, "Well, Master Willy, there's nothing like a letter for explaining things. I'll get one there for you without the old boy seeing it. I mightn't do it first go off but I'm bound to get the attention of one or other of the ladies sooner or later."

But when Ned scouted the farm on his first visit he saw no one at all. Later the same day the only person he saw and the last one he wanted to encounter was Simon Bentwood himself. He was hobbling across the yard with the aid of a stick.

The following morning he rode past the gate and there met Randy Simmons. To him Randy was an old man, a good farm worker. He had heard nothing against him except that he chatted a lot in the village inn. But then all the old codgers chatted a lot when they had a pint of ale in them. In an off-hand manner he enquired of his master and mistress, and to this Randy replied, "Oh, all be gone into Shields. Me here, I'm king of the castle with only young Larry Fenwick to do me biddin', and he's as thick in the top thatch as a crumpled cow's horn."

"Would you do something for me?" Ned asked.

"Aye, aye, lad," Randy replied, "if it doesn't cost money."

"Would you give a letter to the young lass? It's private like, very private, you understand?"

Randy gazed up at the young fellow before grinning at him and saying "Oh aye, I understand, I understand a lot I do; nothing much escapes me. One eye over the fence and one ear under it, you learn a lot that way." He jerked his head towards Ned, who replied with the same gesture that they understood each other; at least that's what he thought when he handed the letter over.

Two hours later Randy Simmons, on entering the kitchen, happened to drop the letter from his apparently flustered hand as he encountered his master.

"What's that?" Simon demanded and Randy Simmons grabbed the letter up from the stone flags, muttering as he did so, "Nowt, master, just a letter."

"Well, if it's a letter, let me have it."

Randy placed the letter behind his back, saying, " 'Tain't for you, master."

" 'Tain't for me!" Simon repeated Randy's words, then held out his hands, adding, "What letters come into this house are for me. Let me have it!" With the appearance of genuine reluctance Simmons handed the letter over, and then the world had seemed to explode in that farmhouse kitchen.

Reading part of the letter aloud to his amazed and now really frightened wife, Simon Bentwood ground out, "My dear of dears, Ned will get this to you to tell you that, unfortunately, Josefina has to sail earlier than expected, so I shall be leaving on Saturday morning for Liverpool. But I shall be back on Tuesday."

He held the single sheet of paper in both hands and, in his rage, shook it as he glared at his wife. Then with heightening passion he ended, "My dearest dear, nothing or no one can separate us.

Just cling on to that. You are mine and I am yours for as long as we may live, and after. I shall be there on Tuesday night as usual. Until then, my love, your own Willy."

At this he crushed the letter in his hand as he screamed, "As long as you may live. And begod! Your time is short, Master William Sopwith. If I have anything to do with it your time is short," then he had made to rush out of the kitchen, but the cramp in his back caught him and he leant face forward against the wall and beat on it with his bare fists.

After some minutes during which he had continued to gasp with pain, he turned and, looking at Lucy, cried, "Where is she? Get her!"

It said a lot for Lucy's courage when, standing stiffly, she said, "Not until you calm down."

"You! You! woman." He brought himself with a great effort from the wall; then stumbling his way towards the dairy where Randy Simmons had already warned Noreen of impending dis-aster, having explained that it wasn't his fault, that he had been looking for her when he had come up with her father and became flustered.

Simmons had got no further with his mumbling apologies before the door burst open and without uttering a word Simon Bentwood grabbed his daughter by the collar of her dress and dragged her struggling and crying out into the yard and back into the kitchen; and there, throwing her into the old rocking-chair with such force that but for Lucy's hand it would have tipped over backwards, he bent above her bawling now into her face, "You dirty little strumpet you! To think I'm seeing you day in and day out and never guessed. I'm a bloody fool. Blind, like him. Well, listen to me, miss." He had grabbed the front of her dress and brought her upwards to him. "And listen hard. I'll see you dead first afore he comes within miles of you again, let alone touch you. Do you hear me? I'll kill him. Do you hear me? And happily swing for it afore I see you mixed up with that lot."

"Then . . . then you will . . . you will swing, because he's for me, and me for him, no matter what you say."

The blow from the flat of his hand knocked her backwards. And now Lucy was clawing at him, crying, "Leave her alone or I'll take the poker to you!"

"Out of me way, woman!" With one backward thrust of his arm he knocked his wife flying and almost overbalanced himself;

then hauling Noreen bodily out of the chair, he dragged her through the kitchen, across the hall and up the stairs. When she clung on to the bannisters he brought his free hand with such force across her wrist that she cried out. Kicking open the door of her room, he flung her inside and, looking at her where she fell, he cried at her, "And here you stay until I have your word, whether it be days, weeks or months. I'll feed and water you like an animal but you won't move from this room until you come to your senses."

On this he had gone out and turned the key in the lock. It was the first time in his memory that key had been turned and he had to use all his strength to wrench it around. And when it was done, he thrust it into his pocket and went outside, where he ordered Randy Simmons to saddle up the trap again. Then he made his way to the Manor.

6

Willy, after all, did not accompany Josefina to Liverpool. The doctor having diagnosed slight concussion ordered him to rest for some days, and it was when the doctor was examining him that Willy asked him a question. "Could a blow on my head improve my sight, I mean in the right eye?"

"Improve your sight?" The doctor pursed his lips, then said, "I doubt it."

"The last time you came about three weeks ago, I think it was when Lizzie Gamble broke her ankle, you were wearing this same suit were you not, doctor?"

The doctor looked down at his attire. "Yes. Yes, I suppose so," he said.

"I thought I detected a stripe in the material then. Rather unusual material, I thought, not . . . well, not a sober cloth, as it were."

"No, you could say that, not a sober cloth." The doctor smiled broadly.

"Well —" Willy put out his hand and drew a finger nail down one of the narrow stripes of the doctor's coat, saying "At that time I couldn't really distinguish the colour of the stripe, but now I can see it's blue on a grey background. Am I right?"

"Yes, you're right."

"Then that gives me the answer to the question I asked you. Could a blow on the head restore one's sight?"

"Ah! yes, yes. . . . But it may be only a temporary thing. As Doctor Blackman has already told you, in your right eye it's the nerves that are affected and bodily and mental strain can act on these. Then again, with the blow the retina could have been dislodged. And now moved again. I don't know."

"But I have received a bodily strain, so to speak, and either the eye nerves have been affected, in reverse to what he suggested, or the retina *has* moved again."

"Ah; yes, yes, could be perhaps." Again the doctor was nodding his head. "But I wouldn't rely too much upon the change."

"If it's only the nerves that are affected, couldn't I have an operation?"

"On the nerves at the back of the eye? Huh!" The doctor laughed now. "I doubt it. Nerves are funny things to play about with in any part of the body, but the eye is the most delicate. Still, let's see how long the improvements lasts, eh? and we might try spectacles again, although I know they were of little benefit to you before."

"Just as you say, doctor. By the way, shall I be able to travel, I mean will this dizziness go within the next day or so?"

"Oh no, no, there must be no talk of you travelling for at least a fortnight. What you must do now is rest."

So Willy said his good-byes to Josefina from his bedroom in the old nursery quarters where they had grown up together, and he was saddened to a depth that he hadn't imagined by the coming loss of her. The eruption on that particular Sunday some weeks ago was forgotten, at least by him, and he held her hands tightly as he looked at her, and with his improved vision he saw that she was very beautiful, exquisitely so. His throat was full as he said, and with a truth he was facing for the first time, "I'm going to miss you, Josefina, so, so very much."

She stared at him in silence. Her dark eyes were bright, seeming to give off a deep purple light. Her small mouth was pressed tight. But she didn't speak, and so he went on, "Why must you go? We have been so close all these years. If we *had* been brother and sister the tie between us couldn't have been stronger."

Now she opened her lips and her voice did not match her small, delicate frame but sounded deep and full of meaning as she said, "But we are *not* brother and sister. Mama, as she said, has had her doubts all these years, in fact she is convinced that her husband had nothing to do with the makings of me. But this I think has only come to her of late, whereas for me I have known since I passed out of childhood that I in no way belong to this race . . . your race."

"Oh, Josefina, don't say that. You'll always belong to us. You . . . you have a special place in my heart."

"Have I?"

"Yes, yes." He drew her hands towards his chest and pressed them there until she said with slow separated words, "But not special enough."

181

Both his eyes widened and the light that was without a hazy rim in his right eye saw the look in hers and slowly his hands released their hold on her and his head dropped forward while his mind cried, "No, no!" and his senses cried back at it, "Yes. Oh yes!" Josefina thinking of him in that way, and for how long? This was why she couldn't stand the thought of Noreen. Oh God! the complications and the hurts and the weight of guilt, for he knew now that he was responsible for her going.

She had risen from the side of the bed and helplessly he looked up at her and his next words sounded inane to his own ears as he said, "It . . . it needn't be good-bye, you could come back for a holiday or we —" His voice trailed off for he could not add, "Noreen and I could visit America."

She stood looking down at him for a moment, her expression holding a look of slight scorn mingled with sadness. "If I were contemplating coming back for a holiday," she said, "I wouldn't then be leaving now. As to you coming across there, that would be a waste of time, that's if you wanted to see me, for I don't intend to stay long on the ranch, I mean to find my own people. I won't be happy until I do, be they what they may. . . . Good-bye, Willy." She leaned forward and as he reached up to kiss her cheek she placed her lips fully on his. It was the first time it had happened and their touch was like a spark from a fire alighting on his mouth, and instinctively his arms went up and held her tightly, and she to him; then, her hands on his chest, she thrust him back on to the pillow and, head bent, she ran from the room.

Slowly he lay back and stared before him. Josefina feeling like that. . . . And how did he feel? He moved his head slowly. He couldn't explain how he felt. He only knew that he was sorry to the heart of him that she was going and that he would never see her again.

When his gaze moved round the room, the images were dimmed again with the moisture in his eyes. "I love Noreen," he said to himself. "Oh yes, I love Noreen." And there was no doubt in his mind but that he did love Noreen. Yet why was he feeling like this about Josefina for his instinct was urging him to get up and to dash down the stairs and beg of her, "Don't go. Don't go, Josefina."

You couldn't love two people, not really, not at the same time, and in the same way. It was impossible.

He could not take into consideration that he was his mother's son and had inherited her problem.

7

"Mam. Mam. Do something, will you?"

"I will, lass, as soon as I can."

They were each kneeling on the floor speaking through the keyhole.

"I'll go mad if I have to stay here much longer."

"If you give him your word he'd let you out."

"I can't do that."

"Don't be ridiculous, girl; pretend, say you will, swear you will, and then once outside I'll get you away. I've got it all ready, I mean some things packed, and money for you."

"Oh, Mam!" There was silence for a moment. Then Noreen's voice came tear-laden and trembling through the keyhole of the stout oak door, saying, "Go to the police, Mam; they could make him let me out."

"No, lass, no! I've gone into that. It's a private matter. A father is allowed to chastise his daughter, that's what the constable said."

"Mam, I'm smelling, I haven't had a decent wash. It's . . . it's thirteen days since I've been in here and my slop bucket's full again."

Lucy turned her eyes towards the stairs and put her head to one side as if she were listening; but it was not for her husband coming home because he had just gone off to the market after having opened this door and thrust a meal inside.

This morning he had not brought any washing water because he was in a hurry. Whenever he did bring her a ewer he would shout through the door for Noreen to stand back, and do the same whenever he brought her an empty pail and took the full one out.

It was the full bucket of slops that Lucy was seeing in her mind's eye as she looked towards the staircase. Turning her head sharply back to the keyhole, she said, "Listen, Noreen, listen. Now pay attention. He'll have had a drink when he comes in but he won't be full; he's wise enough not to overdo it because then I might get the chance to search him for the key. He's slept in the other back room since he put you in there. Now pay attention. I'll tell him you must have your slop bucket emptied. Now have it in your hand when he opens the door and make to put it on the floor within reaching distance of him, then swing it up and let him have it over him . . . Do you hear?"

"The slops?"

"Yes, yes."

"Right, Mam. Right."

"Then make for the door. I'll do my best to keep it wide. When you get downstairs go through the front room, I'll leave the right-hand window open, make for the cow field and the bottom gate. . . . You listening?"

"Yes, yes, Mam. Go on, go on."

"Well, go to the old barn at the bottom, I'll leave the bass hamper of your clothes there and enough money to keep you going for some weeks. Make for the Jarrow turnpike. It's not far from there to the terminus where you'll get the horse bus. Do you follow me?"

"Yes, Mam, yes."

"He'll never think about you going that way, he'll think you'll go straight to the Manor. But for God's sake, girl, if you value that young lad's life, don't go near that place. Do you hear me?"

There was a pause before Noreen's voice came to her, saying, flatly, "I hear you, Mam."

"And you promise you won't go there?"

"I can promise you that, Mam."

"Because you know he'll kill this time, don't you?"

Again there was a pause before her daughter said, "Yes, I know that. But I'll tell you something, Mam. If I had a knife in here the night instead of a bucket of slops I'd drive it into him. I would, I would."

"Oh, Noreen, Noreen, don't say that. He's acting like this because of his feelings for you."

"Huh! feelings. It's not feelings for me, Mam, that's caused him to be mad, and you know it. He must have had some outsize opinion of himself when young and couldn't imagine anyone passing him over. He still can't. . . . You know what's the trouble with him?"

"Enough. Enough. Listen. Listen."

"I'm listenin', Mam."

"When you get to Newcastle take a cab to Garden Crescent. Have you got that?"

"Yes, Mam."

"There's a boarding house. It's respectable, it's run by a Mrs Snaith. Remember that, the name's Snaith. 2 Garden Crescent. Oh, if only I could get something under this door." Lucy now actually clawed at the carpet that was tight against the bottom of the door. Although worn with constant rubbing it was still impossible to slip a piece of paper over it and beneath the door.

"It's all right, Mam. Mrs Snaith, 2 Garden Crescent, Newcastle. I'll remember."

"And don't write me, lass, not here. Write to him and tell him he must never try to see you 'cos you're going to start a new life. . . . And you'll have to. You understand that?"

Lucy waited for confirmation of this, and when none came she said, "Noreen! Noreen! you've got to forget him. If you want him to remain alive you've got to forget him. Get it into your head, lass."

"If I ask him to come away with me he would, Mam."

"Oh, come down from your cloud, lass, how would he earn a living away from the Manor?"

"He wouldn't need to, he'll have money of his own."

"Not until he comes of age, lass. And then all these things are complicated. I think it's the mother who holds the purse strings there, and she's sheltered him all his life."

"He's no weakling, Mam. You don't know him."

"All right, he's no weakling, but he's an almost blind man, and how long do you think romance will last living a hole and corner life? You're sensible, you've always been sensible. He's been brought up as a gentleman; you yourself could rough it and your feelings remain the same, but it's different for a man, I'm telling you, I know. They are full of self-importance, from the smallest to the biggest. Aw lass' – she finished in a tearful voice – "put him out of your mind. There are others in the world who will jump at you. You're young, this will pass."

When no answering voice came through the keyhole, Lucy got to her feet and stood leaning against the support of the door for a moment, her eyes closed, her head bowed. Then bending again, she put her mouth to the keyhole and said, "Put on as much clean underwear as you can," after which she turned and opened the door of the wardrobe on the landing where most of Noreen's clothes were kept because the bedroom with its sloping roof would not allow of such a large piece of furniture, and taking from it a coat and a working cloak, she went downstairs and began to prepare for her daughter's escape.

On his return, Simon Bentwood was slow in getting down from the trap. Lucy watched him from the kitchen window and noted with relief that he was impeded as much by his back as by the drink he had taken.

With regard to the latter she was informed of the amount almost immediately for Eddie, scurrying into the kitchen, whispered, "He hasn't had a lot, Mam, three pints and two whiskys. I was watching from the window. It's his back; he could hardly get up into the trap."

Lucy made no answer but stood waiting for her husband's entry. The moment he entered the door she could see that he was suffering great pain for he had difficulty in lifting one foot over the step into the kitchen. Without comment, she watched him take off his hat and outer coat; then he sat down at the table, and cast his eyes over the bare boards before raising them to Lucy and saying, "What's this?"

She answered straightaway, "I'm not making any more meals in this house until that girl is cleaned up and is properly fed. She hasn't had a bite since breakfast, and worse, the room's stinking, her bucket is overflowing. If you don't come to your senses soon she'll die of a fever."

He stared at her. Then, his tone without anger, even moderate sounding and slightly weary, he said, "She could be out of there within minutes if she gave me her word, but until she does there she stays and nobody can do anything about it. Do you hear that, Lucy? Nobody can do anything about it. I'm her father and it's within my power to keep her under control as long as I like."

She bowed her head and remained silent for a moment, and then said. "Will you give her a clean bucket?"

When he made no reply she looked at him and with raised

voice cried, "Well, if you can't make the stairs let me take one to her."

The very suggestion seemed to lift him from the chair, and when he was standing straight he said, "Bring it to me!"

Immediately she went into the scullery and brought an empty pail, but as she handed it to him he said, "Give it to the boy."

This was a contingency for which she wasn't prepared; nevertheless she handed the bucket to Eddie and when his father pointed towards the door the boy went before him into the hall and up the stairs. It was a good minute later when Simon joined his son for he'd had to place two feet on every stair before being able to make the next one.

Now he was standing outside the door. Slowly he put his hand into his back pocket and, taking out a key, placed it in the lock. He paused a moment, then turning the key he pushed open the door, stood for a second before reaching out towards Eddie and grabbing the empty pail from his hand, then taking three steps into the room he faced his daughter. Her face was deathly pale, almost haggard looking, her eyes wide, staring, and her lips quivering.

Simon swallowed deeply, cleared his throat noisily, then said, "Well, are you going to see sense, girl?"

When she didn't answer, only stared defiantly back at him, he thrust his hand behind him and said, "Come and take the pail, boy."

Now Noreen's gaze flashed to her mother standing on the landing, then bending swiftly she picked up the pail and as Eddie approached her she screamed at him, "Out of the way!" and at the same time she heaved it upwards and threw the contents at the man before her.

Simon, aware of her intention just a second too late, had thrust out his arm towards her but when the avalanche of filth spewed over him he let out a most inhuman cry, staggered backwards, slipped, and with arms flailing in an effort to catch hold of something to break his fall he fell flat on his back and with an agonising groan lay there.

Noreen did not even see him fall for she was out of the door, past her mother and down the stairs; nor did Lucy go to the aid of her husband but, running after her daughter, she hissed, "Don't forget the address. And pick up your cloak." Noreen did not wait to give an answer to her mother. Like an escaping prisoner, as she certainly was, she flew through the sitting-room and out of the window, and as swift as any hare she made her way to the old barn where would lie her passport to freedom, freedom her mother would never have provided her with if she had known what she was carrying inside her.

8

"Mama. . . . Mama! please, please, be quiet. It's no use talking any more. I mean to go over there and find out what's happening to her. I went along with you last week when you asked me to wait, I've gone along with you this week when you've begged me to wait, but I can wait no longer. Unless she was tied up she would have got word to me in some way, I know she would. She's strong-willed, determined if you like."

Tilly sank down slowly on to the couch and, taking a handkerchief from the pocket of her dress, she wiped the beads of sweat from her brow.

It had been hot all day, in fact June had been behaving as one expected it to do for the past two weeks; there had been no rain, the sun had shone all day long and the nights seemed to be almost as hot as the days.

All the windows on the ground floor of the manor were open, yet no breeze stirred through the house.

She brought the handkerchief round her lips and, reaching out, picked up a glass of sherbet from the table and sipped at it. After replacing the glass on the table again she moved her lips slowly one over the other before she said, "What you don't seem to understand, Willy, is that Simon Bentwood is capable of killing, and rather than have you have his daughter I'm sure he will attempt it, even knowing the consequences of such an act."

"Mama" – he was bending down towards her now – "why did you have me trained in wrestling?"

When she looked up at him and made no reply he demanded, his voice almost on a shout now, "Go on, tell me, tell me why you had me trained to defend myself."

"Don't shout at me, Willy!" Even as she said the words she was surprised that she had to speak in such a way to this son who up to a few short weeks ago she had deemed to be the most even-tempered creature in the world, and when he slowly straightened his back and stood rigid before her she looked up at him and said patiently, "Willy, you are dealing with a madman. How can I get that home to you? Simon Bentwood has become unbalanced." She now put her hand out towards him and, gripping his wrist, she said, "Do one more thing for me: wait until you hear from Steve. You said yesterday he was going to make enquiries."

"I'm sorry, Mama, I can't. I can't stand another day without knowing what's happened to her. Do you know that I haven't slept for nights?"

No, she hadn't known that, but she used his words now, saying, "Well, if that is the case, you're in no fit condition to meet up with that raving lunatic of a man." Her voice had risen now, and she pulled herself to her feet and as she did so there was a tap on the drawing-room door. It opened, and Biddle stood there and announced solemnly. "Mr McGrath to see you, ma'am."

Tilly did not move towards Steve as he entered the room but Willy did. His hand guiding him along the back of the couch, his face slightly to the side, he hurried towards the mist-shrouded figure and as Tilly watched his hand go out to Steve, and Steve take it firmly within his and turn him about, then guide him back towards her, she experienced the grinding rib cage pain again which had nothing to do with her son's unhappiness but which recalled the words he had said to her some time ago: "At one time, I thought he was my father."

It was the first time she had seen Steve to speak to privately since their interrupted conversation. She had seen him twice since, both times he was on horseback and in the company of . . . the woman. And on the second occasion she knew that he had deliberately turned off the main coach road to avoid meeting her.

Acting the hostess, she said, "Can I get you something to drink, Steve?"

To her surprise he accepted the invitation, saying, "That would be welcome at the moment, Tilly. A beer, if that is possible."

Yes, a beer would be possible, and from the cellar too, but it wasn't usually drunk in the drawing-room. However, marriage into the Drew family had so much altered Biddle's attitude that the request he should serve the guest with beer in this room would register no effect on his expression.

As she rang the bell Willy was saying to Steve, "Have you heard anything?" and before the door opened Steve had answered,

"Yes. Yes, I have." But once Biddle had entered the room he did not speak again; not until Tilly had said to Biddle, "Will you please draw a fresh flagon of ale from the cellar and bring a platter of bread and cheese at the same time?" and the door had closed on the butler did he look from one to the other and say, "I must warn you that it isn't pleasant news."

Willy made no comment, and Steve went on, "If one is to believe Randy Simmons's chat he's, I mean Bentwood's, got her locked up in her bedroom and she's been there for the past fortnight,"

"*No! No!*" Willy turned about hastily and made to walk towards the open window, and when he stumbled against the chair and it toppled over, Steve, rising hastily, made to go to his aid, but Tilly's hand on his sleeve stayed him, and when he looked at her she shook her head.

Now they both watched Willy swing around as he cried, "Well, this is it! I'm going over there. Will . . . will you come with me, Steve?"

When there was no direct reply Willy shouted, "All right! All right! I'll go on my own, but go I will."

"Hold your hand a minute, wait. Wait. Come and sit down." And saying so, Steve went towards him and drew him back to the middle of the room and pressed him down into a chair. He himself sat on the edge of the couch and, leaning forward, he gripped Willy's knee as he said, "You've got to go careful in this business, Willy. If you barge into his house, even into his farm-yard, and he does you a mischief you won't get much sympathy or even justice, you'll be at fault."

"I don't want sympathy, and if there's any justice the police should go to the house and lock him up."

"Now! now! wait. Put your studying cap on and think it out. It's a private matter; she's his daughter. What does she want to do? Well, she wants to run off with a young man. Now he doesn't see eye to eye with her about this, so what does he do? He locks her in her room. The same thing's been done countless times before, Willy, in an effort to make young lasses come to their senses."

"She's . . . she's not just a young lass, she's a very sensible person, clear headed . . . she thinks. . . ."

"Well, if that's the case she'll likely think of a way out of this situation. Look; will you leave the matter in my hands for another day or two? I'll take a walk round there and when he's in the fields, Bentwood I mean, I'll try to have a word with her mother." His voice now went into a gritty growl as he added, "And at the same time I'll collar Mr Randy Simmons and threaten to choke the life out of him if he carries any more tales. He's an old rat that fellow. He was a mischief-maker when I was a lad and the years haven't improved him. Well now, what do you say?"

"What's that? Aw no!" Tilly looked towards the door. They all looked towards the door from where beyond in the hall there came a sound as if Biddle had dropped the tray and the glass had splintered. But when there followed a commotion of scuffling and muddled voices, Tilly glanced quickly at Steve and he at her. Then they both ran towards the drawing-room door. But before they reached it, it was opened, not thrust open, but kicked open, and there, like an infuriated bull, stood the man who was in all of their minds.

"Where is she? Come on! Where is she?"

"Now, look here, Mr Bentwood." Steve had taken a step forward, only to be checked by Simon Bentwood's voice bawling, "You keep out of this, McGrath, this has nothing to do with you. Or then perhaps it has, you being her fancy man."

The echo of his last word had scarcely died away before Steve had sprung over the distance between them. But all Bentwood's faculties were alert, the drink had worn off, his back for the moment had eased as it was apt to do at times, helped he had imagined by the cold sluice he had given himself under the pump to rid his body of the stink and filth of the slop bucket; so he met Steve's attack not with his fists but with his boot. Bringing it sharply forward he caught him in the groin and sent him reeling to the side in agony. Then he was in the drawing-room and advancing to where Willy was waiting for him, his body stiff, his arms slightly bent, his head turned well to the side.

The pose checked Simon Bentwood's onslaught and within an arm's length he stopped and again he bawled, "Where is she?"

Before Willy could answer, Tilly's voice broke in, crying, "She's not here. Your daughter's not here."

Simon Bentwood did not take his eyes from the young man before him and again he demanded, "Where is she? You dare to stand there and tell me she's not here, go on!"

"*She's . . . not . . . here.*" The words were spaced and firm; then Willy added more to them: "But if she were here, I can assure you I wouldn't let you near her."

"You! you blind son of a bitch of hell." Now it was he who sprang, his right hand extended in the act of delivering a blow. But surprisingly it didn't reach its target and there was no one more amazed than Bentwood when he found himself spun round, his arms wrenched behind him and into a grip like that of a vice while a knee found the sorest spot on his spine, and, his body bent over, he was forced to groan aloud.

In the seconds it had taken this to happen, Tilly had raced from the room past Biddle and Peabody, who were attending to Steve, and it was only seconds again before she returned and, looking to where her son was still holding Simon Bentwood, she shouted, "Let him go. Let him go, Willy."

Willy could only dimly see the outline of his mother standing in the middle of the room. For the moment his vision seemed to have worsened and he imagined she was standing holding a gun to her shoulder. Her voice confirmed his dimmed image, for she now cried again, "Let him go, and if he dares to raise a finger to you I'll shoot him."

Slowly Willy relinquished his hold on the big, flabby figure and he could see enough to know the man stumbled some steps forward and groped for the support of the back of a high chair. He saw him straighten his back, then look slowly around the room.

Perhaps it was not only the sight of Tilly standing levelling a gun at him that raised the fury in Bentwood but the fact that she seemed surrounded by all her lackeys, for besides the two flunkeys three outside men were standing by her now. Two of them he recognised as the Drew fellows. And then there were the women crowding round the door, a host of them, all ready to defend her and her blind brat.

He fixed his gaze on Tilly now, then on a bitter laugh he cried, "You would shoot me, would you? If I remember rightly you used to be against guns at one time, wouldn't hear of a rabbit being potted. But that was afore you crossed the seas and became a squaw. Did you shoot Sopwith afore he shot you for mixing it with the blackies? . . ."

The report of the gun startled him and lifted him from the ground for the bullet had passed through the pad of his coat taking the skin off his shoulder with it and had lodged itself in the panelling near the window behind him.

In the stillness that pervaded the room he put his fingers inside his jacket, and when he pulled them out they were wet. He stared at them for a moment, then looked towards her. She had the gun cocked again. She had shot him, Tilly Trotter had shot him. She could have killed him. Perhaps she meant to kill him. He wanted to say something but he was too shaken and he stood with his hand extended in front of him listening to her saying, "I aimed for your shoulder. Now I'll give you exactly five minutes to clear my grounds, and should you ever enter them again, Simon Bentwood, I won't aim for your shoulder next time. One more thing, from this moment I give you twelve months' notice to quit your farm. . . . Arthur. Jimmy." She did not look towards the men as she spoke but went on, "See that this man leaves my property."

When Jimmy and Arthur Drew approached him, Simon Bentwood, as if coming out of a dream, growled at them, "Keep your place, you two. She hasn't finished me off yet; I'm still capable of dealing with lackeys."

"Arthur."

The command checked Arthur Drew from taking the battle further.

Simon Bentwood now moved from behind the chair and in passing down the middle of the room he had to come within two yards of Tilly and he paused for a moment as he glared at her and he said, "I'll make a case of this, shooting's an offence. There'll be no one to meet you coming out of court this time. There's still justice here, and I'll see you along the line yet."

Although she knew that his threat was empty because he was trespassing and had forced an entry into her house, she shivered as she recalled her ordeal the first time she had been in a court; and it was true, he had met her, he had been there to comfort her. He had been the only one to comfort her. But she couldn't imagine that the bulky form walking slowly through the door was one and the same man as the kindly thoughtful young Simon Bentwood. It was terrible to acknowledge the fact that love could have such power as to change a man into what Simon had become.

The room began to buzz: the girls were around her, Peg, Fanny, Lizzy, Betty, and Christine Peabody. "Are you all right, ma'am? Are you all right, ma'am?"

"Yes, yes, I'm all right. Bring in some tea and . . . whisky," she said to Peg, and to the others she said, "Yes, yes, I'm all right. Just leave us."

She placed the gun on the table and as her hands left hold of it she clasped them together in an effort to stop them trembling, before walking down the room to where Willy was standing beside Steve. Peabody and Biddle were still present and it was Peabody who said, "I . . . I think, madam, that Mr McGrath should have attention."

She had to lean right down in order to see Steve's face for he was bent over, one arm still hugging his waist.

"Is it bad?"

He made no answer, not even to move his head, and so she turned to Biddle and Peabody and said quietly. "Can you assist him upstairs to the grey suite?"

"Yes, yes, ma'am."

One on each side of him, they went to help him up, but he shrugged them off; and Willy, moving to the front of him, said quietly, "Once you get straight you'll be able to walk, Steve. Look, lift your arms."

Steve slowly raised his head and looked up at Willy and did what he was bid; and Willy, linking his forearms under Steve's oxters, gently brought him upwards, then placing one hand firmly on the bottom of his spine he pressed it, saying, "That better?"

Steve gave him a sickly smile now as he said, "Yes. Strangely it is."

"Phil Spoke knew a trick or two."

"He must have," Steve nodded at him; then looking at Tilly he asked, "You all right?"

"Yes." There was a slight quiver to her voice but she repeated, "Yes, I'm all right. Can you manage the stairs?"

"Thanks all the same, but if you don't mind I'd rather make for home."

"But I think you should be attended to."

"It'll . . . it'll just be a bruise. Winded me for a time." He nodded at her.

She stared at him, then said, "Very well, but you won't be able to ride." She turned to Biddle now. "Tell Myers to bring the coach round as soon as possible;" then turning again towards Steve, she took his arm, saying, "Come and sit down."

Slowly and stiffly Steve walked up the room, but when Tilly indicated the sofa he shook his head, saying, "I think I'll be better standing, if you don't mind."

She looked at him now in deep concern. "I wish you'd stay and let me see to you."

"Don't worry about me, I'm used to managing. It's yourself you've got to think about." With this, he turned to where Willy was standing near him and, moving his head slowly he said, "Now have you changed your mind about letting your friends deal with that maniac?"

Willy did not answer but facing his mother and Steve, he said slowly, "She must have got away. Why didn't she come here to me?"

"Well, I should have thought that was obvious, lad, she knew she would endanger you."

"Where could she have gone?" He turned his dim gaze from one to the other, and when neither of them spoke he said, "I'll find her. She can't have gone all that far, she wouldn't know how for she's never been further than Newcastle in her life."

As Tilly looked at her son she hoped from the depths of her heart that his search would be in vain because instinctively she knew that if he were to find her he wouldn't enjoy her for long. One way or another, Simon would see to that, for she wouldn't always be there with a gun.

9

The village was agog. My God! she had started again, that one up there. She had shot the farmer now, and him just going asking if she had seen his daughter. And her fancy man going for him! Well, Farmer Bentwood had seen to him, laid him on his back for close on a week he had, almost put an end to his whoring too, so it was said. But to think she would actually take a gun up and shoot the farmer, him that had been so kind to her in her young days. Why, she had been the cause of his first wedding going wrong; hadn't she made a scene on his very wedding night, when he'd gone running to her aid and left his bride soured.

Old Mrs McGrath, now a toothless hag, retold the tale for the hundredth time to her grandson, even going as far as to brag it was her hand that had taken the light from the witch's bastard's eyes. But her own son had warned her an equal number of times to stop her chattering, and he warned her now to keep the door closed and her voice down when she spoke of that 'un up there, because, say what you like, she had power. It had already been proved in both ways in their very own family; hadn't she killed one of them off and raised another to a position he would never have reached on his own, for what had that young snipe learned in a pit that he himself and his brothers hadn't. Looking back, he reminded his mother that her youngest son hadn't had a word to say for himself when a lad, timid he had been, skinny, undersized, and look at him now, six foot if an inch and broad with it, and learned they said, book read, and spoke no more like the rest of them. Now who but one with a strange power could have brought that about? he asked his mother yet again, so it behoved her to speak in whispers when she was alluding to that 'un.

The day following the events at the Manor Randy Simmons brought the news to his master that his daughter had been seen tearing towards the turnpike road the night before, and the same pair of eyes had watched her wave down the horse bus before it

197

reached the turnpike; and she had been alone except for a bass hamper that she carried.

After hearing this news, Simon Bentwood looked for his wife and found her in the dairy, her arms turning the wheel of the churn. She didn't stop her work when he came and stood close beside her. Putting out his left hand, for his right one was hanging stiffly by his side, he gripped her free arm and said, "You manoeuvred it, eh?"

Lucy stopped wielding the churn handle and, taking up a large wooden spoon from the bench to the side of her, she brought it down sharply across the knuckles that were gripping her flesh.

At this, he almost screamed at her, "Go on! woman, put my other one out of action. Is that what you're aiming at?"

She walked away from him, placing the churn between them, and then she said, "Yes, if you handle me in such a fashion again, yes. And aye, I did manoeuvre it. I wasn't going to see you drive my daughter mad up in that slit of a room, so I told her what to do. Throw filth over him, I said, because what was in her bucket would match your mind."

"Be careful, woman! careful. I warn you."

"You can warn me of nothing, Simon Bentwood, no more, no more. I've put up with you for years because I loved you. I've lived with the fact that your mind was on that woman every minute of your waking hours and I tolerated it because, as I said, I loved you. But no more, after the way you've treated your daughter and aimed to break her spirit into submission because you couldn't bear to think that she would find happiness with the son of the woman that spurned you. I could see you dead to-morrow and not mourn." She paused now and stared into his face. His brows were beetling, yet the expression on his face seemed to express more pain than rage, and when she ended, "I never in my life imagined I would say those words to you, but they're true. And I will add to them this: from now on I'm no longer your wife. I'll cook and clean and work, but I'll no longer share your bed, not ever again. You'll have to find solace elsewhere, Simon, to ease the hunger in your heart, but it'll never again come from me."

She ran her hands down each side of her white apron before ending, "Now if you'll leave me I'll finish the butter, but if you don't then you can get your henchmen to come and do it for you." She watched his lips part slowly, his mouth open wide as if gasping at the air. She waited for him to speak but no words came. His lips closed, he made an attempt to straighten his back; then winced inwardly at the pain before turning away and walking slowly out.

She did not turn to watch his going but, gripping the handle of the churn again, she swung it down and up; and now her own mouth was open wide and the salt tears were raining from her eyes down into it.

Tilly visited Steve on each of the first three days after the incident at the house. She had wanted to attend him but he had pushed her off as if she were a young girl who had never witnessed bare flesh, so she arranged for Peter Myers to see to him. But it was from the doctor she derived the extent of the injury Steve had received. The impact had split open his groin almost two inches and it had to be stiched; moreover, his whole hip was bruised.

Tilly had arranged for Fanny to ride over in the trap, taking a hot meal to him and, whilst there, to tidy the cottage. She would like to have carried out the latter duties herself, and doubtless would have done if Willy hadn't been claiming most of her time.

Willy had become a problem. Never had she imagined this quiet son of hers could become so intense and show such determination. In a strange way she could see Matthew in him, for Matthew's one aim in life had been to conquer herself; it seemed now that this trait had also developed fast in Willy. He was more like Matthew's son than Mark's but, of course, she should not be surprised at any traits that made their appearance in her son that resembled those in Matthew, for were they not half-brothers?

Willy was determined to find Noreen, and his main idea was that the best place to look for her would be in Newcastle. But he couldn't search alone, and so without even asking his mother's leave he had ordered Ned Spoke to take him in, not on just one or two occasions but every day. He had not even enquired if she would need the coach. This annoyed her, and so she brought it into the open on the evening of the fifth day.

It was almost dark when he returned. She had gone to the drawing-room door to watch him entering the hall and she saw by the way he walked and the groping movement of his hands held out before him, that his sight at this stage must be very dim, and so she directed him towards her, saying, "Have you had anything to eat?"

He lifted his head and, walking more steadily now, he crossed to her, saying, "Yes, we had a bite around teatime."

She looked from his pale, dust-covered face to his equally dust-covered suit, which spoke of the miles he must have tramped round the city, and certainly not in the main thoroughfare, and she had the desire to put her arms about him and comfort him, while at the same time she knew, should she do so, she would be seeing the boy he once was and not the man he had become.

She walked just ahead of him, her voice leading him into the middle of the room and to the couch, and there she said, "What will you have? Some soup and cold meats?"

"No, no, I want nothing to eat, but . . . but I'd like a drink, a whisky."

The surprise she felt she didn't show in her voice as she repeated, "A whisky?" He hadn't been a spirit drinker, not even a wine drinker, if he drank anything it was the usual ale.

She had rung the bell and Biddle had brought in the tray and decanter. She sat down on the couch and, following a moment's silence, she said, "This can't go on, Willy."

"Why not?"

"For so many reasons." She turned her body towards him and her voice was sharp now: "You'll wear yourself out. Moreover, Ned is wanted here, as is the coach. You did not even ask if I might need it."

There was silence again for a time before he answered, "No, I didn't because I thought you would understand. Anyway, I would think I was past the stage where I've got to ask permission to use the coach. As for Ned, I was under the impression that you gave him me as a guide years ago. He is my man."

If in the future were she to try to pin-point the time when her boy finally went from her, she knew it was now on this beautiful June evening, two days after his twentieth birthday with the scent floating in from the garden, with the air still and the house quiet and seemingly at peace. That love that was tearing at her son had thrust itself between them, severing the bond that had linked them from his birth, and with this knowledge the pall of aloneness settled on her once more. Had there still been Steve in the background waiting, his patience of years proving his stability, the pain would not have been so acute.

Josefina gone, Steve gone, and now Willy. What was it about her that time and again thrust her out into the wilderness? What had begun it all, this thing that caused her to be misjudged, ostracised, that caused men to love her and hate her and often brought death in its wake? Money . . . yes, money. She felt herself nodding at this realisation. It was as if for the first time her eyes had been opened and she saw from where stemmed her fate, the stolen money, stolen by the McGraths, and discovered by her grandfather and taken from its hiding place by him and Simon Bentwood's father and hidden in the well of the farm. And it was she herself who, as a child, innocently revealed to old woman McGrath, Steve's mother, that she possessed a sovereign, a sovereign to go shopping with when it was known that her grandfather had never worked for years, and they were supposed to live from hand to mouth. From that day the McGraths had planned to recover what they thought was theirs, and when all else failed Hal McGrath had determined to get his hands on the money by marrying her. That had been the beginning. And yet not quite: There had been her desire too to read and write. This had brought her within the vision of the parson's wife, and the parson's wife, who was young at heart, had besides teaching her her letters, taught her how to dance, and with dancing the image of the witch had been born. And it was strange when she came to think of it, she had never danced since. She was now fifty years old and she had never danced. She had faintly hoped to do so on that New Year's Eve years ago, but that was the night the mine had been flooded, and that was the night Steve first kissed her as they stood together watching the New Year come in.

"Will you want the carriage tomorrow?"

"What?"

"I said will you want the carriage tomorrow?"

"No, no."

"I can go in the trap, it makes no difference."

"No; take whichever you want."

"I'm sorry."

"It's all right . . . Go to bed. I'm going up too."

Willy pulled himself to his feet and when he was facing her he said slowly, "I can't help myself, Mama, I wish I could, but she's . . . she's all I want from life. It's odd, the feeling she creates in me when I'm with her, it's . . . it's as if I'd come home. I can't explain it. I . . . I understand how Josefina wanted to return to Texas."

He stopped speaking and turned his head to the side now as if Josefina had suddenly appeared, and he recalled a dream that had been vivid in the night, but had escaped him on awakening leaving only a vague, confused feeling. But now he was remembering it, because in his dream he had been searching in an unknown place and it wasn't for Noreen but for Josefina. He put his hand to his head. Sometimes over the last few days he had thought he wasn't only going stone blind but stone mad.

When he felt the touch on his arm he allowed himself to be led from the room and up the stairs. All his life he had been led here and guided there, and he now felt a fierce urge to throw off the arm that he had leaned on for years and scream to the gods to give him light, at least light enough that he would never need hers or anyone's guiding hand again.

10

During the weeks that followed and slipped into months there grew in Tilly a feeling of helpless despair as she watched her son get into the coach that was to take him to Newcastle or Gateshead or Sunderland or Durham. His search had taken the form of a mania; he had become the object of gossip to the extent that bets were laid on his finding young Noreen Bentwood before her father did, because it was well known that Simon too was searching, not so frequently perhaps but with more advantage.

During the last two weeks however, there had been days when the carriage had not gone out and Willy had stayed at home and spent the time in his rooms or walking in the gardens. He could do this alone because he knew every path and turn up to where the land drifted away into fields.

These days had brought relief, she knew, to Ned Spoke, for she guessed he had become weary tramping the streets, his eyes continually searching. But when she had questioned him about the procedure he had made no word of complaint for she knew he was devoted to Willy. This the young man demonstrated when once she said to him, "See that he gets a good meal when he's out, Ned," to which he had replied, "He won't go into an hotel, ma'am, because you see I can't sit with him, my being dressed as I am. And then I'd be like a fish out of water eating in them places, so it's usually rough grub, pies and peas, or pork dips an' such, but it's fillin' an' wholesome and he eats." And he added, "Well, he knows he's got to, ma'am, if he wants to go on."

Occasionally Steve would relieve Ned. At least on half a dozen Sundays he had acted as Willy's guide. The last time was the Sunday just gone. It had been a very wet day. September was nearing October, the trees had turned, the grass was yellowing and the land was getting ready for the winter, and on their return Steve had remarked on this, saying to her, "Something 'll have to happen to put a stop to this afore the winter sets in or you're going to have a sick man on your hands, Tilly."

When she had said, "But what can I do?" his answer had been, "I don't know, I don't know. What has to be done he'll do himself I suppose." And then he added, "The pity of it is he thinks if he doesn't have her he'll never have anyone. He can't imagine anyone else wanting him, not in his condition. This is what make the whole thing so very difficult. I've told him, or words to the effect, that there's more fish in the sea than have ever been caught, but that slid off him."

More fish in the sea than have ever been caught. He must have come to the same conclusion with regard to his own affairs. He himself had picked on another fish, hadn't he?

Since this business of Willy's daily treks had come about, Steve had made no further reference either to the woman or to marriage, but she knew it must be very much on his mind because she had seen the woman at the cottage twice during the week he had been ill. Her horse standing at the gate had been the cause of her turning her own animal about and riding back home. On another occasion Fanny had told her, "I didn't stay to do anything, ma'am, because the lady was there again."

Fanny hadn't said the woman, but the lady, and Fanny knew a lady when she saw one.

Tilly knew it in herself that she dreaded meeting Steve's "lady", and because of this she generally took a different route when going to the mine. Here, she saw him at least once a week when on a Friday he, his under-man, John, and herself held their meeting in the new office buildings she'd had erected. Previously Willy had made the fifth member at the meeting, but no longer, and his absence would be commented upon by John as if it were the first time he had not put in an appearance.

John, as dear as he was, could be very irritating at times, Tilly found, especially when he voiced openly what he thought of Willy's behaviour. Inconsiderate to say the least. And the whole thing lacked dignity. Chasing a farm girl! Well, that's what it amounted to, didn't it? She didn't come back at him and say that if Anna had been a farmer's daughter and had shown an interest in him at the time when he imagined that no one would ever want him or love him because of his stammer he, too, would have done the same as Willy was doing now, for she knew from experience that the years dimmed memories of failings and one's reactions to them. That was why the old could never understand the young.

*

Then came the day when Tilly met Steve's lady. It was at the beginning of November. She herself was feeling at a very low ebb for she had nursed Willy through a severe cold that had bordered on pneumonia. One good thing had come out of this, for now he seemed to realise how fruitless his search was. He was physically weak and mentally dispirited and on this particular morning when the post arrived she was glad to see two of the letters were from abroad. One was in Katie's handwriting, the other Josefina's.

Over the last few weeks she had dealt with her mail at a small desk she'd had placed in Willy's bedroom, and now entering the room, she said cheerfully as she held up the mail, "Two letters from Texas."

"Oh?" His interest sounded as weak as he looked. She did not immediately open the letters but went to the fire and, taking up the tongs, placed more coal on it. Then pulling her chair towards the brass fender, she placed her feet on the rim, reached out to the desk to the side of her and picked up the first letter. It was Katie's, and it began simply:

"Dear Tilly, I take pleasure in answering your letter. I am pleased to say I am very well at present and so is Doug. Miss Luisa, too, is well, although she misses Mr Mack very much. We all miss him very much, Doug most of all I think, but as my ma would have said, Tilly, one's sorrow can be another's joy. Which isn't a very nice thing to say at this time, but you see it's like this, Miss Luisa has taken Doug into partnership, and that is a big thing, isn't it, Tilly? Just fancy, Doug in partnership on this ranch. But, of course, he's taken it as another excuse for not coming to England because since fencing off the land there's thousands of heads of cattle to be seen to. Eeh! its a sight, Tilly . . . the drives. And to think there wasn't a single head of anything left after the war. I said to Doug the other day, you would enjoy it, the riding; as for meself, you know me. Tilly, I'm not built for a horse.

"Now about Miss Josefina. Well, like I told you in my last letter, she only stayed here a few weeks and spent most of the time asking our Mexicans where she could find her mother. Then, off she went and I really thought, Tilly, I would never see her again for it was plain to see that she had her back up against white people. Well, I suppose that was only to be understood for, going by the looks of her, she is a half-breed and you know what things are like out here. Well, three weeks ago there she is come back getting off a scrub cart, dusty and tired and looking smaller than ever, and she looked different, so sad. Well, it was like this, Tilly. She finds her mother and was horrified, that's her own word. I hope I've spelt it right. Well, she said she was horrified at the conditions under which her mother lived and she wasn't pleased to see her, I mean her mother wasn't pleased to see Josefina. All she wanted was money. And she told her that she wasn't born of Mr Matthew but the man who fathered her was called Abelorda Orozco. He had once been a short time hand on the ranch. He was living with her there in the house and whatever he was like must have come as a shock to Josefina for she found it difficult to speak about him, Tilly. And you know what, Tilly, she started to cry. Even as a child, although it's years ago, I never knew Josefina to cry, and I couldn't imagine she'd ever be given to crying."

Tilly stopped reading the letter and looked over the top of it towards Willy. Indeed, Josefina must have received a shock and be in great distress, for she herself, too, had never seen her cry, not even on that day of the great outburst, nor when she had finally said good-bye to her on the boat, and they had held each other tightly for a moment and looked into each other's eyes. There had been a mistiness there, but no tears.

She returned her attention to the letter:

"Miss Luisa will be pleased to have her stay for she is lonely. She spends a lot of her time up here . . . Miss Luisa. The latest is she is talking to Josefina about starting a school of sorts. There are now about ten Mexican children in the huts and quite a number scattered further afield, and you remember Number Three? well, he married a half-breed Mexican about ten years ago. But I think I told you that. And he has five children but they don't look half-breeds for they're all pure black and lovely bairns. At times with one and another the place seems swarming with bairns, it's like being back home and, oh Tilly, how I long to come back, just for a little while, not for good 'cos I've got to like it out here. Well, I had to, hadn't I? Well, Tilly, no more news now 'cos the men are riding in and that bloke of mine will go and eat one of his own horses if the meal isn't on the table. Give my love to all of 'em . . . I'd better tell you afore I finish, Tilly, that I've written to Peg and told her I'd love to have her out here. I hope you won't mind, Tilly, but I long to see someone of me own. You know what I mean. Love again, from Katie."

As she placed the letter on the table, Willy turned his head slightly towards her from the bed and said, "Well?" And she answered, "I haven't opened Josefina's letter yet. That was from Katie."

"What has she to say?"

"After I've read Josefina's letter I'll read it to you."

Josefina's letter began:

"My dear Mama, Strange but I still think of you as my mama, yet I have just recently returned from seeing my real mother and my mind is still saying, she was right, she was right, meaning you, for I haven't yet got over the shock.

"I imagined when we met she would take me to her heart. I was prepared for her and her family being poor, but not the kind of poor I was presented with, dirt, laziness, squalor, and a way of life that I am ashamed to put into words, yet I shouldn't be because I know I was born to it

"I am ashamed to admit now that I left the ranch with hardly the courtesy of a thank you to either Katie or Luisa and they both had been very kind to me, but when I returned humbled in spirit I was brought low by their reception of me which was so warm and welcoming.

"Luisa had ideas with regard to me putting my education to use. She talks of starting a school here for the children of mixed races. I should be enthusiastic at the prospect but I am only half-hearted with regard to it. I feel I must still be in a state of shock.

"With regard to what you tell me about Miss Bentwood, I cannot believe that she will be gone for good. If she loves Willy then she will return. Or if he loves her . . . as I know he does, he will make the means to find her.

"I miss you, my dear Mama, more than I can tell you, and over these past tempestuous days I have made comparison and thought how lucky are the people who work under your care.

"My love to you and Willy, Josefina."

The movement she now made brought Willy's attention to her again. "It was a long letter," he said.

"Not as long as Katie's . . . which do you want to hear first?"

"It doesn't matter . . . Well, let's hear what Josefina has to say."

So Tilly began to read Josefina's letter, but she noted before she was half-way through it that Willy had turned on his side, his face towards her, and that the look of despondency had for a moment left him. She omitted to read out the part concerning himself and Noreen, and as she ended he said immediately, "She should come home." Then after a moment's silence he added, "Does she know about Noreen?"

To this she answered briefly, "Yes, I wrote her."

"And she hasn't referred to it?"

There was a long pause before she said, "No."

She watched him lie back on his pillows, she watched his hand move across his usually clean-shaven chin that had a deep shadow of stubble on it for as yet today he hadn't shaved and he would allow no one to do it for him.

His voice was low as he said, "She sounds different, broken somehow, her spirit gone." He turned his head slowly towards her again. "She was always high-spirited, wasn't she?"

"Yes, yes, she was."

"You know, we lived together all those years and appeared so close but I've thought of late that I never really understood her, or her need . . . her many needs."

"That wasn't entirely your fault, she had a secret self. I was excluded from it, too. I've wondered lately if it's a good thing to take people from the environment into which they are born. Heredity is in the blood and it will out in the end, yet, if I hadn't taken her, imagine the life she'd be leading now. One does what one thinks is best. But then, what is best? I know one thing, unless you are born into the class no amount of self education is going to prepare you for acceptance into it."

"You could grace any class."

He had held out his hand towards her as he spoke, and she rose from the chair and took it; and she stood in silence for a moment looking down at him before she said, "There's never been more than half a dozen people in my life who have believed that, but thank you, dear." She bent down and kissed his cheek, then said on a sigh, "Well, it's Friday again, I must get to the mine. I'll send Ned up to you. The papers have come from Newcastle. He can read you the headlines. And I won't be long, a couple of hours at the most."

She was going towards the door when he said quietly, "I miss you."

She paused and turned her head over her shoulders and answered as quietly, "I'm glad to know that." But even while

208

saying it she knew in her heart that she was now but a poor substitute, for what he needed.

The meeting was over. It had been much the same as usual, even briefer because John was not there to ask questions and raise irrelevant points which he felt he must do to prove his interest.

After the meeting she had gone some way into the mine accompanied by both Steve and Alex Manning. She had talked to the men and here and there enquired after a family, congratulating a Mr Morgan who told her that his son had got a book prize for reading at the village school and his daughter a certificate for her regular attendance at Sunday School.

This over, they walked up out of the drift, there to see on the road beyond the huddle of stables and outhouses the woman. She was seated on her horse and she and the animal appeared as a beautiful picture in a grubby frame.

As she walked slowly to the top of the drift, Tilly kept her eyes fixed on the woman. She knew that Steve had glanced quickly in her direction, but she did not look at him. Her whole attention was on the creature before her, and she saw her as creature, a beautiful creature. She was attired in a dull brown corduroy velvet riding habit. Moreover, she was riding as a lady should, side-saddle. The whole made her own attire with top boots and breeches mannish and gauche in comparison.

"Why! Phillipa; I didn't expect you." Steve had gone on slightly ahead of her and was now holding the woman's hand, and she, looking down at him laughing, said, "We just returned last night. I came by the cottage, but you weren't there. And your fire's nearly out. Do you know that?"

"Huh!" He was laughing as he looked up into her face. Then seeming to remember Tilly, he turned and said, "My dear, this is Tilly . . . Mrs Sopwith. I've mentioned her to you."

"Yes, yes."

The woman was nodding down towards Tilly now, but Tilly stood looking up at her making no movement until a hand stretched out; and then she had to force herself to lift her own, and as this was being shaken with the woman said, "I am very pleased to meet you, Mrs . . . Sopwith. And pardon me for saying it but I must do so right away, I admire your attire. It's so sensible." Then releasing Tilly's hand, she looked at Steve as she ended, "I'm going to have an outfit made like that."

"It won't suit you."

"No? . . . Why not?"

"Because . . . Well —" He turned and grinned at Tilly now. Then looking back at the seated figure, he laughed out loud as he said, "You're bursting out all over, you've got to be slim, flat, before you can wear breeches like Tilly here." He jerked his head towards her while still looking up at the woman.

Flat, which really meant unwomanly. That's how he saw her. Oh, let her get away out of this.

"I must get my horse. It . . . it has been nice meeting you. Good-bye."

"Oh . . . oh no, you don't." Steve had his hand on her arm. "We'll both get our horses and we'll all return to the cottage. I want you two to get to know each other. It's about time." On this he looked up at the woman, saying, almost with a command, "You stay put, we'll be back in a minute." Then taking Tilly's arm, he hurried her across to the stables. But once inside, she released herself and, facing him, she said, "What if I have no wish to become further acquainted with your lady friend?"

"Well, Mrs Matilda Sopwith" – he was poking his head towards her – "for once I'm disregarding your wishes. Yes, for once in my life I'm disregarding your wishes. Now get that into your head. The time has come for plain speaking and I can't do it here, so if you'll allow me." He bent down and she put her boot on to his hand, and the next minute she was in the saddle and riding out of the stable.

The journey to the cottage was lively, but she herself took no part in the banter. The grinding pain was in her chest again. Men were cruel. All men were cruel, but at this moment she thought Steve was the cruellest one she had met as yet, for he was getting his own back for the years of dalliance, for that's how he must have looked at the time he had spent at her beck and call. And now he was paying her back, proving that a man past his prime but who could still be taken for forty was able to capture the affection of this young woman. She might be touching thirty or thereabouts, but she was still young . . . and beautiful with a figure that could not carry breeches and a riding jacket, and was much more alluring to a man because of it. . . .

They were in the kitchen. The keetle had boiled; she, the woman Phillipa, had made the tea. She seemed to know where everything was kept in the cottage, and when the three cups of tea were poured out it was she who handed one to Tilly, then one to Steve. And as she picked her own up from the table, Steve went to her side and, putting his free arm around her waist, pulled her tightly towards him. And like this they confronted Tilly as she sat barely able to hold the cup and saucer steady in her hand. And then his next words almost sent them flying, for what he said was, "Tilly, meet my daughter, Mrs Phillipa Ryde-Smithson."

Tilly gulped, such a deep gulp that it brought her chin moving towards her shoulder and her right hand jerking to steady the saucer that her left hand had almost let drop. She looked up at them. They were both grinning at her, for all the world like two children who had sprung a surprise on an elder.

When she found her voice all she could manage to say was, "Your daughter?"

"Yes, Tilly, my daughter." The grin had gone from his face. He looked at her steadily before adding, "It's a long story. I'll get down to it shortly, but in the meantime I'd like you two to get to know each other, and so if you'll excuse me I'll take my cup of tea into the back and have a wash."

It would be difficult to say if there was ever a time when Tilly had felt more embarrassed than at this moment. She could find no words with which to express her feelings. Nor apparently could Mrs Phillipa Ryde-Smithson. But it was she who spoke first. Drawing a chair up to the table, she sat down and she tapped the saucer with her spoon and kept her gaze fixed on it as she said, "As Steve said, it's a long story."

Tilly noted that she had called him Steve, not Father. "And he'll tell you the tale much better than I can as he knows more about it, but all I can say is that I am very proud that he is my real father although Daddy, as I call him, is a wonderful man and I love him dearly. But they also know that I have a special affection for Steve, and strangely they have too." Now she lifted her gaze to Tilly and her large grey eyes twinkled as she said, "It was very naughty of him to keep you in the dark. You thought I was his woman, didn't you?"

Tilly felt the colour flooding over her face and she said on a slightly defensive tone, "Well, not exactly his . . . his woman, I thought you were to be married. He gave me that impression."

"Naughty of him! Very naughty of him! He's a tease, you know."

No, Tilly didn't know that Steve was a tease, but what she was gathering, and quickly, was that this woman, this daughter of his, had undoubtedly been brought up among the class. Her manner, her way of speaking all portrayed this: the words naughty, very naughty, the way she said them, he's a tease, all held an indefinable something that spoke of a different world, a world in which she herself lived but was not of it because she hadn't been born to it. This woman was Steve's daughter and Steve had been a working boy and was still a working man, yet this girl had evidently been brought up in an environment which had soaked into her until now she appeared . . . of the blood, so to speak, which belied the conversation with regard to heredity that she'd had with Willy just that very morning.

"Your son is not well at present?"

"No; he, I am afraid, has just escaped pneumonia but he is recovering."

"I should like to meet him some time if I may."

"You will be very welcome."

There was a silence between them now, until Steve's daughter broke it by putting her head back and calling, "Have you dropped down the well?"

"No, m'lass, I haven't dropped down the well." Steve came out of the scullery rubbing his hair with a towel, and Phillipa, getting to her feet now, said, "I must be off. Lance is meeting me with the coach in Harton at three o'clock. He's attending a meeting on the Lawe with sea captains and such about some cargoes."

"How long are you here for?"

"Oh, a week at the most."

"What about your horse, if Lance is meeting you?"

"Oh, we'll stable it and one of them will pick him up tomorrow. By the way, Lance would like you to come over on Sunday if you've nothing better to do."

"I have nothing better to do." He smiled at her.

"Well, good-bye" – she had turned to Tilly – "I was going to say Mrs Sopwith, but may I call you Tilly? I've always heard of you by that name."

"I'd be pleased if you would. . . . Good-bye."

"Good-bye."

Tilly watched Steve throw aside the towel, rub his fingers through his hair, then escort his daughter to the door and down the path. She saw him put his hands under her oxters and heave her upwards, and although the rampant jealousy of this young woman had gone, the sight of the tenderness with which he treated her and the friendliness that existed between them, which was almost like a comradeship, touched some sore point in her heart and she turned from the window and went and stood before the fire, looking down at it, waiting his return.

His face was straight when he entered the room. And it remained so while he poured himself out another cup of tea and sat down on the settle; then in a sober manner he said, "Sit yourself down; you're in for a long session."

Seated before him, she kept her eyes intently on his face. When he was young his affection had created in her an irritation mingled with pity because of the love she could never give him, and as a man his concern for her had created in her nothing but a deep thankfulness, until it had grown into something much stronger, but never had she felt resentment against him. Yet at this moment when she knew that she must still be in his thoughts as dearly as ever and that her rival, so to speak, was no rival at all, she felt an irritation rising in her that bordered on aggressiveness, and just as it happened at other times in her life when she'd had the urge to strike out, so now she wanted to bring her hand across his face, which, had she done so, would no doubt have revealed to him her true feelings more than any words might have done. . . . All these months he had been laughing at her; the secret that she thought she held was no secret at least from him; he had made her suffer in imagining that he was tired of being the friend, the sustainer in time of trouble, and was putting a definite end to it.

As he put the empty cup back on the table he broke in on her thoughts, saying, "I don't suppose you remember the day I came to the house and stood round near the wall and I told you I loved you and even tried to blackmail you into returning some affection by reminding you I'd killed our Hal for you . . . eh?" He brought his eyes to hers but she made no answer, and he went on, "No, it's likely too far back to remember. And it's of no consequence. Anyway, from then I still kept on hoping, that was until I heard you'd taken up with your master. It was then I left home and travelled about a bit. I was in lodgings when I met Phillipa's mother. She was the same age as me, just on nineteen, and it was strange but I'd never had a woman in my life afore because, you see, I only wanted you."

She didn't lower her eyes and cast her glance down on this, but she looked straight at him and listened to him now as he continued, "I was scared to death when I knew Betty was going to have a baby, and her brother and father were for hammering me and dragging me to the church. But I couldn't face it. I did a bunk. And so did Betty. She went to Hartlepool to an aunt of hers who wasn't very fond of her parents. It was in a roundabout way that I heard the child had been born and that it was a girl and that it was to be put out for adoption. Funny, but that did something to me. I sought Betty out and told her I was making decent money and would support the bairn. She agreed. She was working in a mill at the time. Then within a couple of months she wrote me and told me that she had met a lad who was willing to marry her but that he wouldn't take the bairn on and so she was again going to put it out for adoption. Now it's strange how things come about, but the owner of the mill had a daughter who had been married eight years and without the sight of a child in view and, as things get about, she had heard of the obstacle to Betty's marriage while she was visiting her father. She and her husband lived on the island of Jersey. So Betty was approached with regard to the adoption. But at the time she didn't know who it was who wanted the child, she only knew it was going to a very good home. So she told me that she was going to let her go. Well, what could I do? I remember going to see her, and there was the child in the cradle. And I knew then that I didn't want to let her be adopted but that there was no other course open. By the way, the name on her birth certificate was Mary not Phillipa, but it should happen that her adoptive grandmother had been named Phillipa and her new mother decided to call her that.

'Well —" He now rose to his feet and went to the mantelpiece and took a pipe from the rack and from a tin a long plug of tobacco; then sitting down again, he proceeded to shave the end of the plug into his pipe as he went on, "Time passes. It has a habit of doing that, but every now and again I would think of the child: she would be three; she would be four; she would be ten; what was she like? During all this time I'd had a longing for bairns, for a family of me own, and twice I'd been right on the rim of getting married. Oh yes" – he nodded at her as her eyes widened –

214

"within a fortnight at one time. And I had to run again." He smiled wryly now. "She was going to have me up for breach of promise, that one. I settled with her for nearly all me savings. The other one was sensible, she knew I wouldn't make a good husband.

"When Phillipa was eleven her adoptive mother died, but before she did she told her who her real parents were. Well, the news was a shock, as could have been expected, to this young girl. But she was filled with curiosity, and so she makes a trip from Newcastle to Hartlepool on her own and there she found that her own mother had died the previous year and her husband years earlier, but that she had a father, a real father, who was alive. The old aunt gave her this information. Her father's name she learnt was Steve McGrath and the last that had been heard of him was that he was working in a pit further north.

"Anyway, two years later when she's on holiday from her private school, and was supposed to be visiting a school friend she finds me, so it was about seventeen years ago when a young and beautiful girl knocks on the door. I can see her now" – he turned his head to the side – "standing very upright, straight faced, just about there" – he pointed to the table – "and saying, 'I'm Phillipa Coleman. My real mother, I understand, was named Betty Fuller, and you, I understand, Mr McGrath, are my father.'

"You know, Tilly" – he leant towards her now, the look in his eyes was soft and tender like they must have been on that day – "if God had opened the clouds and dropped an angel at my feet I couldn't have been more surprised, or pleased. But pleased isn't the word to describe my feelings on that day. This girl, this lady, because she looked every inch a young lady, was my daughter, and, you know, it was strange but from the word go we clicked, just like that." He snapped his fingers. "And that's how its been ever since. Well, the next visitor I had was her adoptive father, Jim Coleman, a man who loved her as if she were his own. Well, we talked, and the outcome was I was invited to his home, his mainland home. He had two, one in Newcastle, strangely enough, and the one in Jersey; and stranger still, we became friends. Then there came on the scene Mr Lancelot Ryde-Smithson. That's a mouthful for you if you like. He was the man who wanted to marry her. She was sixteen and he was seventeen years her senior, but she loved him and he doted on her. He was French on his mother's side and a charming man, and very wealthy into the bargain. Well the Ryde-Smithsons are, aren't they? You know" – he nodded at her – "the steel-works and such."

Ryde-Smithsons, the steel-works and such. Yes, indeed.

"Anyway, Mr Ryde-Smithson and I talked. We were men of different worlds, but almost the same age and we understood each other. And that's how it's been up till now. I was at their wedding, a big affair, just before you arrived home from America. It was held at her father's place in Jersey. And you know, Tilly, it was a wonderful feeling to be accepted by everybody, but . . . but mostly by her and Lance. He was a great man, he still is. They live in France most of the time. I've been there to their home and played with me grandchildren. Aye, grandchildren, I'm a grand-father. Two lovely children, Gerald is twelve now, and Richard ten. And you know something more, Tilly? If I had any sense I'd have been away from your mine and this place years ago because I've had offers that would make a man dizzy, and from Mr Cole-man, an' all. And why haven't I accepted any of their offers? Well, Tilly, some people would say it is because I am a bloody fool. And sometimes I thought they were right. Oh yes, yes." He shook his head and his face unsmiling, he repeated, "Yes, yes; many a time I thought they were right. And not more so than early on when you went off abroad with Mr Matthew. That nearly finished me. Well, it did finish me, and I've asked myself time and time again why I stayed on in this place in that bloody little mine because, Tilly, it is a bloody little mine; bloody in more ways than one. There's hardly a day goes by but I fear to see water rushing towards me. Oh yes, I know everything's been done that can be done, but nevertheless it is a bad-tempered bloody little mine. And this cottage" – he waved his hand round – "very nice, very nice, but I exaggerated its charm when I first came into it. And you know why, I've got no need to tell you, it was just so that I'd be near you. Anyway, your presence was full about me here, you'd lived in it. Then off you go to the Americas, so why did I stay? There was Phillipa and Lance and Jim Cole-man, all of them wondering what on earth was the matter with me, turning down a nice house in Jersey or a fine house in Jesmond as Jim Coleman once offered me. But not for nothing of course, he was a business-man. As he said, he wanted someone who could handle men, and apparently, Tilly, I have that talent. And there I was letting it go rotten here, so to speak." He sighed now and, looking into her face, he said, "I'm laying it on thick, I know, but

I've waited a long time. Tilly. And over these last years acting as your sort of henchman, friend of the family, yet not accepted at the Manor because of what one might hear from the village, that damned narrow-minded sanctimonious little cesspool. I sometimes think of this place, you know, Tilly, when I'm sitting in Jim Coleman's dining-room at a table laden with silver, some pieces so heavy the weight would fill a skip, and accepted there, an' all. But here I'm Stevey McGrath, son of that old hag in the village, with a brother that's got a reputation that stinks and a nephew that's been along the line twice. Anyway, Tilly, there it is, I've had me say. It's been grinding in me for years. And I've got to say this, I don't think . . . well in fact, I know I couldn't have stood the situation as it's been between you and me if I hadn't had Phillipa as an outlet, so to speak, for the strain's been hellish at times. So there it is Tilly." He looked at her softly for a moment without speaking, and at this point she could have dropped into his arms, but he began again, and what he said now brought her slumped body straight and tightened the muscles in her face. "And now, lass," he said, "I'm going to give the ultimatum I should have given you years ago. You marry me or I take the belated offers and move. I'll give you a little more time to think it over because there's the responsibility of Willy and next year he'll be coming into his own I suppose, and if he were to marry, well, that would be one of your problems solved. Yet if Noreen doesn't turn up I doubt if there's much hope of marriage coming his way, and so you might feel obliged to stay with him. But whether you'd see me as dowager master of the hall" – he pulled a face here – "dowager isn't the right word but you know what I mean. Anyway, it's up to you. I might as well tell you while I'm on, Tilly, that I've had a very good offer and it's open until February next. That leaves you three or four months to sort things out finally, although I'd be happier if I could know by . . . well say December."

Tilly stared at this man, this person standing before her whom she had grown to love as she imagined she had never loved Mark or Matthew, and he was talking about his love for her in a fashion that one might use in a matter of business, small business, for his statements had been cool, concise. He had made no attempt to take her in her arms and kiss her, no attempt to speak of his need of her or give her the opportunity to speak of her own need of him. She couldn't sort out her feelings at the moment, she only knew she felt utterly deflated while at the same time hurt, and angry.

For a moment he appeared like the old Steve when he put his hand out and gripped hers, saying, "Don't look like that, Tilly. All this I know has come as a bit of a surprise to you, but life's like that. You should know better than anyone that life is full of surprises, especially where feelings are concerned. Anyway, my dear, it's up to you."

Yes, it was up to her.

Slowly she pushed his hand away from hers and, rising to her feet, she looked into his face and she repeated her thoughts and his words, "Yes, it's up to me, Steve. Thank you." She inclined her head towards him and she took no notice of the pained and troubled look that came into his eyes but, turning from him, she went towards the door, opened it and walked slowly down the path. She knew he was close behind her but she didn't look at him, not even when he helped her up on to her horse, not until he said, "Tilly" and the name was filled with a deep plea did she turn her gaze to him and say quietly, "I'll be seeing you, Steve." And with that she rode off.

11

He was gone from her, as surely as if he had married that woman who had turned out to be his daughter. The Steve who had coolly given her an ultimatum was in no way related to any of his other selves which he had presented to her over the years. All these had held that quality of kindness and devotion that she had come to expect. Never, never could she have imagined that Steve would change, not towards her, for hadn't he been obsessed with her, and that was the word, obsessed with her from when he was a boy, in a way as much as Matthew had been.

But Steve *had* changed, and not a little of the hurt inside her was due to the fact that she didn't know anything about this other Steve. The man who had presented the ultimatum was a man of parts, a man who mixed with the gentry, while she herself who had lived with them, been mistress to one and married another, was still on the outside of the charmed circle wherein moved the class. But he was mixing with them, thick with them so to speak, for the Ryde-Smithsons were class, and the Colemans, oh yes.

For years now she had longed to be one with this man and she knew that she had deluded herself into thinking that marriage to him was impossible because of the vow she had given to Matthew never to marry again, for inside herself she recognised the truth, and the truth was that the shadow of that vow had grown dim, very dim a long time ago, and that one of the real reasons that had kept her from marrying Steve was merely the fact that she couldn't see him acting as master in this, a manor house. Yet she knew now that he had in a way as much experience of such houses as she had, more in fact, for he had been accepted by their occupants: as he had so graphically stated, he had sat at their table where one piece of silver was so heavy it would weigh a skipful of coal.

The Steve who had dedicated his life to her was no more and she could blame no one but herself for the loss, but the hurt this knowledge brought to her was intensified by the fact that during his periods of frequent absences at week-ends he had not been relieving his needs up in the cottage in the hills with some woman, or indulging in the inn on the high road, but was being entertained by his daughter and her people. She would have rather, much rather, known that he was assuaging his natural appetite than playing the father and being accepted by a class of people with whom she had imagined he could never mix, the class which, incidentally, ignored her.

He had given her until December to decide. Well, she had decided already.

In the weeks that followed this revealing day Tilly's spirit had risen up in her, especially so at night when, her pale reflection staring back at her from the mirror, she had cried at it: Who does he think he is anyway? Steve McGrath who has hounded me with his love all my life now to give me an ultimatum? And to say he couldn't have borne the situation between them if he hadn't had the consolation of his daughter. It was galling to think now that she herself hadn't really held him all these years.

On one occasion she had paced the floor for hours and the soft padding of her steps had penetrated upwards, and Willy, sleep eluding him too and with ears highly attuned to every sound in the house, had made his way downstairs and, knocking on her door, he had called, "What is it? What's the matter?" and she had answered, "Nothing. Nothing." Then after a moment he had asked, "May I come in? I can't sleep either."

She had stirred up the fire and they had sat side by side before it in silence for a time, until he said, "It's Steve, isn't it?"

She was sharp to answer, "What makes you think that?"

"Because I suppose my ears have taken over from my eyes and I read a lot from inflexions, and yours has very little warmth in it now when you talk to him."

She hadn't answered him for a time, then said, "We had a difference," and to this he replied, "Well, I hope for both your sakes it doesn't last. He's a good man, Steve, you know, Mama. There's not a better. He's honest, true, and he's been a good friend to you . . . and to me."

Honest? she had thought. Devious would be a better word to apply to him.

Changing the subject, he had said suddenly, "I have a feeling, Mama, that Noreen is dead. I dozed off while I was reading and I saw her. She looked changed, really grotesque, but I put my hands out to her and she slapped them away. Then I opened my eyes and the feeling became stronger. It was as if she were in the room with me. But there's a certainty in me now that we'll never come together."

"Don't say that, dear, just keep hoping. We could hear any day from the agent we engaged; he has already traced her to two places since she left the lodgings."

Willy had said nothing to this but had risen from the chair and made his way towards the door. There he had said, "Goodnight, Mama," and she had answered simply, "Good-night, Willy."

And then he had added, "Think about Steve."

Think about Steve? If she could only stop thinking about Steve. . . .

And now it was December. The snow had come early this year. Twice there had been heavy falls. They'd had no post for three days, but on midday on this Wednesday Jimmy got through to the village and met the carrier and returned with a sheaf of letters, one of which was addressed to Mrs P. Crosby.

After giving Biddle the letter to take to Peg, Tilly went up into her room and the first one she opened was from Josefina. It was short and very surprising and right to the point. It began simply:

"Mama, I am coming home. I have booked my passage and sail early in January. I cannot wait to leave this land and be once again with you, and with Willy, even with his wife, if Miss Bentwood has returned. I imagined that a rejected love was the most cruel thing anyone could suffer, but I have discovered that there are feelings that can be injured more deeply. Rejection of one's colour can carry sufficient hurt but when you carry the imprint of two on your countenance then the hurt reaches depths which you didn't imagine lay within you.

"I realise now that you protected me, even cosseted me, and I long to return to that protection. Your loving Josefina."

Tilly sat back in the chair and covered her eyes with her hands for a moment while her teeth pressed into her lower lip. It was as if a daughter of her own flesh was expressing a longing to be with her again. After what had happened of late with Willy and Steve, especially with Steve, Josefina's return would be all the more welcome, and she experienced a feeling almost akin to joy as she thought of them both being in the house again with her, Willy perhaps seeing Josefina in a different light, that is if Noreen didn't appear on his horizon again. And as day had followed day she had become more assured that this latter would not happen.

She had just opened the letter from Katie, which confirmed what Josefina had written, when there came a tap on the door and when she said, "Come in!" Peg entered.

Immediately Tilly sensed her confusion, and she guessed before Peg spoke what was causing it.

"Can I have a word with you . . . ma'am?" There was always a hesitancy with all of the Drews between her title of ma'am and her name, even after all these years.

"Of course, Peg. Sit down."

Peg sat on the edge of the small padded couch that stood crossways in the middle of the room, and she dropped her head and unclasped her hands before, suddenly groping in her pocket, she drew out a letter, saying, "I've had word from our Katie."

"Yes, I thought it would be from her." Tilly nodded, then slapped at the letter in her own hand. "I've had one too."

"You haven't read it then?"

"No, not all yet."

Again Peg looked down. Then her voice a mere mutter, she said, "She's sent me the money for me passage, she wants me to go out. What am I to do?" She raised her eyes now and looked straight at Tilly.

"What do you want to do, Peg?"

Peg glanced to the side; then lifting her hand, she straightened her cap, pushing at the starched frill that covered her ears before saying, "I'm not ungrateful. Believe me I'm not ungrateful. You've done so much for all of us, but I'm gettin' on, Tilly, and somehow I'd like to end me days with our Katie. I'm sorry." Peg's head dropped lower until Tilly said softly, "Peg, look at me." And when Peg had lifted her head she went on, "I'm not going to say I won't miss you, I shall, there'll only be Fanny left, but you've got to live your own life. And there could be a lot of it left to you yet, for you're so sprightly and don't look half your age. And so you write straight back and I'll do the same; and I'll also make arrangements for your passage on the next boat out."

"You won't want me to serve me notice?"

"Don't be silly." Tilly now got to her feet, Peg also rose, and they stood confronting each other as Tilly said, "There's no need to talk of notice between you and me or any of your family, my family, because that's how I consider you all, as my family, the only real one I ever knew after I lost the old people. And what's more you'll not go out empty-handed, you'll go out as a well-dressed, well-endowed woman. And if the men are after you for nothing else they'll be after you for your money." She now punched Peg playfully in the shoulder. But Peg, bowing her head again, began to giggle like any young girl until her laughter suddenly sprang into tears. And then they were holding each other, Tilly, too, crying now as she said, "There, there. It'll be a wonderful life for you. You'll enjoy it. Just think what it's done for Katie."

After a moment they separated and both stood wiping their eyes, smiling now, and Peg said, "What about them Indians?"

"Oh, well, I should think by now they're all dead and buried. Katie's man has likely polished them off. Oh" – her voice became serious now – "don't worry about the Indians. As Luisa said, the Civil War was worse to put up with than the Indians. There's great things going on out there. I often think how different my life would have been if Matthew had survived. We would have had our own big ranch and thousands of head of cattle and horses, and" – she nodded towards Peg now – "that's what you could have one day, you'll see. There's lot of lonely men out there."

"Oh, Tilly. Oh no, not me. Never again; not at my age."

"Don't tell them your age, well, knock ten years off. Anyway, Doug's a big man now being partner with Luisa, a lot of marvellous things can happen and will happen to you. Well now, go on downstairs and tell the others. I doubt if the lads will be pleased. Yet on the other hand —" she pulled a long face and nodded towards Peg as she ended, "they might take a leaf out of your book and the rest of them follow you. And then where will I be?"

"Oh, there's no fear of that, Tilly; the lads know where they're well off. Aye, as our Sam often says, it was a lucky day for the Drews when they *drew* up alongside of you that special Sunday."

"And a very lucky day for me, too, Peg, oh yes. But go on now."

"Thanks, Tilly. I'll never forget you. None of us ever will."

223

The room to herself again, Tilly stood looking towards the door. Peg had said she would never forget her. That was very magnanimous of her because at times if she hadn't hated her she must have disliked her when she saw her as the stumbling block between Steve and herself, for Biddy had made no secret of the fact that in her opinion Steve would have taken up with Peg had Tilly been out of the way. But Tilly had known this would never come about because Steve would never have stayed in this quarter of the country if it hadn't been for her, even before he discovered his daughter. . . . *Oh, his daughter*. She turned away with an impatient twist of her body and went to the desk and finished Katie's letter, which told her exactly what Peg had just said.

The remainder of her mail was dealing with business. After she had gone through all the letters and filed them for answering she rose and went to the window. It had started to snow heavily again, big white flakes, falling slowly and so thickly that she couldn't see down into the garden. She sighed deeply. At this rate the road could be blocked again and they could be hemmed in for days, even weeks. There seemed nothing to look forward to, until she reminded herself of Josefina's coming. And on this she gathered up two letters from the desk and went out of the room towards the attic floor and the studio where she could hear Willy playing the piano. He spent most of his time now playing the piano or the violin. He seemed to find comfort in the pieces that he chose, all slow movements. That was how he must be feeling about life, slow, tedious. And for her, too; oh yes, yes, for her too it was slow, and tedious.

12

There was a fug of warmth in the room which contrasted with the bitter snow-driven wind outside.

It was just on one o'clock. The street grating, under which and supported by two planks of wood was a piece of plate glass, at no time allowed very much light into the basement room, but today it could have been a brick wall so thick was it covered with the black slush from the treading feet.

The lamps fixed to the walls on each side of the table were so placed that they illuminated only the table itself and the double oven fireplace exactly four feet from the end of it. Perhaps this was as well for they shut out from Noreen Bentwood's gaze a regiment of cockroaches and fearless rats that infested the margin of the basement. So dim were the outskirts of the room that to the vermin it must have been constant night, and the cockroaches, if not the rats, seemed to take this for granted. The two cats that should have been parading the premises were so satisfied with food that they slept most of their time, except at night when they escaped to pursue their instincts.

Proggle's Pie Shop was situated in an alley off the waterfront. It was open from six o'clock in the morning until twelve at night and was never known to be empty. It was also known that Proggle never kept his cooks longer than two to three weeks at the most. This latest one though had stuck it for seven weeks, but of course that was because her belly was full and she was for the House. But like many before her, she'd leave that visit until the last second if she was wise.

It was also said that the pastry which had lately come out from Proggle's kitchen was the best the customers had ever tasted.

It was this fact and this fact alone that had caused Proggle to keep the lass on so long and to grant her concessions, such as letting her start at eight in the morning and finish at eight at night. At three halfpence an hour and her food, he considered he was paying her well. And so good a hand was she at pastry-making he had offered to take her back when her confinement was over, that's if she could get someone to take the bairn for adoption. He had talked the matter over with her, saying, "What you mustn't do, lass, is put it out to farm, 'cos if it hasn't got rickets when it goes in, it'll have 'em sure as God made little apples when it comes out, for no matter what you pay those bitches they feed the bairns nothing but pap, mouldy bread and whey, sucking at pap bags all day long tied in their boxes. Rabbits in backyards have more scope than those bairns. I've seen 'em; so don't have it put out, lass, have it adopted, or send it back to your people, 'cos who-ever they are they brought you up right. I can see that in many ways."

He was kindly, was Joseph Proggle, when kindness would benefit him in the long run, but he was right about the baby farmers. Noreen had seen this for herself. There was one place two doors down from where she lodged where the children didn't cry out aloud, they merely whined in chorus and continuously.

Noreen lifted up the heavy sneck of the oven door and drew out the iron shelf on which were two dozen round pie tins, the pie crusts raised with a shiny crown from the colouring of burnt sugar with which they had been brushed.

When she reached the table she did not slide the shelf on to the edge of it, as she usually did, but dropped it with a light thud; then one hand on the corner of the table, the other hugging her waist, she bent over for a moment while drawing in deep breaths of the stifling air.

It was some seconds later before she straightened herself and, taking up another iron sheet filled with pie tins, she placed these in the oven. Following this, she took a ladle and went to the fire again and there stirred a thick mass of peas simmering in a huge black iron kale-pot, before returning to the table once more, tip-ping out the pies on to a wooden tray which she then carried to the end of the room where, inset in the wall, was a lift. Placing the tray in this, she knocked twice on the wooden side, and a minute later when she saw the shelf move upwards she turned away and, going to the table again, took from a brown bowl a great slab of pastry, threw it on to the floured table and began to roll it out.

She was only half-way through this process when again she stopped and once more one hand was gripping the edge of the table and the other hugging her waist. It couldn't be, not yet, if her timing was right. And oh yes, she knew that was right. There were another three weeks to go. So what was this strange pain that was gripping her now?

Pulling a box towards her, she sat down on it and clasped her hands on the table top and, looking to where a narrow black mass was moving backwards and forwards against the far wall, she whispered, "Oh God! don't let it happen so soon. Oh God! God!" As she moved her head the tears sprang into her eyes and rolled down her cheeks; and now, her chin drooping towards her chest, she whispered, "Oh, Mam. Mam! Oh, Mam. Mam!"

She did not think of Willy. Strangely, she rarely thought of Willy these days. At first the temptation to write to him had been so great that she had actually stamped a number of letters and got as far as the post office with them. But there she remembered her father, and she knew that if Willy were to take her back to the Manor – for where else could he take her – he would not live long, as her mother had suggested, to enjoy his triumph.

For some time now she hadn't cared whether she lived or died; in fact, there were nights in that dreadful little room she had rented with the sound of all human activities penetrating her ears far into the night, she had prayed that she wouldn't see the morning.

Of late there had come over her an apathy. The only person she wanted to see was her mother, but at the same time she knew that her own condition would horrify her, at least at first.

"Now, now! what's up with you, lass?" Joseph Proggle had come down the steps in his slippered feet, and his approach startled her. Jumping up from the box, she muttered, "I . . . I was only resting, Mr Proggle, just for a minute."

He peered at her in the dimness, saying, "You're not comin' on, are you?"

"No, oh no" – she shook her head emphatically – "I was just a bit tired."

"It's early in the day, lass, to be tired, not yet on one, an' the shop packed to suffocation. They're pushing them down scalding, they are. Those peas ready?"

"Yes, Mr Proggle."

"Well, dish 'em up an' get another lot on 'cos the way the weather's shapin' it's gonna be a full house. And I've got an order for six dozen pies for the night, sailors havin' a beano along at the Blue Sail."

He peered at her as she stood rolling out the pastry; then he

227

said, "I'll get Jenny Blackett to come in and give you a hand round teatime. How's that?"

"Thank you, Mr Proggle. It'll be a help."

"She can clean up if nothin' else. . . . My God! look at that cheeky bugger." He took an empty pie tin from the table and heaved it at a rat that was making for the middle of the room. "What's those bloody cats up to?" He now took his foot and kicked at the larger of the two cats curled up to the side of the oven and when it awoke with a squeal he cursed it further, crying, "You'll end up as pie meat, me lad, if you don't do your job. You don't feed 'em, do you?" He had turned to Noreen now, and she shook her head, saying, "No, no."

"No, that's right, don't give 'em a scrap, let 'em work for their livin' else we'll have that bloody inspector here again. . . . Inspector!" He spat on the floor, then said, "Well, hurry up, lass. When is the next lot due?"

Noreen turned and nodded towards the other oven and paused before she said, "About five minutes, Mr Proggle."

"Good, good. Send them up straightaway."

She nodded again, then went on with her rolling.

It was around about this time in the day that Simon Bentwood left his horse and trap at the farrier's with instructions to the man not to unharness the animal as he would be no more than half an hour before he was back, because with the change in the weather he'd have to take the road home as soon as possible.

But the conditions in Newcastle were nowhere near as bad as they had been when he left the farm. Although it was snowing here there were no drifts, the streets and roads were just black slush. He made his way down to Market Street past the new Law Courts and into Pilgrim Street where he stopped before a doorway on which was a curved brass plate indicating a number of offices therein. On the third floor of the building he knocked on an opaque glass door, then went in.

A clerk was sitting behind a small desk. He did not look up immediately, he was writing in a ledger, his hand moving slowly, and his paper cuffs hanging almost two inches below the frayed sleeve of his jacket made a small grating sound not audible until Simon stood looking down on the bent head in silence as the man contined to write.

"You deaf?"

The hand moved over two or three further words before the head lifted, when the elderly clerk, looking over the top of his glasses, said, "Not that I'm aware of, sir."

The tone immediately aroused the aggressiveness in Simon. "None of your bright lip, mister," he said. "You tell your boss I'm here."

He watched the man rise slowly from the chair, go towards another glass door, knock on it, then enter the room.

It was almost three minutes later when he returned. Stepping aside he left the door wide, saying, "Mr Robinson is free now to see you . . . sir."

Simon gave him a scathing glance as he passed into the small office where the agent was sitting behind a long substantial looking desk and on an equally substantial looking leather chair, and he greeted Simon affably, saying, "Ah! Mr Bentwood. Good-day to you. It is strange that you should come at this time."

"Why? You have news?" Simon sat down opposite the desk, and the agent, nodding his head briskly, said, "Indeed! Indeed! And I would have had it out to you but for the weather." He did not add his thoughts: "and to Mr William Sopwith at the same time." Hansom his clerk and he had a small wager on who would reach Proggle's pie shop first. Mr Sopwith had the advantage of a carriage but this man sitting here had the fury of a father to give wings to his feet.

"Well, get on with it, what do you know? Have you found her?"

"Well, yes and no. . . ."

"Yes and no? What answer is that to give! You have or you haven't?"

Mr Robinson sat back in his chair and tapped his fingertips gently together as he said, "It all depends on a name, a change of name. We have found three young women who apparently don't want to be found. One goes under the name of Hannah Circle, which is not her name at all; likewise Mary Nugent; and the third one is a Miss Lucy Cuthbertson. Each of these young women has a reason for not wishing to be found. . . ."

"*What did you say?* Lucy Cuthbertson?"

"Yes, Lucy Cuthbertson."

Simon was now leaning forward in his chair. "What's she like? How old?"

'Well, it's very hard to gauge a young person's age when they are with child, as are these three young women, but Miss Cuthbertson. . . ."

"What did you say?"

"I said Miss Cuthbertson. . . ."

"Afore that. With child you said?"

"Yes, that's what I said, Mr Bentwood. Now as regards this young lady, she could be eighteen, twenty, twenty-two, what can one say, because the position she holds at present is, I should imagine, very taxing. I have only seen her twice, and then in a dim light when I presented myself as a vermin inspector in her kitchen."

"You what!" Simon's eyes were screwed up.

"A vermin inspector. One has to take on different guises in this business. I had heard there was a young woman working for a certain pie maker near the waterfront and that she was near the time of delivery, so last week I presented myself, as I said, as a vermin inspector. Does the name Lucy Cuthbertson ring a bell for you, sir?"

Simon was staring down towards the floor through narrowed lids. She was going to have a child. His Noreen was going to have a child. And who could be the father but that blind bastard. He would kill him. Sure as he was sitting here he would kill him. But to get to her first, to get her home. Oh yes, to get her home. He blinked and said, "It was her mother's maiden name."

"Oh." Mr Robinson's eyes widened. "I think we are on the right track then, sir. Anyway, I would suggest that you go to the shop and ask to see her. Do you know where Proggle's Pie Shop is, sir, on the water . . .?"

"Yes, yes." Simon had risen to his feet. "Who doesn't known Proggle's Pie Shop?"

As Simon now made hastily towards the door, Mr Robinson rose to his feet, saying, "I trust if the young woman is whom you hope her to be, you will call and settle your account . . . or should I send the bill on to you?"

Simon paused for a moment, turned his head and said, "Don't worry; either way you'll be paid."

"Of course, sir. Of course."

In the street now, his walk almost a run, he dodged in and out of people on the crowded thoroughfare and slithered as he crossed the road between the packed vehicles; then his breath coming short and sending out waves of mist to mingle with the thickening snowflakes, he came to a stop outside the pie shop and stood for a moment, his eyes closed, while the appetising smell of the pies filled his lungs as he drew in a deep breath before pushing his way into the crowded shop.

It was some minutes before he could get to the counter. At one end of it a young boy was scooping ladlesful of mashed peas into bowls while at the other end a small sharp-faced, greasy-haired man was swiftly bundling pies into sheets of newspaper seemingly with one hand, while with the other placing numbers on tin plates that were being held out to him by the customers, and, like a magician with a third invisible hand, he was taking money and returning change.

When Simon managed to push his way along the counter and to stand before him, the man glanced at him for a moment, saying, "Plate or paper?"

"Neither. I want to see Lucy Cuthbertson."

As if some unseen clockwork had stopped the movements of his hands, Mr Proggle looked at the well-dressed man before him, who by his voice was not a gentleman, but by the cut of his clothes was certainly someone of quality. Swiftly resuming his servicing, pushing the paper wrapped pies or the plates this way and that, he asked, "Why do you want to see her?"

"I'm her father."

Again the hands came to a temporary halt and the man, now jerking his chin upwards, said, "Oh aye. Well, you'll have to prove that."

"I'll prove it, where is she?"

"You'll have to wait, I've got me hands full."

Simon now looked over the heads of the crowd of men, women and children and his eyes came to rest on a dark hole that led into the shop, and so, pushing his way through the throng, he paused at the top of the stairs and glanced back at Mr Proggle, who was staring towards him; then he descended into the cellar kitchen. . . .

The first glimpse he had of his daughter, his beloved Noreen, pierced him as would a knife driven into him by a friend. His lass who had been brought up as good as any lady working in this

231

filthy hole. She had her back to him but there was no need to wonder if he was on the right track.

When Noreen turned from the oven, the big iron shelf in her hand, and saw him standing in the dimness at the foot of the stairs she had to take two running steps in order to avoid dropping the shelf and its contents on to the floor. Then she stood leaning against the corner of the table staring at him, some instinct born of the tie of blood urging her to fly to him and throw her arms around him and feel the protection of his strength, while the knowledge of his temper and the possessiveness of his love brought her back straight and her face stiff as she watched him approach slowly into the radius of the lamps.

When he didn't stop at the end of the table but kept coming on she backed from him towards the ovens, saying as she did so, "You lay a hand on me and I'll scream and I'll have that shopful down on you."

"Aw, lass! lass!" The tone of his voice, the sorrow in it, the compassion in his look, took the stiffness out of her entire body, and when he stopped within an arm's length of her she saw that his whole face was quivering.

His voice low now, even pleading, he said, "I'm not going to lay a hand on you, all I want is for you to come home."

Again there was the urge to throw herself at him, but the realisation of why she was here in this filthy verminous, stinking place came to the foremost of her mind, and she cried at him, "And be made to toe the line again, locked up? Or perhaps you haven't noticed" – she now slapped her stomach hard – "I'm not alone any more, I'm carrying Willy's bairn. And what'll you do if I go back? Kill him, as you promised? or will you send for him and say marry my daughter and make an honest woman of her? But before you comtemplate doing either let me tell you that it was me who did the wooing. Oh yes, you can droop your head, I wanted him, I wanted his child. I thought in my ignorance that if you knew I was bearing you'd see things differently. But you went mad before you even knew we had come together. And now you say come back?"

Simon still kept his head bent. He knew he wasn't dealing with a girl any longer but that here was a woman who would go her own way no matter what he did or said. But all he wanted at this moment was to get her back into the shelter of his home because unless he succeeded in doing that he would have lost for good, not only her but Lucy also; and of late it had come to him that strangely he needed Lucy, for lying alone at nights he had realised that what he had thought of as her complacency, good-humoured complacency, had been a form of strength, deep strength. And she had shown him to what depths that strength could carry her these past months, for as sure as he would have killed Willy Sopwith had they met up, she would have done likewise to him if he had laid a hand on her. And he knew now that he needed her, he needed her as much as he needed Noreen, more in fact, because Noreen would, he hated to admit, have inevitably gone from him one day to another man. But Lucy would always have been there. She was there now, and yet she wasn't there, but once she had her daughter back and knowing he was the means of bringing her back quietly, peaceably, accepting the condition she was in, she would return to the once pliant wife he had come to rely on while not realising it.

He said quietly, "Your mother misses you. She's not herself any more, she wants you back. And there'll be no trouble. I promise you. I give you my word on it, there'll be no trouble." He did not add, "As long as Sopwith keeps out of the way," for he knew he wouldn't be accountable for his actions if he were to come face to face with the fellow, for the desire to pay off the score between Tilly and himself was still burning in him and could only be achieved through her son.

"Do you mean that?" Noreen's throat was swelling, and he answered, "I do." But when she said, "And you won't tie me down in any way?" there was a slight pause before he repeated her words, "I won't tie you down in any way."

She now dusted her hands one against the other, then looked from side to side, saying, "I'll . . . I'll be leaving him in the lurch, he's. . . ." She got no further; evidently in pain she pushed past him and gripped the edge of the table and again her hand went round her waist.

Now Simon was holding her, saying, "What is it?"

She shook her head, unable to speak for the moment; when she did she answered simply. " 'Tisn't due for three weeks."

"But the pain, how long have you had it?"

"A couple of days."

"Come; get your cloak."

As Simon spoke Mr Proggle entered the kitchen, saying, "What's this? What's this? Now look, where you off to?" He put his hand out towards Noreen, but it was Simon who answered, saying, "She's off home where she should have been all the time."

"She . . . she can't go like this, she's by the week. She's leavin' me in a pickle and I won't pay her, not me. I can claim for the four days; by the week she is."

"What does she earn a day?"

Mr Proggle seemed surprised by the question and the fact that the man was putting his hand into his pocket, and he muttered "Penny ha'penny an hour. Good wage at that; six shillings that is."

Slowly Simon counted the six shillings on to the table; then staring at the man, he said, "You should be prosecuted for keeping anyone working in this hell hole." He pointed now to a cat chewing at the carcass of a rat and to the beetles scurrying around the skirting board, and his lip curled away from his teeth as he said, "Slaves have better quarters."

"A man has to earn a livin'."

"You mean, has to make a fortune. And that's what you're coining up there" – he jerked his head – "and out of the unfortunates. Out of me way!" He threw his arm wide and nearly knocked the man on to his back; then with his other hand around Noreen's shoulders he pressed her forward and up the stairs. And now guiding her through the shop amid the curious glances of the customers, they made for the street. There she stopped and, turning her face upwards, she let the snowflakes fall on it for a moment before gazing down the narrow cobbled road towards the waterfront and the dim shapes of the masts of the boats lying along the quay.

"I've got the trap at Fuller's, do you think you can walk that far?" She nodded but made no reply; nor did she resist when he put his arm around her shoulders and helped her up the slippery bank towards the main thoroughfare.

It was when they entered the farrier's and she saw Lady, her head tossing with impatience at being still harnessed to the trap, that she almost broke down and wept. Going to the horse who seemed to recognise her almost instantly, she laid her face for a moment against her cheek. Then moving towards the step of the trap, she was about to lift her foot on to it when again the pain seized her, worse this time, bringing her almost bent double, and Simon, holding her tightly, said anxiously, "Shall I take you to a doctor?"

"No . . . no." She straightened up. "Just get me home."

Home. It had a wonderful sound as she uttered it, and it sounded wonderful too to his ears.

Lifting her bodily now, he placed her in the trap, pulled the canvas hood – an invention of his own, he had made to keep out the winds – firmly into place; then having settled his account, he took his seat beside her and they moved out and began the journey home. . . .

When they crossed the bridge and left Newcastle it was as if they had entered another world, a white snow-bound world. Whereas the streets behind them had been lined with slush, the roads before them were bordered in deep white drifts, and the further they went towards Jarrow the deeper became the drifts and the harder the going. At times Simon had to dismount and kick the light snow away to allow the horse passage.

He had lit the lamps shortly after they passed through Gateshead and now at four o'clock in the afternoon the night had come upon them and it was impossible to see beyond the radius of light given off by the dim lamps.

Time and again he tucked the rug around Noreen and asked the same question, "Are you all right?"

Sometimes she answered "Yes", and sometimes she merely nodded. These were the times when the pains were gripping her. And she knew now, without having previous experience, that the child within her was trying to kick its way into life. . . .

It was almost an hour and a half later when they reached the turnpike. At this rate another half-hour and they'd be home, but the road that lay straight ahead to the farm was now almost impassable with drifts three feet and more high. There was nothing for it but to take the side road. This would lead through the wood for at least half the remaining journey but there the trees would have taken a great deal of the snow and stopped the drifting.

He got down from the trap yet once again and turned the horse to the right and up the somewhat sheltered side road that led into the wood, the far edge of which actually bordered his own land or the land that he had thought of as his own and which he had been given notice to leave. But this thought did not enter his mind, all he wanted was to get his lass home and not least to witness Lucy's joy at the reunion.

He had been re-seated in the cart for less than a minute when from out of a snow-covered ditch to the right of them there sprang a young doe. How it had strayed down this far would never be known because the nearest herd was in Blandon Park, and that was all of eight miles away. When the horse reared, then tried to go into a gallop, Simon pulled on the reins and yelled, "Whoa there! Steady! Steady girl, steady!"

But the animal was tired and frightened and it continued to try to go into a gallop; and for a number of yards it succeeded in an ungainly fashion, but then of a sudden it seemed to leap into the air before disappearing into the ground. As it let out an unearthly neigh both Simon and Noreen joined their voices to it as the trap, capsizing, rolled right over pinning them both beneath it. . . .

They were all very still until the horse kicked out with its back leg, and as the hoof struck Simon in the middle of his back he made no sound for he was already unconscious.

There was silence again for quite some time; then Noreen, her voice like a faint whisper, said, "Dad! Dad!" then louder now, "Dad! Dad!" She tried to move and found her arms free but the seat of the trap was pinning her legs below the knees, and as she muttered, "Oh God! Oh God!" her upper body relaxed and she lay back in the cushion of the snow, and her last conscious thought was, "Well, I'm glad we made it up."

13

When Steve came up out of the drift entrance he paused for a minute, saying to one of the men beside him, "Good God, look at that! That's a contrast if you like. If you want to get in the morrow I can see you having to get your shovels out early on."

The man nodded, saying, "Aye, aye. The women kept it clear yesterday, but it was nowt like this. Aye, you're right, it'll be shovelling white instead of black." He gave a throaty chuckle, then went on his way, saying, "Night, boss," and Steve answered, "Night, Dick."

In the office, Alec Manning was at the desk writing in the ledger, and Steve hanging his lamp on the wall said, "It's been coming down thick and heavy, eh?"

"Yes; it started again about two hours ago."

"Well, that was just about the time I went in. And by the way, they've got about another thirty skips extra out of that seam the day; must have been glad of the warmth."

"Yes, I suppose so. And speaking of warmth, some of the fellows were at me about the free boots for the bairns come Christmas, and wondered if they couldn't have the money instead."

Steve turned sharply towards him, "Why is that?"

"Oh, they said the money could be spent on coats and such like and they can cobble the boots up."

"Cobble the boots up?" Steve nodded his head. "Or get a skinful with the money? I doubt if she'll agree to that."

"I didn't think she would, but anyway they asked me to tap you so you could tap her."

"Well, I think I can tell you what her answer will be afore there's any tapping done. The more you give some folks the more they want; they get an extra dollar at Christmas. Who else gives them that? You ask them that and tell them if they don't take the boots for the bairns they won't get the dollar. That'll make them think differently. Are they all in on this?"

"No, I don't think so; just Conroy, Wilson and McAvoy."

"Oh, McAvoy. He'd see his bairns and his wife going naked, that one, as long as he could get his slush. He's the one who wouldn't send his lad to school, you remember? Anyway, I'm not bothering about them now, I'm ready for me bed. That's if I can get there. By the way, if I'm not in in the morning you'll know what's holding me up."

"Don't worry, I'll be on hand. Rosie grumbles at times about the house being so near the pit, but this is one of the times I'm thankful it is. And so is she. And that's another thing, you know, you needn't make the journey home, there's always a bed there."

"Thanks all the same, Alec, but there're two rabbits in the yard that need feeding, and three pigeons, not forgetting the cat. Of course the cat could have the pigeons, then finish up on the rabbits if the worst comes to the worst!"

They both laughed, then nodded at each other, saying, "Well, good-night."

In the stable, he lit a lantern, attached it to the side of the saddle, patted the animal while he laughingly half sang a verse from Cowper's hymn:

> "God moves in a mysterious way
>   His wonders to perform;
>   He plants His footsteps in the sea,
>   And rides upon the storm."

He was feeling happy tonight, yet on the face of it he had no reason to be. Tilly's attitude told him plainly what her answer was going to be. His plain speaking had made her mad, which, in a way, was a good thing, it all depended how you looked at it. He was spending Christmas with Phillipa and Lance and the children. He supposed it was this prospect that was affording him this feeling, yet all the time his mind, when not taken up with work, dwelt on Tilly.

When a voice came out of the darkness, saying, "You're going to have a job further along, Mr McGrath," he looked down into the two faces peering up through the falling snow at him, and he said, "Well, you've managed it."

"Just about, but it's worse further on. Doubt if the lads will get in from beyond the turnpike the night."

The other man laughed now as he said, "Never thought I'd say I'd be glad to get down below, but this is one time I will."

"Good-night, Mr McGrath."

"Good-night, Higgins. Good-night, Smith."

He hadn't gone more than half a mile further on when he realised what the men meant for the horse was now up to its knees in snow in the middle of the road, and it wasn't drifting here. Some way before he reached the cottage he dismounted and ploughed forward on foot, leading the horse now, and it was just as he came in sight of the gate that another dark figure stumbled into view gasping, "Is that you, Mr McGrath?"

"Yes, it is. Who's that?"

"Scorer, sir. Billy Scorer."

"Hello, Scorer. Been finding the going hard?"

"Aye, I have, sir. And there's trouble back there, dreadful trouble. You're the first one I've met. There'll have to be help got. It's a horse'n trap tumbled into a ditch or a small gulley, and there's a woman and man pinned 'neath it. It was the horse that drew me attention, neighin' it was, cryin'."

"Whereabouts was this?"

"Just off the turnpike, a couple of dozen yards just afore you get to the wood."

Steve looked about him in bewilderment for a moment; then said, "Well, I'll have to stable the animal, he couldn't get through in this. Hang on a minute, I'll come with you."

"I think it'll take more than two of us. I tried to pull the woman clear but she seemed out for the count, didn't help herself. From what I could see with me light she didn't look hurt. I mean there was no blood or anything, but she's pinned somewhat."

"I'll be with you." Steve was shouting back now as he led the animal up the path and into the stable. There, pulling the saddle off him, he pushed him into his stall, placed an armful of hay and a bucket of water within his reach, then picked up the lantern and hurried out to join the man. . . .

It was a good half-hour later when they reached the side road. They hadn't met a living soul on the turnpike. There was a deep silence all around them and Billy Scorer remarked under his breath, "Can't hear the horse now, but it's along this way; unless they've been found already."

"I shouldn't think so by the look of the road." Steve swung the light of his lantern over the smooth white surface ahead of them and added, "Likely they'll all be covered by now."

"No, listen; that's the horse again."

They both made an effort to hurry now, lifting their feet high above the snow. Then the light of their lanterns showed up the tangled mass of horse, trap and two twisted figures.

'Dear God! what a mess." Steve shook his head, then said quickly, "Look; I think the first thing we've got to do is to get the horse out of the traces and then we can lift the trap, but we can't budge it as it is now. But wait, hold your hand a minute. Here." Steve held his lantern out to Billy. "Keep it high and I'll see what shape they're in."

Slithering into the deep soft mass of snow, he let himself down to the bottom of the gulley; then shouting, "Move it to the right . . . the light," he saw dimly the face that looked as white as the snow in which it was pillowed but half-covered by the side of the trap, and now he whispered, "Good God!"

Hanging on for support to one wheel of the vehicle, he swept the snow from around Noreen's face and shoulders. Then his hand going inside her cloak felt for the beat of her heart. He waited a moment, then let out a long breath before easing himself around her to the other figure. And here he expected to be confronted by Willy, but the man lying on his side, his head hatless, his face almost buried in the snow, showed him immediately who he was, and again he whispered, "Good God! Simon Bentwood bringing his lass home and to end like this."

He now pushed his way through the drift to where the horse lay, and as he did so he shouted up to Billy, "Further along this way. Keep the light up."

The horse was still, its eyes wide open, the look in them almost of human appeal. He patted its head, saying gently now, "All right, all right, old fellow. We'll soon have you loose."

Making his way round its head, he clawed himself up the incline which was less steep here, and now hastily said, "Stick the lantern in the snow and help me get him loose. But look out for his legs; if he can rise at all he'll lash out."

Once they had pushed the snow away from around the horse, the unloosening of the traces was a comparatively simple matter, but when the animal was freed it didn't kick and struggle to be up and away, and Steve had to prod the poor beast, saying, "Come on, come on, on your feet. On your feet."

It was some minutes later when he looked up at Billy and said, "I think the poor fellow's had it." But the animal, perhaps realising for the first time that it was free, gave a mighty snort and a heave and pulled itself to its feet to stand there quivering. In doing so, it moved the shafts of the trap and Steve, reaching quickly forward, grabbed at the iron frame that had supported the hood and, hanging on to it yelled, "Pull back! Pull back!"

Second later they were both grappling with the frame and Steve was yelling again, "Pull back towards you. This way to the left." Then his voice again on a yell, he cried, "Do you think you could hold it?"

"Aye, aye."

At this he scrambled round to the back of the trap and there, bending low down, he thrust his hands into the snow and under Noreen's shoulders and gently eased her towards him.

Pulling her well clear, he laid her down, and then made his way to Simon. And to his surprise he saw that Simon was free. The half-buried cart wheel had missed him by inches. But it took him all his time to pull the unconscious form through the few feet to where Noreen lay. Once he had done so, he called to Billy ,"You can let go now."

When the trap had sunk once more into the snow, Billy came round the end of it and, holding the two lanterns aloft, he asked quietly, "They alive?"

"Yes; but they won't be much longer if they've got to lie out here. We've got to get help." He gazed down for a moment on Noreen where, through her open cloak her stomach rose, and he added in his own mind, "And quick!"

"But where from? Where's the nearest, would you say?"

"The Manor."

"Aye, the Manor. But it'll take another half-hour to get there in this. By the way, the beast's got up the bank. Perhaps you could ride it."

"No; it would never make it. I'll be quicker on foot . . . Will you stay with them?"

"Aye. Aye, of course. What else?"

"I'll be as quick as I can, Billy. But here." He pulled off his thick overcoat, saying, "Put that round her."

"You'll freeze, man, in this."

"Not if I keep running I won't. And look there." He swung the lantern backward and forward. "That looks like a shawl of some kind. Drag it out and cover them. But see to her. I'm away."

Without any further words he scrambled up the bank, and when he came to the horse, standing mutely now, he slapped it on

241

the flanks, saying, "You'll be all right, boy, you'll be all right."
Then to his surprise the animal began to trudge after him. . . .

He was gasping for breath when he came to the gates. Finding
them locked, he rattled the bars, then pulled violently at the iron
bell-pull. But no one came out of the lodge, so he kept clanging
the bell, and he was wondering if he should make his way along
the boundary and climb the wall when he saw a glimmer of a
light from a lantern in the distance.

Ned Spoke peered at him through the bars in surprise, then at
the horse standing there before saying, "Mr McGrath?"

"Open up, Ned quick; there's been an accident along the road.
I want help."

Within minutes they were hurrying up the comparatively clear
drive and to the house, and at any other time Steve might have
been brought to a halt by the fairy tale scene of the lighted
windows set amidst the white world.

He was kicking the snow from his boots and leggings when the
door opened and Biddle, like Ned, exclaimed in surprise, "Mr
McGrath!"

Steve did not mince words but said briefly, "Your mistress.
Get her quickly."

"Yes, yes, sir, Mr McGrath." And turning to Christine Peabody, who was passing through the hall, he said, "Tell the mistress Mr McGrath's here. 'Tis important. Quick now!"

Steve was still standing in the hall when Tilly came running
down the stairs. She stopped at the foot and stared at him. The
fact that he was wearing only his working jacket, breeches and
leggings, and that there was snow still clinging to him, brought
her hurrying forward now saying, "What is it?"

"There's . . . there's been an accident. Can I have a word with
you? We'll need men and . . . and a couple of stretchers." He
moved now almost ahead of her towards the breakfast-room, and
when they were inside he turned to her, saying, "It's Bentwood
and the lass. He must have been bringing her home. The trap
went into a small gulley. We've released them but they're both
unconscious."

When she put her hand to her mouth he said, "There's something more I think you should know, the lass is full with a bairn
and by the size of her almost on her time, I would say."

The whispered "No!" reached him and he explained softly,
"Now you can understand Willy's concern. Anyway, we've got to

242

get them out of that as soon as possible. I don't know to what extent either of them is injured but they were both unconscious when I left them."

"You, you want them brought here?" It was a question rather than a statement and tinged with disbelief and he said, "Where else? The only other place is the Rosier pit cottages and you wouldn't have them go there, would you?"

"No, no." Her voice was a mere whisper. She closed her eyes and shook her head. Then going swiftly to the door, she muttered, "I'll get my things."

"There's no need for you to come."

"I'm coming nevertheless. If the girl's in the condition you say, well" – she turned her head and looked at him for a moment – "the responsibility lies here as you've already indicated."

"Willy. Will you tell him?"

"Not until we get back. He's up in his own room, he needn't know. Will you go to the stables and round up the men?"

"Well yes; but there's only four out there, isn't there? So you'd better tell Biddle to come along an' all, we'll need four for each stretcher. I've Billy Scorer along with them. That only makes seven."

"I can be the eighth."

"Don't be silly." He had turned on her, speaking as a man might to his wife, and she as sharply replied, "I am not an old lady yet."

"Aw, you know what I meant, Tilly. But there's no time for arguing, if you want them alive we'd better look slippy."

If we want them alive! As she flew up the stairs and got into her riding habit and donned a thick coat and fur hat she endeavoured to press away the thoughts: Did she want them alive, either Simon Bentwood or his daughter, the girl who was now carrying her son's child, her grandchild? And the honest answer she could give to this was, for Willy's sake she wished the girl to be still alive but not her father, for if he lived she knew that sooner or later she would lose her son.

It was almost two hours later when the men, stiff and frozen-looking themselves, carried the prostrate forms upstairs and into the rooms that had been prepared for them. While Biddle and Steve saw to Simon Bentwood, Peg and Fanny Drew undressed Noreen, and Lizzie Gamble, Peggy Stoddard, Nancy Garrett and Christine Peabody dashed up and down the stairs carrying water bottles and oven shelves wrapped in blankets, and during all this time Peabody stood in the kitchen dispensing hot toddy to the men; and Tilly faced her son in her bedroom and listened in silence as he stormed at her for having kept the knowledge of the accident from him.

Tilly was weary, she felt frozen to the bone. She had drunk a large glass of raw whisky, yet it seemed to have scorched only her throat.

"What would the men think?" he asked her now, and for the first time she answered him, saying, "That you were better kept out of the way, you'd have only been a hindrance."

"My God! the things you say to me!"

"Huh!" It was a weary sound. "The things I say to you, Willy? Have you ever considered the things you have said to me lately? Ever since this girl came into your life you have hardly spoken to me but there has been a streak of recrimination in your words. Well now, what I'm going to say to you now holds no recrimination. Noreen has come back into your life, but she's not alone, she is full with your child, at least I would hope it's yours."

He did not exclaim, "What!" he did not immediately storm out of the room and grope his way to find her; he made no movement whatever; even the muscles in his cheekbones remained still; it was as if for the moment he had been deprived of life while being told he was the creator of it.

She rose from the chair and put her hand on his arm, saying, "You didn't know?"

He drew in a long, slow breath, then made a small movement with his head; then said slowly, "Where is she?"

"In the Blue Room. She . . . she has regained consciousness. She came to before they lifted her out of the ditch, but she's very weak and . . . and —" she pulled him to a standstill as he went to move away, then finished softly, "the child is about to be born."

"Aw no!"

"Yes."

"The doctor?"

"We'll have to manage without one."

She took his arm now and led him out into the corridor, down the gallery and into the west wing. This part of the house was rarely used but, as in the past, three or four bedrooms were always kept ready in case of visitors. Tilly had continued the practice although they hadn't been used for years. Now in two adjoining rooms the fires were blazing; Simon Bentwood lay in what was known as the Yellow Room and Noreen in the Blue Room.

When the door was opened in the Blue Room Tilly beckoned Peg out and Willy went slowly forward to where he could see the outline of the bed; then he was moving up by the side of it and now he was peering down into the white face and the eyes that were staring up at him.

"*Oh, Noreen!*" As he breathed her name he felt his mother pushing a chair for him and he sat down; and then his hands went out and cupped the face turned towards him, and again he whispered, "Oh, Noreen!"

When she didn't speak or make any movement, he muttered, "I didn't know. Why didn't you get in touch? This is terrible, terrible. Oh my dear, my dear."

He was aware that the door had closed and that they were alone, and now he bent his head forward and placed his lips on hers, and when there was no response he asked softly, "Are you in pain?"

"Yes."

It was so like her not to waste words, his sensible, level-headed Noreen.

"Oh, I've missed you, Noreen. I've searched and searched day after day. Where were you?"

"Newcastle."

"Newcastle?" He lifted up her hand now and brought it to the top of his chest and, pressing it there, he said, "I went through every street in that city, every alleyway, every court. Ned got tired of looking – and you were there all the time. Oh my dear. My dear." . . .

"Please, please don't cry." It was the first animated sign she had shown, and she put her fingers up and touched his cheek. "Don't worry. Whatever happens, don't worry."

As he went to speak she placed her fingers on his lips, saying slowly and hesitantly now, "Listen to me, Willy. Don't upbraid yourself ever, do you hear me? What happened was because I wanted it to happen, 'twasn't your fault, so you have nothing to reproach yourself with. Remember that."

245

As he held her hand tightly between his own, his vision seemed to clear for a moment and he saw her face so different, so much older than the memory of it he had kept in his mind during these past months. Her cheeks were hollow, her skin looked grey. Then of a sudden he watched her features go into a grimace. He saw her teeth clamp down on her lip, and in this instant he recognised the face of the woman he had seen in his dream. When she brought up her knees and groaned aloud, he said, "What is it? What is it, Noreen? I'll . . . I'll get Mama."

She gasped and held on to his hand for a moment. Then her legs slowly straightening again, she said, "Can . . . can you send for my mother?"

"Yes, yes, of course." He jerked himself up from the seat, almost gabbling now, "We'll . . . we'll get her here." He turned from the bed and groped his way hastily towards the door, for now his vision seemed so blurred he could not even see the outline of the room. Before he opened the door he was calling, "Mama! Mama!" and a second later Tilly who had been waiting outside, said, "Yes, what is it?"

He caught at her extended hand. "Noreen . . . she's in pain, and . . . she want to see her mother. Do . . . do you think we can get her through. . . .?"

Tilly did not answer immediately, and then she said softly, "We'll do our best. You come away. Peg!" she called, and Peg came forward and Tilly said, "Stay with her until I get back."

In the hall she hesitated for a moment before saying to Peabody, "Tell Arthur and Jimmy I'd like to see them."

She knew that both men, like the rest, would be very tired for it had been no easy task, she knew personally, to carry those two stretchers all the way back here, but she also knew that if she were to ask the Drew men to walk into hell for her they would do it.

A few minutes later she was facing them saying, "I know this is a bit thick and I hate to ask it of you, but she's in a bad way and she's asking for her mother. Do . . . do you think you could get her?"

Without hesitation it was Jimmy who answered, "If it is possible we'll get her here, Tilly. There's one thing, it's stopped snowing."

It was Arthur who now put in, "And when we're that far, we'll call in in the village and pick up the midwife. If we can get Mrs Bentwood here, we'll get her here an' all."

She nodded at Arthur now, saying, "That would be a good thing if you could persuade her."

"We'll persuade her all right." Arthur nodded at her.

"Thanks." She looked from one to the other and made a gesture towards them with her hand, then said, "Wrap up extra well and take a flask with you."

"Aw, we'll see to ourselves, don't worry."

As they turned to leave, Steve appeared at the foot of the stairs. He did not speak but he beckoned to her with a lift of his chin, and as she approached him he said softly, "He's conscious. I told him the lass was all right but he's asked for his wife."

"I . . . I have just sent for her."

He stared at her for a moment before saying, "Well, I doubt she'll have to hurry, I think he's on his last legs." Her eyes widened slightly as he added, "I think his back's broken, and there's something gone inside, he's bleeding."

She lowered her head now, and then she asked, "Does he know where he is?"

"Oh yes, yes, he knows where he is. When he first opened his eyes and looked around he . . . he spoke your name, your old name."

She did not ask how he had said her name for she knew it would have been laden with recrimination; yet Steve's next words belied her thoughts. "He didn't speak it in bitterness," he said; "I think he knows his time is short and if it's in your heart to forgive I think you should look in on him, for no man should die in aggravation such as he's held for so long inside of him."

She turned her head to the side and she kept it like that for some time, so long in fact that she became aware of feet and legs scurrying backward and forward across the hall; then lifting her head she looked at him and without a word passed him and walked slowly up the stairs. He followed.

When she opened the bedroom door she paused, and Steve had to press her forward in order to close the door. Then she was walking slowly to the foot of the bed. There were lamps burning on a table at each side of it and the lights seemed focused on his face like two beams. His eyes were open, the skin gathered in deep furrows at the corners as if screwed up against pain. His lips were apart and his tongue kept flicking over the lower one as if he were thirsty. This caused her to drag her eyes from him and say below her breath, "Does . . . does he want a drink?"

247

But before Steve could answer the voice came from the bed, low and thick. "No, I want no drink, I want nothing from you." There was a long pause while their gaze linked; then his voice came again, "You've ... you've done enough for me, Tilly, haven't you? You've come in because you know I'm done for but you know in your heart you did for me years gone by. You ruined my life you did. And you know something?" He hand now came up and gripped his throat, and when he swallowed deeply Steve went to him and, bending over him, said, "Don't talk."

Simon swallowed again, then looking at Steve, he said, "I'll talk all I want." Now he turned his eyes again on Tilly and, his words coming slower, he went on, "What I was gona say was, you were never worth it. You know that? You were never worth it. Lucy was worth t ... ten of you ... ten of you. Do ... do you hear? Lucy was. ..."

Again his hand went up to his throat; and now Steve, putting his hand under Simon's head, raised it slightly, then twisting to the side he took a glass from the bed table and held it to his lips. For a moment Simon gulped at it before pushing it aside, and when Steve laid his head back on the pillow he looked up at him and, after a great intake of breath, he muttered, "She's done for you, too, hasn't she? Henchman, lap-dog, that's what she's ... made of you."

"Yes, very likely."

The quiet retort seemed to silence Simon for a time. Then he said, "My girl?"

"She's all right."

Simon turned his gaze on to Tilly again who was now standing gripping the brass rail at the foot of the bed, and his voice a croak, he said, "She's carrying a bastard born of a bastard. Well, you might get the bairn but ... but you won't get her; I'm ... I'm takin' her along of me." His voice trailed away as a stream of blood ran slowly down the side of his chin, and as Steve bent over him, Tilly turned from the bed and stumbled out of the room and into the corridor. And there she made for one of the deep stone window-sills and dropped on to it and, her hand gripping her brow, she bowed her head.

Love and hate she knew were divided by a mere gossamer thread, but death was supposed to soften the emotions. That man in there had once loved her, and she him. Oh yes, she him. And it was she who should have hated him for being the instrument of shattering her girlish dreams. But she had never hated him, her feelings had not gone beyond dislike and revulsion. But her later rejection of him and the knowledge that she had become mistress to a gentleman had seemed to turn his brain.

"Come away from that cold seat." She lifted her head sharply. For a moment she had thought it was Biddy speaking to her – Fanny was very like her mother – and she allowed the younger woman to raise her up. But when she would have led her across the gallery and down the stairs, she stopped her and said, "No, no, Fanny; I'll go to my room. Is . . . is Willy still. . . .?" She turned her head in the direction of the bedroom where Noreen lay, and Fanny said, "Yes. Yes, he's with her. Don't worry about her, we'll see to her."

"Is she in labour?"

"Well now, she's in pain and has spasms, but it's nothing like the labour I've had with either of mine. Look, you go and lie down or put your feet up anyhow on the couch. If anything goes wrong I'll call you. You've had about enough."

As if their positions were reversed, Tilly walked obediently away from Fanny. Once in her room, however, she didn't put her feet up but kept them tramping the carpet. The only outward sound in the room was this padding sound, but inside her mind there was a great commotion. Voices were yelling at her, all her own but from different ages: as a child who had asked herself quietly why she hadn't anyone to play with, it wasn't only that the village was a way off; then the young girl screaming underneath the weight of Hal McGrath's body, yelling, "No! Oh no!"; the nightmare of the stocks; the even greater nightmare of the courthouse and the question, "Are you a witch?"; the voice that yelled in deep bitterness against those who had burned down the cottage; the loneliness that had cried out against the feeling that was engendered against her by the one-time staff of this very house. She had not cried out when twice she had been turned out of this place, that treatment had only filled her with sadness, but she had cried out greatly in bitterness when her son was blinded. Her cries had turned to screams when the Indians had massacred all but her and Matthew; but in the end they had got Matthew. All through her life she seemed to have been crying out, mostly against injustices. The loves she had experienced had always caused her in the end to cry out.

When the noises in her head became so loud she gripped it with both hands and became still, saying to herself, "Stop it! Stop it!"

This was not the first time she had experienced this cacophony of her own voices yelling against her destiny, but tonight there was a difference because all the voices, although yelling loudly, sounded weary. And she was weary, so very weary. Going to the bed, she lowered herself slowly on top of it and, turning her face into the pillow, she wept.

14

It was four o'clock in the morning but it could have been four o'clock on a busy afternoon for the house was abuzz with activity. The men had returned with Lucy Bentwood and the midwife around midnight. They were all exhausted, but Lucy would not rest until she had seen her daughter. The fact that Noreen was pregnant had come as an added shock to her; she had imagined the midwife had been called for one of the maids, neither of the Drew men had enlightened her otherwise. But as she had looked down on this almost unrecognisable girl pity and compassion had fought and conquered the feeling of dismay and shame.

When they were enfolded in each other's arms and Noreen was crying, "Oh, Mam! Mam!" Lucy had been too overcome to utter any words, but her soothing hands had spoken for her.

Later, when she had stood by her husband's side and he had held out his hand towards her the very act had been one of supplication and it had surprised her. And when she placed her hand in his he whispered, "Lucy, I . . . I found her," she nodded; then said, "Yes, yes, Simon, you found her," and he must have recognised the note of forgiveness in her voice, for swallowing deeply again, he said, "The child; take . . . take it home. Don't . . . don't leave it here."

She could not say to him, "It must be with its mother, wherever she stays."

Again he had to gulp before speaking and, his voice a mere whisper now, he said, "I'm . . . I'm sorry, Lucy. You . . . you were a good wife. You . . . you didn't deserve my . . . my treatment. And for what, I ask you? For what?"

"Don't talk; lie still."

"I'm . . . I'm going to lie still for a long time, Lucy; will you say you forgive me?"

She could not see his face and her voice was breaking as she said, "There's nothing to forgive. It's life and we've lived it as God ordained. Good comes out of bad."

"You were too good for me. I . . . I should have had her, and she would have brought me more torment than . . . than I've gone through already . . . Wish there was time to show you I . . . I could be different. Hold my hand tight, Lucy."

She held his hand tight and he closed his eyes and seemed to sleep. . . .

At one o'clock Noreen's labour pains had started in earnest. With Lucy on one side and the midwife on the other they urged her to press downwards, making encouraging noises, wiping the sweat from her brow, suffering the pain of her clinging nails. Then as the time wore on and the pains became more frequent her strength seemed to become less.

It was during one such period that Tilly opened the door and, beckoning Lucy towards her, said softly, "Steve thinks you should go in," at the same time motioning her head back towards the corridor. "I'll stay here."

Lucy paused for a moment, looked back towards the bed and the straining girl, then without a word she passed Tilly and made for the room along the corridor.

Tilly took her place at the other side of the bed from the midwife whose face was running with sweat, and the woman shook her head and muttered, "Summit 'll have to be done, she's about pulled out."

Tilly did not ask, "What?" but she bent over Noreen and said softly, "Put your hands behind you, dear, and grip the bed rails."

Almost immediately the midwife's voice came at her harshly, saying, "She's tried that! I tell you she's got no pull left in her."

Tilly looked at the woman. From the moment of her entering the house she had seemed to bring the atmosphere of the village with her. She must have come under protest or perhaps out of curiosity, but now she was looking almost as weary and tired as Noreen.

When Tilly spoke to her now it was as the mistress of the house. She said, "You look very tired; go down to the kitchen and send one of the girls up."

"And what could they do, ma'am, at a time like this?"

"As much as you're able to do at the moment."

"Are you tellin' me I don't know me job, ma'am?"

"I am simply telling you that I think you need a rest."

The woman straightened her back, then almost glared across

252

at Tilly, saying, "Well, don't blame me, ma'am, for whatever happens when I'm out of the room."

Before she finished speaking there was a tap on the door and Peg entered carrying a tray holding bowls of broth, and Tilly, turning to her immediately, said, "Take it across the corridor into the little library, Peg, please, Mrs Grant is going to take a short rest, then come straight back here."

Although there was protest in the midwife's pose as she went out of the door, Tilly also gauged there was a certain amount of relief, for the woman had been on her feet for almost four hours.

When Noreen began to moan, Tilly caught her hands, saying "There, dear, press down. Try. Come on, try."

The girl made an effort to obey but there was little pressure in her straining and when she relaxed again, Tilly looked down on her in not a little alarm: if something wasn't done, she, too, would die. The thought brought her glance towards the far door and the dressing-room in which she knew Willy was pacing. It had taken Steve to get him out of the room and she herself had turned the key on this side of the door, but now instinctively she ran to it and unlocked it, saying as she did so, "Come in. Come in."

When he was abreast of her she whispered at him, "She's ill, very ill, and weak. Take her hand; talk to her."

She led him quickly to the side of the bed and when he placed his hand on Noreen's she saw that it was received with no answering grip, but Noreen turned her eyes towards him and said softly, "Willy?"

"Oh my dear, my dearest, are . . . are you all right?" It was a stupid question to ask but it was a man's question, and her answer startled him.

"If . . . if the baby . . . is all right, let . . . let Mother have it, will you?"

When he made no answer she said again, "Will you, Willy?"

"But . . . but you're going to get well; you're going to be all right. Won't she?" He turned his head towards the hazy figure of his mother standing at the other side of the bed, and when she didn't speak he gathered up Noreen's hand to his chest and pressed it tight against him as he muttered, "Noreen! Noreen! you must get well. I . . . I need you. I love you."

The only answer he received was a groan as another spasm of pain hit Noreen; at the same moment the door opened and Peg came scurrying into the room muttering by way of apology for not

253

returning immediately something about the midwife knocking over the broth.

Beyond the open door Tilly saw Steve standing beckoning to her. Going quickly to him she pulled the door behind her and looked at him as he said softly, "He's gone."

She had been expecting this news yet it brought a strange reaction: she wanted to cry again and a voice from the far past came rising up from the depths of her, saying, "Oh, Simon! Simon!" And the picture that now floated before her mind's eye was that of the kindly, considerate young farmer who had literally kept them from the borders of starvation for years; and following on this there came an accusing voice that had attacked her again and again, saying, "What is it about me that changes people so?"

" 'Tis better this way; but it's odd that he should have to die in your house . . . Aw Tilly!" Even the way he sighed on her name she took to be a condemnation of that which was in her and which could not be named.

Her back stiffened slightly and her voice conveyed the stiffness as she said, "Would . . . would you tell her . . . her mother" – she inclined her head towards the bedroom door – "she's needed?"

If he noticed her change of manner he ignored it and asked, "How is the lass?"

"In a bad state, I should say."

A sharp cry came from behind the closed door and he turned abruptly and hurried away leaving Tilly standing where she was voicelessly praying now: Don't let it happen to the girl. She wasn't thinking at this moment of the effect on Lucy Bentwood should she lose both her husband and her daughter, but of her own son and the burden he would have to bear if Noreen's death came about through the carrying of his child and the hardship she must have endured during these past months.

As Lucy passed her they exchanged a glance but did not speak, and when Steve, reaching out, opened the door for them the scream from the bed hit them and caused all their faces to move in protest. . . .

As the late dawn broke the child was born. It was a girl and barely alive, but as it gave its first weak cry Noreen Bentwood joined her father.

15

The village was again agog. Nothing seemed to bring it alive as much as the happenings in the Manor surrounding . . . *that one*. There had been shipwrecks in Shields when people standing help-less on the shore had watched men drown; there had been cases of cholera, enough to cause widespread apprehension of coming epidemics; there had been pit strikes; there had been strikes in the shipyards when the Jarrow men became a ferocious fighting horde, their anger ignited by injustice. Then there had been the local scandals. The daughter of a prominent business-man living not far from the village had run off with a stable hand, and she just fresh out from a convent education, and he not able to read or write, so it was said. And yet all these things great and small seemed to fade into insignificance whenever something occurred . . . up there, through . . . *that one*. And now God above! would you believe it, Farmer Bentwood searching for his daughter finds her working in the kitchen of a brothel, so it was said, and al-though her belly's full with the blind one's bastard he brings her home, at least makes the effort to. And she must have been willing enough to come with him. But then what happens, some evil spirit guides him on the wrong road and there *that one's* fancy man finds them. And the result; aye dear God! – everyone in the village shook their head when they whispered the result – both to die in her house. But for the farmer to die there . . . well, it was weird for she had plagued that man all his life. Hadn't she ruined his first marriage? And hadn't she tried to shoot him once? And now finally he dies in her house, and his beloved daughter with him. Was it not weird to say the least? they asked of each other. And had anybody reckoned up the people who had died after coming into contact with her?

They had waited to see her attend the funeral – it would have been just the brazen thing she would do – but she hadn't been there. Her son had though. Yes, and walking unashamedly along-side the poor widow, overshadowing her own son Eddie.

The villagers didn't go on to say that afterwards Lucy Bentwood had returned not to the farm but to the Manor; but they were up in arms at the fact that young Eddie had gone back and sacked Randy Simmons. Now what did you think of that, and him being on that farm since he was a lad? He had been given notice to quit his cottage an' all, no pension. Of course, everyone knew that Randy wouldn't starve, he had feathered his nest in one way or the other over the years, but that wasn't saying he should be put out of his cottage and no compensation. They were surprised at young Eddie though. But likely he had only been carrying out his mother's orders, for it was well known she never had much use for Randy.

But when it was all boiled down, it was still all connected with *that one* up there.

They sat one at each side of the fireplace in the drawing-room, each with a cup of tea in her hand, and when Lucy sipped at hers Tilly followed suit.

There were words to be said, matters to be arranged, but she couldn't find an opening. Yesterday this woman had buried her husband and her daughter, and the fault lay here in this house, for if her son had not given this woman's daughter a child then likely she would not have run away, and so there would have been no need for Simon to go in search of her. The snow would not then have got them, and they would have been alive now.

Only an hour ago when Willy had said for the countless time that he didn't want to give up the child, she had been forced to make him share the burden of the coffins he had followed yesterday. Unlike herself promising Matthew that she wouldn't marry again, Willy had said that he had given Noreen no answer to her request that he'd let her mother have the child because at the time he was stunned by the thought that she knew she wouldn't survive the birth.

Tilly was startled out of her thinking when Lucy said quietly, "Don't carry the burden for what has happened on your shoulders, nor let your son carry it, it was inevitable. I don't know what

Simon had promised her in order to get her to return home but I feel she would have demanded that in no way would he do any harm to your son. And knowing him, he would have promised her this whilst at the same time being determined to wreak vengeance for what had happened to his daughter. Although he had not known it, he had been in love with her. Oh yes, yes" – she nodded towards Tilly's widening eyes – "he had in a way put her in your place."

"Oh no, no! You're wrong there. He ceased to care for me many, many years ago."

"He had never ceased to care for you."

They stared at each other in silence.

"He was besotted with you. It was a bitter knowledge I had to accept, and it would have been easier to bear if he had acted normally and not tried to erase his feelings through hate, false hate."

Remembering the last time she had looked down on Simon Bentwood's face and his words to her, Tilly was forced to say, "I . . . I think you're mistaken. His hate was real, not simulated."

"Then why did he die calling for you?"

Tilly made a movement to rise to her feet, then resumed her seat and, her head moving slowly from side to side, she said, "It must have been in delirium because at our last meeting he told me exactly what I was worth to him, and his meaning was plain: he had wasted his life following the dross while ignoring the gold that was you."

"He said that?"

"Yes."

"And he meant it, and had he been spared to live you would certainly have come into your own." Tilly looked down now on Lucy's bent head whose muttered words were scarcely audible: "I stopped loving him a long time ago but I still cared for him and his needs. And then I stopped caring. That was the worst part, I stopped caring. I . . . I loved my daughter, yet in a way I was jealous of her, for I knew if he had had to make the choice who would have the last crust in a famine, he would have given it to her. Strange" – she raised her head now – "he never cared anything for his son. Most men long for a son. And the boy was aware of his neglect from when he was a child. And I know now, and it is strange that I should say this, but my son is glad that his father's gone because his fear has been buried with him. He was afraid of him, you know.'

257

Lucy now took another sip from the almost cold tea; then putting the cup and saucer down on the table that stood between them, she said, "At times I've pitied myself because I was being forced to live a life without love, and I envied you; but now I know that my life has been like a calm sea compared with yours and the injustices you have been made to suffer. Beautiful women like you have to pay the price for their beauty. In your case I think it's been too much, so what I say to you now, I said before, throw off any burden you might feel concerning my loss, because I shan't be unhappy: I have my son who I know loves me dearly, and because of your son's consideration I have a granddaughter to bring up. At the same time though, I shall remember that she has another grandmother here and also a father. And now I must be getting back."

Tilly watched Lucy take the napkin from her knee and fold it up before laying it gently on the corner of the table. She watched her dust her fingers against each other, adjust the bodice of her black taffeta blouse, smooth down the sides of her thick black cord skirt; then as she slowly rose to her feet, Tilly rose also and impulsively now she held her hands out towards this woman who had suffered through her for years. And when she felt them taken and gripped the tears sprang to her eyes. They stared at each other for a moment in silence, until Lucy said thickly, "I'll away and get her then." And to this Tilly, being unable to speak, merely nodded.

Left alone, Tilly turned and stood gazing down into the fire. She knew that she should go in search of Willy for it was no easy thing she had persuaded him to do, and she knew if she faced the truth that persuading him to relinquish his claim on the infant was at bottom her own desire to be rid of the child, for at this stage of her life she didn't want to take on any more responsibility and certainly not that of an infant, for it would be herself who would have to bear the responsibility of its upbringing. Its presence, too, in the house would have been an obstacle to the plan that was forming in her mind, if it was not already formed, but which she would not at the moment bring to the fore. Even so, knowing all this, she still asked herself if she was really wise in letting the child go, for its presence might fill the gaping years ahead. Anyway it would always be near for what she meant to do was to give the freehold of the farm to Lucy and her son. This would achieve two things. It would ensure that her grandchild would always be near at hand, but more so it would go a long way to easing her conscience.

It was almost the New Year again and Steve had not asked for an answer to his ultimatum. Of course, he wouldn't, not under the circumstances.

He had been very good during this whole unfortunate business; in fact, for one period he seemed to be running the house, quite unintentionally she realised, for he was not trying to show her that he was capable of acting as her regent. Anyway, when he came for his answer it would be the same that she could have given him months ago in the cottage.

Of all the things that had happened to her emotionally in her life she knew Steve's defection was a most painful thing she'd had to endure. It was as if they had been married for years and that he had suddenly told her he had another woman . . . and had had her for some long time.

She closed her eyes tightly on the thoughts of how deep had become her jealousy of his daughter.

16

She said to Willy, "I don't think I can make the journey to Liverpool to meet Josefina; you'll have to go with Ned."

"But she'll think it odd."

"No, she won't. Tell her I'm not feeling very well, she'll understand."

"It's a long way to come just to be greeted by me."

Willy was sitting aimlessly in the big chair, one arm hanging over the side, his fingers moving slowly in the long hair of the dog at his feet, and Tilly wondered how long it would be before he would realise how much Josefina loved him. Sometimes she wondered if he already realised it. Last week he had suddenly said, "Only five more days and she should be here – that's if the boat docks as expected. It'll be like old times." Then he added, "Can one really relive old times?"

"You can but try," she had answered.

"She must have been very unhappy over there to want to come back because when she left she was so adamant that she would never return. . . . I missed her, you know."

'Yes, I'm sure you did. And I did too."

"I think I'll start at the mine again once she's settled in. I can't just sit here idling my days away. By the way, Steve hasn't been this week, has he?"

"No."

"Was he at the meeting on Friday?"

"No; he has gone off for a long week-end with some friends."

"Have you two really quarrelled?"

"No; why should we?"

"Oh, Mama, don't treat me like a fool. I've loved too, remember, I know what it's like, and Steve's love for you must be a very unusual love to have served you all these years."

'Well, he's not going to serve me much longer."

There, it was out.

"What!" The slackness left his body, he was sitting straight up in the chair. "What do you mean?"

"He's got the offer of a new post, with Coleman's firm."

"Coleman's the engineers?"

"Yes."

"And he's going?"

"Yes; as far as I know he's going."

"When did all this come about?"

"Oh, some time ago."

"I can't believe it. Did he actually tell you this?"

"Yes, Willy, he actually told me this. And what you don't know, Willy, is that my dear friend has for some years been moving in high places. He has a daughter. . . ."

"What! Steve has a daughter?"

"Yes; she's a full-grown woman, over thirty, and she was brought up by the Colemans, and from there married into the Ryde-Smithsons. You don't get much higher than the Ryde-Smithsons."

"*Steve! Our Steve?*"

"Yes, Steve. Our Steve."

"Have you met his daughter?"

"Yes." Tilly watched him sink back into the chair and nod his head slowly as he said, "So that's what it's all about. Well! Well! Talk of surprises, I wouldn't have believed it. No wonder you have been feeling down. I'm sorry." He pulled himself to his feet and made his way towards her, and when his arms came about her she lay against him for a moment, saying with a break in her voice, "Such is life, Willy; it's . . . it's full of surprises."

"And you've had more than your share. Well, I never thought he'd desert you, no matter how big the carrot was. I'm amazed, really I am. . . ."

There was a tap on the door and Biddle entered, saying, "Mr McGrath has called, ma'am."

"Speak of the devil." The words were muttered before she nodded towards Biddle, saying, "Show him in, please." Then quickly she turned to Willy, saying, "Where are you going?"

"Into the library. I don't want to be in on this, I might forget how good he's been to me and say things I'd be sorry for later." He now turned from her and groped his way steadily down the long drawing-room to the door at the end, and as he went out of it Steve entered the room from the other end.

He gave no immediate greeting until he was standing in front of her, and then some seconds passed before he said, "Nice to see the sun out, isn't it, even though it's struggling?"

"Yes" – she turned her head towards the long window – "We could do with some sunshine."

"How are you?"

"Oh, I'm all right . . . Sit down. She pointed to the chair opposite, and when he had sat down she resumed her own seat.

He was looking very spruce, very smart. He was wearing a new suit, she noticed, pepper-and-salt colour and of a good tweed. He had short gaiters over the tight trouser bottoms; his boots were brown and highly polished. At his neck he was sporting a gold tie pin in the shape of a riding crop. His hair was well brushed, still brown on top but greying at the temples. His face was lined but more with character than with age. Yes, he would cut a good figure in the society in which he was about to move; his daughter would have no need to apologise for him, oh no.

That he was returning her appraisal was given with his next words, "You look peaky," he said.

Her back stiffened still further. "Well, if you remember I've been, in fact we've all been, through rather a trying period."

"Yes, yes." He nodded pleasantly at her. "I could say we have. Yes, I endorse that."

I endorse that. He was using words that would fit into his new way of life. The bitterness gathered in her, forming a knot in her chest, not a little with the knowledge that there were worlds dividing the once adoring lad and this sophisticated man.

"Are you up to talking business?"

"Yes, I'm up to talking business."

"Good." He was smiling at her again. His whole attitude seemed to point to his being well satisfied with himself and when he said, "I'd better get on my feet, it's usual isn't it when one comes a-courting?" Her mouth fell into a slight gape. He was making fun of her, and to say the least it was in very bad taste. She listened to him in amazement as he now said, "About me ultimatum."

Perhaps it was her irritation and feeling of annoyance that made her remark, even bitterly, to herself that in spite of his polish he still reverted to the idiom "me".

"What's it to be?"

She stared at him for almost a full minute before rising slowly from the chair and facing him and, as slowly, saying, "I think you're already aware of the answer."

"Aye." He looked to the side and raised his eyebrows. "Yes, I felt that's what you would say after the way I put it to you. I'm not surprised. Well now, that's out of the way." He opened the last button of his jacket, pulled the points of his waistcoat down, then said, "Me other business. It's about the cottage, I want to buy it."

Rage was rising in her. He had dismissed her refusal as the merest trifle, not worth a second's consideration. She had never thought there would come a time when she would hate Steve McGrath almost as much as she hated his brother, but it was almost upon her. And he wanted to buy the cottage! She repeated now in cutting tones, "You want to buy my cottage? You're sure you don't want to buy my mine too?"

"Well, not at the present, Tilly; funds wouldn't run to that." His smile broadened. "But I can manage the cottage and the alterations I have in mind."

"Oh —" her lips pouted, her head wagged and she repeated, "alterations you have in mind."

"Yes. It is poky, you must admit, so I thought of sticking on a parlour. Not a drawing-room" – he looked around the room, his head making a waving motion the while – "just a nice comfortable parlour. The present room I'll turn into a kitchen, for that alone, and I'd like a little dining-room and a couple of bedrooms up above. I would arrange all the windows to be mostly at the back, because it's a very nice view from there, isn't it, being on that bit of a rise? I've also seen Mr Pringle who owns the fields at the bottom. He's quite willing to sell a few acres because they run soggy in the dip and the cattle get bogged down there sometimes in the winter. When I've been thinking about it, I've had to laugh to meself because that's how manors and big houses started, didn't they, mostly anyway, from a little cottage and a bit added on here and there? This very house" – he waved his hand about – "I learned recently had only eight rooms when it was first built, and now how many has it got? I bet they can't count them. Of course, I won't be able to achieve it at one go but that's the kind of pattern I've worked out. So what about it, eh?"

She just couldn't believe her ears. There was something wrong here. What did he want the cottage for and all the extensions if he was going away? She tried to speak but her words were choking her and she had to swallow deeply twice before she could bring out, "Why do you want to buy the cottage if you are taking on a new position?"

"I never said I was taking on a new position."

Again she swallowed. "You indicated in your ultimatum that if my answer didn't suit you, you would then take up Mr Coleman's offer. Such a lucrative one you gave me to understand."

"Oh that! And aye, it was very lucrative, as you say." He jerked his chin upwards. "But I told him straightaway no. I never had any intention of taking it on."

"But you said. . . ."

"Aye, I know what I said." His voice had lost its bantering tone. His face was straight now and the muscles began to jerk in his cheekbones, and then he muttered thickly, "I had to do something to bring you to your senses and to stop you actin' like a young lass who didn't know her own mind while all the time you did. I was sick of being played about with, being used, I wanted to know where I stood for once. And now I do."

As she watched the stiffness leave his face and a twisted smile draw up the corner of his mouth, the anger in her swelled. To think he had put her through all this for months, and on top of all the other trouble. He had been laughing up his sleeve at her while knowing what she must be suffering.

She could have been yelling at the sightseers who were looking at the burning cottage, or staring at Alvero Portes before she sprang at him, or standing in the square confronting the villagers, her anger was as deep as any she had felt before, and she reacted to it.

When her hand came slap across his face he staggered back for a moment, then covered his burning cheek with his palm. Slowly now his mouth opened as he stared at her; then a most unusual thing happened. It took the fire out of her anger and she slumped like a pricked balloon when, his head going back, he let out a great roar of laughter. It rose and rose and the tears gushed from his eyes as it became louder.

Willy heard it in the library. It brought him up from his chair but he didn't move towards the drawing-room; but it caused him to smile, the first time his features had moved in this direction for weeks.

The laughter was heard as far away as the kitchen and caused Fanny to exclaim, "Oh, isn't that good to hear somebody's laughing?"

It caused Peabody in the hall to unbend so much that he forgot himself and addressed Biddle as Clem, saying, "Well! well! Clem. What do you make of that?" And what any of them would have made of the scene in the drawing-room would be hard to say, for now Steve was holding Tilly tightly in his arms. His face was wet, his mouth wide and his eyes looking straight into hers, he was saying, "You don't hit a man unless you either hate him or love him, and there's one thing I'm sure of, you never hated me. Aw Tilly! Tilly!" Again the laughter slid from his face and, his voice thick and coming from deep in his throat now, he said, "I haven't any need to tell you how I feel, you've known it since I was a lad, but I must put it into words. I love you, Tilly, with no ordinary love because I've lived you and breathed you since I can first remember. You've never been ordinary, not even as a lass, and when you became a woman . . . well, you had something, and all the men who met you knew it. It is a strange quality you have about you, Tilly. But I'll say this for you, you've never played on it because I'm sure you don't realise you've got it. It's a kind of power you have, either to make or to break a man. And you know, that's been proved. But I didn't want it to happen to me, the breaking I mean. Although taking the crumbs you've dropped over the years has been hard, I've put a face on it just to remain near you. Discovering Phillipa as I've said afore, helped, but nothing or no one could fill your place. I was rough on you a few months ago but I could see it as the only way to end this impasse because what I don't want, Tilly, is you as a mistress. Many a man would say I've been a damn fool because with a bit of manoeuvring that could have come about some years ago. . . . Don't move." He shook his head at her. "You're not going to get away. And deny it as much as you like I know I'm right, and you do an' all. I want you as a wife, Tilly. I've always wanted you as a wife, and that's what you're going to be to me at last, isn't it? Willy will eventually marry Josefina, it's a foregone conclusion. You know that as well as me, and you'll have to be prepared for more tongue-wagging . . . Oh aye. And those two as much as they love you they won't want you here. You'll have to face up to that too. That's why we're going to live in the cottage."

She was limp within his arms. She wanted to say something,

upbraid him for the way he had gone about this business, but all her mind was saying was, "Oh, Steve! Steve! Oh, my dearest Steve!" She wanted to say the word "dear" or "dearest" aloud, words that he had never heard her apply to him, but she was unable to speak, so she let her lips speak for her. When she placed them on his there was a space filled with stillness before his grip became like a vice and her whole body seemed to merge into his for a moment, two moments, three, a passage of time going right back to their childhood.

They were both different beings when still holding her he pressed her gently from him and, drawing a deep breath, said, "Tilly. Tilly. Mine at last. I . . . I can't take it in yet, but I will. . . . Oh Tilly!" There was a break in his voice. Then as if in an effort to cover his emotion he reverted to a jocular tone as he said, "I've got a name for the house when it's finished: Trotter Towers. What about that?"

'Trotter Towers." She bit on her lip and said again, "Trotter Towers." Her mouth went into a wide gape. "*Trotter Towers*." When a great gurgle of laughter rose from where it had lain dorment for so long and they fell against each other once more, their mirth mingled and the house became alive with it.

"*Oh Steve! Steve! Trotter Towers. Trotter Towers. Trotter Towers. You and me in Trotter Towers*."

The fears of the years seemed to slide from her as if in one of the Brothers Grimm's fairy tales she saw the tower rising from the stones of the cottage and, standing guard, was Steve, and as long as he was there she knew she would be safe against attacks. She was wise enough to know she'd still be attacked, for even when she changed her name from Sopwith to the once hated name of McGrath, she'd still be known as Tilly Trotter. But what matter; she was loving again and being loved. Oh yes, she was being loved, by this man who had never stopped loving her.

Her body was lost in his again, she had no breath, no desire to think except that she was loving for the last time, and it felt as if she'd never loved before.